CH00469063

Making a Silk Purse

or

It's a Wonder He Lasted as Long as He Did.

By Lindsay Allen

Lindsay Allen

You can't make a silk purse from a sow's ear is a widely used proverb said to mean that you can't make something of high quality from poor materials. It was first found in Alexander Barclay's Eclogues (a Scottish clergyman 1475? – 1152) and the Rev Jonathan Swift (1667 – 1745) is widely credited with coining the phrase.

Although, I did work as a Bluecoat at Pontins in 1983, 84 and 85 (South Devon and Blackpool), there was never one at Whitley Bay. All the characters and events in this book are fictional.

Lindsay Allen

Making a Silk Purse

Prologue

18th August 1984 – Sunny Dunes Holiday Camp, Whitley Bay

It was mid-August at Sunny Dunes Holiday Camp and on that morning Debbie had slammed her chalet door too loudly. She wasn't bothered because she knew full well her roommate, Siobhan would remain undisturbed in the death-like sleep of oblivion that only a day off can bring. Feeling a change in the air, she saw the leaves on the trees were turning the sickly, yellowish green that signposted the arrival of autumn. Above her head, a scrawny seagull circled and peered with its nasty little eyes for leftover chips on the ground. Unaware of any seasonal changes, the bird had only food on its mind. This was not the case with Debbie, who pulled her blue blazer tighter around her shoulders, feeling the prickle of a chilly draught. Only yesterday evening, she had noticed how much earlier the nights were drawing in.

As the summer marched forward, Debbie became increasingly aware of the limited time she had left here. Sadly, these carefree days of undemanding duties and nights spent sitting up until all hours drinking, laughing and joking with her friends were numbered. Unlike the other Bluecoats at this Pontin's Holiday Camp, she was a student and this had been a holiday job. For Debbie, the season had started late, after the University term had finished, so for her there would be a premature ending to her fun. The unwanted finger of academia was beckoning for her return to a different world of lectures, tutorials, essays, a complicated thesis to produce but worst of all ... those dreaded final exams.

Catching a glimpse of herself in a mirror as she passed through the amusement arcade, Debbie's mood changed for the better. As usual, when kitted out in her war paint she was pleased with what she saw. Her dark hair looked like a work of art after she had glued it into its stiff porcupine quills. The white face and carefully applied make-up contrasted strikingly with the boring conservative jacket, sensible knee-length skirt and plain court shoes of her Bluecoat uniform. Admittedly, not everybody appreciated her style but those that mattered did.

Debbie sashayed through the amusement arcade with its flashing lights and blinging fruit machines. Her path meandered across the orange and black zig-zagged carpeted floor in order to avoid the ad hoc placement of one-armed bandits, coin shoots and teddy-pickers. As *Nice Day for a White Wedding* by Billy Idol blared out from a speaker, her steps adjusted to follow the upbeat rhythm of the song and her lips mouthed the words. Although she was surprised that a couple of geeky teenage lads playing the Pac Man Machine failed to notice her, she didn't care. Without fail, Darren in the change booth always waved at her appreciatively, which he did at that very moment, as if on cue. She reciprocated the gesture and rewarded him with one of her signature smiles. She had been told on good authority that he fancied her but feared he was punching above his weight, which he was.

From leaving their chalets, until once more off duty and out of the public sight, it was a prerequisite for any decent Bluecoat to have a smile permanently tattooed on their face. This didn't sit easily with Debbie's notions of her own image but she had perfected an acceptable compromise. She daily swanned about the campsite, wearing what others saw as something between a grimace and a smirk. Passing through the Orangery tea-room, she startled two elderly ladies sporting buttercup yellow and coral coloured frocks. They had been staying there for two weeks now and reminded Debbie of the old dears off *Fawlty Towers*. While waiting for their afternoon tea-dance to happen, they seemed a permanent fixture in the glasshouse, watching the paddle-boats bobbing up and down on the lake.

Outside the swimming baths, Kevin the life guard, with his dark, curly moustache and speedo trunks asked her the time. His voice as usual was accompanied by an unpleasant sneer. Debbie thought there was certain dodginess about Kevin and there was something about him she couldn't quite like. Generally, the indoor pool seemed to be a dubious place, where random members of staff seemed to hang around for no particular reason. She couldn't quite put her finger on what was the matter with Kevin, but without a shadow of doubt he certainly needed to wear some tracksuit bottoms and cover up his nether regions.

'Someone's cutting it a bit fine, aren't they?' Kevin shouted at her and put his hand on his waist, to draw attention to the place where nobody needed to look.

'Well, hardly' Debbie muttered under her breath and started running towards the Entertainment's Office to report for duty. She was pretty sure that this morning she would be greeting the new arrivals on the entrance gate at eleven, as that was what she usually did on a Saturday. However, sometimes the rota changed and that was why all the Bluecoats had to attend the daily ten o'clock briefing.

As she pushed through doors, she was astonished to be greeted by a sea of ashen faces, almost as white as her own. Something was clearly amiss and an ominous question mark hung in the air. It seemed that by being last to arrive, she hadn't been party to some vital information that had been shared with everyone else. Not knowing what to do for the best, Debbie ran across the floor taking charge of the only seat left available in the room. Usually the chairs weren't arranged in any particular order but this morning, they formed a sinister ring round the edge of the room. Debbie felt like she was joining a magic circle of Bluecoats who, rather than pulling any rabbits from hats had congregated together to receive bad news from the doctor.

'What's going on? What's wrong with everyone?' Debbie asked the room but no one replied.

Fat Suzanne deliberately ignored her and Debbie watched the tears trickling down her face, causing the mascara to run in black streams down her wobbly cheeks and through her three chins. Karen, who worked with Uncle Benjie the children's entertainer, had linked arms with her friend and was also weeping. Her normally fluffy blonde curls looked as if they badly needed a comb through them. Next to her sat Barry, in his habitual tracksuit, who worked alongside her chalet-mate Siobhan on the sporting activities, pretending to read a newspaper. His girlfriend Liz was leaning against him and twirling her long, dark brown plait round her finger as if the repetition would make the problem go away. Marcus, as usual seemed engrossed in some historical magazine but as his eyes had remained fixed at one spot in the middle of the same page for so long, it was clear he was taking nothing in. Over by the sink, she could see her friend Stephen's lip quivering beneath his long bleached white, *Flock of Seagull's* quiff.

'Debbie. We don't really know but we think that ...' Stephen began.

'Stephen, be quiet. You know we can't talk about it. Not yet,' hushed Roger, the Head Bluecoat, giving Stephen a harsh glare.

'Well if you'd got yourself here on time Debbie, you'd know what this is all about, wouldn't you?' Suzanne wiped her face, making its mess even worse. 'But we've all been asked not to talk about it. So, we are doing as we've been told. Aren't we, Karen?' Her habitual smugness triumphed over the current grief and her sycophantic pal nodded in agreement.

Surprisingly, Stephen was sitting next to his chalet mate Mike, whom he normally avoided, as they didn't get on. Mike was staring forlornly into his cold cup of coffee, as if the end of the world had already happened. Meanwhile, Roger was trying his best to hold things together but was perpetually shivering and sniffing. Debbie thought he must be starting with a very bad cold and she watched him as he took out a handkerchief from his pocket to wipe a trace of blood from his nose. In this room, which was almost always filled with raucous laughter and noise, nobody was speaking. The only sounds to be heard were those of sobs, snuffles and the clearing of throats.

After a short time, Debbie realised that muffled voices could actually be heard from inside the Entertainment Manager's Office. The door was closed but there was definitely the low hum of a conversation. She was sure this weird situation was almost certainly down to some mischief on the part of that Tony Noble. She remembered her confrontation with the horrible Entertainment's Manager only a few weeks ago. The awful things he had said and done played once more through her mind like a spiteful needle stuck on an unpleasant record. Whatever was going on presently was most likely because of him and if nobody was going to tell her she would just have to find out for herself. However, when she stood up and headed over to the door, Roger sprang in front of her and barred the way.

'Debbie, you can't go in there.' Putting his hands on her shoulders, Roger shook his head. But then she became even further alarmed because she felt strange, jittery pulsating twitches running up and down his arms as if he had been plugged into an electrical socket.

'What's wrong?' Debbie asked. 'What's the matter with everyone?' Something odd was happening, but what? How was she supposed to know what she was doing that day, if she hadn't looked at the rota? And more to the point, why was everyone behaving so peculiarly?

'It's Tony ... he's dead.' The words tumbled out of Roger's mouth as if he had no control over what he was saying. After this proclamation Karen completely lost her battle with grief and a loud keening filled the air. The silent spell had been broken and the Bluecoats tried to reassure each other with comforting words, hand squeezing, hugs and wails in some attempt to counterbalance this shocking announcement.

Debbie, staggering backwards, grabbed Roger's arm to steady herself. 'But he was fine last night wasn't he?' she stuttered. 'He was ... laughing and drinking pints. Just being the usual Tony. How can this be? People don't just die like that, do they?'

'Keep your voices down everyone.' Roger attempted to quieten them by flapping his arms. 'We don't want them to hear us in there. They told us not to discuss it didn't they?'

'What does it matter? How can they expect us all to keep quiet Roger? It's bloody ridiculous,' snapped Stephen.

'Debbie.' Roger was trying to keep is voice calm but it sounded anything but. 'Jill came in this morning and she found him. He was lying in there on the floor.' Roger couldn't meet her eyes and kept them fixed on the floor. 'She's in there with him now, with Stan.'

Jill was the Assistant Entertainment's Manager, Tony's right hand woman, among other things, and it was unusual for her not to be keeping everyone in check. Each day Jill drew up all the rotas and timetables. She made sure everyone was where they should be and behaving as they ought. Normally this growing hysteria wouldn't be tolerated but this wasn't normal was it? Certainly, in Debbie's experience, Entertainment Managers weren't in the habit of dying overnight. Debbie thought with some envy of her chalet mate Siobhan asleep in her bed and ignorant of all of this terrible drama.

Also in Tony's office was bluff Yorkshire man, Stan Braithwaite, the Sunny Dunes Campsite Manager. It was unknown for him to set foot in the Entertainment's Office. Usually, when the Big Cheese Stan and close friend of none other than Fred Pontin himself, snapped his fingers, his minions (of which Tony was one) came running to him. Everyone on the site was at his beck and call. Mostly, he was to be found smoking cigars in his tacky office, with its red velvet upholstery and leopard skin drapes. Debbie had only been in there once when she first arrived, but the room had certainly left an impression and not necessarily a favourable one.

Despite having her own personal grievances with Tony, she wouldn't have wished this upon him. Although the man was a vile bully and a lying bastard, this news was just so shocking. However looking around the room of distraught faces, Debbie wondered just how genuine all this grief was because almost every single person assembled there had some axe to grind with the man.

Debbie was sure, judging by his craggy skin and white hair, that the Entertainment's Manager must have been pushing sixty at least but this was no age to drop down dead was it? Debbie had never actually come face to face with death before. She didn't quite know how to process its finality. For up until now, the immortality cloaks of her close friends and family had never been touched.

'But he was fine last night wasn't he?' Unable to think of anything else nice to say about the man, she returned to her earlier thoughts. 'He was ... laughing and drinking pints. He can't be dead ... that's impossible isn't it?' Debbie remembered the previous evening when Tony had been his normal sleazy self with his rude innuendoes, grubby jacket and filthy laugh. She had thought how he sounded just like Sid James' characters in the *Carry On* films but much more nasty.

'I don't know. I haven't seen him. It's just what they said.' Roger was now sweating profusely and looking even more ill than usual. Little beads of moisture had been collecting in his ginger moustache making it swell and look like a slug. He hadn't been himself lately and this morning's events clearly weren't helping matters. Roger attempted to turn away, lost his balance and lurched sideways. Stumbling against the wall, he bashed his head. He winced and rubbed his rapidly enlarging bump, hoping that Debbie wasn't going to once more encroach into his personal space.

'Well *they* might be wrong.' Debbie's words sounded more optimistic than her voice. She thought that despite Tony not presenting himself as a man in fine form, there had to be some chance he could be resuscitated by doctors. She thought about the man lying on the other side of the door. Although he never seemed to eat, an unhealthy paunch hung round his middle like a rubber ring, causing buttons on his grubby shirts to strain precariously. The stench from his foul breath might be the result of his decaying teeth but a more likely source was surely something rotting inside. Last night, as he had been calling the bingo, she had noticed him becoming over-excited and his face had turned a most worrying shade of puce. As he had announced that the next ball out was two little ducks, the sight of him was actually quite terrifying. Such had been his state of frenzy on the quack-quack-quacks, his bloodshot eyes had almost bulged out of their sockets. Yet, the thought of him lying dead and motionless on the floor seemed inconceivable. Particularly, since she couldn't imagine him with his hands empty, as she didn't think she had ever seen him not nursing a fag, a pint or both, even at this hour of the morning.

Debbie looked about the room once more to gauge the reactions of the others. Over in the corner, Suzanne along with her sidekick Karen, was still crying. Marcus's eyes remained glued to the same spot on his page. Mike was now staring into middle distance and Stephen sat mesmerised as if in a trance. Roger was an even more extreme version of the gibbering wreck he had been for days. She thought once more that so many people in the room had such good reason to loathe Tony.

'Was it his heart? Had he had a heart attack?' As Debbie searched around the room she expected an answer. None came; everyone was trapped in their own little bubbles. Why was nobody taking any action? Debbie just couldn't understand it. 'Why isn't the ambulance here?'

'I don't know. It's just not got here yet.' Roger looked uncomfortable, shifting his weight from one foot to the other, looking as if he couldn't decide on which foot to stand or that he was in desperate need of the toilet. 'It's just Jill and Stan in there at the moment. I don't know what they are doing or saying but I wish everything would get a move on and sort itself out.' It was as though Roger just wanted the fuss to be over and done with. As if he had somewhere more important he needed to be. 'Apparently, the ambulance is on its way … and so are the *police.*' He blurted out the last word and dashed towards the window when he heard the screech of a siren.

'Well the doctors might be able save him …' Debbie knew heart attacks didn't always kill people. Her Granddad had one five years ago and he must be much older than Tony. He was fine and dandy now. Unlike Tony, who she pictured lying like a resigned king on office floor with its black and white chequered chessboard lino. Jill, his self-appointed queen, would be strategically manoeuvring herself around his body, trying to revive her lover and fearful for the loss of her own privileged position. Stan's mind she imagined would primarily be concerned with the impact of this inconvenience upon his profit margins. But this was all wrong and Debbie thought once more of her granddad. It should surely be all about saving Tony's life and time was of the essence in situations like this.

'They should've been here long before now.' Debbie was certain the paramedics ought to have been busy defibrillating or whatever they did with their various pieces of equipment. As she looked out of the window, she saw that a panda car had pulled up and two policemen were walking towards the office. One was middle aged but the other was much younger and closer to her own age. 'But wait … what has any of this got to do with the police?' She noticed Mike trying to catch her attention from across the other side of the room.

'Debbie.' Mike threw his cold coffee into the sink and rushed over to her. 'It's too late for any of that. Don't you see? Tony's body in there is stone cold dead. Don't you get it?' he hissed. 'He's been dead all night. There's nothing anybody can do … it's too late. There's a bloody great knife sticking out of his back. It's more than likely a murder case and all of us are suspects. Really, is it any wonder the police are here?'

Chapter 1

14th July 1984 – Sunny Dunes Holiday Camp

Debbie's Arrival

When Debbie first arrived at the Sunny Dunes Holiday Camp it was quite late on Saturday night. She'd had a long train ride and then a further bus journey since leaving Birmingham early that morning. This wasn't the first time she had been a Bluecoat, she had worked the previous summer down in Paignton in Devon but this place was obviously very different. For a start it was much larger and from the moment she entered the gates she was hit by the thud of music from the bar and the cacophony of screeching seagulls. She was told by a surly security guard, who seemed suspicious of such a late arrival, to head for the Entertainment's Office which was to be found just behind the ballroom to the left. Debbie was a little miffed that the man hadn't offered to help her with her heavy suitcase. She was exhausted and he was clearly no gentleman.

She walked past the children's train with its colourful carriages and smiling clown's face resting for the night. Tugging her case along the path festooned with jolly buntings, she passed a large hall where holiday makers were being treated to a nasal warbling rendition of *I Will Survive*. Debbie was certain that was no woman's voice singing. The air was thick with the salty smell of the sea and seemed greasy from the aroma of fish and chips which permeated everything. It reminded her of the holidays of her childhood with her parents. A little further on, she spotted in big yellow and orange illuminated letters the words, REGENCY BALLROOM. Drawing closer she could hear the haunting sounds of an organ playing. Through the windows she watched elderly couples displaying varying levels of expertise while quickstepping, shuffling, twirling and hobbling around the dance floor. It reminded Debbie of a photograph of her grandparents in their younger days, before even the 2nd World War. Pausing for a moment to watch the ghostly dancers, she felt as if she was eerily stepping back in time.

At the back of the ballroom she saw the Entertainment's Office sign on the door which meant she was in the right place. When she knocked on the door a voice immediately invited her to come inside. Warily, she stepped into a messy room furnished with a collection of mismatched tables and rickety chairs. The walls were plastered with rotas and timetables attached with drawing pins. A further door at the bottom of the room was ajar.

'Hello. Is this the Entertainment's Office? Am I in the right place?' She called towards the open door.

A voice croaked from within, as if its owner had been chain smoking for the past forty years. 'Come in here my dear. I guess this must be Debbie… at last. Let's have a look at you then.'

 Debbie walked through a thick fog of blue smoke into the inner office where a sharp-featured late middle-aged man, with a white comb-over and red face sat behind a desk. In one hand he clutched a glass tankard of beer and in the other a fag was held by his nicotine-stained fingers. Next to him, was sitting an attractive woman in her late twenties. She wore her hair in brassy-coloured ringlets, had a haughty look and long eyelashes which immediately put Debbie in mind of a camel.

'Yes that right.' Debbie nodded. She looked from one set of bloodshot eyes to another of the brightest sapphire blue. That woman had to be wearing contact lenses she thought.

'So you must be our new Bluecoat then. Debbie, isn't it?' The man smiled at her unnervingly, to reveal yellow crooked teeth that looked like pieces of popcorn.

'Yes, I'm Debbie. Debbie Carter.' She smiled back with her mouth closed, licking the inside of her teeth to check hers were still straight.

'Well I'm Tony. Tony Noble — your Entertainment's Manager. Pleased to meet you.' He leaned across the table to shake hands with his new Bluecoat. Debbie found his tight grip clammy and moist. 'And this … is my gorgeous assistant Jill.' He winked at her lasciviously and Jill's girlish giggle sounded inappropriate coming from a woman who must be pushing thirty. Debbie found it disturbing watching Jill's demeanour shift from mannequin's dummy to giddy teenager. Tony shuffled some papers on his desk and briefly scowled before baring his terrible teeth in a grimace at her. 'I see you've worked as a Bluecoat before then, Debbie.'

'Yes, last year. I worked down in Devon at a holiday camp in Paignton.' Debbie had enjoyed her work last summer and when she had reapplied for a job as a Bluecoat this year, she had been surprised she hadn't been sent back there. However, once her term had finished they were already a good few months into the season so she supposed it was just where there was a vacancy.

'Well I think you'll find things a little livelier here. Don't you think Jill?' He nudged Jill roughly with his pointy elbow. She narrowed her eyes and rubbed her arm.

'Be mostly pensioners there I'd have thought.' Jill then wrinkled her pretty little nose in distaste at the thought of all of those horrible oldies. She tossed her mane of golden curls and batted her lashes to remind Tony of her own still youthful charms. Debbie noticed that under the table, Tony's bony hand was soon pawing Jill's equally skinny knee in a proprietary manner.

'Now it's a little late for going on a tour.' Tony removed his grip from his assistant's leg to lift his cuff and consult his fake Rolex watch for verification. He thought it was really was a bit of a cheek, this new Bluecoat arriving so late and probably his wife would have expected him home by now. 'So we'll do that in the morning. That ok?' Then his priorities suddenly changed. All thoughts of his neglected spouse were mysteriously forgotten and replaced by the more enticing prospect of further liquid imbibement. 'So, can I offer you a drink of something pet … maybe a whiskey or a can?' Tony pulled a half empty sticky bottle from the drawer in his desk and refilled his own glass with a generous measure.

'Could I have a can of coke please?' Debbie was really tired and not in the habit of drinking whiskey. All she really wanted after her long journey was to be shown to her chalet and go to sleep.

'I don't think Tony keeps kiddy's pop in his fridge.' Jill chuckled. 'I've a bottle of wine open. Would you like a wee glass?'

'Yes please then. Just a small one.' Debbie noticed a slight Scottish lilt to Jill's voice. Her smile wasn't all together pleasant but she had at least made a gesture of camaraderie by sharing some of her own wine. Jill locked eyes with Tony once more, and then glanced at the clock on the wall to remind himself of the time.

'Then I'll show you where your chalet is.' said Jill.

'There's no rush Jill. We are just showing our new Bluecoat a little hospitality.' Tony took a slurp of his whiskey.

Debbie watched the perspiration on Tony's brow and he gave her another of his unpleasant smiles. 'I was surprised you arrived so late actually …'

'There was a delay on the train,' she replied. 'I'm sorry I thought I'd have been here earlier …'

'Here you are Debbie.' Jill thrust a small glass of something sweet and bubbly into her hand. 'Now you drink this quickly and I'll take you to meet Siobhan.' She stressed the name using a strange tone and her eyes glinted with mischief, as it there was something untoward about this person.

'Siobhan?' Debbie immediately feared this was to be her chalet-mate. And from Jill's tone she thought there must be something weird about her. She imagined a devil with cloven hooves, horns and a forked tail. Surely she didn't have to share a room with anyone? She'd had a place all to herself last year. Debbie didn't want to share with this strange Siobhan and from what she had seen of this place so far, she was beginning to wish she had been sent back to Paignton.

7th April 2014 – Trinity Square, Central Gateshead

Having Bigger Fish to Fry

Trinity Square in the centre of Gateshead was particulary bleak that morning. The recent building refurbishment was really no improvement on the iconic *Get Carter* car park that Alf Robert's (the former Mayor of Weatherfield from *Coronation Street*) had once been thrown off. Indeed, the only real benefactor from the development seemed to be Tesco, whose store had expanded enomously like a gigantic lump following a blow to the head. This had led many to speculate that perhaps Gateshead town centre ought to be re-named Tesco on Tyne.

Martha sat on the bench opposite the supermarket. She was an elderly woman with a messy grey nest of a bob, crumpled ill-fitting trousers and a shabby quilted blue jacket. To her right was the multi-screened *Vue* Cinema, promoting its two for one ticket offers in bold red letters and to her left were the usual Greggs, Boots, Burger King and Poundland, common to any conurbation large enough to provide a steady footfall on a daily basis. Watching the comings and goings of the shoppers through the centre of the twenty foot tall and almost as wide silvery halo sculpture, in the middle of the precinct, was a regular pastime of hers. She chewed on her pencil for a moment, before doodling a few stick men and writing down her thoughts in a well-thumbed paisley notebook.

Then Martha turned her attention to her beloved pigeons. At least thirty of the cute grey birds were strutting, swooping and pecking at the concrete in front of her with their little pointy beaks. She thought their delightful coo was soothing and peaceful. In fact, she was sure that if the sound of purring pigeon could be bottled, it would be more effective at treating depression or anxiety than anything a quack of a doctor could prescribe. Their tenacity was also something Martha admired, for those beady, sharp eyes were relentlessly on the lookout for morsels of food and crumbs. Trinity Square was as good a spot as any for leftovers, as it's purveyors of cheap fast foods supplied those who needed them least with the sugar and carbohydrates required for their daily fix.

Martha was positive that over time the birds, along with the Greggs customers, were becoming larger and larger. If this trend continued, the poor birds would need to be especially wary at Christmastime, for it was more than likely they could be culled to provide a cheaper substitute for the plump, festive birds sold in the store close by. Still, she liked to feed them, and reaching into her battered carpet bag, she took out a handful of seeds and scattered them on the ground. The number of birds multiplied tenfold and she gave a little smile of satisfaction as they feasted on their food.

'Good God. You stupid woman! What are you doing?' A man in a grey suit with a venomous face was standing right in front of her and barking crossly.

'What's wrong?' Martha suddenly jerked her head back and stared at him in amazement. 'I'm only giving the birds a little something to eat.' She wondered why this rude person was shouting at her.

'They're bloody vermin! You're encouraging them!' He wagged a finger in her face.

'And what business is this of yours?' she said tartly. 'I often come and feed these poor pigeons and I'm not causing any harm.' Martha noticed some passers by smirking and stopping in their tracks to watch this amusing altercation. It wasn't as if she was the one raising her voice and disturbing the peace.

'Really? Well, what about the effects their filthy mess all over the place? And you do know they spread diseases, don't you?' The obnoxious man brushed one hand off the other, imagining himself flicking away some dirty pigeon mess. Much to his annoyance, Martha just ignored him, took the seeds out of her bag and continued to feed the birds.

He edged closer to Martha warily, as if worried she too might be a source of avian contamination. Moving his hand forward, he attempted to snatch the paper bag from her but she was too quick for him. She stuffed the package into her pocket and flashed him a look of defiance.

'Just get lost you old witch and take your ... disgusting pigeon bait with you.' He snarled at her.

'I've just as much right to be here as anyone else.' Martha saw that a crowd was beginning to form around them.

'As the Deputy Manager of Tesco's.' He straightened his tie and pointed to the shop entrance behind him, in case there was any danger she didn't know to which shop he was referring. 'I have every right to remove a person making a nuisance of themselves. Which you most definitely are.'

'No I'm not,' she snapped back. There was no way she was going to allow this pompous git to get the better of her. She noticed the name on his badge - Mr M. Robinson (Deputy Store Manager).

'Do I have to contact the Police?' He jabbed his finger at her her but was suddenly stopped in his tracks. A skinny youth clutching a collection of bottles with a crazed look in his eye, ran straight into him. As he shoved the Deputy Manager to one side and pushed him over, the boy dropped one of the whisky bottles he was carrying. Smashing on the ground, the amber liquid seeped over the concrete with its accompanying unpleasant smell. Unperturbed, the lad carried on running across the square with the rest of his nine bottles of spirits.

'Stop there, you bloody thug! You've just knocked me over. Come back here now and apologise.' The hooligan was oblivious to Mr M. Robinson's shouting and disappeared around a corner.

'And I'm the one causing a problem, am I?' Martha asked as she watched with glee the Deputy Manager staggering to his feet with nasty stains on his smart trousers and a piece of broken glass sticking out of his knee.

'Stop thief!' Came the cries from the staff running from out of the store.

'He's nicked our booze,' shouted Dave from the cigarette kiosk, as he pounded across the square gasping.

'And it's not the cheap stuff either. It's from our premium range,' spluttered an out of breath Keith from the fish counter.

'He's done what?' yelled Mr Robinson as he realised that the booze had been stolen from *his* Tesco store.

Now he had much bigger fish to fry than mad Bird Woman, thought Martha. With great amusement, she watched him join the other Tesco employees in the *pointless chase* which put her in mind of two the two popular quiz programmes on the television. Unsurprisingly, they were not fast enough. Martha gave a hoot of delight, as the thief had long disappeared and outsmarted the inept Tesco security squad. This was more than enough excitement for one day. As it was almost noon and the vile stench of whisky was making her feel sick, Martha decided it was time to return home.

Chapter 2

14th July 1984 – Sunny Dunes Holiday Camp – Debbie and Siobhan's Chalet

Something to Tell Her Friends

Once Jill had quickly kitted Debbie out with her uniform and shown her to her bleak chalet, she was soon on her way back to the Entertainment's Office. Debbie understood the measure of what was going on there. The two of them were clearly having an affair and she suspected that Tony was married. While Jill was pretty enough in a vacant Barbie-doll-like way, her looks were deceptive because she was obviously shrewd and calculating. More than likely she had used to full advantage her feminine wiles on Tony and it was surely no coincidence that she was now Assistant Entertainment's Manager. This was certainly a very different holiday camp than the one she had worked at last summer — bigger, brasher and more sordid. She wondered what the other Bluecoats would be like and more particularly her chalet mate.

The wallpaper in the chalet appeared to have been painted a nicotine shade of yellow but this was obviously some time ago, as great chunks were crawling down the walls like peeled curls of potato skin. She wondered if Siobhan, yes that was the name that Jill had mentioned, smoked. Judging by the smell it seemed more than likely. Over the far side of the room the bed had a blue and red duvet cover with a diagonal design and a football magazine lying on the pillow. On the wall nearby were smiling photos of an ordinary-looking, mostly ginger-haired, family. This must be Siobhan's bed and she wondered what Jill had been implying about her earlier. Judging by the photos, she was most likely a redhead with a hot temper. So maybe that was what Jill had been referring too.

The other bed had a shabby yellow, orange and black cover, which was the same horrid design as the curtains and was tucked severely into the mattress. A pillowcase in a dirty shade of candy-floss pink with a blue Pontins logo peeped out grubbily from beneath. This was not the most inviting of places to sleep. Debbie sat down on her lumpy bed and wished she were back in Devon where her room had been nothing special but it had been all hers and better than this. She looked across at the cassettes next to the little plastic player and was disappointed to see *Barry Manilow, the Nolans* and *the Carpenters* — most definitely not her musical taste.

Suddenly, the door flung open and a young woman, of about her own age with no-nonsense, short, platinum blonde hair, pale, freckled skin and a big grin burst into the room.

'Hi, you must be Debbie.' She spoke with a broad Northern Irish accent and gave Debbie a long up and down look. 'Wow, I've never met a Goth before. This will be something to tell the folks at home. I'm Siobhan by the way. Pleased to meet you.' And Siobhan proffered a hand to be shaken.

Debbie accepted the very firm handshake. 'Hi, yes, I'm Debbie.' This Siobhan wasn't what she had been expecting at all. 'I take it this must be my bed then.' Debbie had never met a Northern Irish person before either.

'Yes and I know it looks grim but there's a Brentford Nylons in the town, you know? You can get some decent bedding like mine quite cheaply there, to be sure.' Siobhan plonked herself down on her comparatively luxurious bed and stared at Debbie as if she were some creature in a zoo.

'Yes, I think that might be a necessity as soon as possible.' The cover on Debbie's bed not only looked disgusting but felt clammy and not too clean.

'Well, after a long day here. One thing you really need is a good night's kip. Can't do much about the lumpy mattress but what the … say Debbie, would you like a cup of tea? Do Goths drink tea?' She went to plug in the ancient kettle which certainly wouldn't have met modern-day safety standards.

'No, only blood.' Debbie said this dead-pan and Siobhan looked nonplussed. 'Only joking and yes please I'd love a cup of tea.'

'Ha ha.' Siobhan gave a deep throaty chuckle. 'Good one. I'm glad to see you've got a sense of humour — you'll need one working here.' She took a cigarette out from a packet of Regency Regals. 'D' you want a tab?'

'No I don't smoke.' Debbie had been right. She was sharing with a smoker and consigned herself to a season of passive nicotine inhalation.

'So, how come you're just starting now? The season's already half way through. There's only another three months to go.' Siobhan wondered if perhaps her extreme appearance had caused some bother at another camp and she had been forced to move. She knew they were a bit more lenient here than at other Pontins, which was one of the reasons she had been pleased to have been placed here herself.

'I've been at college and term only finished a few weeks ago. This was the first vacancy that came up.' Debbie explained, wondering how this would go down with her new chalet mate.

'Well, well … a swotty Goth, eh? That'll raise a few eyebrows.' Siobhan snorted and gave her another of her what were becoming, quite endearing, guffaws. 'You'll have to watch out for some of the other Bluecoats.' She was blowing smoke rings and trying to appear wise. She reminded Debbie of the caterpillar from *Alice in Wonderland*.

'What do you mean?' Debbie was perturbed. Would the other Bluecoats not like her because she was a Goth, or even worse in their eyes ... a student?

'Well here's your tea m'dear.' Siobhan tapped the ash from her cigarette into the sink and left the cigarette to balance there while she poured water and milk into the mugs, leaving the teabag in to brew. 'Good strong Irish tea from home, you know, my mam sends it to me. The sort you can stand a spoon up in. Sugar?'

'Who will I have to watch out for?' Debbie was feeling quite worried and it seemed to her that Siobhan was delighting in playing cat with her as the mouse.

'I take it you've met Tony?' Siobhan took a final drag from her cigarette before stubbing it out in the sink. 'Well ... not that I'm one to gossip, but ...' She tapped the side of her nose knowingly. 'Shall we just say he's a one for the ladies if you get my gist? And you'll be his type if you know what I mean?'

'His type? He has a penchant for Goths then?' She certainly hadn't been expecting this.

'No, just something new, unusual. Yes, he'll definitely see you as exotic.' Once more Debbie felt as if she were some strange creature on exhibition in a freak show.

'Siobhan, there's obviously something going on with him and Jill.' Debbie thought she had better mention this because Siobhan was clearly just amusing herself with her ridiculous speculations.

'Oh yes, but that doesn't stop him. He'll get into anyone's knickers he can.' It was Debbie's turn now to laugh and she was beginning to warm to this funny forthright girl. 'But that Jill, she's another one you'll have to watch out for. She doesn't even like Tony really, do you know? Oh no, it's just the power *she* likes. Bossing us Bluecoats about that's what *she* likes. Last year *she* was just an ordinary Bluecoat, you know? Well, I think it's obvious how that promotion came about.' Siobhan tilted her head knowingly to one side. 'Anyway watch out for her. You're pretty, so she'll hate you.'

'What about you?' Debbie thought that in her own rather strange, pale boyish way Siobhan was attractive enough.

'I'm definitely not his type.' Siobhan made a puffing sound with her mouth.

'If you don't mind me saying your Irish look is quite … unusual you know.' Debbie wondered how Siobhan would take this and hoped she hadn't offended her new roommate.

'Debbie, I'm a lesbian.' Debbie hadn't been expecting this. She had never met a lesbian before and now she was sharing a chalet with a Northern Irish albino one. Now that was something to tell *her* friends.

10th April 2014 – The Lazaridis House – Jesmond, Newcastle

The Horrible Cleaner

Jillian had a hairdresser's appointment shortly and before that was enjoying a flat white coffee from her latest gadget in the conservatory. From out of the windows, she could see her lovely garden with its weed–free flower beds and recently mowed lawns. These were separated into three distinct stepped terraces that she thought looked like the tiers of a lavish green wedding cake. Edging the grass were her herbaceous borders which in the summer would be crammed with fragrant jasmines, lily-of-the valley and creamy coloured lupins. Jillian was generally fond of pale colours which she always thought looked pristine and tasteful. At the moment, she was enjoying her spring display of white daffodils and magnolia tulips she'd had specially imported from Amsterdam.

In the middle of her lower lawn she had installed an impressive water feature. During a recent visit to Kew Gardens, Jillian had been particularly impressed with the massive water lilies. Some of the spectacular plants' diameters had been even larger than those of satellite dishes. These had been the inspiration for her obviously scaled down but nonetheless equally splendid pond at the bottom of the garden. Jillian thought the beautiful flowers reminded her a little of herself. Each opening bud, flanked by parasol-sized pads, emerged out of the water as if a deity waiting to be adored, rather like Botticelli's painting of Venus. Also in the centre of the pool was a trickling fountain, around which ghost-like koi carp circled, idly blowing bubbles.

Jillian congratulated herself on her fine horticultural taste and the wise decision she had made in selecting Carl, a recently retired police officer, as her gardener. He usually came round two or three times a month to trim the bushes and keep everything in order. In fact he was due to come round later that week and she needed to ask him about the suitability of a certain pagoda she was thinking of ordering. She flicked through a *House Beautiful* magazine for some further inspiration. In the conservatory section she noted with smugness, that her new snowdrift-effect Lloyd Loom furniture, was completely *en trend* for this season. While the chairs and tables in the featured article looked similar to hers and were quite pleasant, hers were infinitely superior and cost at least three times the price.

She heard the dreaded sound of the key in the door and her heart sank. It was her cleaner Elaine and as usual she was too early. She had hoped that she would have more time to herself before the arrival of the woman. Although Jillian couldn't deny that her cleaning skills were adequate enough, her presence in the house was a constant thorn in Jillian's side. Once Elaine started talking, there was no way of stopping her. The constant drone of her thick Glaswegian accent grated on Jillian, as if someone was rubbing aluminium foil over the fillings of her teeth.

'Morning there Mrs Lazaridis.' Elaine's voice screeched down the hallway.

'Oh … erm … good morning Elaine,' Jillian mumbled and took a final sip from her coffee, before throwing her car keys and phone into her bag. 'I must dash, I have an appointment at 10.30.'

By then Elaine was already down the corridor and blocking the doorway. That morning, the unfortunate combination of shocking pink leggings teamed with a short yellow T-shirt did not make a pretty sight. A section of wobbly stomach, the colour of uncooked pastry protruded between the two items of clothing. Jillian could not hide the look of disgust on her face. She straightened the waistband of her beige linen trousers round her own slender stomach and smoothed out imaginary creases.

'Well that's ages off, it's only just gone nine.' Elaine clocked the half drunk cup of coffee on the table. 'Surely you have time to finish that wee cup of coffee? It seems a shame to let it go to waste doesn't it? Perhaps there's a one in the pot left for me too? After the walk and the ride in that Metro I'm more than ready for a ...'

'No, I'm afraid that's not possible. I must be making tracks.' Jillian twisted her lips into a begrudging half-smile, before squeezing herself through the small gap between her cleaner and the door frame. Elaine seemed unaware of any need to move out of the way or more than likely she was just being awkward and unwilling to do so.

Once she had escaped, Jillian shouted from down the hallway, 'You can help yourself to the rest of the pot though.' Relieved at last by her close proximity to the front door and freedom from her horrible cleaner, she added. 'There's a cracked mug next to the sink. You could use it then … throw it away.'

'Fair enough,' replied Elaine, pretending she wasn't seething from another put down from her snooty employer. She plonked herself into the chair where Jillian had been sitting and made herself comfy. 'Is your appointment anywhere nice? Are you meeting with up any of your friends today? Will you be making any wee purchases for yourself or Mr Lazaridis perhaps?' Elaine grinned to herself, knowing full well that Jillian would be irritated by her barrage of questions.

'Just the hairdressers.' Jillian answered, glad to be in a different room from the woman. Not that it was any of Elaine's business thought Jillian. Picking up some mail off the floor she caught a glimpse of herself in the hallway mirror, and was relieved that her own appearance hadn't been compromised by her brushing against that Glaswegian mess.

'I wouldn't have thought you needed to go to the hairdressers again. Wasn't it only last week you were there? Have you got something special on tonight like?' Elaine's interrogation continued, as Jillian tried to blot out the sound and admire her own pleasing reflection.

Jillian yawned.'No Elaine, just some dinner dance with my husband, you know, the usual sort of tedius thing?' Why was she even bothering to answer her cleaner's stupid questions? The woman as always was driving her crazy and she just wished her husband had never hired the stupid cow in the first place. This was all Teddie's fault and now she was forced to find places to go to away from her own home, just to escape from her horrible cleaner. If only she could find fault with her work then she could employ someone more suitable. Maybe Carl would be interested in some extra hours or perhaps his wife? For Carl was bound to have a sensible wife she thought, especially with him having been in the police force.

Chapter 3

15th July 1984 – Sunny Dunes Holiday Camp – Debbie and Siobhan's Chalet

Go Break a Leg

When Debbie's alarm clock went off at 9 am, she wondered at first where she was. The sun was streaming through the thin, orange and black curtains and a loud snore was coming from the opposite side of the room. Of course, that was her lesbian roommate Siobhan and she allowed herself a few more moments in bed to think about the details of last night's conversation. She needed to report to the office for ten, so she had an hour and after sleeping in the sticky bedclothes, she felt in desperate need of a shower. But there was none here, only a bath.

'Siobhan.' She whispered, but there was no reply. 'Siobhan,' she tried a little louder. 'Is it ok if I have a bath?' There was still no answer so she took that as an affirmative, as after all they were sharing the chalet, so she had just as much right to use the very basic facilities.

Debbie hadn't yet had time to unpack, and after the chat with Siobhan, she had only felt up to a quick wash, tooth clean and bed. The only clothes she had placed in the wardrobe so far were the Bluecoat uniform blazer, skirts, shirts and navy pussycat necktie for the evenings, that Jill had kitted her out with last night. She had gathered some underwear from her suitcase along with her nightgown, as she felt a little wary of dressing in front of Siobhan, for obvious reasons.

Then after her shallow bath in the chipped white tub stained with rust, she dressed in the privacy of the bathroom in her new uniform. It was identical to the one she had worn last season. As she slipped on the blue and white striped shirt, grey skirt and blazer, it was like being reunited with dear old friends. She smiled at her smart reflection in the cracked mirror as she applied a subtle pink lipstick rather her usual bright red. The previous year, when she hadn't been obsessed with Robert Smith from *The Cure*, her appearance had been less extreme and her hair much shorter. For the first time ever she worried how the others might react. Carefully, she patted down her spikes a little and dabbed at her face so its whiteness was less pronounced.

Siobhan was still out for the count and Debbie worried she was going to be late for her duties that day?

'Siobhan. Siobhan. Wake up.' She shouted close to the girl's face.

'Ugh. What's the matter? What time is it?' Siobhan groaned, her eyes still tight shut.

'It's quarter to 10 and you have to be ...'

'Arggh. No. Didn't I tell you last night?' Siobhan immediately jammed her head under the pillow like an unusually fast-moving tortoise retreating into its shell.

'Siobhan you must get up now.' Debbie didn't want her new friend getting into trouble and she had presumed they could have gone to the office together on this her first day.

'Debbie. It's my day off on a Saturday. And I was enjoying my one day's lie in of the week. Just go away and let me sleep,' she grunted.

'Oh, I'm sorry.' Debbie realised that Siobhan clearly wasn't happy to have been woken up and it had taken some doing. She certainly hadn't mentioned anything about days off though last night.

'Just get lost. And good luck by the way.' Siobhan emerged once more from under the covers, opened one eye reluctantly and added.

'Your uniform looks smart on you by the way. Go break a leg.' Then she immediately fell back into the deepest of sleeps.

8th April 2014 - Trinity Square Gateshead

The Bloodied Knee

Next to the main entrance of his Tesco store, Mr Mike Robinson had just been overseeing a promotional display for the latest new toothpaste. Cutting a dash in his grey suit, stripy shirt and red tie, he strutted up and down the floor. With his chest puffed like a cockerel, he smiled and nodded at the customers, as if he still worked at a holiday camp. Today the shoppers were to be lured into the purchase of Zesty Breeze by the promise of the most zingy smelling breath, ultra-white teeth and a complementary sparkly toothbrush. Its handle had been made into the shape of a mermaid's tail. No doubt, the intent was to attract the market of pampered little girls and their indulgent mothers.

'Yes Elaine, that looks fine.' Mike half-heartedly assured the overweight shelf stacker, who was balancing on her tiptoes and piling the boxes of toothpaste precariously high. The glittering toothbrush freebees were almost hidden by the haphazard oral-cleansing skyscrapers. Mr Robinson's attention was clearly elsewhere and Elaine, fully aware of the massive health and safety issue she was creating deliberately, was just willing them to topple over and land on his head.

However, Mike's mood swiftly changed when he looked out of the window and saw that annoying Bird Woman in his Trinity Square yet again. As always, she was wearing her nasty blue jacket, scruffy trousers and cheap-looking trainers. Both she and her clothes looked as if they needed putting through a machine on a ninety degrees hot cotton wash. Yesterday, he had fully intended to send the old woman packing, but he had been forced to deal with an emergency situation when some scally had nicked lots of bottles from his store.

He thought back and remembered how the shoplifter had viciously pushed him over and it had hurt. Later on, he'd not only had to ask a girl in the canteen to find him a sticking plaster for his bloodied knee but he'd had to go home to change his trousers because the ones he was wearing now had a had a huge rip in them. What a waste of a perfectly good pair of pants. However, what had really got his goat was that the Bird Woman had been laughing at him. She had been pleased that he had been injured and this was something he was not easily going to forget

He had been just about to go outside and send her packing when he had been accosted by some particularly thick customers. The morons had been unable to get the streaming stick for their telly to work and so they wanted a refund. He was sure there was nothing wrong with it and that they were just wasting his time. And, of course, once he had sorted them out the Bird Woman had disappeared in a puff of smoke. Never mind, she would soon be back and he would be waiting. Bird Woman's days and her pigeon antics were numbered. Mike Robinson, Deputy Store Manager would see to that.

Chapter 4

15th July 1984 – Sunny Dunes Holiday Camp – The Entertainment's Office

Looking a Fright

When Debbie opened the Entertainment's Office door, she was met by a fog of smoke and several pairs of eyes turned to stare at her. Some didn't look very friendly and clearly viewed her arrival with suspicion.

'Well, hello.' A shortish man of around thirty greeted her in a high-pitched voice and the manner of Leslie Phillips. He had ginger hair, a neat natty moustache and little brown squirrel eyes that darted about. As he scrutinised her with interest, his gaze lingered a fraction too long on the top of her head. 'I guess you must be Debbie. We have all been so looking forward to meeting you.' He held out his hand to be shaken and as she did so Debbie noticed his odd juddery twitch. Scanning the room, Debbie thought it was a very different place from the one of last night, being now full of Bluecoats watching her while drinking their coffee, eating toast, smoking and watching her.

'Yes that's right.' Debbie felt outnumbered and uncomfortable. She wished now that she had toned down her appearance further and that Siobhan had come with her.

'I'm Roger by the way.' He clapped his hands and clicked together his heels.' I'm Head Bluecoat so you need to keep on the right side of me.' He winked, sniffed and widened his eyes.

'Yes, and if you misbehave Debbie, he'll have you counting the Donkey Derby programmes as a punishment,' chipped in a tall, burly Bluecoat, laughing to himself as if he had said something amusing. He had a deep voice and the look of a rugby player. He wore a moustache which was dark chestnut brown, the colour of his hair. While buttering a slice of toast messily with a large breadknife, he was oblivious to the crumbs he was scattering everywhere. 'Isn't that right Roger?'

'Well, you'd know all about that wouldn't you? Debbie, this is Mike. He fancies himself as a bit of a joker. Don't you Mike? But counting programmes is more your forte isn't it?' Roger dramatically swooshed his head to one side, minced across the floor and shot him a glance.

Mike ignored this comment. 'Hello Debbie. Nice to meet you,' he said as he bit into his toast.

Well at least these two seemed friendly enough Debbie thought.

'All the gang aren't here yet.' Roger placed a hand on his hip and looked impatiently at the big clock on the wall. 'Some are likely still in bed but I'll introduce you to some of these *reprobates*.' And he emphasised his last word with accompanying jazz hands.

'This is Karen. She's a scouse lass and she mostly works with the *kiddies*.' He said this as though having to work with children was a form of punishment. Karen had curly blonde hair the texture of cotton wool and put Debbie in mind of a poodle. She was sipping her coffee from a Styrofoam cup and for some reason was avoiding making eye contact.

'Hello Debbie. Nice to meet you,' Karen mumbled as she looked at the floor, stifling a snigger.

'Over there with the long plait, that's Liz,' said Roger. Liz smiled and gave Debbie a friendly enough wave from across the room.

'Here's Marcus. He plays the trumpet.' Roger pointed across the room and Marcus nodded at her. He was black with very white teeth and was wearing what seemed to be a pair of gladiator sandals that looked somewhat incongruous with his uniform. He appeared to be reading a children's book about Ancient Rome.

'Hello Debbie. Are you settling in all right?' Marcus's eyes went straight back to his book.

'Yes, thank you Marcus.' Debbie wasn't quite sure what to make of him.

Then the door swung open and in waltzed a skinny bloke of about twenty with a shock of blonde hair styled into the most enormous quiff.

'Oh yes, here's Stephen. This is early for him.' Roger checked the clock, tutted and shook his head. Then his eyes widened as if a profound thought occurred. 'And ding dong! Doesn't it just seem like you two have got something in common?' Roger's glance flitted from one extreme hairdo to the other and a bubbling of laughter filled the room.

'Hi Debbie.' Stephen smiled at her like he really meant it. 'Wow. I love your hair. You look just like Siouxie Sioux.' Debbie decided in an instant that she liked Stephen.

'Hi Stephen.' Debbie replied. He sat down in a chair and gazed at Debbie's hair in adoration as if he were a poet who had found a new muse.

Roger was pleased with himself for making the others laugh but hoped he hadn't upset the new Bluecoat. He continued with his introductions. 'Oh, and over there in the corner, that's Suzanne'. Roger pointed at a chubby girl with frizzy light brown hair, who was holding a half-eaten Marathon bar in one hand and a cigarette in the other. The miserable Karen had moved over to sit next to her and the two of them were glued together in deep conversation. 'Suzanne does the keep fit class this morning, don't you? Say hello to our new Bluecoat, Debbie.'

'Hello Debbie.' Suzanne had one of those smug faces that reminded you of a greedy cat gloating over a saucer of cream. She was one of those people just asking for a poke in the eye. She made a great show of looking Debbie up and down, then fixed her stare pointedly upon the enormous hair, before making her thoughts about the new Bluecoat plain.

'Well, Debbie doesn't it just look like you've had a fright? No sorry … is it that you just look a fright.' Suzanne affected an expression of wide-eyed innocence before scanning the room to gauge the effects of her scathing remarks. Karen put her hand across her own mouth barely able to control her glee at the horrible situation her friend had created.

'Anyway.' Suzanne was on a roll and enjoying the moment. 'They put you in the right chalet didn't they love? How are you getting along with that other freak Siobhan?'

'That's enough Suzanne.' Roger hissed at the rude Bluecoat. 'There's no need to be …'

The door to the inner office flung open and Jill made her entrance with her full make-up, bouncing curls and a clipboard holding the day's rota. She tottered in like a new born fawn, wearing some very uncomfortable looking shoes. Accompanying her was the Entertainment's Manager, Tony in his badly stained suit, clutching an almost empty glass tankard of bitter.

10th April 2014 – The Lazaridis' House, Jesmond

Just Some Dinner Dance

As the door slammed, Elaine noted the usual absence of any goodbye from her employer and poured herself a generous cup of the fancy coffee. So a cracked mug was the only one fit for her using was it? Elaine had selected for herself Mrs Lazaride's new cup that had a pretty white swan with a golden beak. She settled once more into the very same chair her boss had been sitting in only moments ago, threw the white cushions on the floor and made herself comfy. When she had finished her drink, she had thought about smashing the stupid mug. However she thought better of it, as breaking the new crockery could well give Jillian the ammunition to fire her and that was the last thing she wanted.

Both of Elaine's jobs as shelf stacker in Tesco and cleaner in leafy Jesmond had been chosen deliberately because of their potential for her to cause trouble. Of course, Elaine was going to do her utmost to get to her cleaning job early, if only to spoil Jillian's day.That in itself was pleasure enough. Where once she had disliked the woman, the years had only intensified this into pure hatred. She was determined that Jillian should pay for what she once did and give Elaine what was rightfully hers.This was where Elaine needed to be canny and tred carefully taking one small step at a time. It was all well and good to annoy the woman a little but she needed to make sure her cleaning was up to scratch because Jillian would soon be praying for an opportunity to sack her. Anyway, Teddie Lazaridis had been the one who had employed her and she always made a point of being extremely nice to him.There was no way this golden goose was going to slip through Elaine's fingers for a second time.

At Tesco, she was constantly being reprimanded for being late but there was no reason to get there early because Michael Robinson baiting wasn't quite as enjoyable as upsetting Jillian. Nevertheless, it was still quite good fun. It was an amazing coincidence really, that not only had she once worked before with each of her employers, now neither of them had the slightest recollection of her. This, in itself spoke volumes as to how insignificant to both of them she had been. However, this would soon be changing because she had something on both of them and pretty soon they would be rueing the day that Elaine MacPherson had barged back into their lives.

Elaine had deliberately caught an earlier Metro because she had fancied a nice little chat with Mrs Lazaridis and wanted to catch her before she went out. Elaine took great delight at goading her boss and was aware fine well that her presence alone in the Lazaridis house did just that. She knew that her constant questioning irritated Jillian enormously — but that was just the point.

As usual, her employer had made her lame excuse to leave the house but Elaine knew she was just trying to avoid her. How on earth could she possibly need to be visiting the hairdresser again? She was only there the other day for God's sake. In fact, her stupid helmet of a bob was if anything too neat and she thought it sat on her head like an upside down fruit bowl. She would no doubt be wanting to look nice for tonight Elaine supposed.

Just some dinner dance poor Jillian had lamented but Elaine had no idea about such occasions because she had never had a husband to do *that sort of thing* with. She had three children, a grandchild and another one on the way to support. As a single parent she had to hold down two miserable jobs just to keep the wolf from the door. Her only experience of any bloody dinner dance was watching *Strictly Come Dancing* on the telly while eating her tea.

Chapter 5

15th July 1984 – Sunny Dunes Holiday Camp – The Entertainment's Office

An Unloved Dog

Despite kind words from the Chief Bluecoat Roger and some of the others, Debbie had been forced to brush away the tears stinging her eyes. She hadn't imagined that she would be met by such nastiness and hostility.

'Pay no attention to her. She's just a mean cow.' Roger sniffed and rubbed his nose. He had a look of genuine concern on his face and he patted her shoulder making her feel like some unloved dog.

'She's just jealous.' Stephen looked in the mirror to check his own quiff was still perfect. 'The only friend she's got here is that bitch Karen and nobody likes her either.' Satisfied that his appearance was up to his usual high standards, he turned his attention to the new recruit and gave her a pitying once over. 'Debbie love, why don't you go and fix your make-up and then come back here for a coffee?'

Oh great thought Debbie, she must have ugly panda rings all round her eyes where the mascara had run.

The expression on Roger's face, somewhere between appalled and amused, confirmed her worst thoughts. 'On the rota it says you are in the Cine Racing this morning and that doesn't start till 11. So you have plenty of time.'

Cine Racing.That was a new one to Debbie, that certainly hadn't been on the programme in Devon but at the moment she was more concerned with getting her appearance in order, rather than worrying what this activity might be.

'Suzanne'll be away in a minute. She taking a keep fit class at half past nine. Ha ha — she's not much of an advert for any exercise class is she?' Stephen rolled his eyes and sniggered.

'Yes ok.' Debbie managed a half smile. 'Where are the ladies?'

'There's not many ladies around here.' Stephen cocked his head to the side once more, in the direction of Suzanne and Karen who were both busy giggling and sharing their own nasty little jokes. 'They're just out the door to the left.'

8th April 2014 - Martha's Flat, Jesmond

Beneath the Old Woman's Weeds

After struggling to find a parking space for her vintage Beetle in the overcrowded street, Martha fished the door key from her pocket. Leafy Jesmond had never been intended for so many cars, but then that had hardly been a problem in Victorian times when the houses had first been built. Even with a parking permit when most of the residents were at work in the afternoon, it could be tricky enough to find a place but at night time it was an impossibility.

Once she had opened the communal door, Martha sprinted up the stairs to her apartment on the first floor. With relief, she tossed her quilted jacket onto her velvet chaise longue and the scruffy trainers onto her Moroccan rug. Then she pulled off the crumpled corduroy trousers and threw the messy grey wig on to the top of her grand piano. Running her fingers through her chestnut tangle of hair, Martha admired her lithe figure in its black T shirt and leggings in her full length mirror. Not bad for her age she decided as she turned a full circle to inspect herself from all angles. Next, she headed for the bathroom to remove the thick, sticky pan-stick makeup from her face and reveal the clear skin of a well-preserved woman in her early fifties.

She selected a *Debussy* CD to listen to before assuming a perfectly executed, straight plank yoga position. Martha was attempting to find an inner state of calm but couldn't shift from her mind the ridiculous behaviour of Mr Michael Robinson. If he could only have watched himself on camera yesterday he would have been appalled at how stupid he looked. She had been expecting a further confrontation this morning because she was sure she had seen him hovering round the door but he must have had some work for a change to keep himself occupied. Each time she visited Trinity Square, she now deliberately positioned herself in his sight-line to further antagonise him.

It had been a corker when the shoplifter had pushed him over. The shocked look on Mike Robinson's face was straight out of an Ealing Comedy as he floundered about the floor trying to regain his composure. Martha had made copious notes in her jotter about the fish out of water, the vile stench of the whisky and the tiny amount of blood on his torn trousers. This was all going to be very useful material for her latest book. She had been quite disappointed not to have had a repeat performance from the Deputy Store manager today.

The most amusing thing was for Martha was that he had absolutely no idea who she was. If he were only to walk back only a few metres into his precious shop, her name and photograph could be found on any of the many copies of her bestselling novels that the store sold. Destiny Chambers, with her tumbling brown curls and her ruby red lips smiled beguilingly at the reader from the back of any of her books. However, Mr Robinson was at a distinct disadvantage because Martha was totally unrecognisable as her alter ego Bird Woman. Nobody could ever guess, least of all Mr Robinson, that this glamorous lady novelist was hidden beneath the old woman's weeds. However, that wasn't all. Martha had known him before, a long time ago, in what now another life.

Martha wondered what Mr Robinson was doing at this moment. She imagined him telling off the girls on the tills, shouting at the lads in the warehouse and being obnoxious to the customers without even realising it. Before going to make herself a herbal tea, she turned on her computer. It was now two pm and she needed to get writing. She had a deadline that was fast approaching and this morning's research had been disappointing. Bringing up onto her screen what she had written yesterday, she began to make some alterations in accordance with what had recently happened. Then, she heard the sound of her phone ringing. Damn, it was her agent Sorchia and reluctantly she picked up.

'Hi, Destiny darling. How are you? I was just wondering how you were getting on?' Martha winced at the sound of her ridiculous pseudonym. Beneath Sorchia's gushing tones was that familiar note of impatience.

'Lovely to hear from you. Yes, yes, all is very well, thanks, and you?' She needed this conversation like a hole in the head and she was not in the frame of mind at that moment to play Destiny Chambers.

'Well, I'd be all the better for hearing your affirmative answer.' Martha could hear Sorchia taking a deep drag from a cigarette.

'Sorry?' Martha pretended she didn't know to what she was referring.

'Well, the new book?' Sorchia cut to the chase. ''Will your first draft be finished by the end of the …'

'Sorchia, I'm sorry, but you know, I've had problems recently.' Martha snapped back at her like a terrier. 'But I've been writing loads these last few days.' This wasn't strictly true but all things considered …

'But sweetie you said it would be ready by the end of …'

'Sorchia. My mother died only a few weeks ago and I've had lots to do.' Sorchia knew this fine well and had even sent her flowers. Admittedly, they hadn't been very nice ones but nevertheless.

'Yes, I'm sorry to hear that but I thought it might have helped you get over it by immersing yourself in your new bestseller.' Sorchia made an attempt at a breezy nonchalance.

'Sorchia, my mind has been on other things.' Martha took a sip from the herbal tea, trying to remain calm. 'My head has been all over the place but as I told you, I have started writing again this week.' This was true although not a great deal had been written.

'Great, so this latest blockbuster by Destiny Chambers should be finished by the end of the month?' Sorchia was like a dog with a bone.

'No, it won't. Just cut me some slack.' Martha could strangle the woman.

'But it needs to be released to catch the Christmas …'

'Sorchia, it will be ready when it is.' Martha wished she could slam down the phone but she needed to keep the woman on board.

'Ok, but I'm so excited for it.' Martha imagined Sorchia's beam of bright orange lipstick oohing, aaghing and pulsating like a belisha beacon. 'What is it about?'

Martha paused then bit the bullet. 'It's about an old woman who feeds the birds.' That should shut her up thought Martha, stifling a chuckle.

'Are you having a laugh?' This was not what Sorchia had been expecting to hear.

'No, but trust me Sorchia, you won't be disappointed. Now I'm putting the phone down.' Martha knew she must have given Sorchia something to fret about but she just wanted rid of her because she needed to get on with her work.

'But sweetie…' Sorchia weedled.

Martha imagined Sorchia must have thought Destiny was just winding her up. For sure as far as her agent was concerned tedious stories about old women feeding birds wouldn't sell books. This was certainly not the type of heroine Destiny Chamber's audience would identify with.

''No, don't go,' said Sorchia. 'You're kidding me aren't you? You've got to be. Surely there must be a young beautiful granddaughter? And yes, I know … she starts off poor then becomes rich and glamorous and …

'Sorchia, I must go. There's someone at my door,' Martha lied, but she just needed to get Sorchia off her back.

Martha ended the call and put all thoughts of Destiny and Sorchia from her mind to return to her writing. Since the death of her mother, she had spent a great deal of time reflecting on what she wanted from life. Although she and her mother had not been especially close, Martha had always craved her mother's approval. The former English teacher had not been impressed by her daughter's Destiny Chambers incarnation and had been embarrassed by her daughter's silly books. Now she had passed, Martha was hoping that her new pen name would help her create something that both she and her mother could be proud of.

Chapter 6

15th July 1984 – Sunny Dunes Holiday Camp – Returning
from the Ladies

Stupid Sandals

When Debbie returned to the Entertainment's Office, the air was
even thicker with a vile cloud of smoke. Coughing profusely, she
put her hand over her mouth. Across the fug-filled room, she saw
Stephen and Roger both smoking and chatting. As these two
seemed to be the most friendly Bluecoats and because they had
shown her kindness earlier, she sat down at the table with them.
Instantly, they both leapt from their seats to profer her a tab from
each of their packets. She shook her head. Was it only by her
participation in this North-Eastern pipe of peace ceremony that she
was going to be fully accepted here, as they all seemed to have a
perpetual fag hanging from their mouths.

'That's much better' Stephen smiled at her, approving of her
cosmetic repairs. 'So Debbie you simply must tell me how you get
your hair like that.' He leaned forward to touch her spikey hair, then
dramatically pulled his hand away as if he'd been prickled by the
thorns of a rose bush.

Debbie laughed, feeling much more at ease with these friendly
boys. 'It's just hairspray – super strong.' She pulled a large purple
aerospray can, decorated with bolts of lightning out of her bag
which Stephen grabbed and squirted liberally on his own hair.
Once more he returned to the mirror flicking his fingers through his
sticky hair admiring the effect.

' Not bad.' He nodded at his reflection.

Out of the blue, Marcus the Bluecoat, with the unusual shoes who had earlier been engrossed in his book, placed a drink in a Styrofoam beaker on the table. He smiled at her displaying his immaculate white teeth. 'Here's a drink for you Debbie. You can just help yourself to coffee, tea or toast whenever you like, you know.'He indicated towards the messy bench laden with half drunken cups, dirty plates, a large used breadknife and crumbs everywhere. 'I don't know if you take sugar?' Debbie recognised a Brummy burr in his voice, a sound she knew well because that was where she had just been studying in Birmingham.

'No, I don't, but thankyou.' Debbie was ready for a drink and glad to hear a familiar accent.

'Thank you Marcus, but Debbie's our friend so get yourself back to your trumpet and silly history books,' snapped Stephen, pulling his chair closer to his new bestie.

'All right Stephen.' Roger scowled at Stephen. 'Thank you Marcus.'

By now Marcus, who was oblivious to any insult and clearly on the austistic spectrum, was marching back across the room to continue reading his book.

Debbie took a sip from the unappetising cup of what she assumed was coffee but could have just as easily have been tea. It had a strange muddy consistancy, a peculiar colour, and with each mouthful crumbly polystyrene particles landed on her tongue.

'There was no need to be rude to Marcus, Stephen. He was just trying to be friendly to Debbie.' Roger chastised Stephen who was now pulling faces in Marcus's direction.

'Marcus. He's a right weirdo Debbie. Have nothing to do with him. That's not even his real name you know. He's called Mark but he thinks Marcus sounds more Roman. You'd better watch out though. He's probably eyeing you up to be his Cleopatra.'

Stephen's eyes were alight with glee as he loved telling this tale and he lit another cigarette. 'The only reason he's come to be a Bluecoat here is because he's obsessed with the Romans and it's near to his beloved Hadrian's Wall.'

'Stephen. Don't be so nasty. There's no harm in him.' Roger thought Marcus was quite cute with his dark mahogany skin and long eyelashes. Debbie was enjoying this story and she chuckled watching the avid book reader over the other side of the room.

'Can you believe he's wearing those stupid sandals again? I'm surprised Jill didn't pull him up on that one again. He's been sent back to his chalet to change them umpteen times but he couldn't give a toss and do you know what he does every week on his day off?' Stephen took a long drag on his fag. 'It's bonkers. He gets dressed up in his silly armour and goes prancing up and down in some place called the Roman Road. He even gets the bus to somewhere right over in Yorkshire.'

'He goes to Corbridge.' Roger shook his head contradicting Stephen, who was from Manchester and had limited knowledge of the local area.

 'Whatever.' Stephen didn't like being corrected and was bored of the subject of Marcus. He stubbed out his cigarette. 'Anyway, you are on the Cine Racing with me this morning Debbie but don't worry. I'll keep you right.' Stephen patted her hand and winked at her, but in a gesture of camaraderie, as it was quite plain which team he batted for.

'What is Cine Racing? Do I have to run?' Debbie had a deep loathing of anything connected with sport, especially if it involved her being filmed. Sport was not her thing, in any shape or form.

'No, you're just selling tickets to the daft punters. They bet on which horse is going to win the race. It's quite pathetic actually but don't worry we'll have a laugh.' Stephen playfully nudged her arm, she remembered Tony elbowing Jill last night and wondered if she had a bruise today.

'Stephen you shouldn't be encouraging her to laugh at the guests.' Roger in an affected deeper voice, pulled rank and slipped into his Head Bluecoat mode.

'Whatever.' Stephen swooshed back his hair and looked at them both coquettishly from beneath his eyelids. 'Honestly Debbie, you wouldn't believe how seriously they take it? There's not even very much money involved.'

'Not as seriously as the *Bingo* though.' Roger reverted once more to his usual higher-pitched breathy speech patterns, similar to those of Stephen.

'No, that's big cash. And whoa betide you if you make any mistakes calling the numbers in Bingo.' Stephen rolled his eyes.

'And you'd know all about that, wouldn't you?' Roger flashed him a reprimanding look before taking a white handkerchief from his pocket. He wiped his nose and Debbie noticed traces of red. She wondered if Roger was about to have a heavy nosebleed but it seemed not and he stuffed the cloth back into his pocket. 'Anyway, this afternoon, you're on the whist drive with me deary.' Debbie was surprised it wasn't poker, as this holiday camp was seemimg to be to be just one big, sordid gambling den.

By this time, the Entertainment's Office was almost empty, as all the other Bluecoats had gone about their morning duties or had gone back to their chalets. Although the door to Tony's office was closed, Debbie could hear some girlish giggling and deep guffaws. She had a pretty good idea of what was going on in there.

'Honestly. This is just typical,' said Roger. 'Really one of those two should be giving you a guided tour of the place. I'll go and find out what's going on.' He knocked on the inner office door before entering.

'Get out.' An angry voice growled from within. 'You've no bloody business in here. Now just close that bastard door. NOW.'

'Sorry Tony.' Roger pulled an apologetic face. 'But didn't you or Jill want to show around the new ...'

'Bloody Hell. You're the   Head Bluecoat here. You show her around and don't forget to introduce her to Stan.' Tony's head, with an angry expression, appeared round the side of the door. 'You know he expects to meet any new staff. Well, go on and get lost. Just go and bloody do it. And don't come in again unless you are invited.' The door once more was slammed shut. Tony was obviously otherwise engaged and was not at all pleased about being interrupted.

'Oops.' Roger looked a little sheepish.' Looks like you're stuck with us two Debbie. Come along we've got less than an hour.'

8th April 2014 – Gateshead Quayside

The Hungry Triffids

Mike was glad that the day was over and he could escape back to his apartment. Today had not been one of his finest. Some weeks ago his wife had kicked him out of their lovely house in Gosforth and he was now staying in a poky studio apartment, close to the Baltic Art Gallery. While some of these flats boasted sensational views across the Tyne, his had a small balcony which overlooked the car park. Sitting on the small, black vinyl sofa bed, it felt as if the large black and grey flowers on the wallpaper were closing in on him. He imagined they were hungry triffids sizing him up for their next meal.

However, the saving grace of this place was that it was close to his work. Furthermore, it belonged to Philip, a good friend of his who was working abroad and owed him a favour, so he didn't have any rent to pay. Hanging from the frame of a print of a Highland Deer with enormous antlers, was his freshly dry-cleaned suit and a crisply pressed shirt for tomorrow. For some reason the washing machine in the flat seemed to be broken and there was no way he was paying to get it fixed. Luckily, a laundrette was close by.

Still, this was only a temporary arrangement, for once his mate's contract in Qatar was up, Philip would be back and Mike would have to find alternative living accommodation. Hopefully, his wife Linda would have seen sense by then. She was just being so unreasonable. It must have been almost three months since she had kicked him out. He had assumed that by now the two of them would have made amends and patched things up. For God's sake, they had been married for more than twenty five years. Most of this time he had spent working bloody hard, making good money to raise their two sons who had since flown the nest. Although one was still at uni, the other was down in London doing very well for himself as a computer programmer. This should be the time that they, or particularly he, should be enjoying having more cash to spend on himself. Why was the bloody woman being so petty?

Well, while his wife was sitting pretty in their three bedroomed semi with her nice little part time job as a lifestyle coach (whatever that was), he had to cope with the stress of his job and live in this squalid hovel. It just wasn't fair and today had all been too much.

First of all, that fat obnoxious shelf stacker Elaine, had been definitely having a laugh at his expense. He was sure of that and it wasn't the first time. For some reason unbeknown to him, the woman thought she could get away with it. She had only been working there a few months and while her timekeeping was atrocious, she seemed constantly to be pushing boundaries and showing him a complete lack of respect. He had no need to put up with this from a two a penny menial worker and she had better watch her step or her days would soon be numbered. At Trinity

Square Gateshead Tesco store, Mr Michael Robinson was one of the top dogs and not a man to be messed with.

Then, to make matters worse the Bird Woman had reappeared on the scene. He had seen her through the shop doors and it was as if she had positioned herself where she could be clearly seen to annoy him. Already the birds had been gathering and just as he was about to go and sort her out he had needed to deal with some bloody customers. Of course once he had finished with them the old crone had vanished. He would be watching out for her the next time though.

Michael poured himself a whiskey, lit a cigarette and started watching the news when his phone began to ring. When he saw it was his wife, he quickly stubbed out the fag, as she believed he had stopped smoking twenty years ago.

'Hello, my dear and how are …'

'Mike. This has gone on long enough. I want a divorce.' Linda's voice had that steely edge he had heard so often of late.

'Hush dear.' He took a gulp from his whisky. 'Now, don't be hasty. We said we would give things time didn't we?' As if today hadn't been bad enough and now this conversation was just what he needed.

'It's almost three months and I want it sorted.' She heard the clink of the glass as it chinked against the ash tray on the table. 'Are you drinking? Now why doesn't that surprise me? And you needn't think I'm selling this house. Oh no. This house belongs to me.'

'Now come on my dear. Just calm down. Number one, it's too soon and … where am I supposed to live?' Why couldn't she just forgive him and then things could go back to normal.

'Mike, you should have thought about that before, shouldn't you? And this isn't a bolt out of the blue is it? Our whole marriage has been a sham. I'm sure your shenanigans with that floozy aren't the first time you cheated on me. It's just the first time you've been caught. You disgust me and I want a divorce.'

Linda's words stung with the truth and Mike could picture his estranged wife at that very moment dunking biscuits into her tea then shoving them between her pursed sanctimonious lips.

'But love, I'm sorry. I promise I will never do it again.' Michael wished he could turn back the clock and not have been spotted by one of Linda's eagle-eyed malicious friends. It wasn't even as if Samantha had been anything special. He was just having a bit of fun and not doing any harm. For years he had got away with his little dalliances and Linda had been none the wiser. Why did that spiteful cow Sandra have to stick in her beak and spill the beans. If truth be known he didn't particularly love or miss his wife anymore but he totally loathed this present lifestyle.

'Don't you patronise me.' Linda ranted. 'You've probably been having it away with every ... Tracy, Dawn or Harriet ... for donkey's years. Haven't you?' She paused for a moment, to reflect on her wittiness in the replacement of Tom, Dick and Harry to suitable women's names. 'If I had known what you were really like do you think I would have married you in the first place?'

Mike couldn't believe she was still fuming about his behaviour after nearly twelve weeks. 'But we've had two lovely sons and a good life together.' Mike tried to highlight the positives. He had been both a good father and husband. His salary was still going into their joint bank account and the unreasonable bitch was living in their lovely semi in Gosforth.

'Yes ... had. I'm glad you spoke in the past tense.' She quickly retorted.

'Now love, just try to see some sense.' Mike pleaded with her while his fingers were itching to light another cigarette.

'I think the days of you calling me love are long gone. I'll be ringing my solicitor tomorrow.' She hung up.

Chapter 7

15th July 1984 – Sunny Dunes Holiday Camp – The Corridor

Tramp by Name

Elaine had been busy mopping the floor next to the Regency Ballroom, when she saw the new Bluecoat running along the corridor with the strangest spikey hair and make-up running all down her face. Did she not realise this look was no longer in fashion? Punk was *so* 1970's and if she thought she was cool she was sadly mistaken. Elaine patted her own what she imagined was a golden Simon le Bon-like bouffant and wondered whatever was the matter with the girl. There were a few things she would like to say to her. Like why was her hair so strange and why did she not possess a hairbrush? Mind, that Bluecoat Stephen's yellow mop was hardly any better. She would like to stick both of their heads in her bucket to give the floors a good swoosh.

However, just what could that new girl be crying about when she had only just arrived? Perhaps she had just quickly realised she wouldn't fit in. They were a funny lot, the collection of Bluecoats this year. And they were very cliquey. Even the ones like Roger and Jill who had worked here for the last few seasons seemed different, more up themselves compared to how they had been in previous years.

There had been a time when some of them had found time to chat and spend some time with the lowly cleaner Elaine but that no longer seemed to be the case. Only last year, she could remember sharing a fag and a coffee with Jill. Admittedly, Jill hadn't asked for her company but nevertheless … now Miss Hoity Toity thought herself a cut above everyone else. It seemed she actively went out of her way to avoid any contact with Elaine whatsoever. The other day she was diligently hoovering the floor beside the Entertainment's Office, when the recently promoted Bluecoat flounced out of the office. Not only did she put her fingers in her ears to drown out the vacuum's buzzing noise but also she stuck her nose in the air, as if she, Elaine, was generating a bad smell. Someone should have a word with Jill about that awful *Tramp* perfume she wore, but then again tramp by name …

Since she had been made Deputy Entertainment's Manager, Jill seemed to think she was something special. Well, we all know how *that* promotion happened thought Elaine and puckered her lips in disgust. She, for one, couldn't bear the idea of Tony Noble's grubby mitts with their knuckle-duster signet rings and dirty fingers pawing her. The thought of his foul beer breath, manky teeth and gravy-stained jackets made her flesh creep.

But, then again Jill was used to the proverbial casting couch wasn't she? Elaine remembered her from old. They had both grown up on the same Scottish council estate hadn't they? Now, Jill denied any previous knowledge of Elaine and she claimed to have been brought up in Edinburgh. As if. Jill was just a lying cow and was pretending she didn't know her because Elaine knew where she had been dragged up. Granted, Jill was a few years older than her but they remembered each other all right. Back in the day, they had both gone to the same sink school. Despite it failing to provide them much in the way of academic achievement or qualifications, some seemed to have fared better in the lottery of life than others.

Yet, even as a young lass, Jill's promiscuous reputation was common knowledge. *Jezebel Jill* was whispered. *That one'll come to nae good*, was muttered repeatedly by her mam and her cronies. Elaine shook her head. These were facts that Jill had conveniently forgotten and kept well hidden in her dirty laundry and along with her naturally broad Glaswegian accent. Oh yes, credit to Jill in digging a deep hole to hide her grubby past. It might be all well and good for the time being but eventually the truth would out at some point and everybody knew that you couldn't make a silk purse from a sow's ear.

Elaine squeezed her dirty mop into the metal bucket of filthy water, as the repaired strange-looking Bluecoat scuttled past. Although she seemed to have reapplied her make-up, her face still looked like a ghost and as for her hair ...

Really, it so wasn't fair. Elaine was sure she would have made a much better Bluecoat than this new recruit, given half a chance. In fact, upon several occasions she had borrowed the key to the uniform cupboard and tried on some of the spare Bluecoat blazers. And without any shadow of a doubt, they had suited her. Once, while wearing a Bluecoat jacket that was the perfect fit and using a scrubbing brush as a makeshift microphone, she imagined herself hosting the talent competition. Just as she was announcing the winner, she had spotted Jill in the distance down the corridor carrying some boxes. With a deft flick of her shoulder, she wriggled out of the jacket, which crumpled itself messily on the ground. Cleverly, Elaine had made a big show of picking the untidy garment off the floor and returning it neatly to the cupboard. Jill seemed unaware of either her trespass or quick thinking.

If only someone would give her an opportunity. Granted, she knew wasn't the best looking twenty-something year old but at least she could keep *her* hair neat. Although she knew she couldn't sing, dance or be particularly pleasant, she had a good loud voice that would be ideal for calling the Bingo. Particularly, as a lot of the punters were Scottish themselves.

The sound of *Let's Get Physical* by Olivia Newton John was blasting from the Regency Ballroom. Below the small spangled stage, with the sleeping Hammond Organ and drums, the hardly sylph-like Suzanne had positioned herself in the centre of the room with her purple leotard and pink leg warmers. As she kicked each leg as high as she could manage, an audience of middle-aged and elderly women were pleased to discover they could easily follow her undemanding routines. With her eyes fixed firmly on the slowly moving hands of the clock, Suzanne was obviously just looking forward to her next fag as soon as the class had finished. Elaine smirked. Suzanne was about the same size as herself, but given a brightly coloured leotard and a decent chance, she'd be doing a much better job with a keep-fit class.

No, this season's set of Bluecoats in her opinion were an ill-chosen bunch. For years, well, since it had been legal anyway, this sort of job had attracted gay men who made no show of hiding their proclivities. So Roger and Stephen were just mincing in the steps of those who had gone long before. She also had her suspicions about that Mike. At the beginning of the season she had thought there was something kind of sexy about his moustache and muscles, but despite her giving him the full come on with her coyest of smiles, he seemed totally oblivious to her charms. Well, he quite clearly wasn't the hot-blooded hetro male he liked others to believe.

Also this year, there was that butch Irish Siobhan with her ugly sour-milky coloured hair and pale skin, who definitely batted for the other side. She was almost sure the dirty dyke had made sheep's eyes at her once or twice. I don't think so, Elaine had thought at the time, before sticking two fingers up at the pervert and pulling out her tongue. She had noticed the new punky Bluecoat coming out of her chalet. Well they both had very pale skin and horrible hair. Really, pondered Elaine, nothing could surprise her and birds of a feather were well known to be found flocking together.

The would-be Purple Goddess, Suzanne and pathetic Karen, the children's Auntie Bluecoat were just mean bitches cut from the same cloth as Jill. No doubt, they were all shagging Tony Noble. In fact, Noble he certainly wasn't in any shape or form. No, this was Elaine's last season at this dump. If they hadn't promoted her to Bluecoat by the end of September … Tony Noble, Sunny Dunes and Fred Pontin could all go swivel.

10th April 2014 – The Olympian Restaurant, Jesmond

Teddie's Eyes and Ears

Theodore was always impeccably dressed. The suits he habitually wore were smart pin-striped; grey, navy or black. He mostly kept the black for sombre occasions such as funerals and meetings with his accountant. Today, he was wearing a smart navy one with an ice blue shirt and a natty, spotted tie. His shoes glinted with polish like two black beetles. So did his hair and moustache, but in their case assisted by *Just For Men Ultra* and a liberal application of Brylcream.

Theodore, Mr Lazaridis or Teddie as he was referred to affectionately by his wife and close friends, looked a little like Agatha Christie's Poirot when played by David Suchet. This was a comparison he quite liked and deliberately cultivated, although Teddie was Greek rather than Belgian. Sometimes, when faced with a problem he would amuse himself and others by consulting his μικρά γκρί κύτταρα (little grey cells in Greek). Jillian had once found this quite amusing, but by now its constant repetitiveness had simply become tedious.

As the owner of several Greek restaurants in the Tyne and Wear region, Teddie Lazaridis was a wealthy man. His parents had moved from Athens to North-East England in the 1970's and had set up a couple of taverna-style establishments. As package holidays to the Greek islands flourished during the 1980's, so did Mr Lazaridis senior's restaurants, as Greek dining became all the rage. By the time of his unfortunate death, after being knocked over by a bus in Northumberland Street, Apostolos Lazaridis was a rich man. As a result, his son Theodore inherited a string of restaurants, a beautiful house and a tidy sum in the bank. It was not long after this he met his wife Jillian while on holiday back in Greece.

Teddie spent most of his time at the flagship restaurant, The Olympian in Jesmond. It was a beautiful place, painted in the very palest of green and had white frescoes of the Ancient Greek deities in procession around the dining area. These were rather like the Elgin Marbles except better, as these all had their heads intact. In fact, Aphrodite's lovely face bore more than a passing resemblance to that of Mrs Lazaridis. Above the gods and goddesses twined lavish garlands of vines and grapes which looked almost real. From the ceiling, hung gigantic chandeliers whose crystals sparkled and winked in the candlelight like come hither invitations from nymphs. Anyone who knew the Lazaridis couple could guess instantly that Jillian had more than a hand in this decor.

From out of the kitchen wafted the delicious smells of meat, garlic and herbs. The svelte student waiters and waitresses in black and white attire, dashed about like Mediterranean penguins with their utterances of Ευχαρίστώ (thankyou) and Παρακαχώ (my pleasure) while the plinky plonk of Greek bouzouki music played merrily in the background.

It was from here that Teddie conducted most of his business with the help of his right hand man Vasilis (his name was Bill really but Teddie had long ago persuaded him to use the Greek equivalent), who was a large bald man in his fifties. He had rather allowed his love of Greek food to get the better of his waistline. Teddie had a special office which allowed him to not only watch the efficiency and politeness of his waiters and waitresses, but listen to their conversations. When he was not there, cleverly concealed CCTV cameras meant he always had his finger on the pulse.

When the waiter Yianni (John) was sacked for helping himself too liberally to the Metaxa from behind the bar there had been no witnessing of his sneaky tippling. Nobody had any idea of what the waiter had been up to, but somehow Teddie Lazaridis knew. Likewise, no one had a clue that light-fingered Eleni (Helen) had been dipping into the tips jar, that was usually shared out equally at the end of each night but somehow the restaurant owner had caught her red handed. Apart from Vasilis, his staff was completely unaware of the existence of this room and if they had been they would have no doubt have found it more than a little creepy. It was all very mysterious and it seemed that the man had an uncanny ability of knowing every detail of his employees' comings and goings. In the Olympian Restaurant, it was as if Teddie Lazaridis had eyes and ears everywhere.

'Ah, Vasilis, how are the bookings for tonight?' Theodore asked his friend who had just replaced the phone after presumably talking with some customers.

'Pretty good boss,' Vasilis grinned. 'There's a party of twelve for an 18th birthday, a large company 'do' and a couple of Wedding Anniversaries.'

Theodore noticed Vasilis had some strands of green vegetable sticking between his front teeth. He instinctively licked the gap between his own front teeth.

'Excellent. And how is staffing doing?' asked Vasilis.

'Yes, don't worry. Chef is in fine fettle and everything seems just tickety boo.' Vasilis gave a nervous glance towards the kitchen.

'Great stuff because I've got a charity dinner to go to with my wife this evening.' Theodore smiled to himself and wondered which of her lovely dresses Jillian would be wearing for the event. Although she must be pushing sixty and many years had passed since he had met his future wife while on holiday in Corinth, to him she was just as beautiful as the day they first met.

'Ok, have a good one.' Vasilis busied himself highlighting that night's bookings with an orange felt pen.

Chapter 8

15th July 1984 – Sunny Dunes Holiday Camp – A Guided Tour of Sunny Dunes

I Wouldn't Eat the Chips

'Right, come on then Debbie. I'd better do as Tony ordered.' Roger poured the rest of his coffee down the sink. 'We've got an hour before your first assignment – the famous Cine Racing. So, we've just got time for the splendid guided tour — ta dah, if we get a wiggle on. Are you coming along then Stephen? I bet you can't wait to see Old Uncle Stan?'

'Well I'll come with you for a while but only because I like Debbie.' He gave her a broad grin and slapped her on the back. She instantly felt much more positive about this her latest experience. 'But I reckon I'll give him a miss.' Stephen rolled his eyes.

'Who's Uncle Stan?' Asked Debbie.

'Stan Braithwaite or Mr Braithwaite, as we have to call him.' Roger held the door open and gestured for them both to follow through.

'He thinks he's something special but he only got the job of Camp Manager because he's big pals with Fred Pontin.' Stephen appeared to have a poor opinion of the man. 'Wait till you see the state of his office …'

'I'm sure Debbie is quite capable of forming her own thoughts on our dear Mr Braithwaite,' interrupted Roger. 'So, Debbie through that door is the Regency Ballroom and up those stairs is the Regency Lounge.'

'That's where all the cool afternoon whist drives are held,' added Stephen.

'Really?' Debbie had learned how to play last summer but she had never found them very exciting.

'Duh – no, of course not.' Stephen snapped back laughing. 'They are as dull as dish water as you'll find out this afternoon. The only good thing about that duty is they often get cancelled because nobody wants to play the stupid game.'

'The ballroom here is where they have all the old time dancing.' Roger explained.

'You know waltzes and quicksteps and all that kind of stuff.' Stephen's feet slipped into a dainty little 1-2-3 rhythm type dance. 'It's quite a laugh in there in the evening and a good skive. You just sit and play records for the dances, you know.' Stephen pointed through the door where Debbie could see a stage with golden curtains and shiny strips of paper running from floor to ceiling but the music currently playing sounded modern.

'It's not that easy Stephen.' Roger was beginning to wish Stephen hadn't come along with them because as usual he was just being silly. 'The wrinklies get really mad if you play the wrong music for their old-fashioned dances.' Roger spoke as if he had had personal experience of this.

'Anyway,' Stephen sniggered. 'If you look through the glass you can see a big fat purple thing running the keep fit class. Hardly a good example to promote exercise is she? It's a wonder anyone joins in the class.' And the three of them laughed at the sight of Suzanne threshing about on the dance floor along with two elderly ladies and some children. The beached whale wore a purple leotard and was scowling.

Next, Roger led them out through the door to the left. 'Over there is the boating lake and straight ahead is the Orangery. It's just a café and the coffee is just as awful in there as the stuff in our office.' Roger scrunched up his face in disapproval but Debbie thought it looked quite pleasant as they walked past. People were enjoying the sunshine streaming through the windows and the room was filled with artificial trees laden with plastic oranges had a cheery Mediterranean feel.

'All right there, Roger.' A man wearing a tracksuit and handlebar moustache, shouted over and tapped the side of his nose pointedly.

'Yes thanks Kevin. This is the new Bluecoat Debbie I'm just showing her around.' Roger waved at the man

'So, she's Mandy's replacement is she? Hi Debbie. Are you a punk then?' He asked in a mocking tone.

'Kevin is just one of the lifeguards. Pay no attention to him. He's just a tosser.' Stephen shouted the last word so Kevin could hear because he could see Debbie was looking uncomfortable remembering her earlier humiliation. Evidence of her reddening cheeks were noticeable even beneath the white make-up. 'Anyway the swimming pool is over there and your chalet is just behind it. Kevin bugger off. Leave the new kid alone.' Stephen shouted across to the lifeguard who was smirking and seemed pleased with himself.

'I would keep out of his way if I was you.' Roger quickened his pace. 'He's bad news.' Roger mumbled this last part and Stephen gave him a strange look.

'If you look over there Debbie, you can see the sports field.' Stephen pointed over to a large patch of grass that had been badly burned by the sun. 'That's where Siobhan does her stuff, mostly with Barry. They've both got their days off today so you won't meet him till tomorrow. Mind, Barry and Liz are so luvved up at the minute you hardly see anything of either of them.' He pulled a face. 'Look, there's Mike down there trying to organise a football match.' Mike, whose face was bright red, was repeatedly blowing a whistle at a group of little boys who were running around the field and paying him no attention whatsoever. 'Don't worry, the only time we go there is for the Donkey Derby on a Wednesday afternoon.' Debbie knew all about those for they had them weekly at Paignton.

'Oh, and that big building in the middle is the canteen. Did you go in there for your breakfast this morning?' Roger asked Debbie.

'No. Nobody had told me about it.' Debbie shook her head. She was actually feeling rather hungry and had wondered what she was supposed to do for meals here.

'That's just typical of this place isn't it? You must be starving.' Stephen fished in his jacket pocket and took out a packet of sticky sweeties, which appeared as though they had been there for some time. 'Here have one of these.'

'Thank you.' Debbie gratefully put a sugary pear drop into her mouth.

'So Debbie, didn't you have anything to eat either when you got here last night?' Stephen decided to eat one himself and offered them to Roger.

'No thank you Stephen.' Roger looked sceptically at the crumpled packet. 'I've brushed my teeth this morning.

'Siobhan gave me a cup of tea and some biscuits. Tony and Jill just gave me wine.' Debbie played the events of last night once more through her mind,

'That sounds about right.' Roger tutted. 'Well, you can get your breakfast, lunch and evening meal in there. Whenever you want but I must warn you … the food is awful and you have to mingle with the guests.'

'Yes, most of us just get snacks from the shops which are over there.' Stephen popped another sweetie into his mouth but this time didn't offer them around.

'Those are the shops. There's a newsagent, a chemist, the photographer's and a fish and chip shop.' Roger was now further quickening their pace, as he was aware of the limited time they had.

'It's not bad in there,' Stephen nodded towards the shop where through the window a woman in a white coat could be seen peeling potatoes. 'We sometimes get chips at the end of the night.'

'Not bad!' Roger pulled another face. 'They keep the uncooked chips in a dustbin round the back and the seagulls crap all over them.'

As they walked past the chip shop Debbie made a mental note to avoid the place.

'Behind the shops is the Smuggler's Bar and the Children's Den where Suzanne's sidekick Karen hangs out with Uncle Benjie, the children's entertainer.' Stephen raised his eyebrows and Debbie wondered what was wrong with Uncle Benjie.

'There is the Prince's Ballroom. That's where it all happens.' Roger announced proudly. 'Every night Bingo starts at eight ...'

'It's on at four pm too. Everyone is Bingo Bonkers here.' Stephen pulled another of his silly faces.

'As I was saying,' continued Roger. 'After the Bingo, Larry Lawson's Show band kicks off,'

'Watch out though Debbie. You'll need to wear shades or you'll be dazzled by his teeth. Zing.' Stephen bared his own teeth which were an ordinary yellowish colour and slightly wonky. 'Mind you if anyone could do with a visit to a dentist, it's Tony Noble. Ha ha.' The three of them laughed together and Debbie blocked out the image of the nasty lifeguard along with that of Tony Noble's terrible teeth.

'Anyway that's where all the shows, cabarets and dancing mostly take place.' Roger once more was wearing his Head Bluecoat hat. 'And over there, next to the main gate is the wages office where you collect your pittance every week and next to that ... is where you will find Uncle Stan.'

'Well, I'm offski. See you back at the office Debbie.' And Stephen marched back across the square.

'Right come on then Debbie let's get this over with. He's not that bad really.' Roger reassured her.

10th April 2014 – The Lazaridis' House, Jesmond

The Awful Manifestation

Jillian went on a few unnecessary shopping errands after her hairdressing appointment, to make sure that the dreadful Elaine had finished the cleaning before she returned home. She stepped out of her white BMW with a few little bags from the expensive shops where she had bought special cheeses, locally made sausages and some lovely Jo Malone candles. When she opened the vestibule door, the parquet floor was shining, the windows gleaming but most importantly there was no sign of Elaine.

To her annoyance, the whole house gave off a scent of polished cleanliness. Jillian ran her finger along the top of the inside door, hoping to find some dust but to no avail. This did not please her in the slightest and she scanned the hallway looking for evidence of cut corners or shoddy workmanship. There was just something about the woman that she immensely disliked. It wasn't her just her slovenly appearance, harsh Glaswegian accent or general boorishness — there was something more. There was something almost familiar about her, as if she had known her in her earlier life but Jillian couldn't place from where and she didn't want to.

Jillian's own sorry upbringing was not the one she would have wished for herself or one she ever admitted to, even to her husband. The squalor of their home, having to share not only a bedroom but a bed with two sisters, her drunken father and often going hungry was not a place she wanted to revisit. She had eradicated any tell-tale trace of Scottish from her voice decades ago but the shameful memories of the poverty of her childhood she kept locked away tightly.

After the sudden departure of the ungrateful Sonia, their previous cleaner, who it seemed had found a better paid job, her husband had took it upon himself to find a suitable replacement. This should not have been his decision because he had his restaurants to attend to and the household was her domain. While Sonia had been young, quiet and minded her own business, Elaine was old, never stopped prattling and worse of all, very nosey. Her husband had imagined wrongly that she would be delighted when she returned from shopping to discover this horrible apparition cleaning in her hallway.

At first, Jillian was just irritated to see this unfamiliar specimen in her home but when the creature turned round to face her, switched off the hoover and opened its mouth ... Jillian was horrified. Elaine was very antithesis of everything she thought she had escaped from. This woman could have been the ghost of her mother who had come back to haunt her. She had severed all contact with her family years ago and she had no idea as to whether her own parents were dead or alive. Jillian wasn't interested, as to her, that life no longer existed and she preferred to pretend it hadn't really happened. That was until the awful manifestation called Elaine appeared in her life.

Maybe that was just it. Perhaps the cleaner's very presence in her life was a constant reminder her of her of her own sorry past. But no, there was something even more personal regarding her dislike of Elaine. There was an over-familiarity about her, a lack of deference to her employer, as if she had *something* on her. It was as if the woman knew she had known Jillian previously and was going to use this information to her own advantage. From the sound of her accent alone, which Jillian could pinpoint to only metres away from the street where she had been raised, it was more than quite likely it was from here where Elaine recognised her. Jillian winced; this was not something she wanted reminding of. Yet, as she racked her brains, she could think of nobody from her past who bore any physical resemblance to her cleaner.

Jillian knew that her own appearance must have changed slightly over the years, as with age it was inevitable. However in her own case, she liked to think that she had matured like a fine wine rather than aged because she had always taken the best care of herself. When Jillian looked in the mirror she was largely pleased with her reflection and she knew she held on to her looks well compared to her more withered friends of a similar age. She hazarded a guess that Elaine must be a good few years older than herself. However, if the hands of time had been less kind to her, they could well be the same age and heaven forbid, they could even have been at school together. She just felt it in her bones that somehow the woman's presence in her life spelt trouble. Without doubt, Jillian needed to think of a way to de-Elaine her life and quickly.

As she walked through into her sitting room, she imagined where she could re-position some of her very expensive but least favourite ornaments. Places where they could be put to be easily caught by a broom, a bucket or the nudge of an elbow and be damaged. If Elaine broke some of her expensive trinkets that could prove to be Jillian's trump card. However, it would be just as likely that she or Teddie would be the ones that did the breakings. Maybe Teddie could help her. Perhaps he would have some solution to this problem because he must have had lots experience in disposing with unwanted employees.

Jillian ran herself a bath with her favourite L'Occitane Lavender Foam, not too hot though, so her recently coiffured hair wouldn't frizz. She lit some of her new Jo Malone candles before asking Alexa to play some relaxing music. Teddie didn't like Alexa and he was convinced she was some sort of spy, so Jillian kept her hidden in the airing cupboard. Stepping into her luxurious bath, Jillian felt all her problems, including Elaine, drift away. This was Jillian's favourite part of any social gathering, as these charity events could often be quite a chore but there were few things a restorative bath couldn't put to rights.

Jillian heard the front door and assumed it must be Teddie. She put on her oyster silk bath robe and went down the stairs to greet her husband.

'Hello darling. How has your day been?' Jillian was secure in the knowledge that as always, she would be looking particularly alluring to her husband, even though she hadn't yet even added her make-up.

'Not too bad. Not too many problems for my μίκρσ γκρί κυτταρα (little grey cells) to deal with.' Teddie gave one of his self–satisfied smiles, as if he had said something very witty. 'And my dear, I see you are busy with this evening's preparations.'

'Yes, yes,' Jillian pretended she hadn't heard this over-used Greek translation of the Poirot phrase. 'But there is plenty of time for that. Would you like a drink perhaps?'

'Maybe a cup of tea would be nice.' Teddie sat down on a chair and removed his jacket.

This wasn't what Jillian had in mind, she found it easier to express any concerns but most particularly regarding nuisance cleaners, fuelled with a glass of bubbly. 'There is something I want to talk to you about. Why don't we get ready and then have a glass of champagne in the conservatory.'

Jillian beamed disconcertingly at her puzzled husband and Theodore wondered what this could be about.

Chapter 9

20th July 1984 – Sunny Dunes Holiday Camp 20th July
1984 – Tony's Office

You Haven't Heard Her Sing Yet

Debbie's first week at Sunny Dune's was drawing to its end. No doubt that evening, many tearful campers would be wearing their finest glad rags, which had been waiting patiently in wardrobes until Friday. On this their final night, some would be hoping to cut a last splendid dash while lamenting the end of their annual vacation. Many holiday makers returned to this same camp year after year, always at the exact time, as if marking some bizarre ritualistic urge to be annually Pontified.

Furthermore, she had noticed in this past week that a few of the punters even treated the staff with such an over-familiarity, it was as if their weekly package included exclusive friendship with their own particular Bluecoat of choice. Debbie hadn't encountered this strange practice happening last year at the Paignton Camp. Maybe it was just a Sunny Dunes thing.

Every night this last week, Myfanwy and Bryn, a mature couple from Cardiff, had a half of lager waiting for her on their usual table at 8.00pm. They must have been sitting there since just after tea to ensure it was theirs, but this wasn't unusual behaviour for these creatures of habit that Sunny Dunes attracted. Usually, Bryn gave a sly wink to catch her eye, when she walked by just after the bingo had finished. Once her attention had been drawn to the unwanted drink on the table, Debbie was then obliged to sit with them for at least 20 minutes. Myfanwy, in her sing-song voice, would then attempt to regale her with what she thought the most fascinating antics of her copious grandchildren. Debbie, wanting to appear professional in her role, hadn't the heart to tell them that she hated lager. Nightly, she had been forced to feign some interest in her tedious family but at least tonight would be the last occasion.

Likewise, a middle-aged woman called Doris with a steely grey perm and a broad Lancashire accent, expected her to dance the *Night Fever* number with her Down's Syndrome son, Malcolm each night. Larry Lawson, the band leader, played this tune regular as clockwork at 8.30 because it was a crowd pleaser that always filled the floor. After which, Doris rewarded both her son and Debbie with a tub of vanilla ice-cream. Really Debbie could have done without this, as she liked to keep a tight control on what she ate. It did little to dampen down Malcolm's libido either, who was a little too touchy-feely for both her liking and his own good. She would certainly not miss having to ward off his sweaty advances and wandering hands.

All things considered, the week had been a very mixed bag. Without a doubt, she had made some great friends. Her chalet-mate Siobhan was lovely and she was enjoying the company of Stephen who made her laugh by just opening his mouth. He knew all the gossip about everyone and had a bottomless pit of funny stories. This was his first season as a Bluecoat and he was desperately hoping it was going to lead him onto *better things*. What quite he meant by that Debbie wasn't sure, as he seemed not particularly talented in anyway other than being amusing and cool, but maybe that was enough in itself.

Also, Debbie was enjoying chalet sharing with Siobhan. Siobhan had at first taken her under her wing, showing Debbie the best places for bargains and bed linen. Debbie had been over the moon when she spotted a perfect set of black duvet covers decorated with skulls and she persuaded Siobhan to buy an identical set for her own bed. The horrid orange curtains were replaced by some charcoal grey ones with patterns of tombstones. When her posters of Robert Smith from the Cure, The Damned and Siouxsie Sioux were in place on the walls, their pad was transformed. Siobhan didn't mind in the slightest when Debbie decided which music they listened to and put all of her cassettes and footballer posters into her wardrobe. This suited Debbie perfectly and after all Siobhan was still allowed some photographs of her ginger Irish family next to her bed. Debbie was delighted that Siobhan had come round so quickly to her way of thinking. Now she was even teaching Siobhan how to apply black eyeliner and she was showing an interest in hairspray. Once her hair had grown a bit longer Debbie could show her how to do her hair properly like her own.

Frequent visits by Stephen, Roger, Mike sometimes even Marcus, was establishing quickly their chalet as the *in* place to be. Siobhan had never known popularity before and she decided she liked it. When the Bluecoats' duties were finished at around midnight, gatherings at Debbie and Siobhan's pad involving loud music, coffee or wine had been often occurring. There were very late nights, but early mornings weren't a problem Bluecoats had to worry about because nothing really started until ten o' clock the next day.

However, while the male Bluecoats were becoming Debbie's good friends, the same term could not be applied to some of the girls, in particular Suzanne. Whenever Debbie walked into the Entertainment's Office and she was there with her side-kick Karen, the two of them stopped talking. Then without fail they gawped at her and continued their nasty conversations in whispers behind their hands. Nevertheless Debbie had a feeling that tonight she was going to be putting Suzanne firmly in her place. It was the Grand Finale of the week, when the Bluecoats performed their *Around the World Show* and Debbie was going to be doing a spot. She didn't know the whole details of the programme but Stephen had filled her in on the content of a few of the acts.

And if the *Old Time Music Hall*, which Debbie had watched on Wednesday, was anything to go by, Suzanne would be imagining herself as the star the show. Debbie had listened with great amusement to her awful warbly-voiced rendition of *Second Hand Rose*. Wearing a pink feather boa and with her plump body squashed into a hideous frilly dress, a deluded Suzanne clearly thought she looked the bee's knees. Debbie however decided she resembled more of an overstuffed sausage. As Suzanne strutted about the stage, with her trotters stuffed into some too-tight high–heeled shoes, a vision of Miss Piggy came into Debbie's mind,

Yesterday, Tony had called Debbie into his office and she had wondered if she was in trouble over something. She was almost sure that she hadn't been rude to anyone and she had racked her brains trying to recall any possible faux pas on her part.

'Debbie, I was just wondering.' Tony as usual was armed with a can and a fag. She had searched for a clue as to what this was about, looking in turn between him and Jill. The Assistant Entertainment's Manager was busy painting her fingernails a pale delicate pink and showing little interest in the conversation. 'It's about tomorrow luv. You see, that Mandy — the Bluecoat who left before you came.' Debbie thought that Tony looked uncomfortable mentioning her name. He shuffled in his seat and stared down at the table in front. 'Erm …you see, well she used to sing in the Friday Night Show. You know, the show tomorrow night? Well you've not seen it yet but I promise you — it's good. Highlight of the week. Isn't that right Jill?'

'If you say so.' Jill's voice had little conviction and she blew on her fingernails to dry them.

'So, now that Mandy has gone,' continued Tony. 'Most unfortunate business … but never mind we don't need to go into all that.' He took a long drag from his cigarette and then stubbed it out in the overflowing ashtray. 'But you see there's now a gap. There's no-one to sing her songs.' He pulled his lips into a grimace and Debbie noticed once more how awful his teeth were. 'And …

according to your details ... well you sang last year at Paignton and it says you were very good.' He nodded at her encouragingly and rearranged papers on his table.

'Oh. It was nothing really.' She tossed her head self-depreciatively. Tony was mesmerised by her hair because when she shook it, not one single strand moved. 'I just sang a few songs in the Bluecoat shows. You know the sort of thing.' But Debbie was feeling quite flattered by this and wondered what had been written about her in the report on the desk. She looked towards Jill hoping to see if she was impressed by this, but the Assistant Entertainment Manager's head was now buried in a magazine.

'It seems you went down very well indeed.' He held her gaze unnervingly with his bloodshot eyes. 'This is probably why you were recommended to fill this post half way through the season. Not many Bluecoats get taken on half way through the season you know?' Debbie detected a slight note of menace in his voice and shuddered. 'You're a student aren't you? What you studying?'

'History and Theatre Studies.' Debbie couldn't see what interest this would be to him.

'Theatre Studies.' He repeated and fiddled with his cigarette packet. 'So, you must be good at the old acting and singing stuff. Is this right?' Tony lit another cigarette and blew some of his smoke right into her face.

'Well, I don't know.' Debbie spluttered and coughed. How could she possibly answer that about herself? But she had often been told how good she was. 'I have always sung since a child but ...' Debbie shrugged her shoulders. Yes, she liked singing that was true, but she suddenly remembered she hadn't been so proud of some of those dreadful uncool songs last season.

She cringed at the memory of herself decked out as Dorothy from the Wizard of Oz and having to sing *Somewhere Over the Rainbow*.

As if that wasn't bad enough, at the end of the song she had to click the heels of her sparkly ruby shoes together, whereupon a trap door had opened and she fell down into the space beneath the stage. Each week she got more bruises leaving her legs a patchwork of yellows, browns and purples. She was so pleased that none of her college friends had known anything about her performances in those embarrassing shows But maybe Tony was going to suggest she might sing something a bit more with it this year and hopefully less dangerous.

'Well, do you know any Country and Western songs?' Debbie's face fell. A cheesy image of John Denver and Dolly Parton singing a nauseous duet about going down some road in some redneck town sprang immediately into her mind. 'I was going to ask Suzanne to fill in but she does quite enough with her Viva Espana number and that very long flamenco dance …'

'Yes, I do,' said Debbie quickly. That sealed it. Any opportunity to put that cow's nose out of place was an opportunity not to be missed. She knew for a fact she could sing a damn sight better than Suzanne and she would do almost anything to wipe the smug smile off her fat face. She would even fall down another trapdoor if so required. Then she remembered a conversation with Stephen when he had been talking about the shows and some song titles tripped off her tongue. 'What about *Country Roads* or *Don't it make my Brown Eyes Blue*?' She suggested, thinking well, maybe Country and Western wasn't all that bad after all. .

This caught Jill's attention and she knocked over her bottle of nail polish. 'One thing I'd like to see for sure, is this Debbie on stage … all decked out in a nice checky shirt, jeans and I'm sure we could even cover up that awful hair with a big straw hat.' Jill smirked imaging Debbie in an unflattering cowgirl get up.

'Uncanny,' Tony gave both Jill and Debbie an excited thumbs up. 'Those were the exact same songs that Mandy did. That's incredible isn't it? So you'll just need to have a run through with the band.'

'And I'm sure I can find a costume for you. Just my kind of job.' Jill mopped up the spilt vanish with a tissue. 'In fact you're about the same size as Mandy was. What she wore will do just perfectly.' Jill thought the outfit hadn't suited Mandy and would likely do Debbie no favours either.

Debbie put the awful vision of herself dressed in such frumpy gear to the back of her mind, as it was completely superseded by the notion of putting Suzanne in her place.

Tony's brain was quickly moving forward now. 'And on Wednesday in the *Old Time Music Hall* …'

'What about *Burlington Bertie from Bow*?' Debbie raised her eyebrows.

'Debbie you're going to fit in perfectly here. What an asset to the team.' Tony went over and patted her on the back for just that little bit too long. He was however signalling for her to leave, as his mission had been accomplished.

When Debbie was outside the door she heard Jill's voice. 'Mind, you haven't heard her sing yet.'

27th 2014 March – The Vue Cinema, Trinity Square, Gateshead

Roger Keeps Watch

Roger was surprised to find himself liking his job working at The *Vue* Cinema in Trinity Square. After a short walk from his studio flat near the Central Station in Newcastle, he could jump on the Metro and be there in a jiffy. There was something very comforting in the brief train journey across the River Tyne that punctuated his work and leisure time.

His role was undemanding and these days that was just the way he liked things to be. He'd had quite enough of responsibility and all its accompanying stress. Roger's days of high powered jobs, fast cars, flash homes and a wildly hedonistic lifestyle were over. Well not totally, for he still wasn't averse to a little pleasure seeking but after the life he had led he knew he was lucky to still be alive. Although cats were believed to have nine lives, the same couldn't be said for gay men. If Roger got stuck up a tree, he couldn't be counting on a rescue from any friendly fireman; he would have to find his own way down. Too many of his friends were no longer around and all things considered he knew it was a wonder that he was.

At the multi-screen cinema, his job was menial, he didn't even have to sell any of the tickets. All he had to do was check those of the cinema goers and direct them in the direction of the right screen. Even if they went to the wrong one, it was hardly of any great consequence. Nobody would be injured or killed. They would just have to move. Really, a monkey could do this job he thought. While the days passed slowly, that wasn't any great calamity, as he certainly wasn't getting any younger and he needed to enjoy a more relaxed pace of life. Although he still had his own hair, teeth and distinctive moustache, his once fiery locks had now faded to an insipid salt and pepper. Yet, he still had a spring in his step albeit a little less jaunty.

Although the cinema complex opened at 10am, there were few screenings until the afternoon and the cinema was at its most busy during the evenings. On this Monday morning, he sauntered across the foyer to the windows that looked down onto Trinity Square. All was fairly quiet. Most of the workers had already scuttled off to their various places of work and the students were likely still in their beds. While some people were trudging along to sign on for their jobseeker's allowance, others came from Tesco's, their hands laden with shopping bags and heading for bus stops.

A few familiar faces had charge of the benches. A senior citizen with a shabby raincoat he often noticed was sharing a pasty from Greggs with his equally bedraggled dog. Two teenagers, no doubt skiving off school, sped across the square screaming while riding skateboards and the old lady was again feeding the pigeons from her threadbare bag. He laughed to himself, he knew someone who wouldn't like that and he watched to see what would happen next.

'What do you think you're playing at? There's customers who might be needing your attention.' Came the reprimand from the Cinema Manager behind him.

'Oh sorry. There was nobody there. I was just looking out the …' Roger wasn't too keen on being answerable to this jerk of a man. At times like this he did miss his old life but he held his tongue because he needed this job.

'You're not paid to be looking out of windows are you? Now go do your job.' The jumped up little man just loved the sound of his own voice.

Roger shrugged his shoulders and meekly went to take his position at the entrance to the screens.

Chapter 10

20th July 1984 – Sunny Dunes Holiday Camp – The Princess Ballroom

Her Mind Was Clearly Elsewhere

It was Friday night and the last game of Bingo for the jackpot of £100 was underway. All the punters eyes and ears were fixed on Tony, who was sweating profusely under the bright lights of the stage. The ping-pong balls swam about in the bingo machine like frantic multi-coloured tadpoles. A silence filled the room, as the microphone crackled and Tony announced the various lucky numbers flying up the shoot: Kelly's eye, legs eleven and two fat ladies.

Suddenly, there was a shout of 'House' accompanied by a chorus of groans, tuts and curses. As Mike went to verify the winning ticket, at least a hundred pairs of dagger-eyes looked in his direction. Debbie was amused that this game was taken so seriously but then again, a hundred pounds was a considerable amount of money, in fact more than twice her weekly wage.

When the clock hands moved to 8pm, the curtains on the stage swung aside to reveal Larry Lawson's Show Band. Sporting a natty emerald sequined jacket, bow tie and overly large false teeth, Larry dazzled his audience with his well-seasoned aplomb. Waving about a little black baton to conduct his band, he danced about the stage like a marionette, his limbs jerking in time to the music as if he were controlled by a third party. The cheery sound of Wham's *Wake Me Up Before You Go-Go* filled the room. Dressed in pristine white, the boys in the band followed his lead playing their instruments with great gusto and sometimes even copying his twitchy movements, imagining that this enhanced their overall performance. Soon, the dance floor was full, bingo disappointments forgotten and the crowd was determined to make the best of their final night for that year at Pontins.

Debbie was going through the words of the Country and Western songs in her head, as it had been a while since she had last sung them. Walking past Myfanwy and Bryn, her mind was elsewhere.

'Debbie,' called a plaintive Myfanwy.

'Debbie love, here's your drink.' Bryn stood up, puzzled why their Bluecoat wasn't giving them her usual attention.

'Oh sorry. I was miles away.' She gave them a half-hearted smile.

'Well it's our last night you know.' Myfanwy pulled out the chair and patted it for their special Bluecoat to sit down upon.

'Here's your lager drink Debbie. The last one.' Bryn looked more than a little mournful and he slowly handed her the ceremonial glass in a formal manner befitting this sombre occasion.

'And I'm so going to miss our little chats to be sure.' Myfanwy pulled her chair closer to Debbie's. 'Just think this time to morrow we'll be home. I can't believe this week has passed by so quickly. Can you Bryn?' Bryn shook his head sadly. 'Still, we'll be back next year, indeed to goodness, won't we Bryn?' Bryn nodded emphatically, resembling one of the little novelty dogs wagging its head in the back of a car. 'Still, we've been shopping today. And do you know I've got some super presents for the grandkids? For Dylan we got him a ...'

Debbie took a sip from her half of lager and her eyes glazed over. The words *Almost heaven, West Virginia* were going repeatedly through her mind and her lips involuntarily without her knowledge formed the words.

'And little Cerys. Don't you think she is going to just love … you all right love?' Perhaps Myfanwy needed to alter her opinion of Debbie. This was their last night and the girl's mind was clearly elsewhere. Probably she was mooning over some boy.

'Oh yes. I'm sure they are all going to love their gifts but I'll have to go.' Debbie stood up as if she had been summoned elsewhere.

'But you haven't finished your drink love.' Bryn was puzzled. After all, she had only been sitting with them for a couple of minutes,

'I know … but I'm in the show next and I need to go and get ready. Sorry.' Debbie pulled an apologetic face.

'Well surely you've time to finish your drink. It's our last night you know.' Myfanwy's lower lip quivered, unable to hide her disappointment. Debbie hadn't been in any of the other shows they had seen this week, so this seemed most unlikely. She had obviously got more important matters to concern herself with. It all left a sour taste in Mfanwy's mouth and now her holiday had been spoilt by the selfish girl.

Debbie was off. She needed to prepare herself and sit quietly to go through the words. If she was perfectly honest she was feeling a little nervous. It was a long time since she had done this sort of singing in public. Although she thought such performances from herself were long confined to the past, she now wanted to do her best, if only to get one up on Suzanne.

27th March 2014 - Ramsay Court, Central Gateshead

Cut Price Fish Fingers

After finishing her shift at Tesco's and doing her skivvying for Mrs Lazaridis, Elaine was feeling knackered. Her feet were aching after a full morning spent relentlessly cleaning, dusting and hoovering. Then, the entire afternoon she had spent traipsing round Tesco's stacking shelves. That Mike Robinson was either sadistic or just plain evil and she was positive that he kept deliberately changing his mind as to where he wanted the stupid special offers displayed, purely to make life more difficult for her.

His latest crowd pleasing offer that day had been, that if you bought six packets of bourbon biscuits you could get a free one of digestives. So, she had been told to arrange the daft promotion, for some strange reason, next to the fresh fruit. But then true to form, he went and changed his mind, Flying off the handle while stamping his feet and shouting at her, he decided they looked all wrong. Next, he ordered she should put them next to the cleaning products, as everyone knew people couldn't resist eating biscuits when they were doing their household chores. Like he would know anything about that she thought. Then, he still wasn't happy. So now, they were by the side of the coffee and tea. Which would have been the obvious choice to her mind, if she'd only been asked in the first place. No doubt tomorrow, they would be sitting in a freezer along with the frozen vegetables and meat

When she finally removed her shoes, in the dubious comfort of her high rise flat, she could feel her toes throbbing like ten lips stung by wasps. Keeping her company was her elder daughter Kylie, who was lying on the sofa like a massive sack of potatoes and ready to give birth at any given moment. She was watching a game show on the telly while her little girl, Krystal was rolling around the floor wailing because her nappy needed changing. Meanwhile, her younger daughter Charlene was vacantly staring ahead and watching the clumps of old paint slide down the wall like candle wax.

'What we having for tea, Mam?' Kylie was doing her best to ignore her own daughter.

'Why don't you change that wee lassie of yours?' Elaine squeezed her sore toes.

'Can't you do it Mam? I already changed her nappy this morning.' Kylie was patting her stomach and trying to make herself more comfy when the door suddenly swung open and in walked her brother Scott.

'Well there's a surprise son. We weren't expecting you this evening.' Elaine pulled an expression somewhere between pleasure and irritation, though probably more towards the latter.

'I was just passing.' Scott grunted and pushed a shabby cushion onto the floor to sit on the sofa next to his elder sister. His younger sister clapped her hands together and dribbled with delight, as she hadn't seen her big brother for a few weeks.

'No coincidence you arrive at tea time is it son?' Elaine slid her feet into some well-worn fluffy slippers that were lying on a nearby rug.

'What we having then?' Scott put his elbows on his knees, cradled his chin in his palms and directed his attention towards the telly.

'I suppose I've got some wee fish fingers sitting in the freezer. As it happens, I got two packets last week, when they were on special offer.'

'Thought it'd be steak or summat special ... what with you and yer two jobs, mam.' Scott smirked and Charlene's gaze was now focused on her brother in adoration. Scott turned to his mam who he thought was looking older and even more worn out. Clearly all this work was doing her no good at all.

'I wish. That Mrs Lazaridis is dead tight.' Elaine hissed the words from between her teeth putting Scott in mind of the snake from Disney's Jungle Book film. 'You'd think she pay more than minimum wage what with all that money she and her husband have.'

'Where is it the bloody cheapskates live?' Scott was watching Bradley Walsh on the box.

'A big posh detached house in Jesmond.' Elaine's face twisted face in envy. 'He's got that fancy restaurant *The Olympian*. It's just round the corner from their swanky mansion.'

'Yes I've seen it.' Scott thought they must be loaded and the cogs of his brains started to turn. 'Can't say I've ever been in it like. Greek isn't it?'

'Yes, he's Greek. She's not mind.' Elaine's face was changing to a peculiar shade of green. 'Would you believe she's from the same neck of the woods as meself.'

'Sound like she's done canny good for herself. 'Scott wished his mam had married some rich Greek bloke. 'I bet there's some belter gear there. Isn't there?'

Elaine's head jolted sharply in his direction. 'You can put that idea straight out of your head.'

'Come on Mam.' Surely nicking the odd item here was a perk of the job and this must have crossed his mother's mind. 'She's not going to notice it if a few things go missing is she? Sometimes things do just mysteriously disappear don't they? Do you remember when that £20 went missing from your purse the other week?' Scott realised perhaps he shouldn't have mentioned this and wisely changed the subject. 'Anyway, are you working there tomorrow? Maybe I could pop round and give you a bit of a hand so to speak …'

'I don't think so son.' Elaine had her own reasons for wanting to hold on to this cleaning job but she had no intention of sharing these with her children. 'Last thing I need is to be up before the beak on a shoplifting charge and see both of my jobs poured down the sink a like a bottle of stale … oh yes and what happened to my bottle of whiskey?'

'What you on about?' Although he wore a puzzled face, Scott wriggled about on the sofa uncomfortably.

'Don't you try to deny it.' Elaine wagged her finger at her son. 'I saw you nicking those bottles of booze from the store the last week you know ...'

'I don't know what you're on about.' He fixed his eyes once more on the screen.

'My little bruv's been up to his old tricks has he?' Kylie asked and elbowed her brother, enjoying his discomfort.

'You'll get caught and banged up, mark my words.' Elaine was worried about the life her son was leading.

'You're both mental the pair of you.' He shook his head angrily. 'Anyway where's me tea Mam?'

'Son, I worry about you, you know. Do you want me to see if there's any jobs going at Tesco in the warehouse.' She bit her lip knowing this wouldn't suit him at all.

'Bugger off. I'm not doing a crappy job like that.' He stood up and started pacing round the room. Charlene couldn't understand what was happening and began to cry.' I knew I shouldn't have come round here. You're always on at me. It's not fair. What about her. She just sits on her lazy fat arse all day.'

'Mam, you tell him.' Kylie shouted. 'I'm about to give ...'

'Stop it the pair of you.' Elaine screamed at them both. She felt her bones creak like squeaky hinges, as she hoisted herself off the sofa and went into the kitchen in search of the cut price fish fingers.

Chapter 11

20th July 1984 – Sunny Dunes Holiday Camp – The Princess Ballroom

Debbie Steals the Show

On her way to the dressing room Debbie was feeling nervous and she was totally oblivious to Doris trying to grab her attention. Her son Malcolm was busy practising his Saturday Night Fever dance moves for their final dance while still in his seat. As he flung his arms about with gay abandon, he was repeatedly hitting a crossed-faced teenage girl who had the misfortune to be sitting next to him. Debbie did however notice her friend Stephen entertaining two elderly ladies in wheelchairs. They were all drinking port and lemons and howling with laughter. After her songs, Stephen would be singing his *I was born under a Wandering Star* but he didn't look to be troubled by the slightest hint of stage fright.

Moments later, she was decked out in the horrid red checked shirt, jeans which were too big and some dirty old cowboy boots. She had attempted to flatten her hair under a straw hat but defiant sprouts were sticking out and she looked ridiculous. Thank goodness none of her uni friends could see her like this, let alone listen to what she was about to sing. What had she been she thinking of?

Standing on the side of the stage she watched Roger singing *Tulips from Amsterdam*. His voice was surprisingly pleasant and he crooned a little like Des O'Connor. Wearing baggy cream trousers and a brown waistcoat he skipped around the floor, his dainty feet traced out the waltz time of the tune. Behind him stood Mike, holding a yellow cardboard windmill. As he span the red wands round, with a bored look on his face, Karen held two plastic tulips and performed a strange clog dance.

Following the outing to The Netherlands, the show travelled to Baghdad and as Larry Lawson played *The Old Bazaar at Cairo* tune, out came Barry and Liz in Arabian costume performing a sand dance. Barry's usual lion's mane of golden locks was hidden under a turban. He was dressed in orange and purple silk like the magician Ali Bongo. Barry was an illusionist and his girlfriend Liz was his glamorous assistant. Dressed in a fetching harem girl type assemble, Liz with her long swishing plait of hair emerged unscathed as she miraculously appeared and disappeared out of boxes, was sawn in half twice and then finally attached to a spinning wheel while Barry threw fifteen knives at her. Meanwhile, Mike stood in the background with a cut-out of a snake charmer. It was all very impressive and Debbie thought Liz very brave.

Next on was Suzanne and Larry Lawson's band struck up with the jolly *Y Viva Espana* introduction. She flounced onto the stage wearing a fancy ruffled red and black Spanish style spotted number, whose stitches were clearly straining at the seams. Beaming at the audience, she trilled her way through the song with her unpleasant voice, great gusto and unwarranted self-belief. Debbie noticed that for some peculiar reason Suzanne was stamping her feet loudly during certain parts of the song. Then she twigged, Suzanne had a very limited vocal range and was attempting to mask the difficulty she was having on some of the higher notes. Meanwhile, Mike skulked about in the background with a menacing cardboard bull.

When the song finished, Larry next launched into a dramatic version of Ravel's Bolero. More Iberian foot banging and handclapping followed, as Suzanne pranced and pirouetted around the hand-held beast, gathering momentum as the tempo increased in a strange flamenco Torville and Dean-like routine. After a long while the dance finally culminated with Mike and the bull falling dramatically to the ground, for Suzanne to place a triumphant foot on the bovine cut-out.

Debbie couldn't quite decide what to make of all this, but those familiar opening bars of *Take me Home Country Roads* pulled her back into focus and she took a large gulp before walking onto the stage. Roger slapped her on the back and she could see her friend Siobhan on the other side of the stage, giving her the thumbs up. She was glad that the bright stage lights meant she couldn't see the audience. Before beginning the song, she glanced behind her to see a large imitation haystack wobbling precariously in the background like an unset yellow jelly.

Thankfully, there was no crackle from the microphone and as she began the song she could just about hear from the monitor that her voice sounded fine. Larry Lawson was beaming at her and he gave her an encouraging wink. Managing to suppress a chuckle, she launched into the first chorus and could hear hands clapping along to the beat of the music. Surely, this was a good sign? Then by the second chorus, folk were joining in with her singing. As her nerves subsided, she realised just how much she was enjoying herself. When the song drew to an end the audience's reaction showed just how much they were appreciating her act.

Then, as *Don't it Make My Brown Eyes Blue* began, she noticed in the wings next to Siobhan was Suzanne, wearing an even more sulky expression than usual. This pleased Debbie greatly and by holding that cow's mardy face in her head, she found herself able to relax into the song, to give her very best performance. She was relishing this moment. All eyes and ears were on her, giving their full attention, but best of all, she knew her act was by far superseding the silly Spanish previous one. Suzanne had been simply the *warm up* and now Debbie was *the act*. When the song finished the crowd's thunderous applause said it all and even Larry Lawson was loudly clapping her. Debbie took a deep bow and skipped off the stage almost bumping into Stephen, intoxicated by the lights and the limelight.

'Wow, that was brilliant Debbie. Good on you.' Stephen jumped up and down congratulating her effusively, before shifting into his own character and ambling onto the stage as Lee Marvin.

'Well done Debbie. That was great. I really enjoyed your singing. You were the best' Roger gave her a sincere smile of appreciation, then a hug and a kiss on both cheeks.

'That was fab. Hey Debbie, you knocked the spots off that Suzanne. Ha ha.' Mike punched her on the arm. Then ran back onto the stage aware he had missed the cue for his next assignment of holding the large silver star above Stephen's head.

'That was excellent Debbie. I really enjoyed your singing.' added Marcus, who was sitting on the ground next to Liz and polishing his trumpet. Liz and Ali Bongo nodded in agreement while enthusiastically clapping their hands at her.

'I was so proud of you Debbie. You've stolen the show.' Siobhan's face was glowing with pride and admiration for her friend.

Tony and Jill walked across. 'Debbie that was brilliant. You'd the bloody crowd eating right out of your hands.' Tony rubbed his own together. 'Now, for the Olde Time Music Hall next week you said you'd do *Burlington Bertie* and … what else was it? Was it *Champagne Charlie*?'

'Well, I can if you like I suppose?' Debbie didn't actually know either of these songs but her head was in a whirl and now was hardly the time for admitting it. From the stage she could hear a gruff voice, as Stephen pranced around pretending to be a camp Lee Marvin.

'Well the cow girl look definitely suits you Debbie.' There was a mocking look in Jill's eyes. 'So maybe drag will too. Ha ha.' Jill's laugh held an unpleasant edge. 'If you can cover that hair with a Stetson, I'm sure a top hat will work just as well too. Anyway, I'm sure your new friend Siobhan can give you a few tips in the being masculine department.' She nodded towards Siobhan who was busy chatting with Roger. 'No, seriously Debbie, that was very good. We were both most impressed weren't we Tony?' Jill didn't sound entirely sincere but there was no way Debbie was going to let this tiny fly in the ointment rain on her parade.

'I'll say. You knocked them dead Debbie.' On the other hand Tony seemed delighted with her performance and that was what counted. Interestingly, there was no sign of either Suzanne or Karen anywhere about and she took their absence to be the greatest indicator of her triumph.

27th March 2014 – The Vue Cinema, Trinity Square

Roger's Reason

It was no coincidence that Roger was working at the multi-plex cinema in Trinity Square in Gateshead. Something had caught his interest there. Prior to this, he'd held a similar role at the *The Gate* Cinema in Newcastle. So, when a vacancy in this cinema on the south side of the Tyne had come up for grabs, his application had ticked all the boxes. Except for his age but the form hadn't asked for this.

Apart from his boss, most of the other members of staff were at least thirty years his junior.They all thought it was odd that someone like him should be wanting to work there in the first place, but after some time decided that it was just Roger that was. The teenagers were all in agreement that this man with his funny little moustache and strange mincing walk was like something from a bygone age. It was as if he were a stereotypical character lifted out from a comedy made long before even their parents had been born.They often parodied him and poked fun at him behind his back. However, they would have found him even more peculiar if they had known anything of his chequered history.

This low paid undemanding job was far about as far removed as you could get from the positions he had held in the past. At one point in his life Roger had overseen a massive chain of sordid nightclubs and sleezy casinos that stretched across the whole country. He'd had the experience of all the related debauchery this entailed in his time. Roger had mixed with some very dodgy characters but he had grown sick of the drugs, weapons, gangs, threats of violence and the constant pressure this involved. Towards the end, it seemed there hadn't been a single moment when he hadn't been looking over his shoulder, dreading the door opening or the sound of gunfire.

Often these days, Roger reflected on his colourful life that had progressed from Bluecoat, to holiday rep in Greece and then further promotion to be an Entertainment's Manager in Brighton. He should have stayed there but no, he had been seduced by the magnetic pull of big money and adventure. Somehow, he had allowed himself to be coerced into running a what seemed to be fashionable nightclub in the North-East. Yet, within a matter of a few short months Rogers life had spiralled into one embroiled in hardcore violence and vice.

In hindsight, it was clear to see that drugs had been the common denominator in all of his problems. Cocaine had been his particular poison and he knew he was lucky to still have a nose. Much of the last twenty years was just a horrible blur with some vague, dubious memories of a chemically induced bliss. He needed to be thankful that he had been handed a get out clause from the unlikeliest of places. By some kind twist of fate though, he had been thrown a lifeline and had escaped from that hell. Drugs had destroyed his life and nearly killed him. He had been clean now for five years now, that was something he could at least be proud of but once you had sold your soul to the devil could you ever really be free? And some were still waiting for their pound of flesh. Over the years Roger had collected an assortment of dodgy acquaintances and people he still needed to avoid. So there were certain places he just kept way from.

These days Roger aimed for a simple life. Although his current flat was very small, he still had bills to pay and his wage from the usher job at *The Vue* Cinema was sufficient, as long as he was sensible with his money. In the past an excess of cash had done him nothing but harm anyway. The location of his modest home was excellent for someone of his proclivities. Nearby, the *Pink Triangle* with its profusion of gay bars meant he was never short of company if feeling a little lonely but most importantly, gangsters seemed to not frequent gay bars or cinemas.

A couple of months ago, finding himself at a loose end on a day off, he thought he would go and have a look at the cinema complex in Gateshead. After getting off the Metro and wandering around the unprepossessing area a little, he found himself in a large Tesco store. It was while he was in there, he caught a glimpse of a familiar figure from his very distant past. Roger felt the ache of nostalgia. This character was from a more innocent time because when he had been a Bluecoat he'd had nothing or nobody to fear. Over the years, it seemed Mike Robinson had changed little in appearance and despite being a little heavier still wouldn't be out of place on a sport's field. However, this was no longer the unsure of himself boy, who had an ill-suited urge to be a comic. Clearly, he had grown into himself and was now a figure of some standing. Roger had watched him, impressed by his strutting around the store full of his own self importance, shouting out orders to his fellow workers and dealing with customers in a brusque manner.

Chapter 12

20th July 1984 – Sunny Dunes Holiday Camp – The Princess Ballroom

Tony's Sad Tale

The rest of the night to Debbie was all a bit of a blur. She remembered Mwfanwy and Bryn congratulating her and saying they now understood completely why she had been preoccupied earlier. In their opinion she was still the best Bluecoat this season. Also, she recalled Doris trying to persuade her to dance for one last time with her son Malcolm. However, at this time Marcus was playing an accomplished rendition of Arrivederci Roma on his trumpet flanked by a cut out of the Leaning Tower of Pisa. In Debbie's opinion neither the tower nor disco dancing seemed appropriate to this particular tune.

Very soon the end of the evening came and everyone joined hands together to sing Auld Lang Syne, as if it were New Year's Eve. When the song came to an end, there were many hugs exchanged and tears shed.

Then Tony took to the stage to give a final farewell to his guests. Gone was the jovial bingo calling Tony from earlier. Now he struck a serious pose and his face froze in an expression of deep sorrow. His cheeks became hollowed and his eyes haunted as if he were wearing a classical tragedy mask. By his side stood Jill with a matching woebegone expression which aged her by at least ten years. Debbie was confused and wondered whatever was happening. Had somebody died? A silence descended upon the ballroom and Tony cleared his throat before launching into his monologue.

'My dearest friends we have sadly arrived at the end of your holiday and I was hoping that you good folk could just spare a moment for those less fortunate than yourselves. If you kind people could be so generous and dig deep in your pockets to donate money to a very worthy cause that is close to my heart, it would be enormously appreciated.' He picked up one of the red collection boxes and gave it a hopeful rattle. 'The *Shiny Star Appeal* is an important and deserving charity that supports terminally ill children and their families.' He paused for dramatic effect and to let this information sink in. Debbie looked around to see all eyes were fixed on Tony, as if he were a magician who had placed them under his spell.

He then continued. 'Many of these very poorly boys and girls have only a pitiful short time left to live. This money, as a gift to them, could provide their families with a wonderful holiday and precious memories for these parents to cherish for ever. Imagine seeing your little seven year old boy, whose fragile body is riddled with cancer shrieking with delight on a roller-coaster in Florida. Or picture your four year old daughter with congenital heart failure, smiling and laughing as she shakes Mickey Mouse's hand at Disneyland.' While Tony dabbed the corner of his eye with a handkerchief, Jill was weeping in sympathy.

'Indeed, I know just how these unfortunate parents feel.' He nodded his head poignantly. 'Once, I had a little boy. He was the sunshine of my life ... always smiling and so full of goodness and joy. That was until a cruel disease took away my Andy. The cancer was called Leukaemia and Andy was so brave.' Tony stifled a sob. 'And, this was many years ago when my wife and I had virtually no money. When Andy was taken ill, my wife worked as a cleaner, took in washing and helped on a farmer's milk round. I was a dustbin man, chimney sweep and would even take on work as a scarecrow.' Tony watched the hundreds of eyes in front of him filling with tears. 'We had to make ends meet. Times were hard after the war. No fancy holidays for poor Andy. Anyway some of our kindly neighbours ... God bless them ... they clubbed together so we could buy him a bucket and spade. We still have on the mantelpiece that picture of Andy playing in the backyard in the soil because ... we couldn't afford to get to the seaside.' Tony now broke down and held his head in his hands to hide his face overcome with emotion. How awful, thought Debbie joining in with the mass collective display of grief. Yet when she noticed Roger, he seemed uncomfortable and was fidgeting, Siobhan was fiddling with some curtains and staring through the window but Stephen ... he was glaring at Tony with a look of pure hatred on his face.

Debbie along with all the other Bluecoats was handed one of the charity boxes. She held this by the string and as she moved about the room, she was completely amazed by people's generosity. The sheer amount of five pound and ten pound notes that were appearing from pockets and purses and being donated was astounding. These folk were not rich by any means and most would have saved furiously all year to afford this holiday but they seem to have been deeply moved by Tony's heartfelt speech. Debbie was impressed. None of the other Bluecoats batted an eyelid, as this was obviously the standard practice on a Friday evening.

Once everyone had retired to bed, the heavy charity boxes were taken through to Tony's office where Jill deposited them into the large, secure safe.

10th April 2014 – The Copthorne Hotel, Newcastle

She Makes Her Flesh Creep

Jillian and Teddie had just sat down for their meal at the Annual Charity Dinner Dance for Underprivileged Children at the Copthorne Hotel. It was always a splendid event. At the front of the banqueting hall was a stage covered with ribbons and sparkly lights, laid out for a twelve piece band. Currently, a trio of piano, bass and drums were quietly playing background music of jazz standards while the meal was served.

Around the edge of the room were positioned eight circular tables as if they were a solar system of planets orbiting the all-powerful star in the centre. Each was covered with a pristine white table cloth, flickering candles and vases of spring flowers. But the table in the middle was draped in golden cloth, had a luxurious silver candelabra, and a massive cornucopia brim-full with exotic flowers. The special table was well-placed underneath a massive glittering chandelier; it was here the important people sat.

Mr and Mrs Lazaridis', who of course were seated at the central table, were tucking into a starter of a rich lobster bisque, soon to be followed by a Beef Wellington main. Jillian imagined Teddie would rather be eating fare from one of his own Greek Restaurants but he wasn't complaining. It was important for his reputation, as one of the most prestigious and certainly richest restaurant owners in the area to be present at such an event.

Jillian knew she was looking magnificent in her new ivory cocktail dress with mother of pearl sequins, as she had just seen herself twinkling prettily in the mirror in the Ladies' Powder Room. Even her husband was looking more dapper than usual this evening in his best black pinstripe suit and she knew they made a handsome couple. At such events money spoke loudly and tonight — her husband's wealth was making plenty of noise.

'Jillian what an absolutely fabulous dress you are wearing. You simply must tell me where you got it.' Barbara Blackstaff, the Mayor's Wife who was sitting opposite her, shrieked and clasped her hands together in appreciation of Jillian's fine frock.

'Oh, it's just a little something I picked up in ... let me see.' Jillian felt flattered, even though she knew herself that she was looking good. 'I think I found this little number in Fenwick's ages ago. I must have had it my wardrobe for years.' This was a lie, for she had purchased it last week from their new spring collection.

'You simply must come shopping with me one of these days.' Barbara was wearing a tangerine coloured kaftan style dress which accentuated her short stocky frame. The inappropriateness of the outfit reminded Jillian of Elaine her cleaner. 'I never know what to wear for these events.' Barbara confessed to an unsurprised Jillian.

'Yes of course. I would love to.' Jillian lied. She couldn't think of any worse waste of her time. No couturier, no matter how accomplished, could possibly make a silk purse out of this sow's ear. Jillian put down her spoon. She suspected this dish must be ladled with cream and one had to watch what one ate otherwise ... she gave Barbara one of her sweetest of smiles to signal the conversation was over.

'Darling,' Teddie turned towards her, while using a serviette to wipe some cream from the soup lodged in his moustache. 'What did you want to talk to me about earlier?'

'It doesn't matter.' Jillian hadn't had the opportunity to speak with her husband earlier and now wished he would look the other way while scooping up his dribbles. 'It was just something about Elaine.'

'Elaine?' Teddie scanned the room looking for an Elaine that he couldn't quite recall. 'Which one is she? You will have to point her out.'

'Elaine's not here Teddie. Silly. She's our cleaning lady. You know?' The very idea of Elaine being at a function likes this was utterly ridiculous Jillian thought. Then she saw Barbara trying to catch her eye once more and she pretended not to notice.

'Λοιπόν (Well), what' she got to do with anything?' Teddie had noticed that the Beef Wellington was starting to be served. 'And why are we talking about her now?'

'Teddie, there's something I just don't like about the woman.' Jillian cleared her throat, aware that her voice was taking on an unpleasant whining tone.

'My dear. You can't fault her cleaning. The house always looks spotless. Πολυ ωρια (*Very nice*)' As the plate of food was placed in front of him, he poked the pastry gingerly.

'Yes, but there's something about her I don't like. She makes my flesh creep. Do you know what I mean?' Jillian's appetite by now had quite disappeared and she took a long drink from her glass of white wine.

'Ω Θεέ μου (My God) Jillian she's always seemed perfectly polite to me.' Teddie was carefully dissecting the pastry to assess the tenderness of the beef within.

'And you can't just fire someone for making your flesh creep. OΧι πολί κακο (No very bad) 'He shook his head as he placed a small piece of meat into his mouth and chewed vigorously.

'But Teddie…'

'Όχι (No) Jillian. This is neither the time nor the place.' Teddie spluttered as he choked on his food.

Chapter 13

20th July 1984 – Sunny Dunes Holiday Camp – The Entertainment's Office

She Likes Climbing Trees

Siobhan was sitting alone in the Entertainment's Office. All the others had hurried back to their own or other Bluecoats chalets, for after work parties. She had a headache and her feet were hurting from walking around in heels all night. After getting herself a glass of water, she took some painkillers out of her bag. She much prefered her daytime uniform, when she could wear a tracksuit and comfy trainers, as her duties were mostly sport based.

When Friday night was over and done with, she was always relieved. For one thing, Saturday was her day off, which meant tomorrow she had the luxury of a much needed lie in. However, much more importantly than that was the knowledge that she didn't have listen to Tony's end of the week speech for another seven days. She just couldn't bear to listen to his wheedling voice trying to squeeze every last penny out of the punters like the toothpaste at the bottom of an empty tube. As the weeks progressed, she could swear that his hyperbole was becoming even more extreme. She felt sick when she remembered what Mandy had told her. From inside his office she could hear glasses clinking. His booming laughter was accompanied by the tinkly one of his accomplice. Evidently, the takings from tonight must have been particularly lucrative.

Outside she heard a whistling and Mike came through the door. Under his arm he carried the cardboard haystack, windmill and bull. He looked surprised to see Siobhan there. 'Penny for your thoughts Siobhan. What's up with you?' He grinned nervously at her, as if he were up to no good.

'Oh nothing. I'm just tired that's all.' Siobhan thought this strange because although Mike had become quite friendly with Debbie, he didn't usually bother making conversation with her.

'Bet you're glad it's your day off tomorrow aren't you?' He leaned the cut-outs against the wall, pulled up a chair and sat next to her.

'Yes, I'll say, to be sure.' Siobhan was puzzled and wondered what he wanted.

'Hey, wasn't Debbie brilliant tonight. I thought that Mandy was good but if anything Debbie knocked her socks off didn't she?'

'Yes, I must admit I was well impressed with her singing for sure. She was great and the crowd loved her too didn't they?' Oh, so that was it. It was obviously Debbie he was interested in and that was why he was cosying upto her because she was her friend.

Mike didn't really know what to say to Siobhan and twiddled with his thumbs for some inspiration. There was an awkward pause until he plucked a random question out of the air. 'How do you like sharing a chalet with her then? Which do you prefer her or Mandy?'

'I like both of them. They're both grand.' What sort of an eejit question was that wondered Siobhan.

'Yes but if you had to choose …' Mike kept turning around to look at Tony's office door which remained closed. Siobhan had the feeling she didn't have his full attention.

'Thankfully I don't. Anyway Mandy isn't here anymore but I'm very happy to be sharing with Debbie. She's lovely and …' Siobhan thought she would put him to the test. 'She likes climbing trees.'

' What?' Mike did a double take. She had jolted his attention back.

'I was just checking you were listening.' This indeed was a very strange conversation and she couldn't see where it could be leading.

'Yes, of course I am. She seems nice enough but what about all that hair? Hey Siobhan.' He stuck his forefinger in the air as if he had just had a brainwave. 'Why did the king ban all the men and women in the kingdom from having haircuts?' He shook his head from side to side and pulled the goofy face he always did when telling his pathetic jokes.

'Well, why did he?' She decided she might as well humour him.

'Because he thought it was an act of hair-esy. Get it? Heresy – hairesy?' His eyes travelled once more to the inner office door.

'Yes, very funny.' Siobhan stifled a comic yawn.

'No, seriously though. She must spend hours in the bathroom to get it like that.' He painted zig zags round his head with his fingers and imagined all the fuss inside the girls' chalet when the girls were getting ready. The air would be all gloopy with hairspray, perfume and women's concoctions.

'Well, I would have thought you'd know all about that with Stephen. I doubt if he gets out of bed with his hair like that does he?' Siobhan was feeling better for having had a sit down and at last her headache was beginning to clear.

'No, I guess not. Don't you thinks it's a bit unfair though? I'm sure all those fumes can't be very healthy,' he added.

'Well she's having to put up with all my smoking, which to be sure must be much worse and anyway I quite like the smell of her hairspray. It disguises some of my horrible tobacco fumes.' Siobhan was seriously thinking about giving up this disgusting habit, only not quite just yet.

'Yes,but I mean Debbie's only been here five minutes and all of a sudden she's getting all the top spots in the shows. I bet she'll be in the Music Hall on Wednesday won't she?'An unattractive note of peevishness crept into his voice.

'Yes, probably. But she's just replacing Mandy isn't she?' What on earth was the matter with Mike and she wondered just what was he driving at?

'But what about you? Why aren't you in any of ther shows?' Once again he glanced at the tightly closed door.

'It's not really my thing.' Siobhan knew she could never in a million years get up on the stage and sing. 'I'm here to do the sports. Oh I see … you fancied singing *Country Roads* and *Brown Eyes Blue* did you Mike?'

'No of course not … but all I get to do is … hold up those stupid bits of cardboard and I'm sick of it.' He glared at the offending items over by the wall.

'Do you want to sing a song then?' She could feel a smile playing around her lips.

'No, but I've been practising an act of my own.' He checked round the room to see if anyone else was listening. 'A comedy act. I want to tell jokes and I've got some really good ones.'

'Mike, why are you telling me this?' If his jokes were anything like the one he'd just bored her with it didn't bode well. 'There's nothing I can do about it.' She wanted to go back to the chalet to celebrate Debbie's triumph with her.

 'The thing is I was going to go in and see Tony now. Do you think now is a good time?' She had never noticed before that underneath the moustache and bravado Mike was like a little boy seeking approval from a grown up and she was feeling uncomfortably like his mother.

'How should I know?' She shrugged her shoulders. Still, it was the first time he had ever bothered with her and she did feel a little sorry for him with his misguided notions of being a comic. 'But I would say not now, as I think he's probably a bit preoccupied. In fact if I was you, I'd brooch the idea with Roger first. Yes, I think he'd be the best bet.' Mike nodded. 'In fact why don't you come back to our chalet now. Stephen will most likely be there and … you can try out some of those jokes on us.' Mike's face brightened even though he didn't really get along with Stephen and the two of them headed for the door.

10th April 2014 – Tesco, Trinity Square

The Re-cycling Bins

Roger had been watching Mike for some time waiting for an opportunity to make his move. He had just finished his shift at the cinema and was making his way to the Metro to go home. Though the entrance glass doors of Tesco, he could see his old chum. Mike was wearing his sharp suit and was dealing with some disgruntled customers in his usual abrupt manner. He waited until the Assistant Manager had finished talking with the people and took the plunge. Without the slightest of doubt whatsoever, he felt sure Mike would be delighted for them to renew their old acquaintance.

'Mike? Mike Robinson? It is you, isn't it?' He walked in front of the deputy manager and stood there beaming.

'Yes, I'm Mike Robinson. Can I help you with something?' Mike snapped. He thought this was more than likely another dissatisfied customer who had been directed towards him.

'It's Roger. You know, Roger Henderson. Don't you remember me?' Roger switched on his brightest of smiles, turning the wrinkles round his eyes into ravines and exposing his nicotine stained teeth.

'Roger?' He shook his head dismissively, making no attempt whatsoever to place this clown. 'Can't say I do. And where do I supposedly know you from?' Mike folded his arms. He was beginning to feel uncomfortable, as this man was standing too close and he could smell halitosis on his breath.

'Pontins. 1984.We were Bluecoats together.' Roger's grin was now stretching from ear to ear and moved even nearer. Suddenly he lifted his arms, as if about to embrace him and a horrified Mike leapt backwards.'Don't you remember me?' continued Roger. 'I was the Head Bluecoat there that year? Roger ?' He stretched out his arms to waggled his theatrical jazz hands while Mike shuffled uncomfortably from foot to foot as terrible memories of that summer washed through his mind. Mike was beginning to feel a little sick. Surely, this pathetic specimen couldn't be that Roger. 'Don't you remember?' Roger sighed nostalgically. 'There was Stephen, Debbie, Suzanne and ... you used to tell all those funny jokes and ...'

'This was all a very long time ago.' Mike looked down his nose at the little man as if he were some sort of inconsequential insect. '1984 ... yes I suppose I was a Bluecoat around about this time.' He muttered into his shoulder.

'Of course you were We were best buddies don't you remember?' Roger couldn't understand why Mike didn't seem as pleased to see him as he was to see his dear old friend. 'It's so good to see you Mike. You look to have done pretty well for yourself.'

'I'm just Deputy Manger here but there's a lot of responsibility you know.' Mike knew for a fact they had never been good friends. In fact after a certain unfortunate event he had kept well clear of Roger. He looked around shiftily, to check if anyone was watching him having this unsettling and awkward conversation with this old queen.

'Do you remember that year? What a summer.' Roger clasped his hands together as if in ecstacy.

'Yes, well, it's great to see you Roger but I have things to do here. So, if you could just move along.' Mike pushed him along with a hand and poked him with a finger, as if he were a cardboard box that had been used for packaging and had now served its purpose.

'But don't you remember?' Roger couldn't understand why Mike didn't want to talk to him. He knew that his brain had been a little addled at this time but nevertheless.

'It's such a long time ago and I find it doesn't do to dwell in the past,' said Mike gruffly. He looked at his watch and wished Roger would just get lost.

'Near the end of the season.' Roger was encroaching once more into his personal space and Mike didn't like it at all. 'Tony was stabbed and the camp had to close early. Do you know if they ever find out ...'

'No, I don't think so. Look, lovely as it it is to see you again Roger, I really must go.' Mike was sweating profusely now.

'But I thought we could maybe renew our acquaintance Mike. Perhaps you'd like come for a drink with me after you've finished work.' Roger patted Mike gently on the arm. Angrily, the Deputy Store Manager jerked the hand away with a flick of his elbow.

'Like hell I would.' He shouted and he noticed the eyes of shoppers and some fellow workers starting to stare. So horrified had been Mike by this idea, that he'd even said his thoughts out loud. Lowering his voice he muttered, 'I can't I'm busy this evening.'

Unperturbed by how uncomfortable his presence was making Mike feel, Roger continued. 'Well maybe tomorrow or another...'

'I'm a very busy man and I don't have time to go out drinking with you.' Mike snarled.

'But I thought it would be lovely to catch up ...'

'Will you please leave.' Mike raised his arm and pointed towards the door.

'But don't you want to talk about ...'

'No. I don't. Now if you aren't going to go on your own account I will be forced to make you.' Mike now had his hands on the smaller man's shoulders and was pushing him towards the entrance.

'Mike there's no need for this.' Roger protested but Mike wasn't listening and was now frogmarching him towards the entrance. When they arrived at the door Roger was perplexed as to why Mike was behaving so churlishly. Suddenly, after one almighty shove the former Head Bluecoat found himself flying through the air before lying next to a collection of Tesco's recycling bins. Roger was baffled and he couldn't understand why his old friend had given him such short shrift.

Chapter 14

20th July 1984 – Sunny Dunes Holiday Camp

– Debbie and Siobhan's Chalet

Big Spender

When they arrived back at the girl's chalet, Debbie was in fine fettle. She had repaired her compromised hair after its hat squashing and she was basking in the glory of the evening. She was humming an up tempo version of *Don't it Make my Brown Eyes Blue* and reliving her moments of glory in the spotlight. Stephen had called back into his place where he had retrieved a couple of bottles of Pomagne from under his bed. How long they had been there, he wasn't quite sure but if he'd been saving them for a special occasion, this was certainly it. He tried to blot out from his mind his usual Friday night fury and his hatred of Tony Noble, so as not to spoil the night for his friend.

'Did you see the look on that cow's face Debbie? It was a picture.' Stephen opened the bottle of fizz with a loud pop and Debbie got two of Siobhan's mugs from the sink.

'Not properly. I was on stage wasn't I?' Debbie was floating on cloud nine. 'But I could sense unpleasant …' She flapped her arms about as if wafting away bad vibes. 'I don't know what it was but there was definitely something lurking in the wings.

'It — was — pure — *hatred* Debbie. She was *so* jealous.' Stephen lengthened his words for emphasis. He was such an amusing raconteur that Debbie couldn't stop herself once more becoming helpless with laughter. 'I wish I'd had a camera with me. It was like this.' Stephen widened his eyes, puffed out his cheeks and flared his nostrils until he looked like a goldfish about to explode.

'Oh Stephen.' Debbie's sides were hurting so much she had to sit down on the bed. 'You are hilarious.' Suddenly concerned, she glanced at her watch. 'I wonder where Siobhan has got to? I thought she'd have been here by now …'

'She'll be along in a moment I'm sure. Meanwhile,' he nodded towards the cassette player. 'Let's get this gloomy music off and play a something a little more *uplifting* shall we?' Stephen pulled some old cassettes out of his blazer pocket.

'But The Cure,' shrieked Debbie. 'What a cheek. They're my favourites.' She wondered what sort of rubbish Stephen was going to subject her to.

'But what exactly are they a cure for? Not misery that's for sure.' Stephen shook his quiff then pulled out her beloved Cure cassette from her machine and slammed in one of his own. 'You and your depressing bands Debs. Here let's have a bit of Shirl.'

As the familiar sound of *Big Spender* filled the room, Siobhan burst through the door and with her was Mike.

'Hi gang. I've brought Mike here with me. To be sure I hope you don't mind.' Siobhan was determined to put her earlier headache to one side and have a great time with her friends.

'Of course not. 'Debbie beamed. ' The more the merrier I say. Here Siobhan. Have a glass of bubbly care of Stephen here.' The rest of the bottle was divided between the two other mugs.

'Yes isn't this nice?' Stephen's face was now deadpan. 'All the chalet mates together.' It was well-known that Stephen and Mike didn't get along that well. Mike wasn't overly fond of Stephen's mincing ways and Stephen thought Mike was a jerk.'

'Here's to you Debbie. I thought your singing was fabulous tonight.' Mike raised his mug and took a drink.

'To our Debbie,' toasted Siobhan and they all, including Debbie, took a generous glug. 'Well done Debbie. I was so proud of you. Mind, what's the craic? What's going on with this pesky music?' Siobhan asked, already feeling much better in the company of her friends. She was actually thinking that their chalet should have been decked out with some black balloons, streamers and maybe even a sequinned glitter ball.

'It's Stephen. He thought Shirley Bassey was more suitable for the occasion of tonight's celebrations.' Debbie gave her own discarded tape a mock, sorrowful look.

'Wait till you see his Burley Shassey on Wednesday in the Music Hall Debbie. I think you missed her appearance last week,' chuckled Siobhan and Stephen's eyes lit up.

'I can't wait.' After only a week Debbie felt she was slotting into life at Sunny Dunes perfectly and she suspected this season was going to supersede Paignton by far.

'Anyway, I've got a rare treat for us all this evening,' announced Siobhan.' Mike has been working on his own act.' Siobhan gave her new ally an encouraging nod.

'Really Mike, and pray tell us what exactly that might be.' Both Stephen's voice and face had a battle to outdo the other in sarcasm.

'Now Stephen, don't be like that,' said Siobhan. Both she and Debbie glared at him. 'Mike wants to be a stand-up comic and I've suggested he should try out a few of his jokes on us.'

'But surely the joke will all be on him — loser,' hissed Stephen not quite under his breath, making sure he could still be heard.

11th April 2014 – The Lazaridis'' House, Jesmond

Teddie's Regrets

Teddie hadn't seen his wife since they returned from the dinner dance last night. He had been much too tired for any further discussion and they had both gone straight to bed. She had still been sleeping when he had left for work early the next morning, as he had an early appointment with his accountant and Jillian liked her beauty sleep. When he returned to the house, she wasn't about. Teddie had forgotten about her book group, which he always thought was a peculiar time to be held on a Saturday night. She had left him a frozen lasagne next to the microwave for him. After the four minutes of heating the small portion, he took a plate from the cupboard and with three meagre spoonful's emptied the container. He wished he had eaten at The Olympian.

As he sat in silence eating his meal, Teddie Lazaridis' started thinking deeply. Much as he adored his wife there were parts about her that he found unfathomable. Even after being together for more than thirty years, there were areas of her life that remained a complete mystery to him. In many ways, this added further to her charm but sometimes it just left him feeling confused. For example, why was she so against their cleaner, Elaine? He just couldn't understand what the problem could be. She was certainly no competition to Jillian in the looks department. Teddie put down his knife and fork carefully on the sides of his plate. He ran his fingers through the wax in his neat little moustache, checking for pieces of stuck meat, as he thought about Elaine with her plain doughy face, fat lumpy body and that coarse, loud voice.

He looked around the tidy kitchen acknowledging that these days their house was never anything other than immaculate and even Jillian had to admit that there was no fault with the woman's work. Teddie took his plate and used cutlery over to the sink. Here he rinsed, dried and then put them away. He had meticulous standards over tidiness. Also, Elaine was always punctual and considering that she was holding down two jobs at the same time, it was no mean feat to zip between Gateshead and Jesmond. Elaine must be thankful for those two nearby Metro stations.

Teddie moved into the lounge and was pleased to find a Poirot episode on the television. He made himself comfy by removing his shoes to place side by side next to the door. Tonight however, he was finding it difficult to follow the storyline, as his thoughts kept returning to the cleaner. He always found Elaine's voice very pleasant as well. Despite its loud volume, he actually liked her Scottish accent. Although admittedly, he wasn't always able to understand everything that she said, he could usually get the gist. There was a bluntness and directness about her that reminded him of some of his old aunties in Greece, who liked nothing better than to have a good old moan.

Elaine was nothing like her predecessor, that Sonia from Croatia who never said a word to anyone and always wore a surly expression. Although there had been attractiveness about Sonia with her slim figure and dark hair, this surprisingly had never bothered Jillian in the slightest. Usually his wife had little time for younger attractive women. However the combination of Elaine's frizzy grey hair, doughy lined face, overweight lumpy body and pudgy fat feet would be unlikely to be considered attractive by anyone. He would have expected his wife to see this as a positive attribute. There must be something else here with Elaine that he clearly was missing.

After making himself a cup of coffee while continuing to think about Elaine, Teddie kept busy exercising his μίκρσ γκρί κυτταρα (little grey cells). Considering what she had to contend with, Teddie thought Elaine coped remarkably well. He was certain that hers was a one-parent family. She must have struggled singled-handedly to bring up her children and now possibly had grandchildren too.

When he spoke next to Jillian he was going to ask his wife to cut her some slack. It was strange however to think that his wife too had been brought up in Scotland, yet the two of them were like chalk and cheese. There was no trace of the Celtic accent to be found in Jillian's voice but then again she was from Edinburgh and maybe they spoke a very different Scottish there.

Jillian was always very vague when she spoke of her childhood and the early part of her life. Apparently, she had no siblings and her parents along with any aunties and uncles, were all long dead. Surely, she must have some cousins though? Jillian was always remarkably quick to change the conversation, when the topic of her family upbringing was raised. Teddie found this very sad, as back in Greece when he was growing up, he enjoyed greatly the pleasure of a wide extended family. Sadly, he saw very little of them these days because his wife no longer liked Greece and now she preferred Spain for their holidays.

He saw that the time was now nine o' clock, his wife would soon be home so he poured himself a Metaxa. Jillian hated the stuff, so he kept it hidden in the cupboard behind some dvds. He was sure she didn't use to dislike it and remembered fondly the time when they had first met when they had drunk Metaxa together. On that occasion, when Jillian first told him she had been an orphan since an early age, his heart had bled with sadness. If anything this completely sealed his total devotion to his goddess - Demeter, Artemis and Aphrodite – she was the embodiment of them all rolled into one.

When he had met the beguiling Jillian, she had been a successful business woman managing a holiday complex near Corinth in Greece. This was close to where his family had originally come from. She was so capable and exuded such energy that the place ran like clockwork. Teddie had been initially flattered and then bowled over that this marvellous woman had shown any interest in him. However, once she had shared her heart-breaking story about losing her parents so young, Teddie had been so captivated by her vulnerability that he fallen even further under her spell. The need to protect her became his raison d'etre. Furthermore, he couldn't believe his good fortune when she agreed to marry him and without a backwards glance, gave up her friends, career and her beloved Pontinental Holiday Camp.

Although their thirty years together had been so happy, he had always assumed they would have had children at some point but for some reason it never seemed to have happened. Jillian had been reluctant to have any investigations done, for she was sure the stork would bring the bundles of joy in its own good time. Well, it was way past any biological likelihood now and while he was disappointed, he secretly suspected she didn't feel the same way. After all this time, his wife still held some cards close to her chest and these secrets had recently started gnawing away at his insides. This little bug was telling him that somewhere along this line there was an Elaine connection, but how could that possibly be?

Chapter 15

25th July 1984 – Sunny Dunes Holiday Camp – The Entertainment's Office

The Tatty Old Scarecrow

After the events of the previous week, Suzanne was like a bubbling cauldron filled with toxic ingredients, furious that so much fuss was being made of that new Bluecoat Debbie and her alleged marvellous performance on Friday night. Even after five days she was still seething. She, for one, thought Debbie's voice was nothing special, in fact it had a rather boring monotone drone and she knew for a fact her own talents were infinitely superior. Debbie had just sung the songs rooted to the spot, as if she were another of Mike's stage cardboards. She'd had an inane grin on her face and barely put in any effort into her performance whatsoever. Whereas when she Suzanne was on stage, she gave it her all. She compared unfavourably Debbie's lacklustre act with her own spectacular rendition of Y Viva Espana. This had then been followed by her own display of unique creativity as she had rewarded her adoring audience to the delights of her fabulous flamenco dancing.

When that upstart Mandy had been given her marching orders, she had felt no pity for her. In fact she had not attempted to hide the fact that she was pleased. Once she had gone Suzanne was secure in her rightful position as the best performing Bluecoat of the season, but she hadn't bargained on the arrival of the punk freak. If that straw hat hadn't been hiding her mad hair, then her act certainly would certainly have got the audience's attention but not for a good reason. If they had seen her stupid hair, the punters would have just laughed at her for being the joke that she clearly was. Suzanne wished that they had.

No doubt at the Old Time Music Hall tonight *she* would be taking over Mandy's *Burlington Bertie from Bow* spot. Suzanne remembered Mandy all right, strutting about the stage in a tuxedo suit, swirling a silver topped cane and all full of herself like a pimped up penguin. The fact that her act followed Suzanne's 'Second Hand Rose' had annoyed her even further, but she had got her comeuppance, hadn't she? So, that Debbie had better watch herself, for Suzanne had her ways of dealing with people and matters not to her liking.

Suzanne lit a cigarette and scowled into her coffee cup. As the door to the Entertainment's Office flew open she hoped it wasn't Debbie or any of her newly formed fan club. Thankfully, it was Karen.

'Morning Suzanne. How's tricks with you?' Even her friend's Scouse drawl was grating on her today

'Well I can't say I'm feeling my best.' Suzanne flicked her cigarette at the tray and she missed. The cigarette and the ash fell on the floor.

'Is this because of last week with ...' Karen began.

'Don't even mention that bitch's name.' Suzanne hissed.

'You're a much better singer than her and she has no ...' Karen flapped her hands about trying to remember the precise word she was searching for. 'Stage presence, that's it.' She clapped her hands together like a sea lion hoping for a fish, feeling pleased with herself for recalling the proper word. 'When you're on stage, you are in command, like the queen.' But this title didn't sound in the slightest bit regal when spoken with a thick Liverpudlian twang. Suzanne glared at her friend, as she thought this term with its homosexual connotations was surely more fitting to either Roger or Stephen.

Oblivious to Suzanne's annoyance, Karen's fawning continued. 'You take control of the whole space. That's why everyone loves you Suzanne. No way can she compete with you. And to be honest what sort of a mess did she look like up there? I'll tell you, all bundled up in her straw hat and checked shirt. She was like a tatty, old scarecrow, standing in a muddy field next to a manky bale of hay.'

'Yes, Miss Ultra-cool didn't quite look her usual self did she?' Suzanne brightened at the thought of Debbie being stuck in field and tied to stick, especially if it was raining. More than likely the rain would turn her horrible hair into a nasty black cauliflower. She made a mental note to hide those communal brollies that were kept in the Entertainment's Office. 'More like Miss decidedly tepidly boring if you ask me.' The two of them descended into hyena-like cackles as the door opened.

'What are you two laughing at then?' Roger was sounding officious, bad tempered and like he was spoiling for a fight.

'Never you mind. It's none of your business.' Suzanne growled before turning her back on him and faced the wall. Karen followed suit.

'Something unpleasant, no doubt.' He shook his head, sniffed repeatedly and looked up at the clock which showed 10.30 am. He seemed uneasy as if he was waiting for something he needed. 'Isn't it time you two were both working? Karen, surely the children will be waiting for Auntie Karen and the Pirate Treasure Trail and you're not even ready in your outfit. And as for you Suzanne ...'

'Whatever Roger. It's another half an hour before Cine Racing.' Suzanne knew Debbie was also down to do this so she needed plenty of time, caffeine, and nicotine as ammunition before she could execute her revenge plan. She had an idea which should work perfectly. Just as it had once before. Karen scuttled out of the door, as she had been in such deep conversation with her friend she had lost all track of time. Meanwhile Suzanne checked through the contents of her handbag.

11th April 2014 – Sandyford, Newcastle

Jillian's Book Group

Jillian was at her monthly reading group and this time it was the turn of Gwendoline Roberts to hold it at her place. There were six ladies in the group who took it in turns to host the event. Some of them went to more effort with the refreshments but Gwendoline was one who obviously didn't. Last time the gathering had been held at Jillian's she had chosen the novel *Zorba the Greek* and her array of splendid fayre had been supplied by the Olympian, her husband's restaurant.

Although, Gwendoline insisted her address was Jesmond, Sandyford would be closer to the mark. Despite her best efforts at belonging to the set, Jillian thought Gwendoline would never quite come up to scratch. After all, her husband was a bookie. Jillian felt there was something shabby about making money from people's gambling addictions. It reminded her of somebody she once knew.

Gwendoline that evening was wearing some unflattering black leggings, which made her too skinny legs appear like those belonging to some nasty insect. This was teamed with a black long shirt with large red poppies that had probably been bought in a sale because Jillian thought it had that look about it. The outfit wasn't something that Jillian would ever have entertained wearing. She had on her crisp linen white shirt along with beige well-cut trousers and some understated loafers which had come with a comfortingly large price-tag.

'Would you care for a vol-au-vent or maybe a top up Jillian?' Gwendoline asked, attempting unsuccessfully to tone down her broad Geordie accent. Jillian, was dubious as what the fishy filling was inside the puff pastry but she suspected some economy staple of sandwich paste and she quickly shook her head. Likewise, she resisted a further glass of wine not due to fact she was driving, but because she was positive it had been purchased in one of those cheaper supermarkets.

'No, you're alright thanks Gwendoline,' replied Jillian. She took her copy of *Brighton Rock*, from her *Mulberry* handbag and placed the book next to her on the buttercup coloured sofa. This was a very yellow room and Barbara Blackstaff, the Mayor's wife, in a salmon coloured dress clashed horribly with the mustard wall paper.

'So what did we all think of the book?' Janet Jenkinson opened up the discussion, smiling expectantly with her lank brown hair and charity shop clothes. She liked to keep these meetings focused. This was a book group after all and the no nonsense approach that she used while running her Girl Guide troupe, she liked to apply somewhat inappropriately here.

'Well, there were certainly some interesting characters, weren't there?' Barbara suggested warily, hoping this bland comment was sufficient to hide the fact she had only read the first two pages.

'Did you think so? I found them rather unpleasant.' Jillian made a stab in the dark at making a sensible comment after reading the blurb on the back of her copy.

'Yes, well this was the 1930's and times were hard.' Marion postulated. She was a retired Head teacher with a steel grey bob and an air of austerity, who peered intimidatingly through her thick glasses like a belligerent old owl.

'And this was down in Brighton wasn't it?' Barbara had just filled up her own wine glass and was looking a little flushed. She giggled. 'I'm sure things were never so terrible up here in the north.'

'Don't you believe it Barbara? I'm sure they were just as bad if not worse here,' contradicted Marion with great pleasure. Feeling like a child that had been reprimanded, Barbara decided she had better keep quiet.

'Oh, and by the way, Ruth can't come tonight. She said to tell you she's not very well. A stomach upset I think.' Gwendoline informed the group and pulled a sympathetic face. Marion shrugged her shoulders as if she didn't believe this all too familiar excuse. 'Anyway, to get back to the book.' Gwendoline made her contribution to the conversation and after putting her pastries on the table, she came to sit on the carpet to join the group. She was eager to demonstrate that she was familiar with the names of the main characters in the book. 'Well, that Pinkie wasn't very nice if you know what I mean ... but I liked Ada and I felt sorry for poor Rose.
'

'Isn't it funny?' Emily said proudly, showing off her familiarity with the text. 'I thought at first it was called Brighton Rock because it was going to be a nice story about people eating rock on holiday. You know, rock, the stripy candy people have at the seaside but in fact it was the weapon used to kill Fred wasn't it?' She was a somewhat earnest girl, who at 17 was the youngest member of the group and Gwendoline's daughter. Normally, she wasn't allowed to attend the meetings but as she was studying Brighton Rock for A level and as it was being held in their house, this time her mother had let her join in.

'Well, I think essentially,' Janet ignored the last comment from the child as she was preparing herself to wax lyrical. She had read a couple of reviews and made copious notes from them. 'The book examines how the good and evil which the Catholic Church preaches to be of paramount importance is superseded by the intrinsic superiority of right and wrong.' Her face wore its smugness like a well-fitting glove as she consulted her notebook before continuing.

'Yes, that was a good point Emily.' Gwendoline interrupted Janet's monologue and praised her own daughter's contribution to the discussion. Sometimes she could swing for that pompous cow Janet. 'Also, wasn't it interesting that Corleoni, Pinkie's nemesis was the same name of the leader of the mafia boss in *The Godfather*?'

'Do you think Graham Green must have been watching the Godfather when he wrote this book?' Barbara was now beginning to slur.

'Don't be so stupid.' Janet flashed the tipsy woman a look of contempt. 'This was written first. No doubt whoever wrote *The Godfather* had been reading this book.'

'Mario Puzo, and it was made into a film by Francis Ford Coppola.' Marion put in her pennyworth only too pleased to also put Janet in her place.

By this time any little interest Jillian had in *Brighton Rock* had completely disappeared and she wondered what Teddie was doing at home. No doubt, he would have finished his dinner she had left for him and would probably be watching some crime drama on the television. She wondered if she dared Lazaridis the subject of Elaine once more because the woman just had to be got rid of. Where was it she knew the woman from? Had they gone to school together? No, she didn't think so but she had the distinct hunch that the cleaner thought she had something on her.

'Jillian? Are you still with us?' Janet was clearly annoyed that Jillian hadn't been paying attention and was staring into space. Obviously she hadn't been following the discussion.

'Oh sorry, I was just thinking about …' Jillian began before Janet spoke over her.

'Well here's a copy of the book that's been *chosen* for next month and it's a bit different from *Brighton Rock*.' Janet twisted her face as she held up a purple book with fancy gold lettering, twinkly stars, puffy pink clouds and what looked to be a Disney princess on the front cover. She tossed the book onto the floor.

'This one was my choice.' Barbara was beaming, as it was by her very favourite author.

'Why does that not surprise me?' Janet rolled her eyes while picking up the offending book and holding it at arm's length as if it were a dead fish. Once more she threw the book down.

'*Follow Your Dreams* by Destiny Chambers. It looks quite frankly — dreadful.' Marion's voice sounded as if she were reprimanding a disobedient pupil and her eyes blinked in disapproval from behind her spectacles.

'Well this woman is a local author — if you can call *her* that.' Janet raised her eyebrows. 'Apparently she lives quite close by.

'Well, if she's local. Then it's only right we support her. After all, its Barbara's choice and we all read what you chose last month Janet.' Gwendoline recalled how she had grimly battled through the first six chapters of Dostoevsky's *Crime and Punishment.*

'Oh, by the way I was over in Gateshead the other day.' Even in her inebriated state, Barbara was relishing the fact she would be next month's book chooser. 'And would you believe they have all her books on special offer in Tesco's for £2.99.'

'Well even that will clearly be a complete waste of money won't it?' Gwendoline muttered sarcastically.

Jillian had taken the discarded book from the floor and was staring at the photo of the glamorous Destiny Chambers on the back of the cover. There was something disturbingly familiar about the expression on her face and the mischievous glint in her eye. Jillian felt the uncomfortable chill of something walking over her grave.

Chapter 16

25th July 1984 – Sunny Dunes Holiday Camp – The Entertainment's Office

Roger Thinks He's About to Get Lucky

Roger was sure those two malicious cows had been talking about Debbie's performance last week. Suzanne would have been crippled with jealousy and her sycophantic side kick Karen would no doubt have been consoling her. The pair of them were pathetic but Suzanne was dangerous and he had his suspicions that she had played no small part in Mandy's dismissal.

Anyway, next Roger went into Tony's office to speak to him about what he thought were some very serious matters. However, he had found him and Jill embroiled in a game of Poker. He had wanted to ask him about the new Donkey Derby programmes that hadn't yet arrived but before he had even begun to speak, Tony dismissed him with a familiar swish of the hand, as if he had much more important issues to attend to. They were playing cards for God's sake. Then when Jill shot him a superior look from somewhere between under her eyelids and beneath her nose, he just felt exasperated with the pair of them. For goodness sake was he, with all of his own problems to contend with, the only one trying to hold the place together. Then, when Tony had the actual audacity to stand up and hold the door open for him to leave at that very moment, he felt furious.

Thankfully, back in the Entertainment's Main Office, he found that Suzanne had gone, which was just as well, as he was all set to give her an earful. Mike was in her place avidly reading a book and making little notes on the back of an envelope. As Roger moved forward, curious to this hardly academic, Bluecoat's choice of research material, he chuckled to see he was reading a book of jokes. And then, as he made himself a cup of coffee, he was almost sure he could feel Mike's eyes boring in to him. But, when he looked up, Mike was seemingly glued to the book which didn't seem to be making him laugh.

So, Roger went to check the day's rota that had been sellotaped to the wall earlier by Jill. It seemed that Cine Racing this morning was to be manned by Mike, Suzanne, Liz, Marcus, Stephen and Debbie. That should be interesting he thought, bearing in mind Suzanne's resentment towards Debbie and he made a mental note to drop in and check on the atmosphere. No doubt, a certain female Bluecoat would be in full Pit Bull bitch mode and ready for the attack.

Once more, he could sense Mike staring at him. He had to admit he found tall, solid, rugby-playing Mike with his dark, brooding eyes and thick moustache more than a little attractive. And, although he had caught him flirting with numerous girls since the season began, he hadn't struck up a serious relationship with anyone yet. He had assumed him to be totally heterosexual but here he was giving off definite signals. Roger felt a frisson of excitement like he had a moth fluttering in his stomach. Perhaps he had been mistaken about Mike and possibly this was going to prove to be his lucky day.

15th April 2014 – 55 Degrees North, Newcastle

Heralding the Time for His First G and T

Stefan had a luxury penthouse apartment on the top of the *55 Degrees North* building in the centre of Newcastle. It was ironic that this had once been the Swan House building where he had come to sign on in the late 1980s. This fact amused him and had sealed the deal for the purchase of his new pad five years ago. His old flat on the Quayside had become too cramped and the area no longer held the same appeal it once had. Without doubt his current vista of the impressive Newcastle skyline totally surpassed that of a poxy slice of the Tyne which was all his last place could provide. Now from the comfort of his own large balcony, he could admire the numerous bridges bestriding the river majestically, before it snaked and slithered its way down to the coast. Each day, if at home, Stefan could watch the ferries departing from North Shields at six, heralding the time for his first G and T.

However, this was the morning; Stefan was drinking his second expresso and had a busy day ahead. Watching the tiny folk down below on the roundabout whether in their cars or pedestrians, he thought they were like little obedient insects scurrying off to their insignificant jobs. Thankfully not for him. He was his own boss and was answerable to nobody. First he had some important zoom calls to make and a few e-mails to deal with. Although these could be attended to from home, that afternoon he would be going down to his studio in Wallsend to work on some exciting new demos for his latest project. Stefan was a successful record producer, band manager and local celebrity. He enjoyed his job, the feeling of having his finger on the pulse but mostly he revelled in the kudos it gave him.

Although the bands he dealt with were largely of the flash-in-the-pan type, this was no skin off his nose. Stefan had this uncanny ability of predicting what would become the next big thing. Somehow he had this knack of bringing together a collection of easy-on-the-eye young lads or lassies, finding them catchy but run-of-the-mill songs, giving them a gimmick and marketing them into a highly successful package. One of his bands, *The Bavarians*, had been massive in the 90's. They had worn tight lederhosen, Tyrolean hats with jaunty feathers and had interspersed their singing with a little novelty yodelling. Similarly, he had later put together three local girls who wore dresses festooned in lights and massive hats like chandeliers. He gave them the name the *Sparkles* and at Christmas 2002 that's just what they did.

A couple of weeks ago he thought he had spotted Leanne Sparkle behind a till in *John Lewis* and he noticed she had gained a lot of weight. Thinking a meeting with her might be awkward he decided against his purchase and quickly left the store. Although Stefan's career had been long and profitable, the same couldn't be said for his protégés. On frequent occasions, he had tried to advise some of the youngsters about being sensible and not squandering what they had earned but they never listened. Vain youth thinks itself immortal and refuses to believe what is happening when after a short life of two or three hits, the moment had gone. But that was the nature of the business, they'd had their brief minute of fame and after all there was always a fresh batch of wannabes waiting for him in the wings.

Anyway, Stefan chose to put some of these more Machiavellian aspects of his wealth to the back of his mind and concentrate on the here, now and his latest band. He checked the time. There were a couple of hours before he needed to leave for the studio where he would be spending the afternoon with his four new lads. Later that evening, he was having dinner with an old friend of his. Destiny was a hoot and they always had great fun together. Nevertheless, at the moment he had something troubling his mind which he really needed to share with her and this wouldn't be giving either of them anything to laugh about.

Chapter 17

25th July 1984 – Sunny Dunes Holiday Camp – The Entertainment's Office

Roger's Faux Pas

Roger could sense that something was in the air. Mike was definitely giving off signals and he had the feeling he was about to get lucky. Checking his pocket for the precious brown paper envelope, he ran for the toilets. Luckily, there was no one around and he headed for an empty cubicle. A few seconds later he carefully wiped the traces of powder from the seat and the familiar euphoria kicked in. Checking his image in the mirror, he ran his fingers through his hair, before straightening his tie and fluffing up his moustache. Hurrying back to the office where Mike was still alone he sat down next to the would be comedian. Beaming at him with what he thought his most attractive of smiles, he pretended to be interested in Mike's book.

With humour being the very last thing on his mind, Roger asked Mike 'Are there some good jokes in there then? '

Mike wrinkled his brow, looked intently at Roger and rubbed his own top lip. 'I moustache you a question.'

'Whatever you like my dear boy, you have my complete attention.' Roger thought how lovely Mike's skin was and his eyes like two dark pools in which he could happily swim.

'I'll shave it for later.' As Mikes head wobbled from side to side and he pulled his gawky comic face Roger was held in complete thrall. All thoughts of Tony, poker and disgruntlement flew out of the window. Roger was floating on air. He wished the two of them could just be alone together … but not here in this, filthy, messy room. He imagined them somewhere very different. Maybe, they could be catching each other's eye on a sunny, tropical beach with golden sands, crystal clear waters and skies of sapphire. Even the nearby park would have been preferable to here. It was actually quite lovely at this time of year, especially in the fragrant rose gardens just behind the men's toilets where Roger had enjoyed a few previous most satisfactory encounters.

'Yes, some of them are quite good.' Mike did a double take, wondering why Roger's face had taken on such a peculiar expression. Unperturbed, he flicked back a few pages in his book. 'What about this one … this is a good 'un. Why did the owl invite his friend over?'

Roger placed his elbow on the table, his chin in his hands and gazed adoringly into Mikes eyes, 'If I was an owl I'd have you over any time.'

'No, that's not what you're supposed to say.' Mike replied crossly, but then remembered he was supposed to be getting Roger on his side. However, even at this point Mike could see his joke had fallen a little flat and the conversation was not going as he had planned.

'You have a lovely voice Mike. Perfect for telling jokes.' Roger pulled his chair closer to the other Bluecoat's.

'Really? Well thank you Roger. No one has ever told me that before.' Mike decided there and then he needed to take advantage of any positives if he wanted his aspirations to come to fruition. 'Roger.' He bit his lip. 'I've been meaning to have a word with you for a while now.' He whispered, as if concerned somebody else might hear.

'Really, I hadn't realised but I'm very pleased to hear it.' Roger shuffled his seat even closer, hanging on his prospective lover's every word.

'It's about.' Mike looked down at his book, with what Roger thought a most attractive flush spreading across his face. 'Well I don't quite know how to say it. It's embarrassing you see.'

'You don't need to feel uncomfortable Mike. Not with me. I do understand you know.' Roger brushed his narrow knee against that of Mike's rather broader rugby player's one underneath the table.

'I've been meaning to mention this for a while. It's frustrating you know.' Mike's top lip was quivering and he was beginning to feel rather sick.

'My dear boy.' Roger looked into Mike's big brown eyes as if spellbound. 'You should have mentioned earlier. I do understand what it's like you know.' His hand was now patting Mike's leg.

'What the hell are you doing?' Horror washed across Mike's face, as he realised where this was leading and even more scarily where he had almost let it go.

'But I thought ...' Roger quickly retracted his hand.

'You thought bloody wrong. I wanted to ask you about me having a turn in one of the shows as a comedian. I'm sick to the back teeth of holding up those bloody pieces of cardboard.' Mike raised his voice.

'But I thought ...' Now it was Roger's turn to feel embarrassed.

'Yes, I know what you thought.' Mike stood up and slammed his book down on the table.

'I'm so sorry. I never meant...' Roger stopped mid-sentence as glum looking Debbie arrived at the scene. Roger felt mortified and wished the ground would swallow him up.

10th April 2014 – Tesco, Trinity Square, Gateshead

From Bad to Worse

Mike had been horribly shaken by the appearance of Roger in his Tesco Store earlier that day and it had put him quite out of sorts. He had not been able to get the man out of his shop fast enough. In his desperation to be rid of the sleazy queen, he had pushed him through the door and bundled his body towards the re-cycling bins like a bag of smelly merchandise well past its sell by date. He just hoped that no one had witnessed his conversation with Roger and prayed to God that the bastard wouldn't come back.

No way, would he have recognised this pitiful specimen of a man, with his faded ginger brillo pad of grizzled hair and horrible wrinkled skin as the Head Bluecoat from thirty years ago. This was a time and a place he had no desire whatsoever to revisit. He tried to push Pontin's memories to the back of his mind but this was impossible. Although Roger could only have been a few years older than himself, he now looked at least a couple of decades his senior. In fact, he was sure nobody would believe they were of the same generation. Mike thought Roger looked like he was ready for a care home. What on earth could he have been doing with his life to accelerate the aging process like that?

There had been rumours of his involvement in drugs back in the day. Mike recalled some dodgy goings on in the swimming baths, but Jesus, what toxic medication could Roger have been taking to do this to himself? Mike knew he hadn't always treated his body as a temple but when he took a glance at himself in the little mirror beside the sunglasses, he was greatly relieved. Thankfully, the image that greeted him was no worse than the one he had seen in this bathroom that morning. As he tried on a pair of aviator sunglasses, he nodded appreciatively at his own reflection. Oh yes, he was still in possession of that certain *je ne sais quoi*. It seemed at least he should be grateful that he hadn't been physically contaminated himself by the unwanted encounter

As he walked over to the book and magazine section in the store, he mused over the thought that the Roger incident was an episode in his life he had tried to delete. Until moments ago Mike had been largely successful in achieving this. Had Roger completely forgotten that embarrassing incident between the two of them and what had almost happened? Even now it made his stomach turn. What about its aftermath and those terrible repercussions for him? How could the man imagine he would ever want to be friends with him?

He tried to shut it all out and picked up a cheesy-looking book called *Follow Your Dreams* from the collection of top ten bestsellers. It was just the ghastly sort of tripe that his wife Linda might read. On the back of the cover, the glossy picture of Destiny Chambers smiled seductively at him. She was quite hot he supposed and he certainly wouldn't kick her out of bed but this rubbish definitely wasn't a thing he would be reading. He slammed the book back on the shelf. Mike wasn't much of a book reader anyway and sports magazines were much more his thing.

Then, as an afterthought, he picked the paperback up again, unnerved because there was something vaguely familiar about this Destiny Chambers. Her long dark hair and rather lovely smile reminded him of somebody he once knew. Now, if she was a blast from his past, he certainly wouldn't mind in the slightest if she came seeking him out. Suddenly, images of Tony, Roger, Stephen, Jillian, Debbie and his father whirled across the ceiling like the segments of a massive kaleidoscope. Mike felt sick.

'You all right there Mr Robinson?' Elaine appeared suddenly from behind the rack of newspapers.

'Yes. Thanks. Elaine isn't it? I was just having a bit of a funny turn.' Mike took a dirty paper handkerchief out of his pocket, that he had earlier blown his nose on, to wipe his brow.

'Oh aye, One of those wee queer turns was it?' The pompous git knew her name well enough thought Elaine. 'Maybe ye need to see a doctor about that one.' She raised an eyebrow knowingly.

'I'm sure I'll be fine.' He stuffed the hanky back in his pocket. 'Anyway shouldn't you be busy somewhere?'

'I'll be away to my other job in a jiffy.' She moved closer to him and lowered her voice. 'I saw you with yer wee pal before.'

'Sorry? What are you on about?' Mike could smell the woman's stale body odour. He looked over his shoulder and about the store nervously.

'You were talking away to that old queen just before, d'ye ken what I mean?'

Mike detected a tone of menace in her voice. 'I don't remember. I talk to a lot of folk.' He felt himself getting hot under the collar. 'It's my job.'

'He had scraggy hair and one of those *mincey* walks.' She put a hand on her hip and waggled her large bottom.

'Elaine. Excuse me … I'm a busy man. And what concern it is of yours who exactly I talk to … well I really have no idea.' He stuck his finger in the air as if he had just remembered something important. 'Oh yes it all comes back to me now.' Mike supposed the best bet was to make light of the encounter, as she obviously thought there was something untoward about it. 'It happens that I think I do recall *someone* fitting your derogatory homophobic description. He was bringing back some faulty … erm … batteries.'

'Faulty batteries eh? It looked to me like the two of you knew each other *and* quite well at that.' She put her head to one side as if challenging him to disagree.

'I don't know what you're insinuating woman but I suggest you crawl back under your nasty little stone and get back to what you're supposed to be doing.' Mike pulled himself up to his full height to tower over this little Scottish toad of a woman.

'Oh I'm away any minute now. But I was just wondering about something. Just a wee small matter.' She fluttered her eyelashes in the least coquettish way he had ever encountered.

'And what exactly *were* you wondering?' He didn't like the sound of this. Why wouldn't she just do one, jiffy on to her other job and leave him in peace?

'I just wondered if there were any wee jobs going.' She stared at him hard without blinking as if this was some kind of threat. 'It's my son Scott, you see. He could do with some work in the warehouse mebbe … or in packing.'

'I don't think there are any vacancies at the moment but I'll bear it in mind if anything … '

'I think you can do better than that.' Elaine's eyes shot towards the window like two bullets, where at that very moment, as if on cue, a menacing figure with distinctive fading ginger hair was walking past. 'Oh would you look at that. Do you think your wee pals coming after you again? Shall I go and have a wee word with him?' An expression of pure evil lit up the woman's face and she noticed they had caught the attention of the two women on nearby tills. 'I'm sure Clare and Dawn would like to know all about your new buddy who in fact doesn't seem to be a new buddy at all does he?'

'Just shut up woman,' Mike snarled and hoped that Roger wasn't coming into the store. Then he mumbled, 'I'll see what I can do about what you mentioned before.'

'So you'll find a job for my Scott then?' Elaine's smirk put Mike in mind of a horrible gargoyle.

'I'll see what I can do.' What was going on? Why was *he* back here again? Did this woman by some weird twist of fate also know Roger?

'Nah, you'll *find* my Scott some work.' The even harder edge crept once more into her rough Scottish voice.

'Yes.' Thank God. Roger had walked on past. 'Whatever. Now isn't it time you were off. We don't want you being late …'

She gave him a conspiratorial look through narrowed eyes. 'Fair enough. So it's agreed my wee Scottie's got a job then and we'll say no more about …' she tapped the side of her nose before flouncing off in the direction of the door.

Chapter 18

25th July 1984 – Sunny Dunes Holiday Camp – Tony's Office

What Tony's Up To?

Both Jill and Tony had been annoyed when that twit Roger barged in. Furthermore, he had made his irritation plain at being given such short shrift and then seemed furious when being shown the door by Tony. Roger clearly needed to be reminded of his place in the pecking order. Meanwhile, Jill had used the opportunity to look at Tony's hand of cards while he made sure his Chief Bluecoat had buggered off and left them in peace. Then, for some strange reason, he held the door slightly open by inserting two of his bulbous fingers into the slight gap. Jill wondered what on earth he was doing, and as their game was obviously abandoned, she used the opportunity to re-touch her lipstick. Clearly he was spying on the Bluecoats she eventually realised, a pastime which she herself was not unknown to indulge in.

She couldn't imagine that Roger was up to anything of interest, as he was in her opinion the most boring stickler for the rules. She found him tiresome and a complete waste of space. Why on earth he was Chief Bluecoat was a mystery to her but then again his stupidity was an asset in some ways. No doubt, he would be blethering on about those damn Donkey Derby programmes again at the next available opportunity. She had only checked them the other day and there were plenty. Probably more than enough of them to last right until the end of the season.

Recently, he just kept getting ridiculous bees in his bonnet about the most trivial of matters and just wouldn't let things be. Last week, he had thought there were insufficient spare bulbs for the spot lights and before that he had been worrying about the staff rota for three weeks' time. It was really most irritating and unsettling too because he would get himself so agitated that his eyes would dart about the room and he would break out into a sweat. Jill wondered fleetingly if maybe he had some underlying medical condition which could affect the conditions of his employment. In fact was he really up to the job?

Anyway, what really had bugged her was the fact that when Roger had stormed in, they had been playing poker. This, in itself in itself was quite innocuous but it was for the best if neither of their names were linked with any form of gambling. Tony had previous form. He had been sacked from other jobs in the past for supplementing his income in a variety of dubious ways to pay off his debts.

Jill herself wasn't particularly bothered about gambling and only feigned an interest to keep Tony sweet. At least once a week after work, she and Tony would head on down to the nearby Pear Tree Casino. While Tony chanced his luck on the Roulette Table, Jill just simply enjoyed soaking up the glitzy atmosphere. She adored being amongst the men in their sharp suits and the women dripping in diamonds. While she was sipping a champagne cocktail, wearing her latest designer dress and holding her new Gucci handbag, she became the Jill she had always been destined to be. Admittedly, Tony was not the escort of her fantasies but one step at a time.

'Tony, you need to have a word with that Roger.' Jill wondered whatever Tony could be finding so interesting through the chink in the door. 'You know he can't just come barging in here whenever he fancies. I mean, he didn't even knock.'

'Keep your voice down.' Tony put a finger over his lip to shush her and Jill went back to reading her magazine, 'There's nothing for you to worry about,' Tony hissed and walked back to take his seat, with a curious self-satisfied grin on his face. 'We were only playing cards.'

'Yes, but it doesn't look good. If you know what I mean?' Jill looked nervy. Tony opened a drawer, pulled out a bottle of whisky and poured himself a glass. 'Anyway,' she continued. 'We could have been doing anything.'

'Hmmm. I'm liking the sound of that.' He took a sip from his whisky and gave her a lecherous grimace. Is that a proposition? I've come over all flustered and saucy.' When Jill quickly jumped up, he leaned over and gave her a nip on the bottom.

Jill sprang away emitting a girlish laugh. 'Not now. I mean you have the meeting soon with Stan haven't you?' She was pleased to remind him about that.

'Ah yes. That's a pity. I'd completely forgotten. It's the effect you have on me. Grrr you just turn me into an uncontrollable wild beast of passion.' Tony's eyes glinted.

'Yes, you have that effect on me too sexy man.' She Grrrd back. 'Now hadn't you better get going?'

'So Babe, are you ok for tonight?' He ran his fingers through his comb-over in a similar manner that which Roger had used on his fuller head of hair, only a few moments earlier.

'Tonight?' She feigned ignorance as to what he was referring to. This was one of their familiar rituals.

'Yes for the Pear Tree after work.' He raised his eyebrows in what he thought to be an alluring manner.

'Oh yes. I'll be up for that.' She blew him a kiss before pushing him out of the door.

13th April 2014 – The Lazaridis' Home, Jesmond

Follow Your Dreams

Jillian had planned that afternoon to Google that author Destiny Chambers, on her laptop. On that fine spring day she was relaxing in her conservatory and drinking a cup of tea from her favourite cup with a swan on the side. Carl had been working in the garden and it was looking splendid with all the early flowers in bloom. Likewise indoors, to her irritation, there were no smears on the windows or specks of dust to be seen anywhere. How could that slovenly pig of a woman be so good at cleaning? She ran her fingers through her freshly coiffured hair and sighed with annoyance.

Destiny Chambers was certainly prolific and Jillian was impressed by her long list of books. As she read the synopsis of the plot of *Follow Your Dreams*, a smile curled around her lips as she imagined Marian and Janet condemning the book as trash and absolutely loathing every word. Of course, she would agree with them but she actually suspected she might enjoy the story. Not that she would admit it.

It seemed Destiny Chambers was a local writer and on the photographs on her website she certainly cut a dash. To Jillian's eyes her look was a bit too contrived and fey. In fact she even seemed a little vulgar with her floaty fancy dresses and high heeled boots. She reminded Jill of Stevie Nicks, which was a look Jillian would never consider emulating herself. However, she supposed Destiny did look quite arty which could be no bad thing for a writer. Yet there was something familiar about this Destiny Chambers and Jillian was almost sure that she must have seen her swanning up and down Acorn Road. Perhaps she lived very close by. Jillian didn't know any authors personally but felt that maybe she ought to.

Although Elaine had finished her cleaning for that day long ago and Jillian had no real reason to leave the house to escape from her, yet she still felt a little restless. She had no meet ups planned for that day and the only purchase she needed to make was a copy of the *Follow Your Dreams*. If she went into a bookshop in Newcastle, there was the real worry that somebody might spot her purchasing to what was in all intent and purpose a trashy novel. She had enjoyed the experience of buying her copies of *Brighton Rock* and *Crime and Punishment*. With her Waterstone's bag swinging she had swaggered out of the shop feeling like a cultured academic. She couldn't say she had enjoyed reading either of them but nevertheless.

This *Follow Your Dreams* was definitely not your typical ladies book group fayre but there was something about the book that had captured her attention. She could have ordered the book online, but Jillian had got it into her head that she wanted to begin reading it that day. And what Jillian wanted Jillian generally got. Except that was not the case with cleaners or with one cleaner in particular.

Now what was it that Barbara had said? The book was on offer in Tesco for £2.99. Well, Jillian definitely didn't need to shop for bargains. The very idea. Unfortunately, there was still danger of people she knew to be lurking even in the Tesco's at Kingston Park but wasn't there another Tesco in central Gateshead? Perfect, for there was absolutely no chance whatsoever of her bumping into anybody she knew there. In fact, Jillian had very little personal experience of driving across the Tyne. It had always seemed to be something to be wary of because she had been led to believe that folks were different on the other side of the water.

Chapter 19

25th July 1984 – Sunny Dunes Holiday Camp - Tony's Office

The Open Safe

Once Tony was out of the door, Jill reflected that she had done her time fair and square in this dump. She needed to engineer a meeting with the real Big Cheese before the end of the season. Next year, she had her heart set upon elevating her position to that of a Pontinental employee. And as she had earned her stripes good and proper through ranks as Bluecoat, Head Bluecoat and Deputy Entertainment's Manager, her role as Entertainment's Manager must surely be in the bag. She had even picked out the resort she fancied – The Holiday Club Poseidon in Corinth. It was a crying shame that Jill, who at the ripe old age of nearly thirty had never even left the United Kingdom. For certain it was time this was addressed and Greece was a place she had always fancied visiting. She painted the prettiest of smiles on her face and mouthed Καλημέρα (good morning) to her reflection in the mirror, as if it were a potential Pontinental punter.

No, without doubt, Tony was definitely becoming a real liability and in many ways she longed for the end of the season. He had served his purpose. Jill had been stuck as Head Bluecoat for a couple of years and under the previous Entertainment's Manager, there had been no chance of promotion. Why were there so many gays in this business? But once Tony was appointed, she quickly detected the puppy dog lust for her in his eyes and the way he hung on her every word. It was as simple as taking candy from a baby. In no time at all the promotion was hers. Yes, well of course there were some drawbacks but up until now the advantages had more than outweighed the disadvantages. That was until recently.

Jill looked at the safe on the wall and a horrible sick feeling engulfed her stomach. What if she was double-crossed by Tony and he had already taken last week's spoils all for himself? She wouldn't put it past the old bastard, for if truth be known she didn't trust him an inch. As the combination numbers clicked into place, the door swung open to reveal at least 50 tins bulging with coins and notes. Jill thought of those lovely Gloria Vanderbuilt jeans and the red Porshe 911 Carrera that she'd had her eye on for some time.

There was an abrupt knock on the door and it flung open before Jill had time to kick the safe closed. In walked bloody Elaine and her eyes were out on stalks. She must have seen the contents. It was Wednesday and by now all that money should have been handed over to the children's charity. But Elaine wasn't to know that was she? And even if their presence still in the safe needed to be explained, that could easily be done, couldn't it? Damn the woman.

11th April 2014 – Ramsay Court, Central Gateshead

Things on the Up

As Elaine returned to her home on the sixteenth floor in the Ramsay Court block of flats in central Gateshead, she wore a smug grin on her face. At last, the pieces of the jigsaw puzzle were starting to slot into place. She knew she was making Mrs Lazaridis' sweat, but the stupid cow still seemed to have no idea why. Was her memory really that poor or had she, which was more than likely, decided to erase certain unsavoury episodes from her memory? Elaine remembered only too well the teenage strumpet Jill, putting herself about in Glasgow and even more so the mercenary Jill at Pontins who she still, to this day despised.

It was uncanny after all this time and with the holiday camp long demolished, that some of the key players in that mid-eighties drama seemed to be re-surfacing. Some of the workers had been originally from round these parts but others like herself, were from places further away. Like Jill, Scottish Elaine had had no desire to return to the place of her formative years, Glasgow. Her mam had long since passed away, God rest her dear soul, and she'd never had much time for her workshy dad or her thuggish brothers. However, even after all the palaver and the subsequent turnover of staff she had kept working at Pontins well into the nineties, ever hopeful of wearing the Bluecoat uniform.

This all changed when she became pregnant by that bloody lifeguard and life for Elaine was to become even worse. Once she'd had her Kylie, then Scott and finally Charlene, her fate was sealed in a life of squalor, hand-to-mouth existence and minimum wage jobs topped up by benefits. She had been living in the once attractively sounding Ramsay Court for over twenty years now but she'd had no friendly interaction with her neighbours. They had been as much support to her as her kid's fathers. Those three ne'er-do-wells, with whom she'd had the briefest of flings, had left her alone and dreading the patter of tiny feet.

When the children had been small, life had been a complete nightmare: wailing voices, angry bangs on nearby walls, constant changing of nappies and her overwhelming exhaustion. She had thought naively that it would have been easier once they had started school. However, she was constantly being hauled into the concentration camps (Elaine had forgotten how much she hated the places) to be interrogated by surly teachers because Kylie had no interest in learning, and Scott had behaviour issues and kept bunking off school. The bastard Head teacher had even implied that poor Charlene, her youngest, was brain damaged and gleefully predicted she would never have the intelligence beyond that of a six year old. Although Elaine had been fuming at the time, one only had to look into those vacant glass-like eyes to know this was sadly the case.

But once the kids were older, Elaine had decided it was time for her to get a bit savvy. So, she started looking out for opportunities to further herself. Once before, a chance for better life had been within her grasp until certain circumstances had snatched it all away. This was all down to Jillian McDonald and this fact she had never forgotten. After the murder of Tony Noble, a crime which to her knowledge had never been solved, she had been led to believe that Miss McDonald had flown off to sunnier climes. How convenient for her. In fact, all the Bluecoats had made a sharp exit as soon as they could when the inept police force eventually realised they couldn't decide which culprit to charge. It was all very fishy how everyone seemed to have an alibi. Yet *someone* stabbed the bloody man and she knew who she would lay her bets on.

For years Elaine had festered, dwelling on that summer of '84 and what should have been hers but there was absolutely nothing she could do. That was until recently. A few months ago she had been flicking through *The Chronicle* , when a photograph taken at some posh charity function caught her eye. Mr Teddie Lazaridis' and his wife Jillian had donated generously to the worthy cause said the caption. Big deal, thought Elaine at first but then she recognised something familiar about that insincere smile of the woman's. A few days later she saw that a successful local restaurant owner and his wife had been opening some new children's play scheme. And there again she saw that bitch's face posing for the camera. Next, she came across the newspaper's covering of the premier of a new musical called *STRIKE* about some unhappy miners at Newcastle's Theatre Royal. All the local big wigs been given special invitation and surprise surprise there she was … Jillian McDonald, her nemesis partaking of a fancy glass of after show champagne. She was wearing a fur coat, tiara and ball gown. Furthermore, the cow must have had extensive plastic surgery done for she had hardly aged in almost thirty years.

So it was time for Elaine to do a little digging. Once again Jill McDonald or Jillian Lazaridis', as she was now known had struck gold. Teddie Lazaridis' was a multi-millionaire and was the owner of several award winning Greek restaurants throughout the North-East. Jill McDonald was living the life of luxury in a massive house in Jesmond as Teddie Lazaridis'' cosseted, pampered wife. Elaine started casing the joint and the more she learned the sicker she felt. This was all so unfair. Hiding behind bushes or peering from bus stops, she watched Jillian Lazaridis' going about her privileged life with her swanky wardrobe, expensive car and total arrogance.

However, one day when she went into the newsagents on Acorn Road for some fags she couldn't believe her luck. There was only a postcard in the window advertising for a cleaner and the contact number was none other than one belonging to a certain Mr Lazaridis'. This was not a common name by any means and it had to be Jill's husband. After a short phone call and brief interview the job was hers. Alleluia, had thought Elaine, at last it would be pay-back time.

Strangely enough, once she had returned into Jill's life other blasts from her Pontin's past were now reappearing. As a result of her recent appointment as shelf-stacker at Tesco, she was answerable to none other than the pompous Deputy Store Manager, Mike Robinson. Although he had somewhat filled out a little and was much more confident, there was no mistaking him as Mike the Bluecoat with his pathetic cardboard cut outs, rubbish jokes and denial of his homosexual inclinations. Elaine had felt a frisson of excitement and opportunity for further mischief.

And just this very week, a nancy boy low-life who was clearly no stranger to Mike Robinson had come harassing him in the store. Oh yes, she had been watching with keen interest the horror on the face of the Deputy Store Manager. Clearly, he was shocked at being approached by this seedy individual and after a short conversation between the two, the old tramp had been literally thrown out of the store. Now Elaine had noticed a certain familiarity about not only the way he held his head but also his distinctive gait. Unless she was very mistaken, it was none other than Roger, the old Head Bluecoat. God only knew what had happened to him over the years for such deterioration in his appearance to have occurred but she was sure there had once been rumours about the two of them. Elaine knew she could use this to her own advantage. This was just what she had done and as a result it looked as if her son Scott would soon be on the Tesco pay roll.

As Elaine travelled up to her flat in the lift covered in vile graffiti and stinking of urine, she hoped Scott was there, as she felt it in her bones that things were on the up.

Chapter 20

25th July 1984 – Sunny Dunes Holiday Camp – Tony's Office

Eyes out on Stalks

Elaine, noticing that Tony was leaving the building, thought it would be a good time to go and clean the Entertainment's Office. Of all the places on the campsite, this was the worst. In her opinion the Bluecoats were like pigs. They were always leaving their half-drunk cups of coffee all over the place and there was always a large breadknife on the bench covered in crumbs and jam. Usually they flicked their cigarette ash all over the floor because the lazy buggers couldn't be bothered to look for or empty the ash trays. But if anything, his office was the worst of the lot. So, this was as good a time as any to get stuck in to his filthy pit armed with her strongest bleach.

Although she hadn't been expecting to see anyone one else there, she shouldn't have been too surprised to find it occupied by his tart. However, what was really puzzling to Elaine was what Jill was doing there at that hour on a Wednesday morning with the safe open? Her mind started whirling like a mop wielding Miss Marple. How was she able to get into it because surely Tony was the only one with a key? And why was it still full of all those charity tins? By Wednesday oughtn't they to have been deposited into the hands of those needy cases for whom the money was intended? Elaine smelt something fishy going on.

'Good afternoon Jill. You don't mind if I clean the office now Tony is out, do you?' Her eyes were fixed on the safe, which Jill's fingers were now fumbling with, trying to fasten the lock.

'No, that's fine Elaine. You must do as you must.' Replied stuck-up Jill, in a much pleasanter tone than the one she that she usually used when speaking to her.

'Well, I'll start with the side over there by the kettle.' Elaine proclaimed loudly, while marching across the room armed with her mop and bucket but her eyes never left Jill for one second. 'If that's all right with you?' Suddenly, her voice became softer and strangely more menacing as she added. 'I see you had the safe open.'

'Yes please do.' Jill replied to her first statement then paused to think of a plausible reason for the second. 'I was just checking all the boxes were in order.' Now with the safe once more locked, Jill turned to face Elaine with a bright red face.

'And are they all in order then? Surely by now those there tins should be with the wee bairns.' She cocked her head to one side. 'I see the kettle's just boiled. I wouldn't say nee to a wee brew.'

'Yes of course Elaine. A cup of tea all right?' Jill was relieved to be back on safe territory. 'Milk and sugar?'

'Yes, and six spoonfuls.' Elaine plonked herself down proprietarily in Tony's chair. 'And are they safe now? Those wee tins?'

'Yes, of course they are safe.' How dare this horrible cleaner cross-examine like this? 'There was a problem getting them to the charity's main office. They were having some procedures done.'

'Procedures? What's that supposed to mean? I dinnae suppose you've any biscuits. I like chocolate digestives best.' Elaine put her feet in their nasty cheap shoes on Tony's table.

'Yes I believe there are some biscuits in the cupboard.' Jill sighed loudly and walked over to the far side of the room. 'But only custard creams I'm afraid.' She put the whole packet next to Elaine's feet, along with the very sweet tea.

'Ah well they'll have te dae I suppose.' She dunked a biscuit in the tea and nibbled at the corner. 'Not bad. His favourite are they? I wouldn't have thought him a custard cream man.' She pushed the rest of the biscuit into her mouth. 'Brandy snap maybe.' She snorted at her own little alcohol related quip. 'But there you go?' She helped herself to a second biscuit.' Anyway, about those procedures? What sort of wee procedures exactly, would stop them accepting the money?'

'I don't know. Maybe they're decorating. You'll have to ask Tony. It's nothing to do with me. Anyway I need to go now. Why don't you get back to what you should be doing.'

As a flustered Jill left the office, a smug Elaine polished off the rest of the biscuits. She pondered upon what she had had just stumbled across and its significance. There was definitely some dodgy business going on involving Jill, for even if she had been bleating, she couldn't have appeared anymore sheepish.

13th April 2014 – Ramsay Court, Central Gateshead

Scott is Horrified

'Hi kids. I'm home.' Elaine burst through her front door and was pleased to see that for once all three of her children were there. Two were watching the telly while the other was staring inanely at the carpet.

'What's got into you?' Kylie was annoyed that her mam had startled her and forced her to move. 'I'd just got meself all comfy here too.'

'I've got some great wee news for us all.' Elaine clapped her hands together in glee. Scott and Kylie were perturbed for they had never seen their mother this happy before.

'Have you won the lottery mam?' Kylie patted her enormous stomach and stretched out on the sofa.

'Have you seen sense and nicked summick from them greedy rich Greek bastards in Jesmond?' Scott wiped a dribble from his nose on his sleeve.

'Better than that. I think this news calls for a chippy tea.' Elaine announced.

'Chippy tea.' Repeated Charlene, as she understood this and banged her hands together.

'Blimey. This has got to be something really good.' The two siblings Kylie and Scott turned to each other with puzzled faces.

'Well it concerns you mostly, my dear wee son?' She squashed herself into the space on the sofa between her two eldest children.

'Kylie.' Elaine's eyes searched the room. 'Where's wee Krystal?'

'Fink she's in the kitchen.' Kylie shrugged her shoulders. 'You know she likes playing with the knives and the plugs.'

'Fair do's. Anyway Scott. Wait till you hear what I've sorted out for you son.' She wriggled up closer to her son.

'Mam, what you on about?' Scott threw a cushion on the floor and moved closer to the armrest in an attempt to distance himself from his mother. He didn't like the sound of this one little bit.

'You'll never guess what … I've got you a job?' Elaine beamed at her son.

'You what?' This was the last thing Scott wanted to hear.

'Come on mam. Who's going to give him a job?' Kylie pulled a face at her lanky useless brother.

'Well, it's at Tescos.' She said proudly. 'So it'll be nice and handy for you lad. I mean you can be there in two minutes from here. I think it'll be in the warehouse at first but …'

'Just stop right there mam.' A look of relief passed across his face. 'No way can I work there. Not never. Have you not forgotten about…?'

'Laddie, no one will remember about that I'm sure.' Elaine shook her head.

'That pompous git's always poncing round the doorway. You know that manager bloke in his swanky suit. He'll recognise me that's for sure.' Scott now seemed pleased and proud of his whiskey raid on the place.

'Son, there are a million scallies in Gateshead who look just like you. He'll nae recognise ye.' Elaine rubbed the greasy locks on her son's head with a combination of distain and affection.

'Are you for real mam?' Scott stood up. He wanted out of here.

'As a matter of fact he's the one sorting your job out.' Elaine was delighted with outcome of the day and this wasn't a feeling she'd often had.

Chapter 21

25th July 1984 – Sunny Dunes Holiday Camp – The Entertainment's Office

Stephen Saves the Day

When Stephen waltzed into the office, he was surprised to see a forlorn Debbie staring at a cold coffee. Her eye make-up was a little smudged and she had been pulling the polystyrene chunks from the rim of her cup which were scattered all over the table.

'Hey what's up with you today?' He was concerned and sat down on the chair opposite her.

'I don't know what I'm going to do Stephen,' she said miserably.

'What are you on about? If that bloody Suzanne has been…'

'No it's nothing to do with her.' She shook her head. 'It's because of tonight.'

'And what's the problem with tonight?' Stephen was mystified as to what she was so worried about.

'*The Music Hall Show*. I'm supposed to be singing at it.' She pulled a big section from her cup and the brown liquid began dribbling onto the table.

'Debbie, I wouldn't have put you down as suffering from stage fright. I just don't believe it. I mean … last Friday you were fab. You just do what you did then and you'll knock them all dead.' Stephen was confused.

'But that's just it isn't it? This bloody *Burlington Bertie* song. I have never heard of it and don't have a clue what it goes like.' And the tears welled up in her eyes.

He struck a dramatic pose with his fingers glued to his head. 'Don't worry. Let me think. I must have heard Mandy singing it dozens of times and as it happens I've got an excellent memory. It's been described as photographic actually.' He nodded sagely, seeming proud of his talent before springing to his feet. 'Listen.' He paused for a moment to gather together his thoughts.

'*I'm Burlington Bertie. I rise at ten thirty and saunter along like a toff.*' He was strutting up and down the floor, singing with great gusto and picked up the sharp bread knife lying on the bench next to the toaster to use as an improvised cane. *I walk down The Strand with my gloves in my hand and I walk back again with them off.*' He exaggerated with great aplomb the putting on and taking off of imaginary gloves. After nearly cutting his finger, he threw the pretend walking stick back on the side and continued. As Roger entered the room the Head Bluecoat shook his head in exasperation at witnessing more of Stephen's daft antics.

'Bravo!' shouted Debbie, because Stephen's performance had cheered her greatly. She clapped and whistled enthusiastically when he took a bow at the end of the number. For whatever Stephen lacked in vocal ability, he more than made up for with the use of the most ridiculous gestures, facial expressions and bawdy innuendo.

'Oh for goodness sake Stephen, surely Tony hasn't asked you to do that tonight has he?' Roger wasn't in a good mood, because of what had happened earlier and he couldn't be doing with Stephen and his daft nonsense. 'No way will Mandy's costume fit you and you're all wrong for that song.'

'I thought he was really good.' Debbie leapt instantly to her friend's defence. 'I wouldn't be half as funny as him that's for sure.'

'Debbie. This song was sung originally by Vesta Tilly. A woman.' Roger said in a patronising tone. 'And she would dress up in a top hat and tails as a man. That's the joke. That's the whole point of...'

'No, of course I'm not singing it. I've my own spot!' Stephen snapped back. He didn't know what was eating Roger but knew for once he'd done nothing wrong.

'What's your song Stephen?' Debbie was curious, as she hadn't caught all the Music Hall Show her first week there.

'Prepare for a treat tonight Debbie. For on a Wednesday night Bluecoat Stephen becomes the great Burley Shassy.' Stephen flung his arms into the air.

'Who's that?' Debbie didn't think she had heard of this person before.

'He's in drag as Shirley Bassey singing *Hey Big Spender*.' Roger pulled a mocking face. 'And his rendition of it isn't that dissimilar to what you just witnessed here.' A cattiness crept into Roger's voice and he felt his mouth wash with bile, as he glanced at the table where he had made his earlier faux pas with Mike.

'Cheeky.' Stephen gave a swoosh of the head and his quiff quivered like the feathers on a cockatoo's crest. 'Anyway, I'm just teaching Debbie the song. She doesn't know it. And she's supposed to be doing it tonight.'

'Oh, I see.' Roger bit his lip. 'Well, Mandy wasn't as ridiculous as that. Do not copy the drag queen, Debbie.' He wagged his finger at her and gave Stephen a disparaging look.

Debbie was surprised that Roger was behaving so churlishly, she hadn't seen this side to him before. 'I wish I could have seen Mandy singing the song. But then again I guess if she was still here, I wouldn't be would I? Why did she leave anyway?'

A strange look passed between Roger and Stephen and both pair of eyes moved uneasily towards Tony's office. They didn't know who was presently in there. Unbeknown to them, there was only Elaine scoffing a second packet of custard creams.

'Here's not the place.' Roger whispered and put a finger to his lip. 'I suggest you two continue with Bertie this afternoon.' He saw the time was nearly eleven. 'You both need to be in the Ballroom now or you'll be late. We don't want to keep the punters waiting now, do we? And Stephen, try to teach her more sensibly.' He spoke to Debbie as Stephen went to make himself and Debbie another cup of coffee to take through to the Cine racing. 'Later on, ask Jill to find the costume for you and get her to sort out a run through with Larry Lawson before tonight.'

15th April 2014 - The Olympian, Jesmond

Moussaka or Stifado?

Martha had arrived at the Olympian Greek Restaurant in Jesmond, ten minutes later than had been arranged, as she knew that Stephen or Stefan, as he preferred to call himself these days, was habitually late. As it was only round the corner from her apartment, Martha had walked. While she waited for her company to arrive, she took a long drink from her gin and tonic and perused the familiar menu. The moussaka was always particularly nice but then the stifado was pretty good too.

Above her, close to the ceiling, the procession of Ancient Greek deities danced, drank and partied along the frescoes. They negotiated a complex obstacle course amongst vines heavy with grapes and bodies asleep or passed out on the floor. It was as if the owner of the establishment, a certain Mr Theodore Lazaridis', who she was on nodding acquaintance with, was trying to actively encourage his patrons to order a silly amount of alcohol to accompany their meals. Noticing that her glass was almost empty, she caught a passing waiter's eye and ordered a refill.

Teddie Lazaridis' ought to be thankful that due his rather high prices, he didn't get gangs of stag dos and hen parties drawing moustaches on his gods and swinging from the large chandeliers. Martha smiled, as her second drink arrived promptly. She liked the Olympian with its well-cooked Greek food, great service, amusing décor and most importantly its close proximity to where she lived. Nevertheless, as a result of holidays to Greece while in her twenties, she always chose to give the Retsina and Metaxo a wide berth.

Eventually, her friend arrived. Stefan was smiling as he sauntered through the door. He sashayed across the floor, in a paisley green silk shirt and tight leather pants, completely oblivious the fact he was at least half an hour late. How very Stefan. She waved, as she was pleased to see him and he stretched out his arms ready to greet her.

'Darling Destiny.' He enfolded her in a bear-like hug. 'It's been too long but my … you're looking fabulous as ever. I just adore that dress.' Stefan quite obviously hadn't bothered to look at what she was wearing as her outfit was far plainer and more sombre than those she usually favoured. In fact her plain grey smock and flat laced-up boots had a definite Amish look about them

'Stefan, it's good to see you … but please.' She removed herself from his grip and sat back down at the table. 'Drop the Destiny. I don't use that name anymore'

'Destiny Chambers. But I just love that name. It's so divine, so you. Whatever are you talking about?' When Stefan eventually noticed her strange attire he was puzzled. Her peculiar dress was certainly not doing her any favours and when he looked down at her feet her usual elegant Jimmy Choos had been replaced by some ugly clumpy boots.

'In fact, don't want to ever hear that name ever again.' Martha put her hands to her ears as if the very sound of the name was offensive. Then she took some severe black-framed reading glasses out of her bag, partly to better see the menu but more importantly to present a studious image.

'Why ever not? It's so glamorous darling. And so you.' Stefan flicked his bald head as he imagined he was still in possession of a magnificent quiff and squinted to read the menu.

'No. It's trashy, frivolous and silly.' Debbie removed her spectacles and ran her fingers through her hair in an attempt to tame her exuberant wild curls. Usually she teased these into gentle ringlets but had decided not to bother that night. 'I'm trying to be a serious writer these days. How is anyone going to take me as anything other than a joke with that ridiculous name? '

For once Stefan was at a loss what to say.

Chapter 22

25th July 1984 – Sunny Dunes Holiday Camp – The Regency Ballroom

Mike's Persuasions

Tony had left Jill in the Office and was on his way to the meeting with Stan, when he saw Mike disappearing into the ballroom. Mike was walking in the direction of the cupboard where all the reels of horse racing films were kept. Tony chuckled to himself, as he knew that at that moment Mike would be blissfully unaware that his earlier sordid little encounter with Roger had been witnessed, but this was soon to be put straight, so to speak.

'Mike can I have a word?' Tony quickened his pace and touched Mike on his sleeve.

Mike was startled and whirled around, as he had assumed he was alone in the room. 'Yes of course Tony.'

'I was talking to your father the other day.' Tony said this matter of factly. He had been friends with Mike's dad since they had done their National Service together years ago and as they lived nearby each other, they had both kept in touch. In fact, Tony thought Mike should be very grateful to him because it was only because of this connection with his father that he'd been given this job. Most of the other Bluecoats had a particular talent, could played instruments, sing or dance but what was Mike good at? Holding up daft bits of cardboard. Yes, Mike and his father, Ronnie Robinson definitely owed him big time.

'Oh yes.' Mike looked flustered and wondered what the two of them had been talking about. Him, probably.

'We've arranged to play a game of golf next week.' Tony's voice had a peculiar edge to it.

'That's nice. I'm sure he'll like that.' Mike wondered why he was being told about this and where the conversation was going.

'On Tuesday,' said Tony pointedly.

'Well that's good.' Mike's nostrils flared in distaste as he noticed the dirty gravy stains down the front of the Entertainment Manager's shirt

'Does he know?' Tony put his head to one side and threw Mike an expression of challenge.

'Does he know what?' Mike raised his eyebrows, baffled as to what the Entertainment's Manager was referring to.

'About your persuasions?' Tony tapped his nose enigmatically with a nicotine stained finger.

'What are you talking about?' Mike's retort was fast but he was beginning to feel uncomfortable.

'Come, come.' Tony's finger was now prodding Mike's blue jacket lapel. 'There's enough of it about here isn't there but I never thought it was actually *contagious*.' He stressed each syllable of this word, as if talking about something extremely pernicious.

'I don't have a clue what you're talking about?' Suddenly an unpleasant image of the mooning Roger leapt into Mike's mind.

But Tony knew this to be complete codswallop, as the lad knew exactly what he was talking about. 'I heard and I saw what went on between you and Roger earlier.' This wasn't strictly true as he hadn't heard all the words exchanged between the two of them, but he had got the gist of it. He had seen Roger making his sick puppy dog eyes as he sidled up to his prey and he had witnessed the hand on the leg.

'What do you mean?' Mike realised that Roger had come onto him but he hadn't encouraged him. Or had he? Perhaps he should have rebuffed his advances earlier. 'It wasn't what it looked like, honestly.'

'Honest, now there's a word. I don't think you've been very honest have you Michael? How long have you been gay and what would your father say if he knew all about your new boyfriend?' After all, Tony had had his suspicions for a while and the earlier incident had merely confirmed these. He had seen the Village People and one of them had a big spidery moustache just like Mike's.

'I'm not gay. That was a misunderstanding. Yes, Roger made a pass at me ... but I'm not interested in him. I'm not like that.' Mike's face was turning tomato coloured and the collar around his neck was almost strangling him.

'I think thou dost protest too much.' Tony was all too aware of the effect this would have on the lad's homophobic father. 'But although your tawdry dalliances are none of my concern, if you don't want me to mention them to your dad ... well I'm sure we can come to some arrangement. '

'Arrangement? Are you blackmailing me?' This beggared belief. That bloody Roger. He'd just been trying to butter him up so he would let him have a go with telling his jokes hadn't he? And now look what this sly, evil bastard was trying to do.

'Mike. If it wasn't for me then you wouldn't have a job here would you?' Honestly, the boy should show him a little more gratitude.

'But I'm not homosexual,' Mike hissed but knew he couldn't risk Tony feeding these lies to his father.

'You just give me a tenner out of your wages each week and we'll say no more about it.' Tony once more tapped the side of his nose and disappeared just seconds before Suzanne walked in.

13th April 2014 – The Central Bar, Gateshead

The Horrid Old Barmaid

After work, Mike had gone for a couple of pints in the Central Bar as the day's events had left him seething. How dare that awful woman Elaine speak to him like that? Who did she think she was? Yet, she had got to him because there was a certain something about her threatening manner that reminded him of Tony Noble all those years ago. Not that he had been Scottish of course, but there was that same threatening tone and even more worrying, the fact that there was something vaguely familiar about her.

He scowled at his pint and glared around the room. Over by the window, there were two old blokes sipping their halves and a loved up couple gazing into each other's eyes. In the centre of the room, was the heavy, dark wooden bar. From behind which, the bottles of jewel-coloured liquids were tempting him to sample their delights like a bevy of beguiling mermaids. Usually, a jolly barmaid called Jess worked here. She was a friendly girl with whom he enjoyed chatting to on many an occasion. But tonight in her place was an elderly harridan with a sour face. This was just as well because Mike was in no mood for flirty banter.

Like the other day in his flat, it felt as if the sides of this place were closing in on him. The wall paper was getting nearer and would soon be touching his face. For some strange reason he had the notion that the pictures might just fly off their hooks at any given moment and the glass smash in his face. Then he remembered that unpleasant incident with the whisky shoplifter the other day and the smirk on the nasty old Bird Woman's face. This bar was a bad choice for someone in his current frame of mind. Often, and with good reason this pub was referred to as The Coffin Bar because of its casket-like shape. No doubt, if all this stress continued the undertakers would be where Mike Robinson would be heading soon for a fitting.

His mobile started to buzz and he took it out of his pocket to see the name of his estranged wife. Well, he could guess what she wanted and was in no mood to deal with her. Even his marital problems of today were the fault of that bastard, Tony Noble. That was him along with his own father. Since as early he could remember Ronnie Robinson, his dad, had had mercilessly teased and bullied him. He had made his son's life a nightmare. Mike was never *clever* enough, Mike wasn't *good* enough, Mike wasn't *man* enough … it was like a mantra running perpetually through his mind even today, verifying his uselessness.

Despite his convincing act as the big cheese at Tesco, he still felt inadequate because it was as if his dad had tattooed the word *loser* onto his forehead. He was fearful of anymore of his hair disappearing because everyone would be able to see. This was the main reason for his infidelities. He felt his behaviour was justified because it was necessary for him to perpetually prove his manhood to himself. For as long as he and Linda had been married, he had his little dalliances here and there but that's all they were. That was until his wife had found out because one of her stupid friends had seen them and got the wrong end of the stick. After all, they had only been spotted having a drink together. It could have been totally innocent. It wasn't, but nevertheless … why couldn't the idiotic woman see she was just making a mountain out of a molehill and let him move back home? However, this wasn't a discussion he wanted to deal with right now.

Noticing that his glass was empty Mike went once more to the bar. 'Could I have another pint of bitter?'

'Another pint of bitter and ...?' The miserable barmaid repeated his words, furrowed her brow and stood with her hands on her bony hips.

'Erm ok.' Mike looked longingly at the bottles twinkling behind the bar. 'I'll have a double whiskey chaser.

'Oh no, you won't mi'laddo.' She glowered at him. 'Not until you show some manners.'

'What are you on about? This is a bar and I want a pint of bitter and a double ...' Mike wondered where Jess was because he could well do without all this nonsense.

'And all I want is a civil tongue from you and the word please wouldn't go amiss.' She added in a sanctimonious tone that reminded him of his estranged wife.

'Could I please have a pint of bitter and a double whiskey chaser, if that's not too much trouble?'

Without speaking she begrudgingly poured the pint and spirit. Then she slammed both the glasses down simultaneously on the bar. 'And that'll be your last for tonight because I think you've had enough already.' She gave him a challenging look but he knew better than to respond. So he returned to his table and his thoughts.

After leaving school and proving himself incapable of securing a place at college or finding a job for himself, Mr Robinson Senior, had persuaded his golfing mate, none other than the Tony Noble, to give him a job. To be fair, Mike quite liked being a Bluecoat at Sunny Dunes Holiday Camp, as it gave him a bit of clout. However, he felt a little jealous when the others were on the stage all doing their turns and receiving applause. He wanted a piece of that pie. So, he had thought to himself, well maybe he could be a stand- up comic like Jimmy Tarbuck or Jim Davidson. He was sure they had once been Redcoats at Butlins, so who knew where it might lead. Wouldn't that just show his father if he was on the telly. Anyway, he had tried a few of his jokes out on his Bluecoat friends and they had been all full of encouragement he recalled. Yet, when his dad heard about this dream, he had delighted in bursting his bubble and shooting him down in flames. *Don't be ridiculous. Nobody's going to laugh at your pathetic jokes. You loser.* The words still stung.

But what was even worse, was his constant jibing about him not having a girlfriend. He was constantly insinuating there was something wrong with him and that he wasn't man enough. When his dad and Tony were on the golf course his shortcomings must have been their favourite topic of conversation. Then, to make matters even worse, when Roger had made a pass at him and somehow Tony got wind of this. The evil bastard had used this information to make his already horrible life unbearable. Was it any wonder that he had not been best pleased when Roger had appeared back on the scene after all these years?

If it hadn't been for been for bloody Roger ... yet what had really freaked him out today were Elaine's insinuations. How could she possibly know about what had happened all those years ago at Pontins? At the end of the day he wasn't gay. He never had been but what would it have mattered if he was anyway? Mike's homophobic father was long since dead and his mother, who wouldn't have cared one way or the other, had dementia and was in a nursing home.

As it happened Elaine had absolutely nothing on him anyway had she? He was positive though that she had been trying to blackmail him. How dare she? She was just a nasty twisted shelf-stacker who didn't know her place. Well, she could forget about any job for her son. One person working in Tesco from her toxic family was more than enough. From now on he would be looking for the slightest excuse to give that woman her marching orders and he was sure it wouldn't take long. He gave the horrid old barmaid a withering look, slammed his glass on the table and left.

Chapter 23

25th July 1984 – Sunny Dunes Holiday Camp – The Regency Ballroom

The Contents of the Packet

Suzanne was already waiting in the Regency Ballroom at her table, ready with her rolls of tickets to sell, when Stephen and Debbie came through the door clutching their cups of coffee. They had a disturbingly conspiratorial look about them she thought. Suzanne didn't like the fact that Debbie seemed to be forging close friendships with the other Bluecoats. Not one little bit. She pretended she hadn't seen them and fixed her gaze on Mike who was busy putting today's reel onto the projector.

'Good morning Suzanne.' Stephen greeted her cheerily, probably just to annoy her she thought.

'Good morning Stephen.' Suzanne growled back but she and Debbie deliberately avoided eye contact.

In front of the stage were five small tables and Suzanne was at the first selling the tickets for horses one and two. Liz was sitting at the second, fiddling with the rolls for three and four while playing with her long plait of hair. Next was Stephen with five and six, Debbie the Freak, as Suzanne liked to call her, had seven and eight. Then finally, in ran a dishevelled looking Marcus to man the last table. Clearly, he had just got out of bed, had toothpaste smeared all over his tie and was wearing his stupid gladiator sandals again. Suzanne glowered in the direction of Stephen and his new best friend, drinking their coffees and sharing confidences. He seemed to be writing something down on a piece of paper for her. Suzanne was dying to know what it was, but she didn't like to crane her neck or appear to have any interest in either of them.

Suzanne looked up at the silver-curtained, sparkly stage and pictured herself on that very spot tonight. Basking in the adoration of her applauding crowd she would be performing her superb rendition of *Second Hand Rose*. She smirked to herself thinking how fabulous she would look in her frilly pink dress, orange feather boa and flower-trimmed bonnet. After her, that bitch was supposed to be performing Mandy's song tonight wasn't she? And as Mandy's ghost taunted her, wafting backwards and forwards across the stage, Suzanne remembered just how much she had loathed her. It had been most fortunate for Mandy that she hadn't shared a chalet with Suzanne, because a certain pair of scissors would have been unable to resist cutting off all that lustrous long ginger hair as she slept. Mandy the minx wouldn't have been half so pretty with a new short back and sides. Those naughty snippers could have had a field day in her wardrobe reducing her cheap tarty clothes to sad straggly weeds and Mandy would have had to save up her meagre Pontin's wages like Bill-yo to buy any new ones. What a shame that would have been.

However, when Mandy got her comeuppance and had been forced to leave, she for one certainly hadn't been in the slightest bit sorry. It was after all only what she deserved. However, Suzanne hadn't figured on her most unfortunate replacement. Oh yes, swotty Debbie could only start halfway through the season because she was a *student*. This was just a *holiday job* for her wasn't it? Some people were just inflated by their own delusions of grandeur weren't they? Actually, that bitch Debbie was ten times worse than Mandy. It really was so unfair. As she watched her nemesis and Stephen in deep conversation, she could feel her mouth frothing as if her tongue were an alka seltzer fizzing in a glass. It had been bad enough at Friday's show, but there was no way that cow was going to ruin this night for her.

Suddenly, there was a sea of faces in front of her and a mad flurry of tickets being torn, money being taken, change being given and banter being exchanged.

'I'll have two on one and two on two love,' came from a man in a Hawaiian shirt.

'That'll be eighty pence please,' Suzanne replied.

'Give me ten on number three,' a woman was asking Liz.

'I hope them's the lucky ones mind,' a man wearing a battered trilby winked at Suzanne.

Then the lights went down, the race began and at last Suzanne had the opportunity she had been waiting for. Now she could sneak off to the ladies. Before doing so, she took a sachet of powder from out of her handbag. She ripped off the corner. When she passed Debbie, the cow was still trying to read whatever Stephen had written on that bloody paper. Nonchalantly, she emptied the entire contents of her packet into the stupid girl's coffee cup. All the other eyes remained fortunately on the screen and she was positive nobody had seen her. Job done. She scuttled off to the toilets full of glee and chuckling to herself.

10th April 2014 – Trinity Square, Gateshead

Fuzzy Memories

When Roger fell against the side of the paper recycling bin, at first he was too stunned to move. He just sat there, ignoring the fact that passing by shoppers were staring and laughing at him. Not only hadn't Mike been pleased to see him but he obviously had no desire to renew their acquaintance. Yet, worst of all he had physically thrown him out of the store. That period in Roger's life when he had known Mike was now a blur, but he couldn't recall that he had done anything to offend the man. However, maybe he was wrong. And even if he had, well surely it couldn't have been anything bad because up until the murder of Tony, Roger's fuzzy memories of that summer were all good or so he had thought.

He managed to struggle to his feet and after propping himself up with an abandoned trolley, he hobbled over to a bench in Trinity Square.

'You all right there sonny?' It was a long time since anyone had called him that name and it made him feel a little better. It was the old Bird Woman that he had watched Mike Robinson harassing from the cinema foyer.

'I'll be all right in a minute.' Roger brushed down his shabby shirt which had some sticky sweetie wrappers stuck to it.

'Was that snotty man giving you a hard time?' She studied him hard wondering what Mike had against this poor soul.

So, the old dear had been watching his humiliation had she? 'It was just a little misunderstanding I think'. Roger forced a weak smile. 'I think, perhaps he mistook me for somebody else.'

'That one's not too choosy who he bullies.' She pulled her jacket tightly round her shoulder because for a spring morning it was quite chilly.

Roger was watching her curiously. 'Yes, I've seen him giving you a hard time.' For someone of her age, who was more than likely living rough on the streets, her eyes were a remarkably clear blue and under peculiar thick orange make-up, her skin was barely lined.

'Indeed, he likes to give me and my birdies plenty of grief.' She put her hand into an old battered carpet bag and pulled out a little packet.

Roger sat and regathered his dignity as she sprinkled a little bird food on the ground. Soon the pigeons came flocking at her feet. 'I saw you from up there.' He raised his eyes towards the cinema. 'You'd best be careful or he'll be out here hollering at you and those birds.'

'I couldn't give a toss. He's a jerk.' She studied the poor man, wondering what his story was, as he had obviously had a hard life. 'So, was it a good film you went to see?'

'No, that's where I work.' Roger decided he liked this little old lady and wished he could give her a free cinema pass to get her out of the cold.

'Oh, right.' At least he had a job she thought.

'I used to work with that Mike from Tesco's many years ago you know.' Roger racked his brains thinking of something he might have done in the past to offend the man.

'Really where was that?' Martha couldn't think in whatever capacity these two could have worked together.

'Oh, it's long been knocked down.' Roger gazed upwards, as if painting a picture in the sky of his younger days. 'It was at a holiday camp called Sunny Dunes.' Martha sat bolt upright. 'It was quite close to here … near Whitley Bay. Do you remember it?' As he turned once more to face her, she slumped back on the bench.

'No that sort of place has never been for the likes of me.' She instantly retorted. 'I've never been a one for holidays and the like. So, what was your job there then? Were you one of the waiters?' Good God, what was going on here?

'No, I was a Bluecoat. Head Bluecoat in fact.' He said wistfully, obviously recalling these bygone days with great fondness.

'I bet you've a few tales you could tell.' As Martha studied the fading ginger hair and the straggly moustache, the penny finally dropped. This was Roger but what in heaven's name had happened to him?

Chapter 24

25th July 1984 – Sunny Dunes Holiday Camp – The Dining Room

Feeding Time at the Zoo

Towards the end of the Cine Racing, Stephen noticed Debbie had become a lot quieter and she seemed to be looking even paler than usual. In fact, he could see unpleasant globules of sweat on her forehead and her skin had taken on an unhealthy, greenish colour, like Savoy cabbage goes when it has been boiled for too long. She said that trying to read the lyrics in the dark must have given her a headache, so she was going to skip lunch and have a lie down for half an hour.

Stephen didn't blame her as lunchtime in the dining hall wasn't the best of places. With all the banging of plates, scraping of cutlery and babbling of voices, it was like feeding time at the zoo. As a dubious perk of the Bluecoat's wages, meals were included as part of the package. However, trying to get some peace and quiet to eat an unappetising toad-in-the-hole or sticky spotted dick was next to impossible. On an almost daily basis, the week's most irritating punters attempted to sit as physically close to him as they could. Inevitably, he always tried to eat his food as quickly as he could, to escape from their mundane questions and boring tales.

Sometimes, the holidaymakers would even be talking and eating at the same time, so in their wide-open mouths you could see disgusting little shards of fish fingers or oozes of mushy peas. It was not unknown for unfortunate Bluecoats to be showered by fountains of cake crumbs when a neglectful diner forgot to close their mouths while laughing. This was very unpleasant and with all matters considered, a bar of chocolate and a bag of crisps in the tranquillity of your chalet was often the wiser option. So, he thought Debbie had made a sensible decision.

Over the far side of the dining hall he spotted Mike, who was sat staring at a plate of sausages and jabbing them with his fork, while an elderly lady tried to introduce him to her white poodle. Meanwhile, Roger was sitting nearby, stirring his bowl of soup round and round with his spoon and looking forlornly out of the window. Outside some annoying little boys were banging on the glass and trying to catch his attention.

'Where's Debbie? I've been looking everywhere for her.' Siobhan joined Stephen in the queue for the food, as her eyes scanned round the room looking for her friend.

'I don't think she's feeling too good. She's gone back to your chalet.' Stephen couldn't quite decide which food he didn't fancy the least.

'Well, you know, I think she's worried about singing that Bertie song this evening.' Siobhan was wearing her football strip, as she had been organising knockout games of five-a-side football that morning. 'She should have just told Tony she didn't know it. I'm sure she could have sung something else.'

'I wouldn't reckon on that. You know what he's like when he gets something into his head.' Stephen rolled his eyes.' After the blue brown eyes song, he had his heart set on her doing Mandy's tranny number, didn't he? But don't you worry about that one. You wait and see. She'll be fine. I've taught her the song. Stephen's worked his magic.' He waved an imaginary wand in her face. 'She will be even better than Mandy. You watch this space.' Stephen gave her a knowing wink.

'Ha ha, you eejit.' Siobhan was pleased he had sorted her friend out because she knew Debbie had been worried. She was glad that Stephen had become her friend too and she enjoyed laughing at his silliness. 'Now, I'm looking forward to seeing what exactly you've done to the song to be sure.'

'Tell you what Siobhan. Let's bolt this food down and we'll go back to your pad for a run through.' At last, they were at nearly the front of the queue.

She nodded. 'That sounds like a good plan.'

'Excuse me, Man Bluecoat and Lady Bluecoat. Can I have your autographs please?' A plump little girl with plaits and thick glasses thrust a notebook and pen into Stephen's hand. She peered at their name badges. 'Stephen and Sheeeobaan ?'

'Yes, of course.' He grabbed the pen. 'And it's Siobhan. What's your name?'

'It's Wendy.' She stared at them both in awe.

'There you go Wendy. Have a nice day.' He scribbled something down in the book, drew a smiley face then passed them on to Siobhan.

'Nice to meet you Wendy,' She gave the little girl one of her brightest smiles, and then checked the room for faces she recognised. 'What's up with those two?' Siobhan's eyes clocked a miserable Mike and an equally sulky Roger at separate tables both playing with their food.

'Well,' said Stephen, 'Mikes just spent the last hour with us in dreary Cine Racing but God knows what getting Roger's goat. Maybe it's *her* time of the month.'

Siobhan sniggered before wincing as she was handed a plate of particularly greasy fish and chips.

After they had finished lunch they made their way back to Siobhan and Debbie's chalet. On the way, they passed Suzanne and Karen who were sitting under a tree smoking and smirking like a couple of witches. They looked at Siobhan, maliciously, with their nasty slitted eyes. No doubt they were making rude comments about her butch-looking football kit. Stephen and Siobhan both looked the other way and pretended that they hadn't seen them.

However, as they unlocked the door, they were both alarmed to discover a distraught Debbie sobbing and lying prostate on the black skull design duvet cover.

'What's the matter with you?' Siobhan raised her eyebrows in alarm to find her friend in this dreadful state.

'I don't know. I've been sick three times and I feel awful.' Debbie's face looked ashen and piece of paper with the *Burlington Bertie* words lay crumpled and discarded next to her.

'Do you think it's something you've eaten?' Siobhan had just had a dubious lunch and was starting to feel a little queasy herself.

'I don't know. I've only had some cornflakes this morning and I don't see how they can do much damage.' She pulled a particularly forlorn expression.

'Well you look terrible.' Stephen picked the words up off the pillow. 'But never mind the show must go on.' He beamed and straightened out the piece of paper. 'Well, have you learned the song?'

'Stephen, stop it ...' Siobhan snatched the paper off him and put her arms round her friend sitting on the bed.

'No, I haven't Stephen.' A look of anger flashed across Debbie's face. 'And I can't see myself singing any bloody song this evening.'

15th April 2014 – The Olympian, Jesmond

Orthopaedic Shoes

Stefan had been looking forward to meeting Destiny that evening but it had been a long day and he couldn't stop the thoughts of his unnerving citing of Roger in the Blonde Barrel the other night. He had been anticipating an entertaining evening ahead of bitchy gossip and amusing chit chat with his old friend. That would be just the tonic he needed. However, from the minute he arrived at the Greek restaurant it was obvious that something was amiss. He knew that her mother had died recently but he assumed she would be over this by now.

He thought at first Destiny was annoyed with him because he was late but that was nothing unusual. She should be used to this, as he was almost always late. It was expected behaviour from him and all part of his wayward charm. Anyway, he'd had to get an Uber here from his place, when all she had to do was walk round the corner.

If truth be known, he didn't really like this restaurant with those creepy Grecian frescoes of Dionysus, Hades and Poseidon glaring down at him from the wall. Also, the monochrome uniformed waitresses, rushing around everywhere made him feel dizzy. They put him in mind of angry glissandos being banged up and down on a piano keyboard. Furthermore, Lazaridis didn't even employ any hot young Adonis-like waiters for him to ogle or flirt with and he wasn't overly fond of Greek food.

As he had entered The Olympian, he saw Destiny waving at him. So, he gave her one of his best luvvie hugs and told her how marvellous she was looking. That was before he realised how absolutely frightful her appearance actually was. With her frizzy unkempt hair, practically make-up free face, hideous grey smock and positively orthopaedic looking shoes, the prospect of a night in Destiny's company was not boding well. Stefan was already bored and he slumped down in a chair with an unusual loss for words.

She proceeded to tell him some self-obsessed drivel about wanting to be taken seriously as a writer. How Destiny Chambers was to be no more and how she was from now on going to be Martha. Stefan wasn't really listening as he was more concerned that there wasn't anybody he knew in the room who would see him in the company of this dowdy creature. In fact, he wished the dinner was over and done with so he could just go home. This was proving not to be the evening he had been hoping for. If someone took a sneaky snap of him and his dinner date, it could be the ruin of his career. He imagined an Instagram post of Stefan Sondheim and his frumpy friend with the caption *Maybe the music mogul will be taking up macramé next* ... Then to make matters worse, to read the menu, she plonked upon her nose a pair of, what could only be described as old National Health spectacles from at least fifty years ago, to make herself look even more of a fright.

'So we are back to Debbie are we?' Stefan sighed.

It took little time for Stefan to realise that he much preferred the company of racy novelist Destiny Chambers rather than boring old Debbie Carter. Destiny Chambers, his writing celebrity and glamorous friend would never be seen dead in that drab grey frock. In fact, he was sure that it wasn't the sort of outfit any companion of his ought to be wearing for any appearance in public.

Over the past few years, Stefan had grown to look forward to spending time with his friend the celebrity writer Destiny Chambers. They always had a good laugh together, swopping gossip and making bitchy comments about mutual friends. Also, Stefan knew that as a couple he and Destiny Chambers made a handsome duo. He was more than happy to see posts of them together cutting a dash on social media. Stefan's wardrobe had more than a passing nod to that of perhaps Lawrence Llewellyen-Bowen (in his earlier more sylph-like days), while Destiny's usual dresses were in the vintage Biba mode of a young Marianne Faithful. Surely, she couldn't have looked at herself in a mirror before leaving her flat. Stefan made a concerted effort to straighten his top lip which he could feel curling in distaste at the appearance of his present company.

Despite Stefan having plenty of contacts in the music and media line, Destiny was Stefan's only link to the literary world, if you could call her writing that. Still, it was another string to his cultural bow and it was usually good for his image to be seen in her company. But in her present state? He looked around the restaurant anxiously. For once, he was pleased there was nobody here that he recognised. With some relief, he forced his lips into a reluctant smile. 'Oh well, never mind.' He said after an awkward silence had hovered in the air between the pair of them for a few moments. Stefan was sure this daft phase of hers would soon pass and he brushed an imaginary speck of dust off his own expensively tailored shirt sleeve.

'No, I'm using the name Martha now.' She spoke in a peculiar monotone voice.

'And for any particular reason?' Stefan's eyes searched around for a waiter, as he was gasping for a drink.

'It sounds a good, solid sensible writer's name.' The prim look on her face didn't suit her and Stefan thought she had aged a good ten years since he last saw her.

'Martha what? Martha Mundane perhaps?' His voice had that unpleasant waspish tone he often used when he was being sarcastic.

'Oh don't be so ridiculous *Stephen*.' After all, she wasn't the only one who had a penchant for changing names.

'Stefan. *Deary* .' He hadn't used that boring name for decades and no longer identified himself with it.

'I haven't thought of a second name yet.' This night was proving to be an unsatisfying chore for both of them.

Chapter 25

25th July 1984 – Sunny Dunes Holiday Camp 25th July 1984 – On the Sand Dunes

Don't You Dearie Me

'Isn't he just the sweetest of dogs, don't you think?' The elderly woman sitting almost on top of him just kept blethering on, while Mike bashed the food around on his plate,

'Do you know,' she continued, 'he's ever so particular about what he eats?' The woman, whose white permed hair was almost identical to that of her dog's coat, was busy cossetting her pet as if it were a baby. 'Won't touch any cheap cuts of meat will you? I have to be very careful about what food I give him because of his delicate stomach. Don't I poppet?' Her cooing squeaky voice was just an awful white noise to Mike and it would have been more meaningful and less annoying if she was blowing a hairdryer down his ear. 'Would you like to hold him? His fur is ever so soft and fluffy. Isn't it my special boy?'

Mike was appalled as the woman actually had the gall to try and shove the pampered pooch and its velvet cushion onto his lap. 'I'm trying to eat my dinner.' He slammed the knife and fork loudly down on his plate and several pairs of eyes turned round to stare at him.

'Oh, my little Snuggles is just being friendly. Aren't you?' And as the mad old bat buried her nose in its lumpy poodle fur, the dog growled.

'I haven't got the time for this.' Mike groaned and picked up his cutlery once more.

'Mind, I'm not surprised those nasty sausages aren't going down too well. I wouldn't give those to my dearest smuggly-wuggly now would I? They're probably made from beaks and hooves.' She gave him an odd girlish giggle, which seemed quite inappropriate coming from someone who was old enough to be his granny. 'Come on, give him a little stroke. He's ever so friendly.'

'For God's sake woman.' Mike stood up, kicked the chair back, nearly knocking it over and stormed out of the room.

'Well, that's not very friendly behaviour for a Bluecoat…' The old woman began, but that was the last of her Mike heard as he slammed the doors behind on the way out.

He needed some air and Tony's poisonous words were flying through his head like toxic arrows. Furiously, he marched across the camp, out of the main gates, across the road and onto the dunes. Throwing himself down on the sand, he stared at the sun which eerily transformed itself into a yellow glowing apparition of Tony's taunting face. One beam sinisterly formed the letters *persuasions*, another spelt *not very another honest*, the next glinted with *tawdry dalliances*, followed by *Ronnie Robinson, gratitude, arrangement* and finally the last punched him with a *tenner out of your wages*.

It was so unfair, Bluecoats were only paid £58.22 a week and £10 less would be a big loss. He took a packet from out of his jacket pocket and lit a cigarette. But there was no way he could allow Tony to tell his father his was gay. He was a big enough disappointment to his father already. Despite having had the privilege of being sent to an expensive private school, he had flunked all his O'levels. After numerous resits, his academic career had ended with him being ingloriously bereft of any qualifications whatsoever. The fact that he had been pretty good at Rugby, but not quite good enough to pursue a career in it, had been his one saving grace. At least his homophobic dad had taken pride in his son's proficiency in a good old-fashioned, hetrosexual, male-dominated sport.

This was all so ridiculous though. Nothing whatsoever had happened between him and Roger. Admittedly, Roger had tried it on with him but he had told him where to go hadn't he? If Tony had watched the whole conversation he would have seen that he had rebuffed that gay chancer. He had told Roger to sling his hook hadn't he? But in all honesty had that been what he wanted really? *Not very honest* rang once more through his mind.

Mike had never had a girlfriend and his parents had remarked upon this several times. Recently, his dad had taken to lewdly winking at him alluding to the fact Pontins must be the perfect place for shenanigans and had made him feel quite uncomfortable. Of course, a light went on in his head. That was the solution to this horrible predicament. He needed to find himself a girlfriend. Actually, he had noticed that Elaine giving him the glad eye a few times a while back. Either that or she had sprayed some of her cleaning products there by mistake. But no, he couldn't stand that accent and … he had some standards. If truth be known he never knew what to say to girls, which was probably because his parents had made him go to the posh single sex school.

Anyway some matters needed to be dealt with first. Unfortunately, he could see no other way out of the situation immediately other than paying that bastard Tony. Although his dad boasted of many *connections*, the only acceptable strings he had been able to pull for his son in the way of job-facilitation, were those of Tony's. And to be fair, it was the only suggestion made by his dad that was of any appeal to him. Out of bricklaying, boiler repairing or Bluecoating, which would most people choose?

'Afternoon dearie.' After Stephen had left Siobhan with Debbie, tea and sympathy, he had decided to get some fresh air. Even though Mike wasn't his favourite person, they were chalet mates and he could see from the scowl on his face that something was wrong. So he thought it would make an effort to be friendly. 'It's a lovely day with the blue sky and sunshine isn't it?' Mike winced as Stephen stretched his arms in a wide circle like the sun to remind him once more of Tony's horrible face.

'Don't you dearie me.' Mike replied in his deepest voice. 'And no it's not a lovely day. I'm sick of the sun.' And he thought, I want nothing more to do with any homosexuals.

'Ooh, I would have said somebody had got out of the wrong side of bed this morning' Stephen gave him a playful punch. 'But it's one o'clock in the afternoon.'

'Whatever.' Mike continued smoking and stared out at the horizon.

'What's up with you then?' Stephen gave him a further punch. This time quite hard. 'Penny for them? I saw you looking all grumpy at that poodle in the dining room. A problem shared is a problem ...' And proffered to link his elbow with Mike's, so the pair of them no doubt could link arms and skip across the beach.

'Get lost!' Mike growled.

'Well there's no need to be like that ducky.' And with a familiar swoosh of the neck, Stephen's hair bounced in the breeze and he flounced off back to the camp.

13th April 2014 – Trinity Square

Swathes of Ectoplasm

Once Jillian had parked her white Audi in the Tesco's car park, she wandered by mistake into the full horror of Trinity Square and was appalled. The place seemed to be full of the type of persons that she would normally cross the road to avoid. Shifty youths hung about in threatening clusters like dangerous packs of wolves. Elderly men and women, wearing old shabby clothes were cluttered on benches and some were even smoking. Jillian, who's once twenty a day habit had been conveniently forgotten, was surprised because she thought it had been long ago banned in public places. She hadn't seen anybody smoking in Jesmond for years, apart from a window cleaner and some rough looking workmen.

While food wrappers littered the ground, sheets of plastic rubbish blew about like swathes of ectoplasm and everywhere pigeons were running amok. A particularly misguided old lady actually seemed to be feeding and encouraging them. Jillian shook her head, because even the naming the place Trinity Square was a complete anathema to her and possibly even blasphemous.

She hurried into the store which was large, but not as massive as the one she had visited before at Kingston Park, which incidentally had a far better class of customer. The riff raff from Trinity Square seemed to have spilled over into the shop. She might as well find the wretched book and get out of the place as quickly as possible.

'Excuse me.' She spotted an officious looking man in a grey suit, who had appearance of someone working there. 'Where is your literature section?'

'If you mean books they're over there, just by the magazines and greetings cards.' He pointed across the store.

'Thank you.' She rewarded him with a nod and curt smile.

'Are you looking for anything in particular?' Mike thought this shopper was classier than most of the other customers and she was wearing nice perfume. So he decided for once to be helpful.

'Yes, I'm after a book by Destiny Chambers. It's called *Follow Your Dreams*.' Jillian mumbled. The quicker this man found her the book, the sooner she could leave. Yet as Mike marched off towards the books, Jillian was annoyed that she had to walk faster than normal in order to keep up with him.

'I've seen that one.' Mike turned round to check she was following. He remembered the photo of the pretty lady on the back cover. 'She's a local writer, you know?'

'It's for my book group.' Although she couldn't care less what this man thought, she didn't want him to imagine this was her usual reading material. 'Not my choice I hasten to add. We don't usually read this sort of rub ... book I mean.' But Mike wasn't listening to her anyway.

'Ta Dah!' Mike picked up a purple and gold book and flipped it over to see Destiny's face smiling at him. 'Here you are, I'm sure you will enjoy it,' then he paused and for some strange reason Jillian thought he was going to tell her a joke, but he just handed her the book.

'Glad to be of service.' He shouted over his shoulder as he disappeared behind some racks of trousers.

While Jillian was reading the blurb on the back of the book she was unaware of a pair of beady eyes watching her.

'Good afternoon Mrs Lazaridis'.' Jillian almost jumped out of her skin when she heard that all too familiar and grating Scottish accent. 'Don't often see you around these parts now do we?'

Damn. How could she have forgotten that this was where else her bloody cleaner worked. 'Hello Elaine.' She said under her breath and quickened her pace.

'Is that a new wee book you've got there?' Elaine was surprised by the cover's flashy appearance compared with the pretentious dull tomes her employer placed strategically around her house. She followed close behind in Jillian's footsteps peering closely to see the book's title. *Follow Your Dreams*. Wonder what that's all about.

Isn't that one by the local writer? Destiny Chambers? Ah yes, I can see her name there ... bloody silly name if you ask me. She sounds more like some sort of naff fortune teller, doesn't she?'

'Right, Elaine.' Why did didn't the woman just leave her alone and stop her incessant babbling? 'I'm in a bit of a rush so I'll let you get on with your work.'

'See you tomorrow then ...' Elaine waved at her.

Not if I can help it thought Jillian.

Chapter 26

25th July 1984 – Sunny Dunes Holiday Camp – Sitting in the Sunshine

Suzanne's Good Turn

'I wonder if that Debbie's still busy practising that song for tonight. Stephen's been helping her with it you know.' Karen wasn't sure if her friend would want to know this information but she thought she would tell her anyway. 'When I walked past the office earlier, I heard him singing and prancing about as usual like a jerk.' She pulled a face. Suzanne and she were both sitting on a wall, enjoying a cigarette in the sunshine before the afternoon's activities began.

'Really.' Suzanne pretended not to be interested. So that's what the pair of them had been up she thought. Of course, those must have been those song words on that scrap of paper. 'Well, that will have been a complete waste of his time then won't it?'

'How do you mean?' Karen asked in her Scouse twang and took a long drag on her cigarette.

'Let's put it this way, I don't think Debbie will be doing any singing, dancing or anything much, other than keeping the toilet company this evening.' The smile glued on Suzanne's face had become almost cemented.

'Why's that then Suzanne?' Karen stubbed out her cigarette with her shoe, to give her friend her full attention.

'Well, I think a certain Bluecoat not too far away from here,' she nodded towards Siobhan and Debbie's chalet. 'Won't be sitting too pretty at the moment. In fact, I have a feeling that it's more than likely she's eaten something that doesn't agree with her one little bit. I predict maybe a case of food poisoning might be on the cards.' Suzanne splayed out her talons admiring the colour of her blood red varnish.

'Oh Suzanne, you're awful. What have you done now?' Karen clasped her hands together in glee applauding her friend's badness.

'Moi? Why do you think it's anything to do with me?' And Suzanne's smug face switched to a look of mock innocence.

'Well, when I saw her about half an hour ago she was looking a bit green around the gills.' Karen patted her cheeks. 'Very pale, like a dead fish. If you know what I mean.'

'Really? But, isn't that just normal for the Goth freak?' Suzanne ran her fingers through her own soft, frizzy brown hair glad that hers wasn't all sticky and spikey.

'Suzanne. You're terrible. What have you done?' Karen's eyes returned once more to Debbie's chalet door and wondered with what symptoms she was suffering.

'Well, let's put it this way.' Suzanne's grin returned. 'I don't think that little bitch will be upstaging me tonight.'

'She could never do that anyway, No way.' Karen shook her head to add further credence. 'But what exactly have you done to her?'

'Well,' Suzanne's voice fell sharply to a whisper and she looked around shiftily. 'When I was at the Cine racing earlier, she and Stephen were being all *pally pally*.'

'I don't know why he wants to be friend with the likes of her.' Karen twisted her face and wrinkled her nose as if there was a bad smell.

'Me neither.' She mirrored her friend's expression. 'But anyway she had this little cup of coffee with her. They both did. Her and her new bestie. So, I thought I would just make *her* drink a little more *interesting*.'

'Oh Suzanne. What did you do?' Karen lit another cigarette.

'Well, nothing, really.' She bit her lip then opened her bag to retrieve an empty packet.

'I just happened to have this in my bag. As you do. And, when I went to the loo … it just kind of fell into her drink.'

'Ha ha.' Karen chortled as she examined the empty wrapper. 'Good for you Suzanne. Laxative powder — that'll teach her. And Siobhan too, it must be stinking to high heaven in …' and as she nodded once more to the green chalet door it opened and out walked a distraught-looking Siobhan.

'Everything all right there?' asked Suzanne.

Siobhan was surprised as these two very rarely spoke to her, unless they had something nasty to say. 'No it's not.' Siobhan said still wearing her horrible football strip along with a worried expression. 'Debbie's not well. She's got a really bad upset stomach, if you know what I mean.'

Duh of course, she knew the euphemism for the most revolting vomiting and diarrhoea thought Suzanne.

'I was just going over to explain to Tony or Jill that she wouldn't be fit to do the whist drive this afternoon.' Siobhan told them.

'Oh, what a pity. Poor Debbie,' said Karen insincerely, as she stuffed the wrapper into her pocket.

'I wonder if it's something she's eaten.' Although Suzanne pulled the corners of her mouth downwards, her eyes still sparkled with mischief. 'She'll probably not be able to do the show tonight.'

'No, I suppose she won't.' Siobhan began walking away from them.

'Wait a minute Siobhan,' Suzanne jumped up to bar Siobhan's way. 'I tell you what. I'm just about to go over to the office myself. Why don't you let me save you a job and I'll explain to Tony about her predicament.'

'No, it's all right.' What was Suzanne up to? She never did other people favours, let alone her.

'No, it's the least I can do. Debbie will be all poorly and sickly. She needs you to look after her doesn't she?' Her voice wheedled.

'Well, if you're sure.' Siobhan wasn't used to Suzanne being kind.

And Suzanne bounced off on her mission, leaving both Siobhan and Karen baffled.

Monday 13th April 2014 – Tesco, Gateshead

Snakes and Ladders

Although Elaine was supposed to have been replenishing the shelves with cans of spicy parsnip and creamy mushroom soup, she had been distracted. She had noticed the unlikely occurrence of one of her employers, Mike Robinson charging across the store being followed by her other, Jillian Lazaridis'. This was something she hadn't been expecting. She watched with interest from behind the trouser racks, while the two of them were in the magazine and book section. They appeared to be having a discussion about something or other.

 Elaine wondered if they would have a sudden light bulb moment of mutual recognition. After all, their identities had been immediately apparent to her, as present day Jillian and Mike weren't that dissimilar to their earlier models. In Jillian's case this was definitely due to cosmetic intervention but with Mike it must just been down to good luck and not having gone bald. However, neither of them had an inkling as to her being the unimportant cleaner from Pontins.

Nevertheless, rather than feeling any resentment about her insignificance, she was all set to use this anonymity as a brilliant opportunity to seek out revenge.

Mike seemed to be finding a book for Jillian and Elaine was surprised because she wouldn't have put him down as an expert on such matters. She was wondering though why on earth would Jillian come to this particular store? Not only was it miles away from Jesmond, but it was full of the common people she despised and it certainly wasn't *her sort of place*. But even more peculiar was the fact she knew full well that her cleaner Elaine worked here and she would have thought that in itself would have been deterrent enough.

 Elaine recognised the fancy book that Mike was showing Jillian with its flashy cover, as she had been drawn to its shininess herself. Not that she had any time to read, but she was amazed that this was the uppity Jillian's choice of reading material. No visitor to the Lazaridis' house could fail to notice the strategically placed, dull-looking copies of the books her pretentious reading group wasted their time with and they were nothing like this. In fact, she was even sure she had seen her Kylie with a copy of something similar, but no, surely she must have imagined it. Her daughter was even less likely to read a book than she was.

Creeping forward among some cut-price cardies, she saw Mike hand a copy of the book to Jillian but neither of them seemed to have twigged their connection with each other. As Mike strode away and Jillian headed for the till, she couldn't resist making her presence known.

When Jillian first clapped her eyes on Elaine the fall of her face was a picture. As if being caught in this store wasn't bad enough, she also tried to hide the trashy book behind her back. But worst of all, was the being on familiar terms with a cleaner and shelf stacker. So Elaine couldn't resist speaking in her loudest Glaswegian voice, drawing attention to both the book and her association with Mrs

Lazaridis'. This made working at Tesco worthwhile for Elaine and she watched with delight the complete mortification of her employer, as she ran towards the checkout, imagining everyone had been listening to their conversation.

Rather than going back to the shelf stacking, Elaine thought she might as well strike while the iron was hot and she went in search of Mike Robinson. He was over in the wines and spirits, making a list as to which had been selling well.

'Mr Robinson. Can I have a word?' Elaine's voice was quieter and more subdued than the one she usually used.

'Oh yes, Elaine. And what do you want?' Mike looked up from his clipboard and he wasn't smiling.

'It's about that job for my Scott.' Elaine gave a wry smile remembering Mike squirming during their previous conversation.

'Sorry?' Mike returned to his notes.

'You promised my son a job in the warehouse.' Elaine reminded him and wondered what else she could gain from this fortunate situation.

'There are no jobs.' He didn't look up.

'But you promised.' Elaine's balloon was already beginning to deflate.

'I did no such thing.' He removed his reading glasses and viewed her sternly. 'And if I was you I'd forget all about that conversation or you'll be given your marching orders. Shelf stackers are two a penny I'll have you know.'

Although Elaine was gutted, feeling once more the harsh reality of the rug being pulled from under her feet, she reminded him of what she knew. 'But, what about that gay friend of yours?'

'Just shut up you poisonous troll,' he snapped. 'Who I know is no business of yours. I'm not answerable to you. You are nothing and don't you forget it. And I think one member of your family working in this store is more than enough. Don't you?' He glared at her and she saw in his eye that all too familiar look of contempt. 'Now, I suggest you get back to your work and keep your nasty little insinuations to yourself.'

Elaine knew it was pointless to say anymore, as she needed more than anything else at this stage to hang on to her own job. With a sigh, she returned to the soup cans, feeling like she had just slipped down a massive serpent in a rigged game of snakes and ladders.

Chapter 27

25th July 1984 – Sunny Dunes Holiday Camp – Tony's Office

Bugger Off Suzanne

While Tony was listening to horse racing on the radio, he heard a knock on the door and without waiting for a reply, Suzanne came barging into his office, all guns blazing. He really needed to have a word with all of his bloody Bluecoats about showing him more respect. After all, this was his office, not a public thoroughfare.

'Tony. It's about Debbie.' She spoke very quickly, babbling wildly and barely able to contain her excitement.

'Suzanne, when you knock on the door you must wait for an answer before entering my personal office.' He thumped his pencil angrily on the table as if knocking a tent peg into some very hard ground.

'Whatever.' Suzanne twirled a lock of her hair round her forefinger. 'Anyway, Debbie *says* she's not doing the whist drive this afternoon *or* singing that *Burlington Bertie* song tonight.' She nodded and folded her arms, as if pleased with herself for relaying this information.

'What you on about? Of course she will be singing tonight. Why ever wouldn't she be?' Tony thought he had just about enough of these Bluecoats and their daft games of one upmanship this season.

'That Siobhan said I'd to tell you she wasn't feeling *up to it*.' Suzanne couldn't hide the delight in her voice.

'Not up to it. What's the matter with her?' Tony looked Suzanne up and down with distain. She was too fat and she reminded him of a pig. A nasty pig at that.

'Siobhan says she's got a stomach upset. But I know for a fact she was up till late last night drinking with that Stephen, and Roger, he was there too. So I reckon it's just a hangover.'

'That's funny, She seemed well enough this morning.' Tony had noticed her laughing and being all childish with Stephen.

'Yes, I thought that too.' She put her head to one side, knowingly.

'Well, with a bit of luck she'll better for the show tonight.' He unfolded the newspaper in front of him.

'I already told you.' Suzanne cleared her throat loudly. 'Siobhan told me that *definitely* she wouldn't be doing that either.'

'I don't care what bloody Siobhan told you. I'm sure she'll be fine by tonight.' He scanned the paper reading the odds on the day's horseracing.

'If you ask me, I don't really think she's up to it,' she hissed. 'I think she knows that and she's just ... pretending to be ill.'

'Suzanne. I think you need to keep your opinions to yourself.' Tony remembered the last time Suzanne had stuck her beak into another Bluecoat's business. It had been obvious why she had wanted rid of Mandy and now a suspicious pattern seemed to be occurring.

'Well I was only saying ...' Suzanne began.

'Well you've said what you needed to, so be off now.' Tony turned up the volume on his radio.

'But I think she's just swinging the lead.'

'Suzanne. Bugger off.'

15th April 2014 -The Olympian, Jesmond

Blast from the Past

Not only had Stefan been particularly late that evening, but his company was proving to be even more tiresome than she had imagined. She ought to have known his reaction to her new creative direction would be negative and she certainly wouldn't be mentioning her Bird Woman alter ego. He would probably just howl with laughter and that was the last thing she needed. She was not in the mood for his usual pathetic flippancy but this sulky peevishness was even worse and she needed to get this dinner over and done with. 'Anyway, have you thought about what you're going to eat?' she asked in a sharp voice.

'Yes, I know exactly what I will have ... but first.' He clicked his fingers as a young waitress came gliding by. 'Waitress, bring me a bottle of your finest Greek white wine and I want none of that Retsina rubbish.'

'Of course Sir. And are you and the Madam ready to order your food yet?' She was a pretty young girl of around twenty who didn't have a local accent and was more than likely a student.

'Give us a moment. I need a drink. My throat thinks my neck's been cut. Jump to it.' And the young waitress in her black and white attire sped off to the bar like a startled zebra.

'Stefan, that was a little rude, don't you think?' Martha was clearly enjoying reprimanding him, and in her current attire she reminded him of a horrible, old schoolteacher he had once had. He wished Destiny would return to keep him company, rather than this sour-faced bitch.

'I was only jesting.' He ran his hand across his head, once more saddened by his lack of hair. 'I'm just tired with all of the comings and goings recently. I have been in the studio all day and have had some tricky people to sort out. And then you confuse me further with your silly name changing but *there's more than that …*' he said enigmatically. Then he paused, as if debating whether to share his thoughts with this person who had until tonight been his good friend. Then, the wine arrived and Stefan boorishly snatched the bottle from the waitress. Pouring himself a generous glassful, he gestured for the girl who was waiting with her notepad to be on her way. 'Give us a few more moments can't you? Then we'll order when we are ready.'

'Of course, sir.' She gave a little curtsy. Mr Lazaridis' trained his staff well.

'Stefan, are you ok? Are you ill? Whatever's wrong?' Martha upon hearing *there's more than that* was jolted out of her own self-absorption and was worried about him. Maybe there was some good reason for Stefan's ill-mannered behaviour. His face had a waxy pallor and he was guzzling the wine like there was no tomorrow. Oh my goodness she thought, perhaps that was it. She didn't like the sound of this. Not one little bit.

'No, it's nothing like that. Physically I'm quite well.' He placed his hands on top of hers and Martha felt some relief she wasn't about to hear he had some terrible illness. 'It's just I've encountered an unwelcome blast from the past recently which has been … how shall I say? Unsettling.' Instantly, their eyes locked in solidarity and their earlier differences became forgotten.

'From the past? Which past?' Although Martha knew instantly as to when he was referring.

'Your past too Debbie. Remember — Pontins 1984 and Tony Noble. You do remember don't you? What happened to him?' As Stefan's eyes became manic-looking, he refilled his glass and he spilled the wine all over the table. Martha topped up her own drink, but alarm bells were ringing.

'Well, of course but it was such a long time ago.' Martha tried to act nonchalantly, but neither of them had dared to speak about this in years. 'I'll never forget that awful day but what's brought him back into your mind?'

'I was in the *Blonde Barrel* with a few mates a couple of days ago.' Stefan's eyes narrowed and his face took on a shifty look. All thoughts of the Martha, Destiny or Debbie dilemma forgotten, she hung on to his every word.

'Yes, that's near the *Life Centre* isn't it?' Martha had never been in there but she knew where it was.

'Yes, in the *Pink Triangle*. Stefan tossed his head. He liked to wear his homosexuality with pride. 'In fact, it's one of my frequent haunts of late. I know quite a lot of the regulars that get in there. But last time I was there something peculiar happened. I knew I shouldn't have gone because I had a headache that night and I wasn't feeling very well. In fact, I should have just gone home. From the moment I stepped into bar, I could sense someone was watching me. It was as if someone's eyes were electric drills boring into me.'

'Oh, don't be silly Stefan. It was probably someone who liked the cut of your gib. Even I know that place is a pick-up joint.' She tried to make light of the matter but from the gravitas on Stefan's face there was obviously more to come with this story.

'Destiny, it wasn't like that. I mean come on … I can tell when someone is hitting on me. There was something sinister about it. Anyway, I made my excuses and left. But before I did, I got a good look at who was harassing me and although it was dark … I think I recognised him.'

'Don't be ridiculous.' Martha snorted as she filled up her glass with the rest of the wine. 'Tony more than likely died years ago and if not, he would be really old by now and certainly not hanging around in gay bars stalking you.'

'No, not Tony. It was Roger ... I'm sure of it ... and he didn't look good.' Stefan shook his head.

'Roger ... what would he be doing here? Last time I heard he was living the high life somewhere exotic. He went on to go *Pontinental* didn't he and then on to managing nightclubs?' Except she knew for certain, that this was no longer the case.

'Yes, I heard that too but there were other rumours.' His eyes widened.

'What sort of rumours?' Martha remembered the dishevelled creature that had emerged from the recycling bins.

'I heard through the grapevine he was involved in ...' Stefan's voice fell to a whisper. 'Drugs, gangsters and shootings.'

'This sounds ridiculous Stefan. You must be exaggerating.' Nevertheless, something radical must have happened in Roger's life for him to have arrived as his current incarnation. Should she tell Stefan what she knew? Whatever dodgy dealings he might have once been involved in, he was now employed in a mundane job at The *Vue* Cinema in Gateshead. So, all in all, it was quite likely he would have been in the *Blonde Barrel* in Newcastle. Furthermore, if he had recognised Stefan, who was after all quite distinctive and well known as a local celebrity, then his staring wouldn't have been that odd. Stefan must by now be used to being a focus of attention.

'He recognised me Destiny.' Stefan had forgotten she was no longer Destiny. 'Not as the Stefan the Music Producer but as Stephen the Bluecoat.'

'How can you possibly know that?' Martha asked him.

No, it wasn't the staring that was the problem thought Martha but the recognition of Stephen as himself from the 1980's. But there was no way Stefan could have been certain of that. Nonetheless, if she was to tell Stefan about Mike, then he would be even more freaked out. She wondered if when Mike and Rogers paths crossed once again, as they most likely would, if Mike's reaction would be so extreme as to throw him into the rubbish bins. While the reappearance of Roger had unsettled Stefan, Mike's reaction had been crazy hadn't it and perhaps not the smartest of moves by drawing attention to both of them? Then again Mike had never been the sharpest of tools had he? Martha's mind was doing summersaults. Also, what about all the connections that Roger supposedly had with gangsters? A resulting vendetta might deliver Mike his just desserts but that would bring even more unwanted attention.

All this was very worrying indeed, wasn't it thought Martha? All these reappearances had to be something more sinister than just plain coincidences. Especially with her and Stefan being local celebrities, they needed to tread very carefully. If the link between them, Roger and Mike was made, it was only a matter of time before some grubby journalist got their filthy hands on the story. Before long, it would be only a matter of time until the whole sorry business of the unsolved murder of Tony Noble was reopened once more.

'Stefan, there is more of this that you need to know.' She doubted very much he would be in the mood for poking fun at the Bird Woman. Not after what she was about to tell him.

'Would Sir and Madam care to order yet?' The waitress who had been circling the table, trying to listen to the conversation for the past few minutes, went in for the kill.

Chapter 28

25th July 1984 – Sunny Dunes Holiday Camp – The Swimming Pool

Roger's Not Going for a Swim

As usual, Roger was up early and on this occasion he needed to be. A certain advantage of being the head Bluecoat this year was that he had a chalet all to himself and he was grateful that once that door was closed, he no longer had to pretend to be anything he wasn't. He shivered, as that morning he wasn't feeling too good, and saw with a profound self-loathing, his sorry reflection in the mirror. His skin had a clammy pasty look and his face stared back at him with the kind of anaemic stony eyes usually found on a dead mackerel. Beads of perspiration squirted from his forehead like the butter through the holes when two cream crackers were squashed together.

He opened his top drawer where he kept his socks. Underneath some blue and red Argyll patterned socks lay a sad empty crumple of foil. He had thought this would be the case and sighed as he tried to steady his shaking hands. Next to his pillow, he found his wallet and to his relief inside there were still three crisp ten pound notes. Action was required immediately. He pulled on his uniform and headed down to the swimming baths.

Although it was only eight thirty, there were already a few folk about. The pool was open from 8 am because some strange people liked an early swim. Some punters were on their way to the dining hall, two ten year old boys were kicking a football about and unbeknown to him a figure in the Entertainment's Office was watching him with some curiosity.

He stumbled into the main poolside where two middle-aged men and a young woman were clocking up their daily lengths. The

Heavy Metal S*moke on the Water* music by Led Zeppelin blasted across the pool. At the top of one lifeguard tower was perched a rather bored looking Kevin, yawning and staring into space. Across the other side of the pool, the other lifeguard Carol, was playing with a Rubik's Cube.

'Kevin,' hissed Roger, running along the poolside and almost slipping into the water.

'Stop running you idiot.' Kevin scowled. 'It's not allowed.' He pointed to a *No Running* sign on the wall.

'Kevin, you've gotta help me. I need ...' Roger was gasping and sounding like a fish out of water struggling to breathe.

'Sssh, not here you tosser. Be quiet.' Kevin growled and jumped neatly down the steps. 'Carol,' he shouted across the water, 'I'm just taking a toilet break. Won't be more than a tick.' Carol didn't acknowledge him as she couldn't hear above the loud music and besides which she was too engrossed in her puzzle. Kevin shoved Roger out of the door and into the staff locker room.

'I've told you before – not here. Are you trying to get us both the bloody sack?' Kevin, in his Speedo trunks, looked menacing, with his thick moustache and wagging finger.

'I know Kevin but I'm desperate. Please ... I need some. Look at the state of me. I can't function.' Roger put his hands together in supplication and fell to his knees.

'You need to get yourself sorted man.' He gave him a push him on the shoulder. 'You need to get a grip, Get yourself under control. This is dangerous when I'm at work you moron, and your cravings aren't bloody dragging me down too.' Kevin scowled and gave Roger a look of contempt.

'I know, but look, here's £30. Have you got my usual?' Roger waved the three notes about in desperation.

Kevin glanced over his shoulder shiftily before opening up his locker. 'I have some here but it's gone up.' He put his head to one side. '40.'

'But I don't have any more,' wailed Roger, tears welling up in his eyes.

'Give me that now,' Kevin gave him a smug smile.' And you can let me have the other 20 at the end of the week.'

'But that's 50! You said 40.' Roger jettisoned air from his nostrils and sucked in his cheeks but at least he was going to get it.

'That's interest. Take it or leave it.' Kevin shrugged.

'Okay, okay then, very well.' Roger sighed. He knew Kevin had him over a barrel but he just needed to feel normal again.

Once the deal was done, Roger just wanted to get back to his own chalet and self-medicate but as he was running past the Entertainment's Office a voice called out.

'Roger. Roger. Come here for a minute please.' Tony, his boss was standing in the doorway smoking. Unfortunately, Roger had no choice but to go over and see what he wanted.

'Oh, good morning Tony.' He gibbered, trying his best to pull himself together and sound affable.

'Roger, would you go and tell Debbie that I would like a word with her now. That's if she's up it of course.' Good God, thought Tony, maybe there was some bug going about as Roger was in a dreadful state. 'What's the matter with you lad? I'd keep out of the swimming baths in future if I were you. What were you doing in there anyway? You weren't there long enough to swim many lengths.'

'I wasn't doing anything. I just needed to see erm … Carol about ... something.' Roger was not only dripping with sweat but he was shivering and twitching. Possibly at any moment he could vomit.

Tony, fearing an outbreak of something akin to the Bubonic Plague took a step backwards into the safety of the office and shouted. 'Well, off you go and don't forget to give my message to Debbie.'

With great relief Roger sprinted along the path and back to the sanctity of his own space. He would tell Debbie in a moment but first things first. He arranged some of the powder into a line on a *Duran Duran* album sleeve.

10th April 2014 – The Blonde Barrel, Newcastle

Roger Sees a Ghost

After the unfortunate incident at Tesco's earlier that afternoon, Roger headed for the sanctuary of the *Blonde Barrel* in Times Square. This was right in the heart of Newcastle's *Pink Triangle*, where all the gay bars were to be found. It was Friday night and a busy time, marking for some the beginning of another hedonistic weekend. The pulsating beat of loud music boomed throughout the room and bodies gyrated and shimmied across the dance floor.

Alongside neat bottoms wiggling in gold lycra pants were tight vest tops showing spidery chest hairs. While young biceps bulged with vigour, elderly arms sagged with loose skin and faded blue tattoos. Yet, all were going for it big time, in an exuberance of colour, foreplay and noise. Some customers seemed more like parrots than people, with their feathers, wigs and bright lurid make-up. Others with horns, gimp masks and bondage gear just appeared bizarre. Although most of the partygoers were male, it was difficult to be certain of gender amongst the high heels, fishnet tights and transgender confusion of the carnival atmosphere.

Roger went up to the long wooden bar and ordered himself an ultra-cool pint of lager. He found an empty table, jumped up on a high stool to relax and people watch. Taking a long drink from his glass he was transfixed by the dancers. The mixture of testosterone, poppers and sweat were a heady mix and Roger inhaled deeply feeling like he was back in the groove. Above his head hung a glitter ball and as it rotated, he felt intoxicated by its myriad of sparkles, that burst across the floor like bubbles in a glass of champagne. Maybe tonight he'd get lucky, for it had been a good while since he had.

There were a couple of blokes playing pool on the red felt table that he half knew and they gave each other a nod of recognition.

'You all right there, dearie?' asked an old queen sitting close by, beneath an elaborate light-fitting, wearing pink lipstick and a needy expression. Roger didn't think he knew him but he couldn't be sure.

Suddenly, there was a rush of fresh noise. A new crowd had arrived. They wore different clothes, had the air of the moneyed, and more of these seemed genetically female. They occupied the large space next to the fruit machines with loud, confident voices and look-at-me attitudes. Letting their presence be known they demanded immediate service. Soon cameras and phones were flashing everywhere. In an instant, all attention had switched to them, as they sat there sipping on cocktails and roaring with laughter like a bunch of over-excited hyenas. Roger wondered who they were and imagined that with all the interest they were generating that they must be celebrities. These days he paid little attention to such things.

One individual in particular however caught his eye. He was sitting apart from the others, deep in thought. Wearing a finely tailored silver suit, tapered shoes, and a bored expression, it was clear he didn't really want to be there. Studying the chiselled face Roger realised, he was seeing somebody he recognised. Once he had known that long face and aquiline nose very well. Gone was the quiff and the boyish appeal but without a shadow of doubt Roger knew who he was. This man had to be Stephen, his Bluecoat friend from Pontins all those years ago. It was like seeing a ghost. What was going on?

Roger had first seen Mike a few weeks ago and now was very much regretting having making himself known to the man but now here was Stephen. This was all very peculiar. Stephen turned towards him, as if he sensed he was being watched and for a brief moment their eyes locked. Stephen's pale face grew whiter and he started to tremble. Without a word to the rest of his party, Stephen flew off his seat and shot out of the door.

Chapter 29

26th July 1984 – Sunny Dunes Holiday Camp – Tony's
Office

Not the Rocky Horror Show

When Debbie woke up the next morning, through the tombstone curtains she could see the sun was shining and she was relieved that she was feeling much better. Still out for the count, Siobhan was snoring loudly. She couldn't remember her chalet mate returning last night but then again she must have been in a very deep sleep herself. Nevertheless, Debbie was deeply puzzled about her own sudden illness yesterday. She was unused to feeling unwell because apart from the odd cold here and there, she very rarely felt poorly. For definite, she could never recall ever having a horrendous stomach upset like that one. She had felt like a battered shuttlecock after a frantic game of badminton due to spending hours toing and froing from her bed to the bathroom and back.

Strangely enough though, she had felt perfectly fine until the Cine Racing. She remembered that before then, Stephen and herself had been having a great time. The thought of him prancing around the Entertainment's Office, using the bread knife as a walking cane, brought a smile to her lips. In fact, she had thoroughly enjoyed him teaching her that song. After working with him, she had actually been looking forward to dressing up in a man's suit and prancing about the stage as *Burlington Bertie*. Even now, she could feel the lyrics of the song lodged in her head and ready to play. She imagined Larry Lawson starting the intro ready for her to begin. Debbie knew for a fact she would have been splendid last night. But no, it seemed that just wasn't to be or was it? Well maybe it hadn't been the case last night, but next week surely she would be given the opportunity to play her part in the show.

She however, could think of one person who would have been absolutely delighted about last night's turn of events. She thought back to yesterday lunchtime, as she was running back to her chalet desperate for the bathroom, she was certain she had caught a fleeting glimpse of two figures out of the corner of her eye. Suzanne and Karen had been watching her and she was almost sure upon reflection that the pair of them had been pointing at her. And they were laughing. Debbie could now distinctly picture the pair of them in stitches, with vindictive tears of delight streaming down their nasty faces. That bitch Suzanne must have been over the moon that she hadn't been able perform last night and Debbie wondered if she was missing something.

'Morning, Debbie. How are you feeling this morning?' inquired a sleepy voice from the other side of the room. Siobhan yawned and stretched her arms above her head.

'I'm feeling much better. I just can't think what the matter with me was yesterday.' Debbie was sitting on her bed still in her black spider nightie with her knees tucked under her chin.

'It was more than likely something you'd eaten. Honestly, the food in this place … but as long as you're feeling better today.' Siobhan was obviously relieved that her friend seemed to be back to normal.

'I guess so.' Debbie was chewing her lip and pondering over yesterday's events.

'Fancy a cuppa?' Debbie nodded and Siobhan crawled out of bed to turn on the kettle. 'Anyway, you don't need to worry,' continued Siobhan. 'Tony knows all about your illness and I'm sure he was fine with it.'

'What do you mean?' Debbie sat bolt upright. 'You're sure he was fine with it? What did he say when you told him?'

'Well, erm … I didn't actually tell him.' Siobhan stared at the floor. 'It was Suzanne. She said she would tell Tony but she said there was nothing to worry …'

'Suzanne. Oh this just gets better by the minute. Do you know when I was running back to the …' Debbie's accusation was cut short by a loud knock on the door and Siobhan was only too pleased to open it.

'How's Debbie this morning?' Roger was standing at the door nursing a cup of coffee and a voice of concern.

'I'm much better thanks.' Debbie answered breezily in the general direction of the door.

'Good. Tony will be pleased to hear that.' Roger called back. 'And he says will you get yourself over to the Entertainment's Office pronto because he wants a word.' After delivering his missive Roger was away.

'That sounds ominous don't you think?' Debbie didn't like the sound of this one little bit.

'He probably just wants to check that you're better.' Siobhan gulped, now feeling queasy herself, remembering what had happened to others who had upset Tony.

'Well I think that depends upon just what was said to him by Suzanne yesterday. Don't you?' Debbie couldn't believe that Siobhan, who she considered her friend, had betrayed her and given Suzanne such powerful ammunition.

Debbie got ready as quickly as she could, which wasn't very fast considering her elaborate make-up and hair procedures, before taking herself off to the Entertainment's Office to see Tony. She thought it was best to get the matter over and done with as soon as possible. It was only 9am and still quite quiet because most of the morning's activities didn't begin until later. Some people however were mulling around outside the canteen after having had their cornflakes and fry ups. Most of the Bluecoats didn't really bother with breakfasts and preferred to spend the extra precious time in bed. Roger was the only one she knew to be an early riser.

When she got to the office it was empty but she could see the door at the far end was ajar and no doubt Tony was waiting for her. She could hear his radio and smell the cigarette smoke. Debbie wouldn't have expected him to be in so early, especially as he didn't live on the site and also liked to keep late nights. She knocked on the door.

'Come in,' barked Tony, not sounding at all welcoming.

'You wanted to see me?' Debbie tried to supress the quiver in her voice as she went into his office.

'Oh good, so you've decided to join us in doing some work today, have you?' There was an unpleasant barb to his voice.

'I'm sorry. I don't know whatever was wrong with me yesterday. I felt so ill. I couldn't stop ...'

'Spare me the details please. You do realise that *most* people here take their jobs seriously.' Tony's brow knotted.

'I do take my job seriously.' She dreaded to think what lies about her had been spun by that spiteful Suzanne.

'Be quiet. You do know that that *you* were very fortunate to get this position here,' Tony prodded the table aggressively with his forefinger. 'It's halfway through the season and everyone else here has been in place since April. We can all be doing without teaching a workshy newbie, you know? And then, to have her ruining all the routines with a no show on the night ... we can all do without that, if you get my drift? It was only because of your now suspiciously glowing reference from Paignton that you were given this opportunity.'

'And I am very grateful.' As Debbie looked into his bloodshot eyes she could feel the tears burning in her own.

Tony lit a cigarette. 'I shall return to the matter of taking your job seriously. Most Bluecoats manage to fulfil their obligations and get themselves to their duties, even if they are feeling slightly under the weather.'

'It was more than that...'

'Shut up.' Tony banged his fists on the table. 'Suzanne explained what the matter was quite clearly. This attitude of yours is obviously nothing new is it?'

'Tony, I can assure you that this won't happen again.' Debbie wished Siobhan had delivered the message herself and not fallen into that scheming Suzanne's trap.

'Mr Noble, to you, I think. You will have to get yourself back in my good books before you Tony me again.' A sudden petulance crept into his voice.

'I'm sorry.' Debbie decided there was something decidedly creepy about him and was now feeling very uncomfortable in addition to upset.

'But, returning to your exemplary reference.' Tony unfolded a piece of paper which he took from an envelope under the newspaper in front of him. *Debbie is always punctual, pleasant natured and well-presented.* I mean, come on, just look at the state of you. We aren't putting on *The Rocky Horror Show* you know. You look like a freak.' Tony snorted and Debbie was speechless. This was proving to be a far worse encounter than one she could have possibly imagined. 'Clearly you managed to pull the wool over somebody's eyes. Obviously, this Mr Sinclair, The Entertainment's Manager in Paignton saw a different side to you than the one I'm seeing.'

'I didn't realise that...' Debbie ran her fingers through her sticky hair, feeling the glue sticking her bristles hair in place and wondered if perhaps she needed to temper down her style.

'Well, perhaps if you showed me what this Mr Simon Sinclair found so appealing ...' He bared his teeth at her. 'Then just maybe we can just overlook this unfortunate incident.'

'Of course, whatever it takes. I promise I will do a really good job with Burlington Bertie next ...' Was he implying what she thought he was? And as he leant across the table closer to her, she could smell the stench of decay on his breath.

'I couldn't give toss about bloody *Berlington Bertie.* Now Debbie, why don't you come and join me round this side of the table?' He pulled back his chair, leered and patted his bony knee inviting her to sit there. 'Let's see if we can sort out this one ...'

Fortunately, she was saved by the bell. At that very moment, as if on cue, the door flew open and in flounced Jill.

'Good morning Tony.' Jill was carrying some certificates and trophies for that day's competitions. She gave Tony one of her cheeriest smiles.

He stubbed out his cigarette, stuffed the paper back into the envelope and shuffled in his chair uneasily. 'Morning Jill. How are you today?'

'I'm feeling great thanks and I'm glad to see you are feeling a wee bit better today though Debbie. You're still very pale though aren't you? Do you think it was something you ate? I hope there isn't a bug doing the rounds. That's the last thing we need.' Jill arranged the trophies on the table in a neat row.

Debbie watched as the mood changed and Tony slid the envelope underneath his large ashtray. 'So I take it that you'll be fine doing the song next week.'

'Yes of course.' Debbie had never imagined she would have ever been so eternally grateful to see Jill.

'And was there something else?' Tony raised an eyebrow and lit a further cigarette.

'No I don't think …' Debbie was unsure as to what she should do next.

'Well, on your way Debbie.' And he waved his hand towards the door.

'Thank you, Mr Noble.' Debbie couldn't get out of the room fast enough as she made her escape.

'Tony,' chuckled Jill.' Since when have you insisted the Bluecoats call you Mr Noble?'

'Since they started barging in here and showing me no respect,' came the almost too quick response from Tony.

15th April 2014 – The Olympian, Jesmond

That's Not Destiny Chambers

Teddie was sitting in his little office at the back of his restaurant. He had made himself a cup of strong Greek coffee, as he did on arrival most days and had opened a packet of Hob Nobs. This was his secret place where he couldn't be seen, but he had nine special cameras and monitors throughout the building so he could check on the happenings throughout his domain. Firstly, he could make sure all of his staff were working hard to the optimum capacity and always being polite. He knew this was of paramount importance, as the reputation of his establishment relied on the consistent use of

Ευχαριστω (thank you) and Παρακαλω (you're welcome) among his waiters and waitresses. This ranked in equal measures alongside the excellence of his φαγητσ (food).

He wanted his customers leaving satisfied, so they would return, which they almost always did. There was a device in the kitchen so he could ensure his high standards of hygiene were being adhered to and one behind the bar for him to keep tabs on any staff member's sly drinking. Teddie Lazaridis' ran a tight ship and would not tolerate any slovenly or inappropriate behaviour in the Olympian. Only his wife and trusted employee Vasilis were aware of his system of quality control and he knew this was for the best.

One of his waitresses, a new girl called Sophia seemed to be being given the run around big time by some awkward customers. Although her given name was Sophie, he preferred his staff to use the Greek equivalent wherever possible. Despite having grown up in a place called Morpeth, a few miles north of Newcastle and having no Mediterranean heritage whatsoever, the girl's dark hair and olive skin were passably Southern European. She was practically running back and forth from table to bar. Teddie would have to have a word with her for this was a health and safety matter. She had nearly knocked Yiannis (John), another waiter with unfortunate ginger coloured hair and milk bottle skin, flying.

Teddie's eyes followed Sophie marching across the floor, as she took the drinks over to the place where no other than Stefan Sondheim, the local music impresario was sitting. Although Teddie didn't know Stefan personally, the man was never out of the papers, telly, or off the internet, so it was difficult not to recognise him. Tonight he looked in a grumpy mood and he had clicked his fingers rudely at Sophia, so it was no wonder she hurried away. Perhaps, he ought to cut his new waitress some slack after having had the challenge of this difficult customer.

Tonight, Stefan had a most unlikely dining companion. While he was wearing some trendy leather pants and a slinky shirt, she wore the dowdiest of dresses and the glummest of faces. Teddie wasn't an expert on women's clothes but he tended to compare all female attire with that of his wife's and he knew for a fact that Jillian wouldn't be seen dead in this number. While he knew that he was on dodgy ground, he couldn't resist turning up the sound on the nearest monitor to the couple. He was curious and wanted to find out not only what they were talking about what was their connection.

'So I'm not using that name anymore. I want to be taken seriously as a writer.' The plain woman sounded peevish. Oh, she's a writer is she, thought Teddie.

'Well I much prefer the name Destiny Chambers than Martha. Even Debbie Carter was better than that.' Stefan said in a surly voice.

Surely, that couldn't be the glamorous Destiny Chambers. He hadn't recognised her at all. Teddie reached in the packet for another biscuit. She looked ghastly. Destiny had been coming to his restaurant for many years and he had spoken with her on multiple occasions. She was almost as famous locally as Stefan but whatever could have happened to her?

Chapter 30

26th July 1984 – Whitley Bay Golf Club

Mike's Game of Golf

Today was Mike's day off. While he was glad to be spending time away from the cardboard cut outs and holiday camp, the downside was that he was expected to spend it with his parents. In some ways it wasn't so bad, as his mam always did all of his washing and ironing for him. Also, she usually cooked him a yummy dinner. He wondered whether it would be beef, pork or lamb and his mouth watered at the thought of the succulent meat, rich gravy and tasty roasties. He wasn't too fussed about the cabbage and broccoli but he did on the whole appreciate his mam's home cooking. She always made a roast for him irrespective of the day of the week because she knew it was his favourite. He hoped it would be beef and apple pie for desert today because that's what he liked best of all.

It was certainly a big improvement on the mass-produced Pontin's canteen fare, but food aside there were distinct drawbacks to his trips back home. Firstly, his little sister Jennifer, who was an annoying 12 years old and a right pain, would have been plotting all week particular ways to irritate him. She really was so pathetic and childish. A few weeks ago she had cut holes in some of his socks. Another time she had added salt to his water glass at meal time. Then, as if these were bad enough last time he had been home, she had jumped out of the laundry basket in front of him on the landing, screamed *BOO* and he had almost fallen right down the stairs. The little creep. Goodness knows what jolly japes she had planned for today. And to make it worse, his parents just laughed at her pitiful antics. If he could be bothered, he would think of a way to get his revenge but if he were to even slightly pull her pigtails, they'd be down on him like a ton of bricks.

However, much worse than that was his father's weekly patter filled with innuendoes regarding his son's *nudge nudge, wink wink* success with the ladies. It was like something off Benny Hill and totally cringeworthy. Today no doubt would be even worse because his father was threatening to take him for the dreaded round of golf.

Golf was a sport in which he had no interest whatsoever. He didn't see the point. What Mike enjoyed most was running around the rugby pitch, scoring a touchdown or best of all was being all together with the lads in a scrum. He thought you couldn't beat it. After all surely sport was about the camaraderie of being part of a team, but golf ... what was the point? He couldn't think of a bigger waste of time than pootling around the golf links knocking the silly little white balls into holes. It could hardly even be classified as a form of exercise. You never saw any golfers break into sweat. What a complete waste of time. Golf was for pathetic *oldies* like his dad or ... Tony.

An image of the man's horrible face appeared up above with its crooked teeth and malevolent grin. Of course, Tony also played golf at the Whitley Bay Club and it would just be his luck to bump into him today. Those awful words Tony had said to him ricocheted from inside his head and suddenly he felt sick.

Mike's parents didn't live too far away from Sunny Dunes Holiday Club and after the short bus ride which he was now doing, he would soon be there. Disappointingly, for the time of year there weren't any clouds keeping the Tony apparition company in the sky, despite Mike's desperate prayers for rain. If only there could be a proper downpour then this embarrassing and potentially awful situation could be avoided. Without any shadow of doubt he was bound to be hopeless at the stupid game anyway compared to his dad, who'd had years of practise.

When he arrived outside his parents 1930's mock Tudor, semi-detached house, his father was ready and waiting in the doorway. He was wearing a flat cap, a red tank-top, tartan plus fours and two-toned brogues. Mike, in his sensible Adidas navy and white track suit, thought that his father looked ridiculous. With one hand Ronnie held his well-worn tartan caddy bursting with a selection of golf paraphernalia. In the other, he brandished his favourite club as if it were actually a cutlass and he was some out-of- time-and-place pirate.

'Right then lad are you all set?' He gave Mike an up and down look. 'Do you want to borrow some of my gear?' Clearly Ronnie wasn't impressed with his son's choice of clothing for this occasion.

'Don't be silly Ronnie. You're twice the size of Mike.' His mother Jean appeared in the doorway, wearing an apron and mixing the batter for the Yorkshire puddings.

'No, I'm sure these will be fine … but then again we can leave it for another day if you don't think I'm properly dressed.' Oh please, thought Mike as he saw horrible Jennifer peering round the curtains and pulling faces from the front room window.

'No, today's perfect son. Look at that blue sky. There'll not be many more of those this year. I tell you, we've to make the best of them.' Ronnie, with a sardonic smile on his face started wheeling the caddy down the path.

'I really don't mind if you want to leave it to a different time …' Mike scanned the sky willing his imaginary Tony ghoul to disappear and be replaced with some big black rain clouds.

'Come on son. A little father and son bonding, that's what we need. And you can tell me all about the action down at Sunny Dunes.' He gave his son a knowing wink, put his arm round his shoulder and thumped him on the back .

'Now make sure you boys are back at 1 o'clock sharp, as dinner will be on the table. And I don't want it going cold.' Mrs Robinson shouted after them, as some Simon and Garfunkel music blared out from a passing by car.

12th April 2014 – Stowell St, Newcastle

Finding Stefan Sondheim

Roger tended to wake up quite early, especially at the weekends. This was largely due to the noisy bustle of people walking only inches away from the window of his ground floor studio flat in Blackfriars Court on Stowell Street, Newcastle. Next door to him, the Chinese supermarket seemed to have a constant stream of loud deliveries particularly early in the morning. Roger shuddered when he thought of the nasty cans of soda they sold there with those horrid lumps of jelly-like maggots swimming around in the pop. He vowed he would never go there again seeking a fix to quench the thirst of a raging bad hangover.

The Chinese restaurants also had early starts in their preparations for lunchtime, especially on a Saturday when they were hoping for good fortune in business. As wheels rattled over the cobbled streets, Roger's sleep was disturbed by the clanking of doors, the scraping of boxes and high-pitched, multi-toned utterances in Mandarin or Cantonese. His shift at *The Vue* didn't begin until the afternoon and for once he would have been grateful for a lie in. He shouldn't complain, the rent for his shoebox was a reasonable price and it was in a central location. He walked through to the kitchen to put on the kettle before folding up his sofa bed, as he liked his place to be as neat as possible. After pulling on some old jogging pants and a sweatshirt from a shelf in his well-organised wardrobe, he tidied away yesterday's clothes then plumped up his two cushions.

Roger made himself a cup of coffee and put on his small television, to see what had been happening in the world. He doubted that anything could be as dramatic as the last couple of days in his own life. Lifting up his sleeve he saw two angry bruises and he remembered the humiliation of being thrown out of Tesco and into the bins by Mike Robinson. He had always remembered the lad as being polite and kind. In fact hadn't he even encouraged him in his misguided aspirations to be a comic? It seemed he had turned into the rudest monster of a man and Roger was baffled as to why he had been treated so shabbily. In fact, he would go out of his way to avoid walking through Tesco and he hoped their paths never crossed again but with a deep sigh he realised this was unlikely.

But if that wasn't enough, last night he had been convinced that he had seen Stephen in the *Blonde Barrel*. One Pontins coincidence was strange but two were definitely unnerving. He assumed that after that unfortunate incident in the summer of 84 everyone had scattered as far away from the North-East as they possibly could. He knew he certainly had. Both Jill and himself had been delighted and relieved to accept Pontinental posts as pronto as possible. Indeed, it was his contacts there that had led to … but no, Roger didn't really want to think about that particularly ill-chosen path.

After a life of ducking, diving and living on the edge, Roger was now happy with his small flat and humble lot in life. His location in Newcastle had been by pure chance and through no choice of his own. Certainly, he had not expected to be bumping into these colleagues from so long ago. He looked out of his window fully expecting to see a middle-aged Suzanne and Karen walk by armed with shopping bags and malicious gossip.

It certainly seemed that Stephen Simpson was part of the *in crowd* in Newcastle judging from the company he was keeping and Roger was curious about him. He fired up his laptop and googled the name. There was a Steven Simpson a butcher, who made special pies in Derbyshire and a Steve Simpson in Cumbria who was advertising his pedigree sausage dogs. Neither the photographs nor descriptions fitted the person he had seen last night. He tried Facebook but still was unable to find a likely candidate for the Stephen he had once known.

Then to his amazement, his eyes were drawn to the telly and there he was.

'And here we have Mr Stefan Sondheim who was present at the event last week.' Stephen was asked by a young blonde woman with an exceptionally orange tan. 'So, Mr Sondheim What is your impression of the new venue?' He was clad from head to foot in black leather and seemed to be at an important opening event for another new nightclub.

'Oh, I think it's great.' He beamed at the camera and placed his face at am obviously practised angle, to show it at his best advantage and hide his double-chin. '*The Roxie* is really going to be putting Newcastle on the map. I mean it's such a happening place with a great vibe. I know my lads are so going to love playing there.'

Then he was gone and the weather report came on the telly. Stefan Sondheim? So that was what he was calling himself these days and Roger supposed it did sound more catchy that Stephen Simpson but wasn't there already a famous composer with that name? Anyway, that explained why he hadn't been able to trace him online. But what exactly was he famous for? Did he have some sons in a pop band? Surely, he couldn't be a famous celebrity for that. And if he did have sons, surely he must have adopted them. Roger turned once more to his laptop.

Chapter 31

26th July 1984 Sunny Dunes Holiday Camp – Siobhan and Debbie's Chalet

The Heavy Rucksack

'Well what did he want? Is everything ok? I am so sorry ...' Siobhan's voice trailed off. She had been chewing on her fingernails furiously for the past hour, waiting for her friend to return from the meeting with Tony.

Debbie had come back into the chalet with her head bent down seeming very subdued. It was obvious she had been crying. She kicked off her shoes and sat on her bed, with her knees tucked under her chin.

'Debbie I'm so sorry. I don't know what I was thinking of. To be sure I knew Suzanne couldn't be trusted. I guess I just wasn't thinking straight. What an eejit. I could kick myself.' She bashed one leg against the other, harder than she had intended and knew she would have a bruise there tomorrow. 'What did Tony say?' Siobhan was getting more concerned by each moment. It just wasn't like her friend to be quiet like this. 'Debbie?' The guilt was sitting on Siobhan's shoulders like a heavy rucksack filled with bricks.

'It's all right Siobhan. It's not your fault.' A tear snaked down Debbie's cheek to join the other streaks of mascara.

'What's happened? What mischief's that miserable cow done now?' Siobhan asked. Debbie didn't reply but picked up a hand mirror, wiped her face and began tugging furiously at her hair.

'Tony can't have been that mad at you,' said Siobhan. 'I mean it was hardly your fault you were ill is it? I mean, strictly speaking, its

Pontin's fault because your stomach upset was more than likely caused by something that you…'

'Siobhan.' Debbie made a sound somewhere between that of a sob and a hiccough. 'Do you think I look like a freak?'

Siobhan thought that Debbie's lovely face now looked like that of a sad *Pierrot* doll. 'What? Of course not. You look always grand. Have you seen that bitch Suzanne this morning?' She really could kill that bastard, shitty girl.

'It wasn't Suzanne, it was Tony. He said I looked like something off the Rocky Horror Show.' Siobhan thought she had never anyone so forlorn and she could feel her own eyes welling up with tears.

'He said *what*?' Siobhan put her hands to her head, having an awful feeling of deja-vu.

'He said I looked a mess. Do you think I do?' Siobhan shook her head and ran her fingers through her own hair feeling the little spikes she had recently been cultivating. She had been willing them to grow longer and quicker, so she could be just like her friend.

'Debbie, you know I think you look fabulous. Suzanne and Karen only make nasty comments about you because they're jealous you know.' Siobhan's mind was whirring fast because if Debbie had gone on the wrong side of Tony this could have dire consequences.

'I'm not so sure any more. But that's not the worst of it though.' Debbie began to doubt herself and wondered if what she had thought happened actually had.

'Why, what did he say? He can't sack you for being ill, you know?' But Siobhan knew that Tony could do whatever he liked and get away with it or so it seemed. He had history.

'You know I have never been so pleased to see Jill.' Debbie shook her head.

'Jill, what's she got to do with all of this?' Siobhan wanted to hear the details of what had actually happened but she was trying not to be insensitive and didn't like to ask. After all, this mess, she thought, was mostly down to her.

'I think he tried to make a pass at me.' Debbie was now wondering if perhaps she had just imagined it all. As she played the events back through her mind, they had a strange blurry dream-like quality about them

'The bastard, I really could kill that man.' And Siobhan gave her friend the tightest hug as she continued weeping. She wondered if this was the right time or not to tell Debbie the full extent of what she knew about Tony Noble.

13th April 2014 - The Crown Possada, Newcastle

A Knife Sticking out of her Back

After he had finished his shift at Tesco that day, Mike left work feeling in a much more positive light than he had for some time. He found himself whistling, as he crossed Trinity Square and headed to towards the Swing Bridge. It was six thirty in the evening, still light and the sun was shining. Above him the kittiwakes were squawking and his mood was spoilt slightly by their horrible white mess splattered like chewing gum on the pavement. Why people seemed keen to encourage them was beyond his comprehension and an unwanted vision of the Bird Woman flashed through his mind. He hadn't spotted her for a while which was good. Clearly the old bag was using some sense and keeping out of his way.

Mike pushed through the door into one of his favourite pubs, the *Crown Posada*. It was a snug Victorian pub with heavy dark green and red panelling. Stained glass windows of Tudor figures welcomed patrons by the entrance and comforting music from a scratchy old gramophone filled the air. Much as Mike enjoyed watching sport, there was a lot to be said for a traditional alehouse without the distraction of television screens or fruit machines. Legend had it that the place had been once bought by a Spanish sea captain for his Tyneside mistress. At first, it had been known as *The Crown*, the Spanish word posada meaning inn or resting place, was later added.

Finding himself an empty table, Mike sat down to enjoy his pint and reflect on the events of the day. He was feeling triumphant after putting that sour bitch Elaine in her place. How dare she assume that he could be blackmailed into giving her no doubt ne'er- do-well son a job. There was something about her voice and herself in general that he really found quite repulsive. Strangely though, there was also something oddly familiar about her too but he couldn't for the life of him think from where. He had only been to Scotland once and that was with his wife because she wanted to visit the famous castle in Edinburgh.

What business of that cow was it who he chatted to and so what if Roger was a gay man? What had that got to do with anything? But that was just what was so unsettling. The conversation with Roger had meant that events from all those years ago had come flooding back. It was all because of that bastard Tony, what he had done to Mike and what he had threatened to tell his father. That's what had freaked him out. He remembered that terrible morning, when they had all sat in the Entertainment's Office waiting. Then, once they had taken Tony away in a body bag , all those dreadful questions had been asked. Amazingly, the identity of the murderer had never been solved but so many, himself included, had such good motives for killing the bugger.

This was what had frightened him so much about seeing Roger. Not Roger's stupid pass all those years ago but the fact that the case might be further investigated. This was something that needed to be avoided at all costs. Yet surely it was impossible that the Scottish shelf-stacker could have known anything about this. Nonetheless, this was further reason that Elaine needed to be removed from her position and Mike imagined, Elaine's body lying prostrate next to the freezer along with the frozen chickens and a knife sticking out of her back.

When Mike went to the bar to recharge his glass, he thought the barmaid looked a little like the woman with the lovely perfume that he had helped find the book she was looking for. He had been surprised that the classy lady had been buying such a trashy book but maybe be it was for a gift. Funnily enough, there was something strangely familiar about her walk but no, it must just be his mind playing peculiar tricks once more.

Chapter 32

26th July 1984 – Sunny Dunes Holiday Camp – Tony's Office

Queering His Pitch

Well, Jill could certainly pick her moments thought a disappointed Tony after his thwarted attempt to seduce Debbie. Also, Jill had only stayed in the office a short while faffing on unnecessarily with the trophies and prizes, as if they were some elaborate flower display. Then in a matter of a few minutes she had flounced off. Strange, for it was almost as if his Assistant Manager had known what he was doing and had been deliberately trying to queer his pitch.

No, that was impossible; if Jill had the slightest notion of what he was up to she would have been furious. Jill could be very spiky when her wrath was incurred. Nevertheless, she had spoilt him having a little recreational sport with the workshy but comely Debbie. Maybe Suzanne had been guilty of over-egging the pudding and trying to paint the new Bluecoat in the worse possible light but Debbie's mysterious illness had materialised out of nowhere. Shortly before she had been having a whale of a time carrying on with that Stephen, hadn't she?

Anyway, whatever else, that glowing reference from Paignton still seemed a little too good to be true, didn't it? Obviously, Debbie was no innocent at keeping on the right side of a boss, was she? It would be interesting to have a chat with this Mr Simon Sinclair from Paignton. Certainly, Debbie's morals were nowhere as lily-white as her face and she would almost certainly have been up for a little jiggery-pokery. Hopefully, she would now be aware of the consequences of what would happen if she didn't toe the line.

Pontins had no place for lazy Bluecoats. Other opportunities for his pleasure would present themselves and he would make sure Jill was well out of the way. Tony smiled to himself, lit a cigarette and opened a can of bitter.

However, upon reflection, it was fortunate for all that his Assistant Manager hadn't arrived a few minutes later, for by then him and Debbie would have been getting it on big time and the shit would have seriously hit the fan. He had a disturbing image of Jill as a feral wildcat, flexing her red painted claws and defending her territory. After savagely attacking a horrified Debbie, the girl would be left with big gashes down her cheeks that no amount of her white face paint would be able to disguise.

No, all matters considered he didn't really want to upset Jill. She had proved herself this season as an exceptional Assistant Entertainment's Manager on many levels. Their private relationship was most satisfactory and she was discreet. His long suffering wife, Maureen was completely unaware of the full nature of their involvement. In the past with previous dalliances, that hadn't always been the case. At least this season he'd had no awkward late night phone calls to explain to his wife. But then again Maureen ought to understand behaviour like this from him was to be expected because a full-blooded alpha male such as himself had special needs.

Jill looked good on his arm at the casino, she was nearly always up for it and most importantly, she was as dishonest as he was. Win, win. He glanced at the safe and thought of the thousands of pounds of charity money inside. A visit to the bank was long overdue. This was most certainly panning out to be the most profitable of seasons.

Since early on in the season, Tony had decided all the Bluecoats this year were a rum bunch. Most, if not all of the male ones were gay and so were even some of the girls. The other females were catty bitches just trying to get one up on each other. He had certainly made the right choice in Jill for his assistant but he was beginning to have his doubts about Roger's suitability for the position of Head Bluecoat.

The main reason he had chosen the lad was because he seemed gullible and a bit thick. He thought there would be a good chance he wouldn't be sticking in his beak where it wasn't wanted and so far he hadn't but he was becoming increasingly more peculiar by the day. Over the past few weeks, Roger had kept bothering him incessantly about such trivial matters. The way he had been blethering on about those bloody donkey derby programmes was ridiculous. It was a matter that had already been sorted by his ever efficient Jill. Also, recently, he had started thinking nothing of barging into Tony's office without knocking and whenever he fancied. Worryingly, this tendency was proving catching. Only the other day, that fat cow Suzanne had done the very same thing. This could be very dangerous for both him and Jill. It could put a spanner in the works. Without doubt it needed sorting and Roger, his Head Bluecoat, should be the person to do it.

And what had been the matter with Roger earlier that morning? The twitching, sweating and unhealthy shade of his skin had made Tony worried that whatever was wrong with him might be contagious. And what had he been doing at the pool at that time of the morning. Roger was no swimmer and something just didn't add up. Tony once more looked out of his window towards the swimming baths and saw a furtive looking Gary, the Camp Photographer, scurrying from the building. His long permed hair had no trace of dampness whatsoever.

14th April 2014 – Jillian's Keep Fit Class, Jesmond

Just a Small Lie

Jillian looked at the clock on the wall and was shocked to see that it was already quarter to ten. If she didn't get a move on she was in danger of bumping into her cleaner. This was something that needed to be avoided at all costs. She had been reading *Follow Your Dreams* for the past hour and it seemed the time had just flown. Although the book was complete drivel she was thoroughly enjoying it.

As she was already dressed in her new beige tracksuit, there was no need for her to change. She flung a few items into her Mulberry bag, added a pearly pink swipe to her mouth with her lipstick and she was off to her car. She was surprised when she noticed Carl's battered old Volvo pulling up on the other side of the road because she had forgotten that he too was coming to do some jobs that morning.

'Good morning Carl. How are you today?' Jillian shot him a cheery smile.

'Good morning Mrs Lazaridis'.' Carl doffed his cap. 'Very well thanks and you?'

'All good. I'm just off to my keep fit class.' She patted her bag. 'You have a key so just help yourself to a coffee or anything that you need.' Jillian wished that Elaine was more like Carl. There was something quite comforting about having an ex-policeman on your pay role. It made her feel safe.

'Very well. I just thought I'd make a start on pruning those bushes.' Carl disappeared around the side of the house with his heavy bag of tools and Jillian jumped into her car.

While she was at the class, she admired her trim frame in the mirror as she participated enthusiastically in the bends, stretches and jumps. As the other bodies wobbled and moaned, Jillian had little sympathy for them as they more than likely stuffed their faces with cakes and biscuits all day. As she shadowed the routines of Emma the fitness instructor to near perfection, the same could not be said for the majority of the class. At the back of the room she spotted Barbara Blackstaff obviously out of breathe, step and time. She was wearing an ill-advised turquoise leotard and an expression of pain.

She wondered how Carl and the gardening were progressing. She had pinned the list of jobs that needed doing onto the shed. Hopefully, Elaine hadn't been bothering the poor man too much. Probably, she would be keeping out of his way. More than likely her family would be the sort to be wary of the law and be used to being on its wrong side.

Once the class was over, a red-faced Barbara was waiting for her in the corridor outside.

'How are you getting on with the book?' Barbara looked relieved the class was over.

'Oh, I haven't started it. I haven't even got a copy yet.' She lied.

'Oh, you will enjoy it. I'm sure of it. Go to Tesco.' Barbara took a drink from her bottle of water. 'There's one at Gateshead. They've got it on special offer there.'

'Tesco isn't very convenient for me. I don't really like going over to the other side of the water.' Jillian remembered the horrors of the previous day.

'Well there's one at Kingston Park too. Anyway, must dash. Can't wait to get back home and dive back into *Follow Your Dreams*. Mark my words Jillian, you'll just love it.' Jillian cringed because she was never going to admit any such thing.

Chapter 33

26th July 1984 – Sunny Dunes Holiday Camp – The Regency Lounge

An Afternoon Whist Drive

Stephen was pleased when he had read on the daily rota that he was down to be on the whist drive that afternoon. Sometimes, with a bit of luck, there wasn't enough interest from the punters and it didn't happen. More importantly though, he was glad because Debbie's name was also written to be on the same activity and he wanted to see how she was. Stephen was puzzled about the cause of her sudden illness. One minute she had been in the finest fettle and they had been having a good laugh. The next she was off running to the bathroom at such a speed it was as if she were training for the next Olympics.

So far, there was only himself and an elderly couple in the Regency Lounge. Although they were busy at the moment drinking tea, they appeared suitable whist material. She had a steely grey perm sitting on her head like a bonnet. He had a bald head and the determined look of a serious card player. Still, there needed to be at least five couples to make the activity viable. Stephen glanced at the clock on wall. It was twenty past two and ten minutes before the event was due to begin.

The Regency Lounge was decorated with faded red and white striped wallpaper. It had a worn colourful carpet with golden crowns and fleur-de-lis. Fringing the edge of the room was a circle of yellow battered chairs. Arranged in the centre of the room were a dozen little green felt-covered tables with four folding chairs set out. There were big sash windows that on the one side looked over the swimming baths. Stephen saw Darren from the arcade heading over to the pool and looking over his shoulder in a very shifty manner. He wouldn't have put Darren down as a swimmer. Still, Stephen had never been in the building, as he couldn't swim.

Two other couples entered the room and sat down at the card tables. The first moved from the outside chairs to join them. It was seeming that the whist drive was likely going to be happening and Stephen went to get the playing cards from the Quality Street tin. As the clock moved towards half past a further three couples joined the gathering and Debbie came running through the door.

'Afternoon Debbie.' Stephen was relieved to see her. 'Are you ok? Well, you must be or you wouldn't be here would you?'

'Yes thanks Stephen. Much better.' But her voice had a quiver.

'What time does this start then?' The bald man was busy shuffling the cards, ready for action.

'Any minute.' Stephen did a quick head count. There were six couples to play including him and Debbie. He addressed the card players. 'I'll be right with you.' Then he turned to Debbie. 'So what was the matter do you think?' He whispered to her thinking she still didn't seem quite her usual self. In fact, her hair really didn't seem as big or her face quite as white. All in all she appeared to have diminished and Stephen was very concerned .

'I don't know. Maybe food poisoning.' She spoke in an unusually quiet voice.

'What's wrong?' Stephen was sure that something was.

'Not now … I'll explain later,' was Debbie's enigmatic reply.

'It's gone two thirty. Let's get cracking.' The eager whist enthusiast poked a finger against his watch face in annoyance.

'Ok. Well, good afternoon ladies and gentlemen.' Stephen gave the room one of his best smiles. 'It looks like we're all up for a super afternoon, don't you think? So … we will be playing twelve hands.

When the last table has finished each game, I ring this for you to move.' There was a tinkly noise from a small bell which he shook to demonstrate. 'The winning couple get 4 points in each round and the winning lady moves to the right table and the gentleman to the left. At the end we tot up all of the scores and the two highest will receive ... ta dah!' And he held up two tiny plastic silver coloured trophies with a little tags bearing *whist player of the week* labels. 'As you can see, no expense has been spared by Mr Fred Pontin.' He gave the gathering a knowing nod, pleased at his own wittiness even though he made this quip every time. 'So let's get these cards dealt and let battle commence.'

After the noises of shuffling and dealing subsided the players all held up their cards to look at their hands but neither Stephen nor Debbie were able to concentrate. Stephen just wanted it to be four o' clock then he could find out what was the matter with his friend.

Wednesday 15th April 2014 – The Olympian, Jesmond

Those Pieces of Cardboard

'Two moussakas and a Greek salad please.' Martha spoke quickly without even looking at the menu. Once the waitress had gone she continued. 'I've seen Roger as well.'

'What? Where?' Stefan's eyes grew round. 'And why didn't you tell me.'

'It's a long story Stefan but I know for a fact that he has a job at the cinema in Gateshead.' Martha whispered, but with all the serious charade thrown out of the window, she was back into full drama Destiny.

'What are you talking about Destiny?' Stefan took a feverish drink from his glass. 'Roger wouldn't be working in Gateshead. Let alone in the cinema. He's run lots of nightclubs. Swish places. Why would he be working in a cinema in …?'

'Shut up and listen.' Destiny was on fire. 'He works in the *Vue* cinema in Trinity Square which I know for a fact because I have spoken to him.'

'When was this?' Stefan's facial muscles contorted strangely as he tried to process all this information.

'I saw him going into Tesco in Gateshead to speak to Mike.' Her eyes looked round the room shiftily.

'Mike who?' Where on earth was this tale going now Stefan wondered?

'Do you remember back when we were Bluecoats all those years ago. There was a Bluecoat called Mike and …'

'Wasn't he the one that used to hold up those pieces of cardboard?' A slight smile made a brief appearance on Stefan's mouth.

'Yes that's the one. Well anyway …'

'Do you remember when that bloody awful Suzanne used to sing that Spanish song he had that great bloody bull to hold?' He gave a loud guffaw of laughter. Temporarily, Stefan had forgotten the full gravitas of the situation and allowed himself a reprise of nostalgia.

Martha brought the conversation back on track. 'Mike works in the Tesco at Gateshead. I think he's some sort of manager there.'

Stefan landed back in the present with a thud. 'What's going on with all these ghosts? I don't like it. Not one little bit.' He ran his long fingers down his cheeks,

'I don't know Stefan.' She looked woeful. 'Anyway, I saw Roger go into the store and speak to Mike. But you'll never guess what happened next.'

'Well, what was it? Nothing would surprise me now.' Stefan refilled his glass and took a long drink.

'The next thing was that Mike literally threw him out of the store. He pushed him out through the door and into some bins.'

Stefan hadn't been expecting this and almost spat his wine back into the glass. 'What? Come off it Destiny. Isn't this just something from a plot in one of your daft books?'

'If sir and madam are ready for their food?' Sophia brought the moussaka and salad to the table. She placed them neatly in front of the two diners who weren't in the slightest bit interested in eating.

Chapter 34

26th July 1984 – Sunny Dunes Holiday Camp – The Regency Lounge

Wiping Off Smiles

Once the whist drive was over, it was Elaine's turn to be in the Regency Lounge but in her case it was to hoover rather than to play cards and drink tea. She tutted at the cake crumbs, which had been scattered like confetti around the copper-coloured hostess trolley. As usual after such events, it was laden with used cups, saucers and plates. Yet another job for her to sort out in taking all the dirty crockery back to the canteen.

On her way to the kitchen with the trolley, she had crossed paths with Jill. 'Hello Jill. How are you this wee afternoon.' Elaine had asked the stuck-up bitch.

There was no reply, because yet again Jill had blanked her and today she seemed particularly full of herself. She was practically skipping down the stairs, clutching an opened letter and she had the most enormous grin on her heavily made-up face. Well, Elaine would soon have a similar smirk on her face when she had her own selection of designer accessories. For the first time in her life she was looking forward to having money to fritter on herself. Oh yes, Elaine's days as a cleaner were numbered that was for sure.

Elaine had her own cunning plan to wipe the smiles off both Jill and Tony's faces. She was now completely sure the contents of that safe weren't intended for charitable causes but were being used to neatly line those two's bank accounts. While it was clear where the spoils from Jill's embezzling were going, Tony's spending was less obvious as it was certainly not being used by himself to buy any new clothes. Oh yes, Elaine had suspected a charity box fraud for some time but now she had got concrete proof. The Entertainment and Assistant Entertainment's Managers were nowhere near as clever as they thought themselves to be. Not only had she seen with her own eyes all that stash of money they kept in the office but she'd also seen the frequent deposits in their bank accounts. The idiots had both left their paying-in books in plain sight on their desk tops, conveniently close to the photocopier.

Painstakingly, Elaine had been busy cutting her letter's characters from magazines and newspapers to glue onto a letter telling them the game was up. It was taking ages and wasn't yet finished but it would be more than worth the effort. She was going to include particular dates and the specific amounts deposited in her missive so they would know she had hard evidence. If they didn't cut her a fair wack then she would be going to the police. She was going to add precise instructions that the money from the week's charity boxes was to be left in a carpet bag which she would put under the hostess trolley in this very place. The Regency Lounge was always quiet of a night time so this would be the perfect spot.

Although Elaine had wondered what the letter that Jill had in her hand earlier was all about, she was certain they wouldn't be anywhere near as interesting as the one she had in her own overall pocket along with a sharp pair of scissors.

Tuesday 14th April 2014– The Lazaridis' House, Jesmond

Tea with Two Sugars

Elaine wasn't surprised that she had seen neither sight nor sound of her workshy son for the past few days. Ever since the mention of the job at Tesco, he had obviously been giving his mother a wide berth. Well, he would no doubt be delighted that despite the best efforts of his mother, the promised warehouse position seemed to have evaporated into nothing. How dare that bloody Mike Robinson go back on his word? How come he'd all of a sudden had a change of mind? When she had at first mentioned his acquaintance with Roger he'd practically wet his pants. She knew that there had been rumours in the past of a homosexual liaison between the two of them and there was never any smoke without fire. At first, Mike Robinson had only been too keen to oblige Elaine by finding a job for her son and buy her silence. However, upon reflection he must have decided, more the pity, that in this day and age it was really no big deal.

Nevertheless, Elaine had her own problems. She still had a son without a job, one daughter with her second bairn on the way, another one that was simple and bills of her own to pay. Maybe Scott's suggestion of a burglary at the Lazaridis' house wasn't such a bad idea but then again, maybe not. Elaine was busy mopping the floor in Jillian's kitchen and out of the window she could see Carl working in the garden. He was a tall well-built man who despite being retired, clearly kept himself fit. He wore a T shirt and Elaine could see the pronounced muscles in his arms as he hacked away at the bushes. No all in all, it would be a stupid idea for Scott to steal from a house where an ex-policeman was often around.

Elaine had always been a little nervous of the police. In the past, well not very long ago actually, she had been known to partake in a little shoplifting. The odd tin of corned beef or packet of chocolate digestives had sometimes found their way into her pockets but nothing major of course. Understandably, this had made her wary of anyone connected with the police force but maybe it was time for a change of tack. Elaine had bigger fish to fry and time was marching forward.

'Carl. I've just put the kettle on. Would you like a wee tea or coffee?' Elaine shouted down into the garden.

'That would be very kind of you.' Carl wiped the sweat from his brow. 'This gardening's thirsty work. Tea please, with two sugars. Eileen isn't it?'

'Elaine,' she corrected. 'Right you are.' Elaine made the tea in one of Jillian's favourite mugs and took it down the garden.

'Thanks. Elaine.' He took the cup and smiled at her. 'So, how long have you been working for Mrs Lazaridis' then?'

'I've been skivvying for her ladyship for a couple of months I guess.' She flopped down onto a nearby garden seat.

'I always find her to be lovely.' Carl took a sip from his tea and wondered when Jillian would be back from her gym class.

'Really? Well I could tell you a thing or two about her...' Elaine noticed a familiar figure in the kitchen window and shot off the chair. She hadn't expected Jillian back so soon and she ran back inside leaving a puzzled Carl to finish his drink.

Chapter 35

26th July 1984 – Sunny Dunes Holiday Camp – The Swimming Baths

The Locker Room

The matter of the unlikely people visiting the swimming baths was bothering Tony and he could feel in his bones that something untoward was afoot. There seemed to be a steady stream of Pontin's employees entering the building on a regular basis including: Darren from the amusement arcade; Gary the photographer; Frank from the accounts department and his very own Head Bluecoat, Roger. Judging by the short length of time they were in there and their suspiciously dry appearance upon leaving, it seemed unlikely they had been swimming lengths.

Also Tony had noticed when he walked past the fruit machines the other day that Darren had been sitting in his change booth with an odd, glazed look on his face. Likewise, he noticed Frank recently sitting on a bench near to the camp's entrance staring as if mesmerised by some rowing boats. He wondered if there was any connection between these young men's strangeness and Roger's peculiarity of late.

Conveniently forgetting that his own behaviour was far from exemplary, he became overwhelmed by a fanatical zeal to find out just what was going on. Rather than chomping at the bit any longer, there and then, he took himself off to the swimming baths.

Arriving at the poolside he found half a dozen children and some pensioners in the water being watched by a rather bored looking lifeguard named Carol. She was sitting on one of the towers and across from her was another ginger haired lifeguard with large ears called John. There was obviously nothing dodgy going on here at the moment.

'Hi, Mr Noble. Are you wanting to see Kevin?' Shouted Carol over the loud music. She was glad to have a distraction.

'Not especially. Why do you ask?' He called back, his ears pricking up with interest at her assumption he was seeking out Kevin. Now why would he be wanting Kevin he wondered?

'It's just that everyone seems to be after him for some reason at the minute.' She raised her hands in bafflement as to why Kevin's popularity had suddenly increased.

This is very interesting thought Tony and he moved closer to Carol so he could properly hear what she was saying. 'Where is now he anyway?'

'He should be along any moment. He swaps places with me at 2.00 pm.' Her thankfulness about this was evident.

'Ok, no worries. I was just checking up on the ... building. To see that it's been ... cleaned. I'll just go and er ... check through here.' Tony sidled off into the lifeguard's office. It was empty with just a few items of clothing lying about and almost silent apart from the slight buzz of vending machine in the corner. Each lifeguard had a locker with their name on and he wondered what personal things they kept inside. All of a sudden, he heard the sound of an opening door and he dived into one of the toilets.

Tony heard voices whispering and he climbed up onto the toilet seat so he could peer over the top of the cubicle to get a better view. It was Kevin arriving for his afternoon shift and he was with one of the waiters from the canteen.

'I've told you Wayne. You can't have anymore. Not if you haven't got any dosh.' Kevin sounded annoyed.

He was definitely selling something thought Tony.

'But please. It's pay day tomorrow. I promise I'll give you the money as soon as I get me wages.' Wayne sounded a desperate man.

'Come and see me tomorrow then.' Kevin folded his arms and glanced around the room before giving Wayne a scornful sneer. Tony ducked down, scared that he would be seen and almost lost his footing. As he struggled to regain his balance, his shoes made a slight squeaky sound. Kevin's eyes shot in the direction of the occupied toilet but the door was still slightly ajar and Tony couldn't be seen. He turned his attention back to the snivelling waiter. 'Get lost you loser. Come back and see me when you can pay for it.' He hissed, his eyes still warily scanning the room.

'But I need some now.' Wayne whimpered.

'Keep yer voice down nob head.' Kevin kept obsessively looking and listening, as if practising his Green Cross Code. When eventually satisfied there was nobody else there, he changed his tune. 'It'll cost you double then.'

'Just give me a little. Twenty quid's worth.' Wayne's eyes watched his dealer with relief as he eventually opened his locker door.

'Thirty, and it will be a little.' He took out a miniscule package, unwrapped it, put a sprinkle of white powder into an even tinier piece of foil and gave it to the grateful waiter.

'Now get lost and you'll bring me the dosh tomorrow. Right.' He gave Wayne a menacing growl and *Bingo* thought Tony.

14th April 2014 – The Lazaridis' House, Jesmond
A Malicious Little Troll

Carl put his mug down on the seat where the cleaning lady had been sitting a few minutes earlier. What a very strange person she was he thought and he didn't much like her. He wondered what rubbish she had been going to tell him about Jillian Lazaridis' because he had always found his boss to be a very nice lady. He enjoyed doing her gardening and being out in the open air. It was certainly more pleasant than the stress of being in the police force. Although he was retired with a good forces pension, the odd gardening job came in handy for the odd little treat or holiday with his wife.

Looking back over his years in the police and about some of the cases he had been involved with, Carl thought it was strange but it was always those unsolved cases that stuck in his mind. The ones when the perpetrators had never been brought to justice. He remembered one in particular from years ago, when he had been a young junior constable. The Entertainment's Manager at a local holiday camp had been shockingly murdered. Somebody had stabbed him in the back with a bread knife. The problem was that almost everyone who knew him had good reason to hate Tony Noble and the investigation had spent weeks going round in circles. Eventually, the case had been dropped because of insufficient evidence and Carl wondered if with the modern technology of today it could have been resolved. Certainly, most of the suspects would more than likely be still alive today, as unlike the victim they had all been fairly young.

Carl continued trimming the bushes and thought about the earlier conversation with the cleaning lady. Was it Eileen or Evelyn? Whatever her name was, he didn't like her. He wondered if should alert Jillian towards the fact that her cleaner was a malicious little troll. Any defamatory comments she had been about to make would have been more than likely fuelled by jealousy, of that he was almost certain.

Chapter 36

July 26th 1984 – Sunny Dunes Holiday Camp   – The Regency Lounge

Crème-de-la-Crème

Jill could barely contain her ecstasy when she discovered the contents of the letter lying on her desk. As she ripped open the envelope, she gave a whoop of joy upon discovering that not only had she been rewarded with the position of Entertainment's Manager at the Holiday Club Poseidon, she was due to start in a mere ten days' time. There would be no lean period this winter for Jill, scratching around for temporary jobs, demonstrating rubbish ironing board covers, or useless teasmades. Oh no, the crème-de-la-crème of Pontinental employees were rewarded with full year round contracts, including generous fully paid vacations as part of their package. Jill felt like she was at last moving in the right direction and had struck gold

Although there was nobody in the Entertainment's Office at present, she needed to be somewhere quiet so she could enjoy reading all of the details about her new job uninterrupted. She couldn't be bothered to walk back the distance to her own chalet. By now she reckoned the whist drive in the Regency Lounge would be over, so it shouldn't be busy in there. Jill skipped out of the office, bounced along the pavement and bounded up the steps next door. There were just a couple of punters drinking tea and she was sure they wouldn't have the slightest interest in her precious letter. She flopped down and reposed in comfort like a classical goddess in one of the shabby yellow chairs.

A closer study revealed The Holiday Club Poseidon was located at a place called Loutraki, which to her further delight she discovered was near Corinth in Greece. The country she had always wanted to visit: land of sunshine, souvlakis and the smashing of plates. She pictured herself in a polka dot bikini sipping retsina on the beach. Ten days. That wasn't very long to organise the purchase of flowing gowns to add to her new Greek wardrobe.

She knew of course that she had made the right decision to travel to Blackpool to meet old Fred Pontin in person. A few weeks after she had submitted her application, he had offered her an interview with one of his minions closer to the North East. But Jill had gone the extra mile and had actually enjoyed her adventure taking her new sports car for a spin across country. She had done her utmost to impress Mr Pontin with her business clout, organisational skills and womanly charms. She had known that wearing her new short tight skirt and low cut blouse would do the trick. He was left in no doubt that any Pontinental establishment under her management would be in the safest of hands. She had left Lancashire certain she'd had a thumbs up from Fred but nothing had been set in stone before the arrival of today's written confirmation.

At last, she would be her own boss and her days of being forced to fawn were over Tony were well and truly over. Jill certainly wouldn't be in the slightest bit sorry to leave them behind. The thought of him slobbering over her now made her stomach turn when compared with the Greek Adonis she might soon be meeting. Did Tony really imagine that she wasn't fully aware of what had been going on in the office with him and Debbie the other day? The fact was that she no longer cared. In the past, it had been in her own interest to turn a blind eye to his pathetic philandering. Although personally she could take or leave Debbie, Jill's pleasure had been in pulling the plug on Tony's advances with the new Bluecoat and queering his pitch.

It was with great relish that she would be telling Tony where he could shove his job and all things considered, it would be good to distance herself from the charity box business. Elaine had suspicion written all over her face and Jill had the feeling she wasn't alone.

The whole matter with Mandy had been most unpleasant but once she'd let be known to them that she knew what was going on, she had to go. While it had been a profitable scam for both of them, they must be by now surely living on borrowed time. The money that was currently lying in the safe, would be just the job for filling her suitcase with sunny clime clothes. However, getting her hands on all of it was more of a problem.

12th August 1987 - Holiday Club Poseidon, Loutraki (Corinth), Greece – Jill's Balcony

Pontinental' s Poseidon

Jill sat on her white balcony, enjoying morning coffee and a cigarette while gazing at the horizon where the cloudless cornflower sky merged with the turquoise of the sea. The Poseidon was attractively perched on a gentle hillside offering its guests not only splendid views of the coast but also close proximity to some of the ancient monuments of Corinth. Only a short walk away was the magnificent Temple of Apollo but few of the punters ventured off the site, fearful of what they might encounter. The closest they came to any experience of Ancient Greek mythology, was meeting the big plastic statute of the Poseidon God that stood at the entrance gate to the holiday club. He brandished his trident in a threatening manner and his green face bore a more than passing similarity to that of Fred Pontin's.

This would now be Jill's third season as Entertainment's Manager at the Pontinental Poseidon and much as she loved living in Greece, she was beginning to feel a little jaded with the holiday club lifestyle. It was relentless and it seemed she was on duty 24/7. Some bikini-clad punters below settled themselves by the pool into their toasting chairs for the day and one of them spotted Jill and shrieked with delight. Jumping up and down she waved as if Jill were a famous pop star. Automatically, Jill painted on her profession's smile and waved back with all the enthusiasm she could muster.

Although the holiday makers imagined themselves having an authentic Greek experience, this was far from the reality. No locals were employed here and certainly no Greek was spoken. The food was guaranteed by the brochures to be *just what you'd eat at home*. None of the *foreign nonsense here* that might bring the *delicate constitutions* of the British down with some *nasty stomach bug*. Likewise, the wine with dinner was a safe *Blue Nun*, rather than that peculiar Retsina which Fred Pontin himself had apparently declared to be *more like a cleaning product than anything his guests should be drinking.*

However on each Thursday to be fair, there was a Greek Night. Plates of Moussaka, which was more akin to a Lancashire hotpot, were served up to the brave guests. While the music from *Zorba the Greek* was played, a young Bluecoat named Nigel from Accrington, paraded about as a *Evzonne* Guard, in his red hat, white mini-skirt and massively pom-pommed shoes.

When Jill had first arrived, all this artifice had seemed really quite charming. After the terrible ordeal at Sunny Dunes Camp she was just relieved to be out of the country and away from the place. Even after three years, there were so many questions that remained unanswered. What had actually happened? Jill now felt truly shameful about the fact that she and Tony had been stealing all of that money from those charity boxes. When she thought of all of those people parting with their hard earned cash, she felt sick. What could she have been thinking of? But then all of a sudden Tony was dead and all that money had just mysteriously disappeared. Who had committed both of these crimes had never been discovered but there were plenty of suspects. She herself was included and after all those awful police interviews, Jill had just been glad to escape from the place. Thank goodness the charity boxes had disappeared and she didn't have those on her conscience.

Yes Jill was certainly pleased it was her day off. She could have a welcome break from organising the Bluecoats, dealing with the guests and persistently smiling. And more to the point she was feeling more than a little excited. Last week, when she had been having a coffee in a little taverna close to the Temple of Apollo, she had got chatting to a lovely Greek man. From the outset he was clearly besotted with her. It seemed he was on holiday, staying with family in Corinth. Strangely enough, although he had been brought up in Greece, he now lived in Newcastle of all places. Here, his father owned not one, but a string of Greek restaurants. The more she found out about Theodore Lazaridis' the more there was to like and guess who she was having dinner with that evening?

Chapter 37

26th July 1984 – Sunny Dunes Holiday Camp –Debbie and Siobhan's Chalet

Feelings of Deja-Vu

Once the whist drive was over, Stephen was desperate to know the details of what had happened to Debbie. So, he suggested that they went back to her chalet, instead of his as Mike might well be there. Yet when they arrived, Siobhan was sitting on her bed waiting for Debbie's return.

'Debbie … Stephen, has she told you what has happened? Has she told you about what Tony Noble did?' Siobhan had been trying to cut down on the cigarettes lately because Debbie didn't smoke. But a heavy fug in the air and a full ashtray proved her good intentions had been forgotten.

'No, not yet, but that's why I'm here.' Stephen shook his head, sat down on a chair and put his elbows on his knees in readiness to listen.

'You won't believe what the bastard has gone and done now …' Siobhan began, as she lit yet another fag.

'Oh there's nothing I wouldn't put past that man. Don't get me started …' Stephen's face usually so brimming with mischief grew serious for once.

'Well I think that Suzanne played a big part in what happened …' Debbie began her story slowly, searching carefully for the precise words to explain the sad chronology of events that had happened.

'I'm so sorry Debbie. I just didn't like leaving you when you seemed so sick …' Siobhan once again, felt the guilt trickling through her body like toxic treacle.

'It's all right Siobhan.' Debbie forced a half-smile. 'She'd just been waiting for any opportunity to get me into trouble.'

'She's just jealous of you, but anyway go on ...' Stephen was rocking backwards and forwards on the chair, urging her to get to the point.

Debbie pressed forward with her tale. 'Well, the first thing was that Roger came knocking on the door early this morning to say that Tony wanted to see me. There was something strange about his behaviour, but that in itself wasn't anything unusual because Roger has generally been very odd recently. Nevertheless, he did seem particularly agitated and I suppose that should have been a warning that something was amiss.' Debbie paused for a moment, to mull over Roger's peculiar sniffing, jerking and nose bleeds, before continuing once more. 'So, I went over to the Entertainment's Office and it was clear from the outset that I was in Tony's bad books. It was obvious that he had been led to believe by Suzanne that I was just swinging the lead.' She narrowed her eyes picturing Suzanne in full flow, spouting her spiteful venom.

'Well that's one thing that doesn't surprise me.' Stephen said while helping himself to one of Siobhan's cigarettes.

'Me neither, but I just didn't think he would be so ready to believe her.' Debbie watched Stephen and wondered if maybe she should start smoking. It seemed she had already become a passive smoker, so it couldn't do her any further harm *and* it might just help. 'Anyway,' she continued. 'He just began having a go at me. Saying I was lucky to have a job here and that my starting half way through the season, was an inconvenience to everyone. Then he accused me of being unreliable, lazy, and worst of all ... that I looked like a *freak.*'

'He said *what*?' Stephen started coughing and scattered his fag ash all over the carpet.

'He said I looked like something off *The Rocky Horror Show*. Imagine how that made me feel?' Debbie's face held the expression of a five year old child — crushed and humiliated.

'The bastard.' Her friends chorused in unison.

'But then things started to get really weird. He seemed to be implying that there was something dodgy about my reference from Devon last year.' As her eyes travelled from Siobhan to Stephen she noticed they were both giving each other peculiar looks.

'In what way?' Stephen asked.

'He seemed to think that Simon Sinclair had only given me a good reference because…'

'Because what?' Stephen had a horrible feeling he knew where this was going

'Well, Simon Sinclair was a lovely man, and he was always very kind to me but not in any inappropriate way. I mean … he was as camp as a row of tents.' Debbie flushed with embarrassment. She wondered if she had offended her friend by making a faux-pas using such a hackneyed turn of phrase. 'Sorry Stephen.'

'No offence taken.' Stephen dismissed the clichéd comment with a swish of the hand as he was dealing with much more disturbing feelings of deja-vu. He and Siobhan locked worried eyes before giving their full attention once more to Debbie. 'Go on,' he said, but had a deep sense of foreboding about what next was to be revealed.

'He was implying that Simon Sinclair and I must have been having a *thing* going on.' Debbie had been mortified because nothing could have been further from the truth. Simon had been a wonderful man who had reminded her a little of Lionel Blair and had taken great pleasure in choreographing all the Bluecoat shows. He had been full of praise and encouragement for Debbie. Simon had always been the perfect gentleman and the complete opposite of Tony Noble. 'And then the horrible man said that if I wanted to keep my job well I needed to ...' Debbie twisted her face and looked uncomfortable. 'Well, he tried to get me to sit on his knee. He was patting his leg and leering at me and it was awful. I didn't know what I should do for the best. Then thankfully ... Jill walked in.' Debbie sighed and felt an instant relief after sharing the details of her ordeal with her friends.

'Unbelievable, that man,' Stephen shook his head while processing this information. Yes, he thought Tony's behaviour had been despicable but he realised the scenario could have been so much worse and would have been if not for Jill's timing. He felt it in his gut that this was not the end of the matter and Debbie needed to watch her back. 'What did Jill say? Wasn't she furious?' Stephen knew that if Jill suspected something going on between her precious Tony and Debbie, then this would only make these grim matters worse.

'No. I'm not sure she knew what was going on. But I didn't think I would ever be so pleased to see Jill.' She looked for a reaction from either of her friends but neither of them seemed to be listening.

Siobhan moved across the room to Stephen and whispered. 'Do you think we should tell her Stephen?'

Stephen nodded and Debbie was confused. It seems she wasn't the only one with stories to tell and it was now Stephen's turn.

'Debbie, there's been an awful lot of strange things going on here at Sunny Dunes Holiday Camp this year,' began Stephen and Debbie wondered what she was going to learn about next.

15th April 2014 – The Olympian Restaurant, Jesmond

Teddie's Ears Prick Up

Teddie had first listened in on the conversation between Destiny Chambers and Stefan Sondheim to assess how Sophia was dealing with this awkward celebrity. He could justify his spying on his staff and customers because this helped the smooth running of his flagship restaurant. Furthermore, it was quite cosy in his little room with a comfy swivel chair and a varied supply of biscuits ready to hand.

Just as he would have imagined him to be, Stefan Sondheim was being rude and shouting at the poor girl. However, Teddie was also intrigued as to why the usually very glamorous writer was decked out in this peculiar and unflattering garb. She looked like one of those Amish women. Teddie knew who Destiny Chambers was for not only did she live locally and was often in the news, but also because she was a regular customer at The Olympian and they had exchanged pleasantries on many occasions. Teddie liked her because not only was she easy on the eye, but she was always very complimentary about his food. He had noticed one of her books lying around recently at home. So, if his wife enjoyed reading her books, she no doubt love to hear any of the latest gossip about her.

It seemed Destiny wasn't to be using this name for her latest book. She wanted to be taken seriously as a writer. So, she was going to use the name Martha now was she? Ah, that must be the reason for the ridiculous attire. He couldn't imagine that her agent would be too pleased about this and Stefan clearly wasn't at all impressed. Teddie was sure the type of women who bought her books would also prefer to read the flowery words of the elegant and charming Destiny, rather than the earnest rantings of some miserable old Martha.

Then, they starting talking about some guy they knew from years ago who was working now at a cinema. Apparently, he had been some bigwig in the past, owning nightclubs and such like. Teddie wasn't really paying much attention because the conversation had become rather boring. He made himself another cup of coffee and was taking a bite out of a Penguin biscuit when he heard the words Bluecoat mentioned. His ears pricked up as the word Pontins was mentioned too. When he had first met Jillian wasn't that who she was working for? She had been running a holiday park in Corinth, that had been part of a franchise called Pontinental. Jillian had explained to him that it was a pun on Fred Pontin's name and he had set up camps at popular hotspots on the continent during the 1970's. However, he was sure that before then she had worked at a holiday camp not too far away in nearby Whitley Bay. It had long closed down but Teddie wondered if these local celebrities had worked alongside his wife. Jillian would just love all this and he looked for his little yellow note book. He needed to write all of this down so he didn't forget the details.

Long ago Destiny and Stefan had worked together as Bluecoats. So had this bloke called Roger who was currently down on his luck. Then there was another person called Mike who seemed to have a special role at the holiday camp holding up pieces of cardboard. He was now working at the large Tesco store in Gateshead. For some reason Roger had been thrown out of the store by this Mike.Teddie's μίκρσ γκρί κυτταρα (little grey cells) were going crazy. His pencil scribbled quickly across the page and he couldn't wait to relay all of this information back to his wife. Wouldn't it be an amazing coincidence if Jillian knew all these people? It could also be good publicity for his restaurant and he took a couple of shots of Destiny and Stefan on his phone cam.

Chapter 38

26th July 1984 – Whitley Bay – The Robinson family house

Family Lunch

The Whitley Bay Family Robinson was sitting around the family dining table waiting for their Sunday lunch to be served. It was a large room with mock wooden beams, casement windows and reproduction portraits of Tudor monarchs on the walls. Jean Robinson was a massive fan of historical novels set in this period, but often Mike found that Henry VIII with his overbearing presence and little piggy eyes watching him as he ate quite put him off his food.

Mike's father, Ronnie was unusually quiet and with a surly expression on his face was reading a newspaper. His sister, Jennifer was in her own little world, dancing in the corner of the room and singing along to her Walkman. By the repetition of the word *Thriller* being shouted in Jennifer's squawky voice, Mike assumed she was listening to Michael Jackson. Although this couldn't have been guessed by the particular notes she was shrieking. True to form, his sister was being annoying but it could have been a lot worse. Nevertheless, he wondered, as he watched her prancing about like the living dead, wiggling her fingers in time to the music, how come they were all stained red. Maybe it was supposed to be zombie blood, to make her feel more in character.

Eventually, his mother, Jean arrived from the kitchen. She had changed into a pretty dress in daffodil yellow and was wearing her favourite perfume, which Mike thought smelled of talcum powder. He supposed his mother was a quite a good looking woman for someone in her forties but Mike couldn't see what on earth she saw in his father. Ronnie's bald head looked like golf ball, his nose was the shape of a potato and he seemed much older than his wife.

Jean was carrying an enormous joint of meat, a dish of potatoes roasted in goose fat and plates brimming with the usual Yorkshire puddings, parsnips, carrots cut in batons, cabbage and broccoli. There were no peas as Jean Robinson couldn't abide little round vegetables.

'So Ronnie,' announced Jean. 'If you would do the honours, I'll go grab the gravy from the kitchen. Come on Jenny love, turn that off and come and sit down for lunch.'

Ronnie obediently started to carve the beef up but Jennifer continued her caterwauling in the corner.

'Come on Jenny you don't want to let your food get cold now do you?' Jean wrinkled her brow, put the gravy boat down on the table and walked over to her daughter. To Jennifer's annoyance, her mother removed her headphones and dragged her to the table.

'But Mam, I was just working on my latest routine ...' Jennifer fumed as her beloved Walkman was confiscated and placed in a nearby fruit bowl for the duration of the meal. Today she had her dark hair in bunches fastened with ribbons on each side of her head and was wearing her favourite pale pink tracksuit. It was covered in dark red stains where she had rubbed her hands.

'Not now, it's time for our family lunch.' Jean gave her daughter a stern look, followed by a full beam of pleasure at the sight of her family all together round the table for a meal. Ronnie was busy putting generous servings of prime rib roast onto each of the four plates. Mike's mouth watered, for as usual, his mother's cooking smelt delicious.

'Well, this looks great Mam.' Mike picked up his knife and fork and banged them together before starting to devour the tasty food.

'As long as everyone enjoys it Mike.' She leaned across the table and rubbed her son's hair affectionately. 'So how did my lads get on with the golf today?'

'I bet Mike was really rubbish. I bet Mike couldn't play golf for toffee.' Jennifer placed one thumb on her nose and wiggled her bloody fingers in the direction of her elder brother.

'Shut up you little cretin. What would you know?' Mike prodded his sister on the shoulder. 'It was really great Mam. I was so sure that Dad was going to thrash me. I mean he's been playing it for years hasn't he? I thought it was just a boring game for oldies but no, now I get it. Would you believe it I only scored four holes in one? It was fantastic.' Mike looked to his father for verification but wasn't surprised when only a sour look arrived in his direction.

'That's great, isn't it Ronnie? 'Jean was feeling so proud of both of her boys and she trilled. 'I bet you were so chuffed that our son seems to have taken to golf like a duck to water.'

'It was beginner's luck that's all.' Ronnie glared at them. 'My old knees were giving me a bit of gip and I couldn't get a proper swing going.' Ronnie mumbled and concentrated his efforts on attacking a Yorkshire pudding.

'Don't worry Daddy. You'll beat him next time,' piped up Jennifer and her eyes lit up as she fanned the flames, enjoying the tension between her father and brother.

'So when are we going again Dad?' Mike was feeling pleased with himself. Just for once he had the upper hand on his father.

'I don't know, I'm very busy at work at the moment,' muttered Ronnie.

'Well I'm not surprised. Not one little bit son.' Jean smiled at her son while she adding some mustard to her plate. 'I knew you'd be a chip off the old block when it came to golf. You know Ronnie, doesn't Mike *always* make us so proud with his aptitude for sports? Do you remember at school how fabulous he was at rugby, basketball and cricket?' Even though she herself hated sport with a passion, Jean always enjoyed watching her son play. 'What about that summer when he was fourteen and he did that fabulous Fosbury Flip in the high jump? The comments on his reports for physical education were always so marvellous weren't they?'

'It was actually called the Fosbury Flop Jean.' Ronnie gave his wife a disparaging look. 'I think Mike's exhibition on that occasion was more of an accident than a deliberate tactic on his part.' Ronnie looked to the ceiling and rolled his eyes. 'Today was just beginner's luck. Don't you think that'll happen again son. Mark my words.' He jabbed a fork with a piece of broccoli on the end of it in the direction of Mike. 'And the only reason the comments on the report seemed so good was because every other grade for the other subjects was so bloody diabolical.'

'Ronnie, not in front of Jennifer.' A shocked Jean stood up to place her hands over her daughter's ears to protect them from the conversation that Jennifer was patently revelling in. 'Now then, Mike's doing all right for himself aren't you dearie?' said Jean. 'You know, lots of young folk would love to be Bluecoats and just look where it has led some people's careers. I mean what about…' She paused and thought for a moment. 'Jimmy Tarbuck and Des O'Connor for example?'

'You need to get your facts straight woman, I think you will find they were Redcoats.' A little smile started hovering around Ronnie's lips. 'But anyway, what can Mike actually do? Can he sing? No. Can he play a musical instrument? No. Can he tell jokes? No.' Ronnie pulled one of his nasty taunting faces at his son which Jennifer copied with delight.

'Actually Dad I've been working on an act as a comedian.' Mike placed the knife and fork down either side of his plate.

'Really?' Ronnie spat out some of the gravy in his mouth along with a great guffaw of laughter. 'And you have actually done this have you? Have you ever done anything at all on the stage?'

'No, not yet but soon I will soon … and my role is very important in the Bluecoat shows.' He picked up his cutlery once more to eat and try to deflect attention away from his show business aspirations.

'I knew it Ronnie.' She beamed in adoration at her son. 'What do you do son? Our Mike in the famous Bluecoat shows. We'll have to go and watch him.' Jean couldn't wait to go and see her only son perform on the stage. Her mind began racing. She would wear her favourite blue frock with the string of pearls that had once been her mother's, and of course she would have her hair set specially at the hairdressers. Ronnie would dress in his smart suit and Jennifer in her party frock.

'I kind of do the stage management and props,' mumbled Mike.

'Stage and props manager. Fancy that Ronnie.' Jean's voice became breathy as it often did when she was excited.

'Admit it son,' growled his father. 'You have no talents or skills whatsoever and the only reason you've got a job as a Bluecoat is because … well let's face facts. It's because Tony is my mate and he owed me a favour. So don't you forget it.' At the very mention of that horrible man's name, Mike felt sick and he just wanted to escape from his awful father and claustrophobic family home.

Mike saw the clock showed two thirty.' I'm sorry Mam. I hadn't realised that was the time. It's getting late and I need to get back because …'

'But you've not had your pudding yet. It's your favourite, apple pie, and it's not very late at all.' Jean didn't want her son to go so soon.

'I really do. You see I'm going out to the cinema with my … new girlfriend tonight.' He informed then with an affected nonchalance.

'Girlfriend. Oh, Mike that's so exciting. What's her name? What film are you going to see?' Jean pictured a possible new daughter-in-law addition to her family.

'Just leave it Mam. I need to go. Have you got my washing?' Mike just couldn't get out of the place fast enough.

'Mike's got a girlfriend. Mike's got a girlfriend.' chanted the annoying Jennifer, jumping up and down in her brother's face.

Jean went to the kitchen and returned with a bag full of clothes all clean and ironed. She winced. 'Except, there's just one problem. Somehow, all of your white shirts have turned pink in the wash. I don't know however that can have happened because I am always so careful …'

Mike stared at the bag horrified. 'I can't wear those Mam. What am I going to do?' Pink girly shirts. The day was just getting worse and this icing on the cake was the last thing Mike needed.

'Well at least you say you've got yourself a girlfriend … *at last*. I was going to say that if the cap fits.' Ronnie smirked to himself, as Jennifer hid her pink tell-tail fingers in her pocket alongside the bottle of cochineal.

13th April 2014 – The Metro from Central Station to Gateshead

Two Brown Eyes

Roger closed the door of his Stowell Street flat and snuck down a back lane. He needed to get a move on, because he didn't want to be late for his shift at the cinema. The cut brought him on to the bottom of Westgate Hill, near the Tyne Theatre and as he turned his head to the left, he saw the new *Roxie Nightclub*. This was where he had seen Stephen yesterday. He imagined Stephen's life to be a whirl of champagne-swilling parties and fun but Roger didn't envy him. Not one little bit. That lifestyle had brought him little joy. Now he had this much simpler one with few worries, a modest flat and regular job. He could pretend that he was safe but was he really? Even now, he was forced to be constantly looking over his shoulder because he knew fine well that certain issues had still not been resolved. Dark figures lurked in the shadows and crouched behind walls. He cast a glance behind him but there was nobody there.

Soon he arrived at Central Station and jumped on a train. He had only one stop to Gateshead and the ride took a mere matter of minutes. The train was quite crowded but he had the unnerving feeling that he was being watched. He felt sick. It must be his imagination. In front of him, at the top of a carriage was a man wearing a black woollen hat pulled down low. He wore a long dark coat and a scarf pulled over his nose and mouth. This was not a cold day. All that could be seen of his face were the two brown eyes … staring at him.

 Roger gulped. The train pulled to a halt. The doors flung open and Roger bolted. He ran like the wind and didn't look behind him. Not even a quick glance. Up the escalator he fled and across the street. Over Trinity Square, he pelted past Tesco and into the welcome darkness of the *Vue* Cinema. Was he safe? Nobody seemed to have followed him but he couldn't be sure. Roger was perpetually exhausted by these worries.

Chapter 39

July 26th 1984 – Sunny Dunes Holiday Camp – The Swimming Baths

Swimming's Funny Effects

It was half past six, and there was about thirty minutes before the bingo was due to begin. Tony finished his can and put out his cigarette, wondering best how to tackle this situation with that scummy drug dealer. After some deliberation, he decided strangely that adopting the moral high ground was the best course of action. All thoughts of blackmail, forcing himself on young women and charity boxes were conveniently set to one side, as he made his way over to the swimming baths on his crusade. Drugs were a serious matter, if Fred Pontin or even worse, the press, got hold of any of this … well, it would spell the end of all of their jobs and Sunny Dunes Campsite. He felt sure of that.

He marched into the building and headed straight for the poolside. Up on one tower sat the ginger-haired vacuous John, whose eyes were moving back and forth following the orange bathing cap of the one solitary swimmer in the water. Opposite him was Kevin, who quickly became agitated, spotting Tony's entrance and shuffled around uncomfortably in his chair as if sitting on a bed of nails. Well, so the filthy pusher ought to be too, thought Tony.

'Kevin. I want a word with you?' Tony's voice boomed above the sound of Prince and *Purple Rain*.

'Well the baths doesn't close till seven so if you want to see me then …' Kevin mumbled although Tony couldn't hear.

'Get down here now.' Tony roared at the top of his voice, as there was no way the toad was worming his way out of this conversation.

'Okay, whatever.' As Kevin slid down the steps, John looked over and took his eyes fleetingly off the lone bather. Kevin sighed, shook his head and shrugged his shoulders before walking over to the door that Tony was kindly holding open for him. Then Kevin was ushered into the staff locker room.

'I know what you are *up to,* you know.' Tony cut to the chase.

'What are you on about? I'm doing my afternoon shift. I'm a lifeguard.' Kevin curled his top lip into an Elvis-like sneer.

'Come come. Don't play the innocent with me.' Tony hissed and put his face, way too close for comfort into Kevin's face.

'I don't know what you're on about granddad.' He pushed Tony's shoulder away. 'But I do think you need to take a chill pill.'

'Chill pill.' Tony smirked. 'That's what you'd advise is it? Interesting.' He raised an eyebrow.

'I don't know what's rattled your cage ...' Kevin put his hands in his tracksuit pockets and pulled himself up to his full height, which was still shorter than Tony's.

'I reckon if you have a long hard think, you'll know exactly to what I'm referring.' Tony held on to Kevin's chin so he had no choice but to hold eye contact.

'Get yer hands off me. Are you sure you've got the right person?' Kevin pushed Tony's hand away.

'Kevin. I've had my suspicions about odd goings-on in here for days now. You'd be surprised what a good view I have from my office. Oh yes. I 've noticed plenty of the Pontin's staff visiting the swimming baths.' He nodded his head knowingly.

'Well it's a swimming pool and they're allowed you know. Swimming's good exercise for you.' Kevin eyed the buttons straining around the stomach on Tony's shirt and thought he could do with shedding a few pounds but wished desperately that the snoop would just bugger off.

'Well I don't think these men were coming to clock up any lengths, if you get my meaning. I think they were coming for something else altogether and something not good for them, if you get what I mean. I know that my head Bluecoat, Roger's been hanging out at your baths for quite often frequently and he's been acting very strangely…'

'Well what's that loser's behaviour got to do with me?' Kevin clenched his teeth together so his words came out like a snarl.

'Not only him but that …' Tony tapped his forefinger. 'Darren, from the arcade.' He tugged on a middle finger. 'Gary, as I think he's called, as well the photographer and oh yes … and that Frank, I believe that's his name. The one who works in accounts.' He waggled all five fingers in Kevin's face. 'They have all been coming in here, looking shifty and then leaving with not a single wet hair. Then walking around the camp scaring the children with their glazed faces and manic expressions.'

'So what? Swimming has a funny effect on some people.' Kevin thought Tony might have some suspicions but couldn't possibly have any proof. Roger was hardly likely to cut off his nose to spite his face and shop him, was he?

'I don't think this is anything to do with swimming Kevin. You're dealing drugs, aren't you.' Tony spat out the words.

'Don't be mental. Why would I do that?' Kevin still hoped he could brazen this one out.

'Well as it happens I was watching you in this very room with that young waiter just a few hours ago.' Tony remembered how uncomfortable he'd been perched in that toilet but it had been worth it.

'What you on about?' Kevin was now like a caged tiger pacing the room.

'I was in that cubicle watching and listening Kevin and I know what happened.' Tony pointed to the door behind him.

Kevin remembered that he had thought he had heard a noise from that direction and now knew the bastard wasn't bluffing. 'I can explain ... He was just a bit short of money and wanted to buy a present for his mam's birthday ...'

'Cut the crap. You're dealing drugs and it's got to stop.' Tony's voice dropped several levels in volume and he changed his tone so that he sounded like a disappointed parent.

'Are you not going to shop me then?' Kevin knew the game was up.

'Well, that depends.' The edge crept back once more into his voice.

'Depends on what?' Kevin was baffled and couldn't see where he was going with this.

'Well, firstly it stops now. You understand?' Tony asked.

Kevin nodded, 'Ok.' He had no choice had he?

'And you will give all the profit you've made to me.' He said this as matter-of-factly as if merely ordering a beer from the bar.

'Hey, but...'

'You choose.' Once more, Tony loomed closely into the lifeguard's face. 'You won't only just lose your job though. This is a serious matter for the police isn't it?'

15th April 2014 – The Olympian, Jesmond

Addressing Certain Elephants

Both Martha and Stefan pushed the food around on their plates as neither had much of an appetite. Both were completely unaware that their conversation was being listened to.

'What's going on Destiny?' asked a glum-faced Stefan.

'I don't know.' She shook her head.

'These coincidences.' He threw down his knife and fork angrily, soiling the white tablecloth with red tomato sauce. 'It's all too much, don't you think?'

'It was never going to go away though was it?' Martha bit her lip.

'Well after all this time. I mean it was twenty years ago wasn't it?' He knew it was even longer than this, but liked to round down on the passage of time.

'A man was murdered. Tony Noble was killed in case you've forgotten.' The elephant in the room was finally addressed and the words said that had been unspoken for so long.

'Nobody's ever going to forget that are they? And it doesn't help with us being famous does it?' Stefan had always feared that someone at some point would have a field day with the information that both Destiny Chambers and himself were suspects in an ancient murder case.

'I'm amazed that social media hasn't already picked up on it.' But she realised that with all these cans of worms being opened, it was only a matter of time.

Martha stared at Stefan's face, seeing the ghost of the hatred for Tony she had witnessed there weekly, when Tony gave his fraudulent charity box speech. Also, the night he had told her and Siobhan the sorry tale of his little brother Andy. Likewise, Stefan remembered Debbie's fury and sadness when Tony had called her a freak and tried to get his leg over.

Chapter 40

26th July 1984 – Sunny Dunes Holiday Camp – Siobhan and Debbie's Chalet

Stephen Spills the Beans

'Do you know I just hate that man so much,' began Stephen. 'And it all started with the charity boxes and his greediness?' After Debbie had shared the details of her nasty experience with Tony earlier, it was now Stephen's turn to spill his beans. 'Do you know on a Friday night, it's like he casts a spell on those poor punters? Some of them save up all year for their holiday here and then he persuades them to stick all of their hard-earned, leftover cash in those bloody boxes.'

'To be sure, I bet some of them haven't even got any money to buy food when they get home,' Siobhan added and went to turn on the kettle. She suspected that this was going to be a long story and some further tea sustenance would be necessary.

'Well, I have noticed how generous some of them are but I suppose it's for a good cause.' Debbie had been flabbergasted but nevertheless impressed that first week, when she had seen all those notes being pulled out of wallets, purses and pockets to be stuffed into the tins.

'That's what they'd have you believe isn't it?' All the usual merriment had completely evaporated from Stephen's demeanour . His voice had become deeper and all the familiar campness had been replaced by the gravitas of a Shakespearian tragedy actor. Only the hair belonged to the Stephen they knew.

'They?' asked Debbie.

'Jill and Tony ... but I'll come to that presently.' Stephen paused and put his head in his hands. 'There is something about myself I need you to know about first and it's something really terrible. You see, I had a little brother called Andrew. He was known as Andy and he was two years younger than me and he had this terrible disease. Leukaemia it's called. It's a type of blood cancer.'

'I'm so sorry to hear that.' Although Debbie had heard of this condition, she knew little about it.

'Anyway, he died when he was ten years old ... but he'd suffered so much and it was awful. All that chemotherapy he went through and well ... I still find it hard to think about. But anyway I'll get to the point I'm making. When I first came here at the beginning of the season, I saw the charity boxes collection at the end of the week and they made me feel happy. You see, I thought that by raising money for children like my little brother, it might make their miserable lives a little more bearable. Andy would always have loved to go to somewhere like Disneyland, but we never had enough money for anything like that.' Siobhan handed Stephen a tissue, as the tears were now streaming down his face.

'Your poor little brother Stephen, but it must have been awful for you as well, to be sure,' added Siobhan. This story was news to Siobhan as well, as it was really only since Debbie had arrived that she too had become good friends with Stephen.

'Yes it was, and my parents too. I don't think that they have ever really got over it.' Stephen blew his nose. 'Anyway, on one Friday night I mentioned my brother to Tony as he was putting out the boxes and I was surprised how interested he was. He was hanging on my every word and then asking for precise details about the treatments and the horrible side effects. I thought he was being caring and compassionate at first but when I look back it was like he was a horrible vampire drinking up my family's grief.'

'Is that why you hate him so much?' Debbie would never have imagined Stephen capable of having a serious conversation like this.

'I haven't even started yet.' There was a glint in his eye and a glimpse of the old Stephen returned for the briefest of moments. 'The next Friday night, you'll not believe this. He was doing his patter and getting the sympathy note from everybody, talking about *his* son called Andy. And the bastard repeated every single word I had told him about my brother. I couldn't believe my ears.'

'The bastard,' gasped Siobhan. 'He didn't even bother to change the name.'

'No he just pretended *my Andy* was his own his own flesh and blood. *His* son, but he's never had any children. He's much too selfish for that.' Stephen cradled the cup of tea in his hands as if he were cold and he was grateful for some warmth, even though it was the middle of summer.

'I know it must have been terrible for you Stephen but at least if some good comes out of it.' Debbie put her hand on his arm and gave it a reassuring squeeze. 'If some of those poor children get to go on lovely holidays with their families and make good use of the precious time they have left well …'

'No, but that's just it. They don't.' Stephen's watery eyes looked into those of his friend with fury.

'What do you mean?' Debbie agreed with Stephen that Tony had been devious and mean stealing his brother's identity but nevertheless it was for a good cause.

'It's Tony and Jill. She's his accomplice and they take all that money for themselves. None of it goes to any sick children.' Siobhan spelt out the truth to Debbie because this was the part of the story that she did know.

13th April 2014 –Tesco, Gateshead

A Piece of Trash

Back on the shop floor in Tesco, Mike was watching a familiar figure sprint across Trinity Square with a look of sheer terror on his face. What on earth was wrong with the man and who or what could he be running away from? He had sensed from the moment Roger made himself known to him that this could only spell trouble. What had happened at Pontins in the summer of '84 needed to stay there. The re-emergence of Roger was just the first step towards the rotting log being lifted to expose that long hidden away conundrum. Soon, the place would be wriggling with Bluecoats, police, questions, accusations until finally the murderer of Tony Noble would at last be brought to justice. However, it wasn't a given they would get the right person was it?

Mike started pacing up and down. He straightened a pile of newspapers before looking once more out of the window to see Roger diving into the cinema complex. He needed to calm down. Just because the man was in some sort of bother, there wasn't necessarily any connection with himself was there? There could be millions of reasons why Roger had landed himself in the shit. The last few memories he had of Roger at Pontins were ones when he had seemed drug crazed and off his head. More than likely, he had umpteen unpaid debts and dealers after him.

Walking over to the clothing section, he spotted a cardy which had fallen on the floor and placed it neatly back on its hanger. Everything was still fine and dandy he needed to remind himself. The sleeping dogs were still lying. Mike's only actual problem was sorting out his divorce which annoying as it was, when all things were considered, it no longer seemed insurmountable.

Suddenly, an image of a befuddled Roger lying amidst all the rubbish flashed into his mind and overwhelmed him with guilt. Possibly he had treated the man shabbily. Without doubt, his old Head Bluecoat had appeared genuinely delighted to see him and eager to renew their acquaintance. Obviously, Roger had completely let slip from his mind that mortifying incident in the Entertainment's Office. However, when all was said and done, it was Tony who had been the villain of the piece. The unscrupulous Entertainment's Manager had been the one who had taken advantage of the situation and made Mike's life a misery. Stupid Roger had merely got the wrong end of the stick. And now, when the poor man was clearly down on his uppers, Mike the bully had thrown him out of the store, as if he were a piece of trash. Perhaps he ought to go over to the *Vue* Cinema to see if he was all right but then, maybe not.

Among the tins of fruit he could see that horrible Elaine who had had the gall to try and play almost the same game as Tony had with him. But Mike was no longer a young lad of twenty, she was of little consequence and times had moved on. But how had she picked up on their being a connection between him and Roger? She was clearly a witch and he pictured her in a pointy hat and long black cloak being burned at the stake along with the Bird Woman. Perhaps Linda, his wife could be added to the gathering too just for good measure? At least momentarily that old crone Elaine had the sense to be keeping her head down and doing her job of stacking the shelves. Mind, he was definitely keeping a watchful eye on her. One false move and she would be finding herself without a job. It would give him great pleasure to hand the dreadful woman her P45. He didn't trust her inch and the sooner she was sacked the better.

Chapter 41

26th July 1984 – Sunny Dunes Holiday Camp – Debbie and Siobhan's chalet

Turn a Blind Eye

That afternoon in Debbie and Siobhan's chalet, the shocking revelations continued unfolding. When Debbie had related what had happened to her in Tony's office, the others kept quiet and let her speak. Debbie realised she ought to be very grateful for Jill's arrival because if not for her, Tony's advances would have gone much further. Siobhan told Debbie that she needed to watch her back at all times as knives were definitely out to get her. She must make sure that she was never alone with that lecherous old goat and steering clear of that bitch Suzanne would be no bad thing either. Siobhan was beginning to wonder if act of sharing a chalet with her jinxed Bluecoats because she couldn't forget what had happened first with Mandy, and now Debbie.

When Stephen had told the heart-breaking tale of his little brother Andy, Siobhan realised that this explained his peculiar reaction each Friday night, when Tony told his sob story to the holidaymakers.

'Of course, it all makes sense now Stephen, so it does.' Siobhan felt she had learned more about Stephen in the past half hour than she had in the last three months. 'I've seen the way you watch Tony when he talks about his little boy that died.'

'Excuse me Siobhan, imaginary little boy to be more accurate,' corrected Stephen, with waspish bitterness.

Debbie cuddled her pillow with the black and white bat design and tried to process all this information. 'I can't believe that he pretended your little brother was his own son.'

'Well, he still does. And I will have to watch him blether on about it again tonight, won't I? Every week it's like he's driving a knife through my heart.' A touch of the old theatricality was returning to Stephen's delivery as he placed his hand on his forehead.

'The whole thing makes me sick,' growled Stephen. 'I mean, haven't you noticed Jill swanning around in her fancy clothes and driving her flash car. We all know where the money for those have come from, don't we? Their wages aren't that good. Did you know Tony's renowned for having a gambling problem as well? He's been declared bankrupt three times in the past. On so many levels he should be not only sacked but locked away in jail.' Stephen lit another of Siobhan's cigarettes and inhaled deeply. He couldn't believe it had taken so long for the penny to finally drop for Debbie. This confirmed his long held belief that students might be able to pass exams but they were as thick as mince in the real world. 'The pair of them must have amassed wads of cash this season.' Once more Stephen was grinding his teeth together.

'And all those poor punters he cheated out of their hard earned money.' Siobhan shook her head.

'I can't believe they keep all that money for themselves. They're just a couple of thieving crooks. And all those poor ill children that should be getting a holiday.' Debbie couldn't understand how the situation had reached this magnitude. 'But why doesn't somebody say something?'

'It's not as simple as that.' Stephen flicked his ash angrily onto the floor as the tray was full.

'No it isn't. Not after what happened with Mandy.' Siobhan cast her eyes down onto the now dirty ash-strewn carpet.

'Now you've lost me.' All this horrible information was beginning to give Debbie a headache. 'I thought Suzanne had just bad-mouthed her like she did me.'

'Well Suzanne no doubt stuck her pennyworth in but ...' Stephen tried to find a space to stub out his fag.

'We never found out all the details,' interrupted Siobhan. 'Because Mandy disappeared off the premises almost immediately after it happened.'

'After what happened?' asked Debbie.

For a brief moment everything froze. 'Well nobody is absolutely sure but...' Siobhan was about to deliver her version of events but was cut short by Stephen.

'Suzanne was jealous of Mandy.' Stephen interrupted. 'Everyone liked her and she could completely knock the spots off Suzanne when she was on stage. That's why Suzanne hated her. Anyway she was clever and brave too. She kept an eye on what was going on. In fact it was months ago, right at the beginning of the season she told me she thought there was something dodgy about Tony and those charity boxes.' He sucked in his cheeks.

'So everyone knows what's been happening except me?' Debbie was now worried and wondering if everyone thought she was completely dense.

'No, not everyone. Some people are so self-obsessed, they don't see beyond the end of their own bloody noses.' He tapped his own.

'The likes of Suzanne, for example,' clarified Siobhan, as if this were necessary.

'Suzanne is under the delusion that her little tale-telling led to Mandy's dismissal.' He puffed out his cheeks pretending to be the round-faced Suzanne.

'She really does have some grand delusions about her importance here,' said Siobhan. Nevertheless, she thought the nasty piece of work had sufficient powers to make people mysteriously ill.

'I don't actually think either Tony or Jill think that much of her.' Stephen had heard them both making scathing comments about her on several occasions.

'So, just how did Mandy come to get the sack and what's it got to do with the charity boxes?' Debbie was keeping a watch on the time, as they would have to get ready for bingo soon.

'Well I reckon, the charity boxes are the key to all of this. You see there was an occasion a few weeks ago when Mandy wasn't very well.' Stephen put his elbow on his knee and his hand under his chin as if thinking back hard.

'Strangely enough, she'd had a stomach ache and symptoms very similar to yours,' informed Siobhan. 'When I saw you back and forwards to the bathroom, it gave me the weirdest feeling of deja-vu to be sure.'

'What are you saying?' wondered Debbie. Had Suzanne poisoned her? If so, when and how?

'Well, I'm sure Suzanne has had some part to play in these mysterious illnesses.' Siobhan nodded sagely.

'Anyway, this is what I think happened,' began Stephen. 'Suzanne used the opportunity of the illness that she had or hadn't caused to bad mouth first Mandy and then you. Then, that dirty old man thought he had you both over a barrel to do … well I for one would rather not think of it. In your case Debbie, Jill thankfully spoilt his plans didn't she? But that couldn't have been the case with Mandy and knowing her like we did … well, she must've just seen red.'

'So it is Stephen. Yes I think that's more than likely what Mandy would've done too …' Siobhan took the dishes over to the sink because she needed to clear up as precious time was running out.

'But what did she do?' Debbie wondered what she herself should have done.

'She must have confronted him with everything she knew about the charity boxes.' Stephen couldn't think of any other likely explanation that would have led to such an immediate sacking.

'But she was in the right because as I now know …' Debbie wished she had known all this and that she'd had Mandy's bottle.

'Tony's best mates with Stan Braithwaite.' Stephen knew that the Camp Manager was one of Tony's golf pals. 'And he's one of Fred Pontin's best buddies.'

'But he and Jill had been stealing the money meant for the sick children,' said Debbie. 'Surely they couldn't get away with all this.

'Debbie. You can't mess with the big boys,' said Stephen sadly. 'That's why everyone just turns a blind eye. And if you want to keep your job you'll do the same.'

16th April 2014- Acorn Road, Jesmond

All's Forgiven Destiny

After the discussion with Stefan on the previous night in the Olympian Restaurant, Martha's mind was in turmoil. She was in desperate need of a walk and some fresh air to clear her head. As she pulled on the previous night's attire, she noticed the light flashing angrily on her landline's answer machine. She also clocked ten missed calls on her mobile too. Unsurprisingly, they were all from her agent Sorchia and there was no need to wonder what she was after. Well, she was in no mood for any writing or Sorchias for that matter, as she had way much too much going on in her head.

She stomped out of her flat and marched down the street in her sensible flat boots. Stefan had seemed deeply troubled about the appearance of Roger and his extreme reaction was bothering her deeply. She couldn't believe that they had openly spoken about the murder of Tony after all these years. It ought to have been cathartic but it wasn't. She thought through the long list of suspects and their different motives for wanting him dead.

There had been Tony's partner in crime, Jill. She had clearly tired of his attentions and would no doubt love to have got her hands on all the charity money to take with her on her upcoming Pontinental venture. It could quite likely have been her. Also something weird had definitely been going between Tony and Mike. She was never quite sure what it was but Tony had a strange hold over him and she had guessed it was in some way connected with his father, with whom he seemed to have had an uneasy relationship.

Without doubt Roger clearly had developed some sort of drug problem at the time of Tony's death and from the look of him recently maybe still had. He must have been desperate for money and could have been capable of anything. There was also something suspicious about that cleaner Elaine. She was always to be found lurking about, listening through doors and peeping through keyholes. Likewise, there had been some shady dealings between Tony and Kevin the lifeguard.

Although Suzanne and Karen had no clear motive for murdering their boss, their nastiness it itself made them suspects. What about that girl Mandy who Tony had molested and sacked? Maybe she had come back seeking revenge. So the list went on, with even herself and her best friend Siobhan included. Martha wondered what had happened to Siobhan and she wondered if she should try and get in touch with her. Martha herself was the only one that she knew for definite hadn't committed any crime but that nevertheless didn't take her out of the frame. Miscarriages of justice happened all of the time. She remembered that horrible incident in his office when he had tried to get her to sit on his lap and called her a freak. She still felt sick thinking of that horrible old man with his disgusting teeth and filthy shirts. In fact it was a wonder Tony had lasted as long as he did.

However, judging from his reaction last night, her best bet for the murder had to be Stefan. She had witnessed week after week the hatred on his face when Tony had been squeezing the cash from the poor gullible punters. When Stefan had told her about what had happened with his little brother Andy and how Tony had stolen the identity for his fictitious son, she could completely understand his loathing of the man. But last night, when he had relayed his horror at seeing Roger in the *Blonde Barrel* and how distressed he had been confirmed her deepest fears for her friend.

Martha turned the corner into Acorn Road and spotted a beautiful dusky pink dress in the window of an expensive boutique. The material was gorgeous, floaty and embellished with tiny mother-of-pearl sequins. It would be perfect for one of Destiny's book signing events and then she remembered … no more pretty frocks for Martha. She sighed and slipped into the nearby coffee shop. She bought herself a flat white coffee and sat down to think about her latest book project. She guessed that she would have to start pulling her finger out soon to get it finished. However, she knew that Sorchia would hate it and so too would the fans of Destiny Chambers novels. Also, worryingly, the bills were mounting up and although her mother's death had left her with a tidy sum she still needed to keep making some money.

As she took a sip of her coffee, she noticed a very attractive man walk through the door. He wore a smart suit, had distinguished dark hair flecked with grey and looked rich. She tossed her hair and gave him one of her most alluring smiles, but to her astonishment he looked right through her. What was going on? Then she caught sight of herself in the mirror opposite. With her unkempt wiry hair with grey roots, make-up free pasty-like face and dull shapeless dress; she had turned into the wretched Bird Woman for real. Sod this for a lark she thought. All was forgiven Destiny and she would have that new dress.

Chapter 42

27th July 1984 – Sunny Dunes Holiday Camp 27th July 1984 – The Swimming Baths

Clutching at Straws

As it was Friday, Roger was feeling flush. His wallet was currently stuffed with notes and he went to score at the baths. In his drawer he had some cocaine left from his last transaction, so he was able to have a little breakfast medication to set the day off with a reassuring zing. Instantly, colours seemed brighter, sounds more tuneful and Roger felt on tip top form to face the day. Although there was a slight drizzle in the air, Roger, who usually hated getting his hair wet, merely quickened his pace and heightened the spring in his step. Today was one of those days when God was in his heaven and all was right with the world.

He imagined this would be Kevin's most lucrative day of the week, for everyone would have collected their weekly pay packet and no doubt some like himself would be off to see the local candy man. On his way he passed a downcast looking Gary walking in the opposite direction. Normally Gary would have spoken, but perhaps he assumed the wet weather would be affecting his photo opportunities for the day and this had put him in a grumpy mood.

Once at the baths, he immediately went to search out Kevin. In his hands he was waving one ten and two crisp twenty pound notes and he beamed at the lifeguard sitting on his tower. The minute Kevin saw Roger he began shaking his head and bolted down the steps as if the baths were on fire. John the lifeguard facing Roger put down the paper he was reading and folded his arms as if waiting for a play to begin.

'No Roger, put them away. I can't.' Kevin was running towards him in an agitated state.

'What you on about? Look I've even got the rest I owed you.' Roger was puzzled because he had thought Kevin would have been only too delighted to see him and his money.

'Just put the bloody dosh away.' Kevin's face was red and he was snarling.

'I said I would settle my debts as soon as …'

'Come through here and let me explain.' He pushed Roger through the doors and into the familiar locker room, much to the annoyance of John who was enjoying all the snippets of drama he had been witnessing that morning.

'I can't sell you anymore drugs Roger.' He spoke seriously and used a voice that Roger hadn't heard before. He sounded older, tired and world–weary.

'Hey, come on. I said I would get you what I owed you as soon as I had been paid.' This must be some kind of joke thought Roger.

'No not just you. I can't sell anyone any gear at all. Not anymore. No weed, no speed, no cocaine, no nuffin.' He looked about the room edgily, as if expecting Tony to jump out of one of the cubicles.
'What do you mean? You have to. I mean I have fifty quid here. I could make it sixty if that's what it …' mumbled Roger pleading.

'I've been rumbled. Aren't you listening to me you numpty? It's that bastard Tony. He's been spying on me and he says if I don't stop he'll tell the fuzz. The police, you know what I mean? Do you get it now?'

But at least, thought Roger, Kevin's voice was sounding more normal again. That had to be a good sign and he clutched at straws.

'Well if I come round to your chalet. Tony'd never know would he?' He searched deeply into the lifeguards eyes.

'I can't risk it. I can't go to jail. My missus is up the duff again. That's the only reason I've been doing this.' Kevin clenched his fists in exasperation thinking of how that blackmailing bugger intended to take everything he'd made so far. It was so unfair and he loathed that man so much he wished he would just die.

'But what about me?' Roger didn't care about the bigger picture. He could only think of himself.

'No can do, sorry an all that but ...'

'I could kill that man.' Roger had already broken out into a sweat and had images of freezing cold, plucked festive birds running about everywhere.

'You and me both.' muttered Kevin.

16th April 2014 – The Lazaridis'' House, Jesmond

Jillian's World Comes Crashing

Teddie had been excited all day and couldn't wait to share the contents of his little yellow book with his wife. She had been asleep in bed last night when he arrived home and was still doing so when he left that morning. Jillian wouldn't believe what he had discovered about Destiny Chambers and Stefan Sondheim. Not only were these local celebrities friends with each other, but it seemed more than likely they would have once been colleagues of his wife's too. He was almost sure that it had been the Pontins at Whitley Bay where Jillian had once worked. He had googled it and found out that it had been flattened long since and made into a housing estate. Its name had been Sunny Dunes Holiday Camp but most interesting of all, was that there had been a massive scandal back in 1984. The Entertainment's Manager had been brutally murdered and somebody had literally stuck a knife in his back.

Teddie had decided not to go in to The Olympian that evening. This was unusual because he almost always did unless he had an important function to attend. Tonight, he was going to treat his wife to the pleasure of his company and give her the benefit of his full attention. Jillian was presently in the kitchen, for he could hear the clattering of dishes and he thought he would wait until after they had eaten to share his information.

'There you are my dear. I have made lasagne. So tuck in.' Jillian smiled and placed a steaming dish of that what seemed to be filled with black pasta on the table, alongside a bowl of limp salad. She filled both of their glasses up with red wine.

Πολυωραια. (very nice). Πειναω πειασμξυος(I'm starving hungry)' Teddie hoped that in Greek his response sounded more enthusiastic and he wished he was eating in one of his own restaurants. He couldn't believe she had yet again cooked lasagne and this time it was clearly burnt but decided against passing comment. 'So, have you had an interesting time today?' He asked making some light conversation.

'Well, I went to my exercise class but you'll never guess what happened.' Jillian's eyes narrowed.

'I've no idea. 'He was finding it difficult to cut through the hard pasta with an ordinary knife. 'Did you see your chum Barbara there?'

'Yes, but that's not what I was going to tell you. When I came back I found that Elaine lounging in the garden and you know what? I can only imagine what she thought she was doing ... was flirting with poor Carl.' She pulled an incredulous face.

'I guess they were just having a break.' He pushed the food around his plate with his fork, to make it appear he had eaten more than he actually had.

'Well, Carl's welcome to a break but she's only paid for a couple of hours and she hasn't got time for such shenanigans.' She raised an eyebrow expecting him to agree.

'Jillian. Αγαητέ μου (my dear),' he couldn't keep his thoughts to himself any longer. 'You'll never guess who was in the restaurant last night.' He pulled his phone and his little yellow notebook out of his pocket.

'Was it Elaine and Carl sharing a meal?' She gave a little chuckle and took a sip from her glass.

'Take a look at this.' He put the phone in front of her. 'Don't you recognise these two?'

'Well that looks like that Stefan that music producer bloke but I'm not too sure about ...' Jillian went to get her reading glasses from the coffee table where they lay next to the book she'd been reading. 'Yes that's definitely Stefan Sondheim. That's his name ... or the one he uses anyway.' She looked closely at the picture and took a further sip of wine. 'But no. I certainly don't recognise his dowdy companion.'

'See that βίβλίο (book) you've got on the table.' Teddie gives a nod in its direction.

'That's just some rubbish for the reading group.' She shrugged. 'It's Barbara's choice. Says a lot about her don't you think?'

'Περιεργως (Strangely enough),Stefan's companion is none other than your novelist Destiny Chambers.'

'Don't be ridiculous Teddie.' She went to get the book. 'Look, there's Destiny. That's what she's like. She looks a bit tarty for my liking but I can't see Destiny Chambers ever going out like that.'

'Λοιπον (Well), that's where you are wrong my dear. You see, I was listening to their conversation through my system.' Teddy nodded emphatically.

'Teddie you've got to stop yourself doing this. It's going to get you into bother believe me …' Jillian was becoming irritated as her husband was lapsing into his Poirot mode and the joke had long worn thin.

'Listen, it was. She wants to be taken seriously as a writer so she's not going to use that Destiny name anymore. She said to him she was going to use the name Martha instead.' Teddie told his wife.

'Martha who? I'll look out for that one not to read,' laughed Jillian cattily.

'But there's more Jillian. Are you sure you don't recognise them?' The twinkle disappeared from Teddie's eye and his face grew serious.

'Well, I told you I recognised Stefan. He's never out of the news is he? But I'm hardly going to recognise that dreadful writer in her stupid disguise.' Why had her husband become obsessed with these two minor celebrities?

'Λοιπον (well) that's the thing.' Teddie began stroking his moustache. 'Do you know before you worked in Corinth, didn't you work at a holiday camp in Αγγλία (England)?'

'And what of it?' Jillian didn't like the way the conversation was going and really didn't like to dwell on this period of her life.

'Λοιπον (well) I gathered from their conversation that they too were Bluecoats and they used to work at the Sunny Dunes Holiday

Camp nearby here. And they seemed worried because in 1984, there was a murder. I looked it up and Tony Noble, I think he was called, was the Entertainment's Manager and he was stabbed. Isn't that where you worked?'

Jillian's face grew pale and there was a hard lump in her throat. 'Yes I think so … but it was such a long time ago …'

'And were you there in 1984?' Poirot's interrogation was metamorphosing into a full Spanish Inquisition.

'I'm not sure …' Why was her husband torturing her with all this?

'Jillian you must remember if you worked there when this Tony Noble was Σκοτώθηκε (killed). I mean a murder's not the sort of thing you are likely to forget is it?'

'Yes, Tony was my boss but I didn't really have a lot to do with him.' Teddie certainly had no need to know about what had really happened between the two of them.

'Isn't it Ξένος (strange) that these two were talking about it last night,' continued Teddie.

His face to Jillian took on the appearance of a malevolent jack-a-lantern. She wished he would just shut up. 'Isn't it stranger still that you were listening to them?' Jillian retorted.

'So you must have worked with these two as well.' He couldn't hide the triumph in his voice.

Jillian resigned herself to the fact that her husband wasn't going to it let go. So she put on her glasses once more to try and seem as normal as possible and studied the troublesome photo on the phone.

'It's possible I suppose that Stefan is Stephen Simpson … but he had a lot more hair then. But I can't place the woman.' She picked up the book once again. 'There is a possibility she might be Debbie Carter but then again she too had an awful lot more hair.'

'So what happened with this Tony Noble?' Teddie persisted and Jillian wished the ground would just swallow her up and take her far far away.

Chapter 43

27th July 1984 – the Family Robinson's House

Pink Shirts

When Mike had arrived back at Sunny Dunes yesterday, he had been only too relieved to escape from his horrible family. He pictured them all as they had been earlier, sitting round the familiar dining table having their roast beef and Yorkshire puddings on a Thursday afternoon. This, he begrudgingly admitted had been for his benefit, as his day off wasn't a Sunday but it was more to make his mam happy rather than anything else. After all, it was the summer holidays and his sister was already off from school. So it was no skin off her nose. Likewise, it made no odds to his dad who had his own building business and could just work when he pleased, or better still, make someone else get their hands dirty.

While his mam was all right he supposed, although she had her moments from time to time, but his sister and his dad … they were both just plain mean. He had wondered earlier why Jennifer's fingers had been all red but now it was patently obvious what the little bitch had been doing. She had added that red cake icing gloop to the washing machine and oh yes, he bet that first she had made sure everybody else's whites had been removed. It wasn't as if some of her past antics hadn't been bad enough, but this one really took the biscuit. And, uncannily she always went unpunished. If he had ever done the slightest thing to the precious little princess, well that had been a different matter altogether. *Leave your little sister alone. You are older and should know better*. It was so unfair because she has always been her parent's favourite.

It wouldn't have been so bad if they had been dyed yellow or blue. It was just the very fact they were pink. When Tony spotted him at Bingo that night, he would be bound to have a field day and even now Mike felt his face burning at the thought of the impending mortification. He could see himself walking into the Ballroom and all eyes turning round to snigger, point and ridicule him in his girly attire.

To make matters even worse, he couldn't even afford to buy himself a new one because after Tony had taken his cut, there was very little left of his pathetic wages. This was all because of him wanting a stab at being a comic and that stupid Roger getting his wires crossed. Tony had just happened to be in the wrong place at the wrong time and having the crafty evil cunning to exploit the situation for his own financial gain. Nothing whatsoever had happened between him and Roger. He wasn't even gay was he? But one thing was for sure he certainly couldn't risk allowing his dad to get a whiff of any of this because then his life would be totally unbearable.

At that very moment in time he wasn't sure who he hated most, his father or Tony. Ronnie Robinson had been so looking forward to thrashing his son at golf and showing off at his swanky club. However, it was unclear who was the most astonished between father and son, upon discovering Mike's natural ability at aceing those little white balls. Ronnie had just stood there aghast, as his son had performed an uncanny succession of straight holes-in-one. One after the other they had kept coming. It was as though he had been born to play golf. His father's face had been a picture and he had still been sulking all the way through most of lunch. Only the opportunity to make nasty comments about Mike's uselessness had cheered him.

Nevertheless, this golf triumph was of little compensation when Mike had spent his night off alone watching *Blankety Blank* on Stephen's black and white portable.

Friday 17th April 2014 – The Lazaridis' House, Jesmond

While the Iron is Hot

'Elaine just what do you think you are playing at?' Jillian was trying to use her haughtiest voice, as she had just witnessed her cleaner once more wasting time once again and fraternising with her gardener but somehow her tone lacked its usual impetus.

'I was just making Carl a wee cup of tea.' Elaine was annoyed at being caught and out of breath from running across the garden.

'You aren't paid for making men cups of tea,' replied Jillian but she seemed distracted, as though her thoughts were elsewhere.

'I had only been out there a couple of minutes …' Elaine said trying to justify herself.

'Just get on with your …' But Jillian couldn't even be bothered to finish her sentence. She held her head in her hands and had a woeful expression.

Elaine gripped her fists together, girded up her loins and looked at the carpet. 'You shouldn't speak to me like that, you know.' There she had said it.

But Jillian wasn't listening because she had already left the room. Clearly, Mrs Lazaridis' had other things on her mind and Elaine was left seething. She had been so close to putting the wheels of her plan in motion but the wretched woman had disappeared. Should she follow Jillian upstairs and continue with what she had to say? Elaine didn't know what the best thing to do was.

Yes, she definitely felt like telling the bitch where to sling her hook but of course she couldn't. Yesterday, a massive gas bill had arrived and she just didn't know where she was going to find the money to pay for it. If only she had been given a chance all those years ago.

She would have made an excellent Bluecoat and who knew where that might have led? But most irritating of all was how close she was to getting her hands on the charity box money. If only bloody Tony hadn't been killed on that very night, then her life would have without doubt taken her down a very different route. There was only one person who could have possibly taken all of that money and that was Jill. At least some of it by rights should have been Elaine's. She remembered all those hours she had spent painstakingly cutting letters out of newspapers and magazines.

Mind you, she had nearly gone and blown it yet again. If Jillian hadn't returned at that very moment then then she would have blurted everything out to that rude ex-policeman and where would that have got her? She needed the dirt on Jillian to feather her own nest not to reward the police. Yes, she would like to see snotty Jill banged up in prison to pay for her crimes but more than that she would like a tidy few grand sitting in her own pocket.

After all, Jillian and her husband were bloody rich. They were hardly going to miss a few measly grand. Would Jillian like her husband to know of her tawdry affair with Tony Noble? She didn't think so. Likewise, would he be impressed by her little scam with the money boxes? What opinion would Teddie, the generous patron of several charities, have of that? Heaven forbid that his wife should have once stooped so low. Teddie Lazaridis' would be mortified and that would be the end of their cozy marriage for sure.

Elaine looked once more out of the window to see a flustered looking Teddie Lazaridis' marching across the lawn. He was having a word with Carl. Maybe his gardening wasn't up to scratch. She pretended to wash some dishes so she could stay where she was and keep her eye on what was going on outside.

Mr Lazaridis' and Carl seemed to be having quite a lengthy conversation. Obviously, Carl wasn't being berated as he was talking to his boss as though they were equals. Funny how Jillian never did that with her but then she had never held a position in the police force had she? Carl seemed unusually animated and he was waving his hands about as if he was embellishing some thrilling yarn. Elaine wondered what ever they were talking about and if she could possibly creep down the garden herself to listen. No, Mrs Lazaridis' was all by herself upstairs and Elaine needed to strike while the iron was hot.

Chapter 44

27th July 1984 – Sunny Dunes Holiday Camp - The Princess Ballroom

Wardrobe Malfunction

It was Friday night and the last bingo session of the week was about to begin. Tony liked to call the numbers for this one as it had the biggest prize. It seemed to Debbie that Tony was attracted to anything involving large sums of money like a magpie to glittery objects. After her encounter with the man in his office, Debbie had grown to despise Tony but after this afternoon's revelations, she now hated him. Next to him, plastered in make-up and jewellery was his side-kick Jill who was looking particularly pleased with herself this evening. Until this afternoon, Jill with her impeccable timing had risen highly in Debbie's estimation but this had now plummeted. The greedy bitch was almost as bad as her partner in crime.

To one side of the stage, Roger was slumped over a table and he looked dreadful. Even from over the other side of the room, she could see his skin was grey and he was shaking. Surely he wasn't having palpitations. Whatever was the matter with him? Close by to him, Suzanne was standing next to an elderly couple she had befriended that week. She was drinking a Babycham with a cherry on a stick, which she had almost finished and would be hoping they would buy her another one. Over the other side, Marcus was sitting at a table by himself reading a book. She noticed he was wearing his sandals. Nearby to him, Siobhan and Stephen were talking together, probably about what had transpired that afternoon.

All the punters eyes and ears were fixed on Tony, who was sweating profusely under the bright lights of the stage. A silence filled the room, as the microphone crackled and then in walked

Mike. Immediately, all attention switched focus to him because for some strange reason he was wearing a shirt in the brightest shade of pink that Debbie had ever seen. This wasn't the tinge of something accidentally spoiled by clothes colours running in the wash. It was the vibrant pink of a flamingo bird. The shirt had either been bought deliberately because of its vivid colour or stained that way to make a bold statement.

But whatever was Mike trying to say? This colour of shirt was not only against uniform regulations but it looked ridiculous and as Mike was wearing a face of the same colour, he was perfectly aware of this.

Tony switched off the bingo machine and instantly the balls fell to the bottom of the tank like dead fish.

'What on earth are you wearing? You ponce,' Tony roared and Mike froze to the spot like a rabbit caught in the headlights. 'I don't know what your father will say when he hears about this along with all of your other shenanigans.'

'But I thought we had an agreement,' spluttered Mike.

'Agreement, my arse. Now stop embarrassing yourself in front of our guests. Get out and don't come back until you're dressed like a man. If we'd wanted another girl Bluecoat … well we wouldn't have picked you would we?'

And Mike's face turned from pink to scarlet as he fled from the ballroom in complete humiliation. The void of silence was broken by an explosion of whispers, laughter and guffaws. Then the crackling microphone buzzed like a swarm of bees and the resuscitated balls once more swam about.

'Eyes down look in.' Tony continued with the bingo unperturbed by the recent strange incident. 'This first one is for a row for fifty quid, but wait for it. The full house is for … one hundred pounds. And first out we have two little ducks …'

'What was all that about?' Suzanne sidled up to Debbie, so shocked by what had just happened that she forgot the passion with which she hated Debbie. She was simply the nearest Bluecoat.

'I have no idea but someone's had a serious wardrobe malfunction,' replied Debbie.

16th April 2014 – 55 Degrees North

Stefan Ponders

Stefan sat out on the large balcony of his 55 Degrees North penthouse flat, drinking a strong coffee and thinking about the last night's revelations. His disapproval over Destiny's appearance now paled into insignificance, compared to what he had learned about Roger and his current situation. Over the years, he had heard Roger Henderson's name crop up in conversations many times, as he had been involved in the running of some pretty prestigious but notorious nightclubs throughout the country. It was well known that these venues attracted some dodgy types and they were not really the sort of place in which Stefan felt most at home. Stefan was no innocent but he tried his best to avoid to getting his fingers burnt which for a local celebrity was pretty important. Roger clearly hadn't.

Anyway, what Roger did was up to him but he just didn't want him raking up murky business from the past which involved himself and Destiny. He remembered vividly that afternoon in the girls chalet, just before Tony had died, when Debbie (as she was then), Siobhan and himself had all laid their cards on the table. When Debbie told how Tony had called her a freak before relaying what had happened between her and Tony. Then, Siobhan had said something like *she'd have to watch her own back in case someone should stick a knife in it.* Well, this must have been what put the idea into

Debbie's head in the first place. That was why he couldn't believe how cool she had been relaying her meeting with Roger. She, even more than himself, needed to avoid the case being reopened, didn't she?

If the investigation began over, the full extent of his hatred for the man would immediately come to light but this time it would be splattered all over social media and who knew what conclusions might be drawn. Stefan Sondheim had a little brother who died of leukaemia. Evil Entertainment's Manager, Tony Noble, who stole the dead boy's identity to swindle holiday makers out of thousands, found dead. Who do you think killed the monster? Stefan spat out a mouthful of coffee.

For once from his balcony, he didn't admire his panoramic view of the city but focused on the other side of the river, where he imagined the sad figure of Roger was showing folk to their seats in the cinema. What was even more peculiar was that it now emerged that Mike, his old chalet mate, who he had never seen eye-to-eye with, also appeared to be working nearby in the Tesco store. Stefan had always suspected Mike had a touch of homophobia lurking somewhere in his closet.

He remembered Mike always wandering about the campsite with his pathetic cardboard cut outs of windmills, bales of hay and didn't he also have to lean along with a Tower of Pisa? Fred Pontin spared no expense in the theatrical scenery department did he? Oh yes, and hadn't Mike at one point even fancied himself as a comic. Stefan recalled not only how dreadful his jokes were but also the fact that he had no comic timing whatsoever. But there was something else too, because Mike seemed to be constantly looking over his shoulder. He had witnessed whispered conversations in corners of rooms between Mike and Tony. It had seemed like Tony had been harassing him and Mike was scared.

Maybe the plonker Mike also didn't want to revisit his Pontin's past but throwing Roger out with the rubbish seemed a pretty sure way of drawing it to further attention. It had certainly caught Destiny's eye which also begged the question of what she had been doing in Trinity Square of all places, in Gateshead. He needed to speak with her more.

Chapter 45

27th July 1985 – Sunny Dunes Holiday Park - The Princess Ballroom

Stephen Doesn't Like to Share his Clothes

Stephen was deep in thought and not paying much attention to the resumed game of Bingo. What on earth was his chalet-mate Mike playing at? Why ever would he choose to wear that hideous bright pink shirt? Nevertheless, if he or Roger had pulled such a stunt, he was sure it would have been no big deal. They were gay and such eccentricities could to some extent be tolerated but Mike wasn't, was he? Maybe he was in denial and that was why the two of them had never really hit it off.

He replayed in his mind the bizarre pink face and shirt incident. Hadn't that outburst by Tony been a little over the top? It wasn't as if he had been setting rubbish bins on fire or stealing anything was it? Not like that bastard Tony himself. Why would Mike's dad be so appalled about his son wearing a blouse? Stephen's own father would have just laughed about it and said it was bloody typical of his daft son's antics. Also, what had Tony meant about his shenanigans? Stephen wondered if this was connected with Mike's laughable (but in the wrong way) attempts at becoming a stand-up comic. After all, he couldn't think what else it could possibly be. And, what was this agreement they were supposed to have? Stephen for the first time felt some sympathy for Mike because it was obvious that the bloody Entertainment's Manager had something on him and Stephen was determined to make it his business to find out what it was.

As the season was progressing, he was starting to hate Tony Noble more and more. His repulsion for the man was always particularly bad on a Friday night, when that monster performed his evil scam. He had a good mind to go around all the punters and tell them what was what. In fact he was beginning to despise the Holiday Camp itself and all the nasty people it seemed to have brought together. Thank goodness he had his friendship with Debbie. However when he looked across the room he saw his new best chum deep in conversation with that bitch Suzanne. What was going on there?

When the season was over Stephen had big plans. He had some mates in Newcastle with whom he was thinking of forming a boy band. Granted, none of them were particularly talented or musical, but he was sure they could jump around a stage looking just as cute as George Michael. Stephen had quite a thing for him but it was such waste that he wasn't gay.

Stephen looked across the room and saw Roger in a particularly agitated state. He was trembling horribly and Stephen was sure if he hadn't been leaning against one of the columns he would collapse. Some of the punters were staring at him too. Stephen was about to go over and see him when he felt a tap on his shoulder.

'Stephen. I hope you don't mind but I've borrowed one of your shirts.' Mike was back and thankfully wearing the correct uniform.

'No, that's ok I suppose.' It wasn't really. Stephen didn't like clothes sharing. 'But what was all that about? Why in God's name were you wearing a pink shirt?'

'My horrible little sister filled mam's washing machine with red dye. All my shirts are ruined.' Mike's face wore a forlorn expression.

'Why didn't you just go and buy a new one. I mean, shirts aren't that expensive.' This came out more waspishly than he intended.

'I know.' Mike looked even more dejected. 'I'll get one tomorrow. I'm just a bit strapped for cash at the moment but thanks anyway.' And he wandered off to the back of the hall.

17th April 2014 – The Lazaridis'' House, Jesmond

A Wonder He Lasted so Long

Teddie had the unsolved murder of Tony Noble buzzing around in his head and he couldn't think of anything else. At the restaurant, Vasilis had been trying to grab his attention, to check an invoice for some supplies for the forthcoming week but he just couldn't concentrate. Then, he realised the person most likely to have some inside information, was working in his home at that very moment. Teddie jumped into his Jaguar and sped off home.

Running around the side of the house, without calling in to see Jillian, he spotted Carl busy digging at the bottom of the garden. Excitedly, he shouted down the lawn to Carl.
'Καλημερα (good morning) Carl. Με ουγχωρεις (Excuse me)'

Carl turned round and was quite alarmed by the agitated Mr Lazaridis,' who was making some very strange noises indeed.

'Mr Lazaridis' what's the matter? Is there something wrong with you?' Teddie with his slicked dark hair and suit, running along the grass put him in mind of a disturbed beetle.

'Με ουγχωρεις (Excuse me).'He flurried a trembling hand across his face to cool himself down. 'Sorry I'll speak in English. I know when I get a little excited I lapse into my native Greek.' He gave the gardener the sort of smile he used when he wanted something from somebody. 'And Carl, please call me Teddie.' He proffered a hand for the puzzled gardener to shake.

'Very well, Teddie.' Carl hadn't been expecting yet another conversation at the Lazaridis' home this morning. 'Is there some way I can help you?'

Teddie cut to the chase. 'You used to be a policeman didn't you?'

'Yes, I retired a few years ago now. Why?' Carl was curious as to where this was going.

'Λοιπον (Well), I was interested in a particular case that has recently been brought to my attention. It was an unsolved crime from many years ago you see.' Teddie twiddled thoughtfully with his moustache.

'That depends how long ago you're talking.' Carl didn't like the many years ago implication. 'I mean, I'm not ancient you know.'

'I reckon we're about the same age.' Teddie looked the man up and down, in appraisal as to how old he was. ' Λοιπον (Well), this was about the murder of a man by the name of Tony Noble. He was an Entertainment's Manager at a holiday camp that used to be down the coast.'

'Sunny Dunes. Yes I remember that case very well.' Carl reminisced back to the summer of 84, to his salad days as a fledgling police officer. When the power, his new uniform, handcuffs and truncheon had felt so exciting. 'You see, it was the first murder investigation I'd been involved in. Funnily enough, I was only thinking about it a little earlier.'

Teddie's face lit up. 'So you were actually there when it happened? Πολυ ωρια(Very nice).'

'What's that you're saying.' Carl thought Teddie kept using some very peculiar words.

'It's Greek.' Teddie was irritated. The stupid ex-policeman ought to have known this. 'It means very nice.'

'I tell you it wasn't very nice at all.' Carl slipped easily back into police constabulary mode. 'I wasn't there when it actually happened, obviously, but I was shortly after and it wasn't a pretty sight. There he was with a great big breadknife sticking out of his back and he was lying in a pool of blood.' Carl stabbed the air with an imaginary knife and fanned out his hands as if making a gory puddle. He folded his arms once more and continued relaying the story. 'You know, it was a wonder he'd lived as long as he did because so many people hated his guts.' Carl was beginning to enjoy himself now. 'That's why we could never solve the case as there were there were so many suspects with such good reason to want him dead.' Carl watched with interest Teddie's reaction to all this. Once a policeman … 'Anyway what's your concern with all of this?'

'Well it's my wife, Jillian. It's her really.' He shook his head

'Oh does Mrs Lazaridis' have a great interest in unsolved local crimes?' Carl had often come across posh ladies having a macabre interest in such unsavoury matters.

'OXι (No).That's not it at all. The thing is. It's quite awkward really but I've just found out something very interesting about my wife. She used to work there as a Bluecoat at this very same time.' Teddie folded his arms and met Carl's eye.

'Never. Mrs Lazaridis' was once a Bluecoat? He wouldn't have thought it would have been her sort of thing at all.' Carl thought back many years to the cast of Pontin's employees and a certain face sprang to mind. 'You don't mean that she was the Jill that was there.' Carl remembered a pretty lady with long blonde hair and an abrupt manner. Like the rest of them she'd just wanted the case over and done with so she could escape from the place. 'You mean Jill McDonald who was Tony Noble's deputy?'

'Yes, that was my wife's name when we first met.' Carl wistfully thought back to their first meeting.

This could never be Mrs Lazaridis' thought an alarmed Carl. She was one of the chief suspects. Jill McDonald had allegedly been the victim's bit on the side and had been involved in the charityboxgate scandal. Blimey, the woman must have more skeletons rattling around in her closet than in an overcrowded graveyard. He couldn't tell Teddie all this it, would break him and what about police confidentiality? No for certain, he couldn't tell Teddie any of this.

'A lot of the details have become foggy over time.' Carl knew this conversation needed wrapping up and quickly.

But Teddie continued. 'And do you know what else? I overheard the other night … I mean I got chatting to some folk, who were also Bluecoats there too from that very same time.'

Phew. Carl was relieved that at least Teddie was off the subject of his wife. 'How did that come about? Where were you?' Carl was puzzled as to how Teddie was so proficient at listening.

And Teddie relayed to an astonished Carl what he had heard while eavesdropping on the conversation between, none other than Stefan Sondheim and Destiny Chambers.

Chapter 46

15th August 1984 – Sunny Dunes Holiday Camp 15th August 1984 – The Orangery

Why was Debbie Still There?

Suzanne was sitting alone in the Orangery next to the amusement arcade, nursing a can of cola and a sulk. Her bottom lip was sticking out even further than her belly over the waistband of her skirt. Staring at the sickly lime green walls and unconvincing plastic pieces of fruit which hung in abundance from the imitation trees, she stewed like tea left too long in a pot. Through the window she could see Frank, that nerd from accounts, who sorted their pathetic wages and put them into those small waxed paper envelopes each week. He had a very odd expression on his face as if he was in a trance. Momentarily, she wondered what was wrong with him, but not for long, as she had her own far more important concerns of her own to deal with.

When she had played the same cat and mouse game before, her trick had worked immediately and Mandy had been given the sack. And, if anything she had blotted Debbie's copybook far worse, so why was she still here? She thought back to her conversation with Tony. Surely, by now the pretentious bitch ought to have been given her marching orders. As she recalled certain phrases she had used to damn her – *not really up to it, pretending to be ill and swinging the lead* – the familiar nasty little smile played about Suzanne's lips.

'Glad to see you're looking a lot happier.' Karen glittered as she tottered across the floor and collapsed in the chair next to Suzanne. That afternoon, the kiddies had story time with Mermaid Moira. So, she was wearing her long golden wig with cascading curls, a necklace of seashells and tight sparkly long skirt. It shone with emerald sequins and had a fishtail attachment which made it almost impossible to walk in.

'You think so, do you? I tell you what would make me lot happier.' Although Suzanne thought Karen looked ridiculous in the costume, she was always secretly jealous of her friend on a Friday afternoon because she knew she would have pulled off the outfit much better.

'What's that?' Karen straightened her necklace as the shells weren't hanging right.

'If you told me you'd just seen Debbie with her suitcase heading for the exit.' Suzanne took a swig from her can and as the bubbles went down her throat she gave a loud burp.

'Well I saw her just before with Stephen and neither of them were looking very happy.' Karen was pleased to be able to feed her friend with any negative news about Debbie.

'What were they doing? Do you think she might have been given the heave ho? Oh please.' Suzanne clapped her hands together with anticipated delight.

'It's possible I suppose.' Karen played with her long corkscrew curls which looked much more like tinsel than hair.

'You know last time with that cow Mandy.' Suzanne recalled with some relish.' Well, she was sacked almost straight away after I put Tony straight with a few facts about her.'

'Yes I bet, he was definitely happy to send her packing. Nobody liked her.' Karen pursed her lips in a manner most unbecoming to a mermaid. 'He and Jill ... well they certainly didn't, did they?'

'Just like Debbie nobody likes her either do they?' Suzanne glanced at the clock, as it would soon be time for her afternoon bingo session.

'Well. I'm not so sure. She hasn't been here that long and ...' Karen began.

'She's been here long enough.' Suzanne hissed through her teeth.

'Yes, I'm sure Suzanne. You know best.' The mermaid concurred with her friend.

'Quite.' There was a pause as the two of them thought over recent events.

'So, you told Tony, she was a lazy cow who couldn't bothered to do her job properly is that right?' Karen was picturing the conversation between her friend and Tony.

'I made it clear that she wasn't up to it. I mean that should have done the trick by now shouldn't it?' Suzanne had an over-inflated view as to her own clout in the hiring and firing at the camp.

'But it was different with her wasn't it?' Karen wriggled in her chair as the sequins were sticking into her side.

'Different - how do you mean?' What did idiot Karen know about anything thought Suzanne. 'She was up herself. What with her lording it over me. Thinking she was a better singer ... you know what I mean? Just like Debbie.'

'But she made those allegations too didn't she?' Karen racked her brains trying to recall the details.

'What you on about?' Was this costume addling her brain wondered a puzzled Suzanne. 'Well I don't know for sure but I overheard Stephen talking with somebody but I can't remember who ...' Karen searched her brain for the details, fiddling with the shells on her necklace as if they were either rosary beads, worry or both

'What are you on about Karen? Mandy got the sack because I put Tony straight about what she was really like. Just like I did with Debbie and that's why I can't understand why she's still here.'

Suzanne thought the silly notions in this stupid siren's mind were the last things she needed to hear.

'I think there's a little bit more to it than that Suzanne.' The mermaid bit her lip.

17th April 2014 – The Lazaridis'' House, Jesmond

The Cacophony of Noise

Jillian was lying on her bed and sobbing uncontrollably. Inky black mascara stains smudged her 100 thread count white pillowcase which was soggy with tears. She had known fine well that Teddie's creepy voyeurism and spying on people could only result in trouble, but hadn't foreseen that she would be the one suffering its repercussions. This bloody business, raked up from years ago, should have been left where it lay. Damn her stupid husband. Had he any idea whatsoever of what a hideous chain of events he had set in motion?

However, who would have thought that two of her Bluecoats would have done so well for themselves? Stefan Sondheim was everywhere: always on the telly, plastered all over the newspapers, he seemed to be never off the radio and his presence on-line was omnipresent. He had featured prominently on the local scene as a successful music producer and impresario for donkey's years and was worth no doubt, millions. How strange that she had come across his face so often and never made the link with that silly, show-off boy from her Pontin's days. To some extent his change of name was to blame but then again he looked dramatically different without that spectacular quiff of hair and the same could also be said about Debbie. Jillian picked up the copy of *Follow Your Dreams* from the bedroom floor. Last night, when she hadn't been unable to sleep a wink, the book had provided a welcome distraction.

She studied the, without doubt, digitally enhanced photo of Destiny Chambers, with her sparkling eyes, perfect skin and long silky tresses. Nevertheless, Jillian had to admit that underneath that ridiculous white make up and preposterous hair, Debbie Carter had been a pretty enough girl and it was possible to see this might be the same person. They even shared the same initials. Jillian wondered about the nonsense her husband had been babbling of her wearing awful clothes and wanting to be a serious writer. What did Teddie know of women's clothing? A smile played about her lips imagining the glamorous novelist in some hideous get up, then suddenly she clicked back into the reality and the inconsequence of it all compared to her own dreadful predicament. She had far too many of her own problems to think of without worrying about trivialities like Debbie Carter.

So there had been sightings of Mike and Roger in the local area too. Had 1984 Pontins been genetically modifying homing pigeon Bluecoats that year? She thought of Mike with his pathetic cardboard cut-outs and pitiful notion of becoming a comic. She remembered Roger, the Head Bluecoat, with his jaunty gait and descent into what can only have been the tragedy of a drug addiction. Then there were those spiteful bitches, Suzanne and Karen. Would they too be arriving here soon to form a witch's coven? Maybe Marcus was still wandering about Hadrian's Wall playing his trumpet and perhaps Siobhan was currently ensconced in some blissful Sapphic relationship in Wallsend.

Jillian hadn't thought of these people in years and with good reason. The death of Tony was awful enough in itself. Although she had never had any real feelings for him and for her he had been just a means to an end, to find him lying dead on the floor had been truly shocking. She had never come face to face with a corpse before. Technically she still hadn't, as he had been lying prostrate but the fact remained that a bloody great knife sticking out of his back, more than made up for that. It wasn't bad enough that she was one of the main murder suspects at that time but her involvement with the charity box swindle simply blotted her copybook even further. How had she been so stupid to get herself involved in all that? The money had all disappeared that same night too. She had no idea where to but for some reason nobody seemed to believe her.

She thought back to that day when she had come into the office and found the extortion letter lying on her table. All the little letters had been cut from magazines and stuck on the crumpled paper which had been all grubby with smudgy finger-marks and spilt cups of tea. The blackmailer's identity had never been discovered. On the night he died, Tony had been going to take the money to the Regency Lounge as the letter instructed. However, it never reached its destination because nearby the empty safe was the discarded tartan carpet bag, lying next to the murdered corpse. Who could have sent that letter?

Jillian squeezed her brain trying to recall the other workers at Pontins, to think of possible threatening letter writers. It was unlikely that any of the Bluecoats would have done this because of the legacy of the unfortunate but foolish Mandy. Although the letter was hardly the work of a literary genius, Jillian imagined most of the staff were barely capable of stringing a sentence together on paper. As a possible suspect, Kevin the lifeguard from the pool in his tiny speedos alarmingly sprang into mind. As did Gary the photographer with his mane of wild permed hair and there was that slimy guy from the arcade whose name she failed to recall.

Down below, she could hear the cacophony of noise from Elaine her cleaning lady singing along with the radio. It was difficult to tell what the song was because her voice was so reedy and loud that she practically drowned out the track playing. Wait though, she had heard that singing before but not recently. It was long, long ago. Since the woman had started working here, Jillian had caught her cleaner watching her in a very peculiar manner. She was always trying to engage her in unnecessary conversation and invade her personal space. Even the other day in Tesco she had been quite literally walking in her footsteps. Quite often, the woman's tone had a threatening edge to it, especially when she asked her inappropriate probing questions. She had never liked the woman from the onset but couldn't fathom as to the reason why. Eventually though, the mist was beginning to clear.

Elaine had never even altered her name like the others. How could it have taken her so long to have made the connection? However, to be fair, although Elaine had never been much of a looker back in the day, the years hadn't been at all kind to her. The plump Bluecoat wannabe had metamorphosed into a bitter and twisted old woman. Although Jillian must be at least a couple of years older than her cleaner, Elaine appeared her senior by at least a decade. Then, Jillian suddenly felt sick as she remembered that not only had the woman been a cleaner at Pontins, but the two of them had even more shared history because they had grown up together on that horrible rough estate in Glasgow.

Who would have thought that within such a short period of time, her world would come crashing down? Randomly, her husband's curiosity had been piqued, when discovering that his wife might have a connection with an unsolved murder case. This had happened in his own restaurant of all places, when he had been listening in on a private conversation between two minor local celebrities.

Somehow a strange catalyst had occurred causing all the old murder suspects to come crawling out from under their stones and start popping up in nearby locations. Not only the former Bluecoats: Stephen, Debbie, Roger and Mike, but also other members of the Pontin's staff too. And, this included the vilest insect of the lot — Elaine, former cleaner at Sunny Dunes who was currently caterwauling in her kitchen downstairs. She moved to the window, fully expecting to see the ghost of Tony complete with an embedded knife, hovering over the lawn. However, to her horror she saw her husband in deep conversation with the gardener Carl, who just happened to be an ex-policeman. Everything was just getting worse.

Chapter 47

15th August 1984 – Sunny Dunes Holiday Camp – Tony's
Office

An Unpleasant Letter

At first when Jill walked into her and Tony's office, she hadn't
noticed the other letter lying on the centre of her table. She was too
preoccupied with the contents of the one secreted in her pocket and
the money in the safe, or rather how long before she could get her
hands on it. There wasn't much time until she would be off to the
pleasures of Pontinental Greece and she was sure others must be
suspicious of the permanent smile she had tattooed on her face.
However, she wasn't going to tell anyone. Jill imagined herself next
Friday night slipping on all of her finest pieces of jewellery and
disappearing with the thousands of pounds at midnight, just like old
Bilbo Baggins at his birthday party in *The Lord of the Rings*.

Then she saw it in the middle of her table and straight away she
thought it looked odd. This could not be a good letter. There was
something instantly disturbing about an envelope where all the
letters forming the recipient's names, **Mr** T Nobl**e and Miss J
Mac**donald, had been cut from magazines, newspapers and God
only knew what else, then stuck on with glue. She immediately
worried just what might be inside.

She was sitting at her desk staring at the letter when the door flung
open. In came Tony whistling *Tie a Yellow Ribbon Round the Old
Oak Tree*, with a smirk of satisfaction on his face.

'Tony have you seen this?' Jill had a sick feeling in the pit of her
stomach.

'Obviously not, as I've just walked in.' Tony quipped.

He had on his patronising face, the one he wore when he thought Jill was stupid. Well, she wouldn't have to suffer that one for much longer would she? 'It's a letter but just look at the state of it. Look at the characters. This can't be good news can it?' Jill held up the envelope and scratched at the letters with her fingernail. 'Look, all the letters making up our names. They've been bloody stuck on.'

'Give the frigging thing here.' Tony snatched the letter and ripped it open. As he started to read an expression of horror spread across his face.

Dear Tony AND Jill

I KNOW What's in that Safe and I know where it has *been* going. You *have* both been stealing the charity money for months and I have proof. On the 12ᵗʰ July £5,000 went into the bank account of Mr A Noble and same AMOUNT into that of Miss J McDonald. I know plenty of other details too and you do not do what I say I am *telling* the POLICE. On Friday night when you collect the next lot you will take that and half the money from the safe to the Regency Lounge. Under the gold hostess trolley will be a *tartan* carpet bag. You will put all the money in there and that will be *the* end of the matter. After all you thieving bastards haven't done too badly out of the Seasons spoils have you?

A SOON TO BE rICHER PERSOn. X

'Oh my God' said Jill as she looked over Tony's shoulder. 'What'll we do?'

17th April 2014 – The Purple Peacock, 55 Degrees North, Newcastle

Destiny's Peacock Pornstar

Destiny was pleased that for once Stefan was on time. Still, The Purple Peacock was very convenient for him, as it was literally underneath his apartment. Everywhere inside the bar was a rainbow of vivid pinks, purples and turquoise. It was a fancily decorated place with golden birdcages, elaborate light fittings and domes like Faberge eggs on the ceiling, a legacy from when it once was the Victorian Royal Arcade.

Last time they had met had been only a couple of days ago, but it seemed an eternity. He had complained because she'd made him travel all that way to Jesmond. It was a ten minute ride for him in a taxi, hardly a trip to the moon. Nevertheless, there was still a lot between the two of them that needed to be said. This place was usually very busy and wouldn't have been her choice of venue. So, she was glad that for the first time she could ever recall, he was here first and if needed to they could always retire up to his luxurious flat.

'Destiny.' Stefan stood up from the throne-like chair on which he was perched and clapped his hands together in an exaggerated show of delight. He was looking dapper in a plum coloured velvet jacket, embroidered brocade waistcoat and very pointed shoes similar to those worn in medieval times which must have been impossible not to trip up in. 'Am I right in assuming from your fab dress, that you are back to normal?' Despite Stefan's best efforts, Destiny could tell by the quiver in his voice he was still not his usual self.

'Yes Stefan you'll be pleased to know that I'm back. Ta dah.' She laughed and the two of them momentarily forgot their grave concerns to engage in their usual theatrical hugging and kissing routine. Destiny was back, wearing her favourite 1920's style, mulberry coloured chiffon dress, elegant patent leather shoes and her tumbling chestnut curls framed a face almost as lovely as the one on her last book cover.

'Thank goodness for that dearie. All that pseudo serious nonsense it wasn't really you was it?' They both sat down on their regal chairs.

'I must admit it was starting to make me feel slightly miserable.' She certainly wasn't going to admit to Stefan, that the straw which broke the camel's back had been upon realising she was invisible to the handsome man in the coffee shop.

'So what will you have to drink? I shall have my usual cocktail.' He clicked his fingers and a waitress came over. '*A Purple Peacock* and make it snappy. Destiny?'

Destiny scanned the menu to see he had selected a vodka based drink with port and lemon. She opted for a martini one, choosing it for its racy name more than anything. 'I'll have a *Peacock Pornstar* please.'

'Glad to see you back on form.' He gave her a wink of approval. 'So, setting aside all the things scaring the hell out of me, there's something that's just puzzling.' Stefan thought her answer to this would break them in gently before the serious stuff was tackled. 'How come you've been spending so much time hanging about in central Gateshead. I mean, it's hardly your sort of place is it?'

'Well, I suppose I can tell you now.' The waitress placed the two amethyst coloured drinks on the table and the pair of them clinked glasses. 'As it's not important to me anymore. You see I had this idea that I would have more credibility as a writer ...' she looked a little embarrassed and took a sip from her cocktail. 'If I wrote a serious novel about an elderly lady leading a sad lonely life.' Destiny realised now how pathetic her notions sounded now.

'Oh please don't start all that again …' Stefan rolled his eyes and almost drained his glass.

'No, this is important.' She stared at the table realising how pompous, silly and up-herself she'd been. No way was she ever going to pen a literary masterpiece. Page turning chic flicks were her genre and she now knew that she needed to stay where she belonged in her niche. She continued. 'I was dressing up as an old homeless woman to get into the character of the book I had started writing.'

'Destiny that sounds ghastly.' Stefan stifled a snigger. It was the first time he had felt like laughing in days.

'Anyway this old woman I was pretending to be liked to feed the pigeons.' Her idea for this dreary book was now sounding worse by the minute. 'So, when I was giving them seeds it really got the goat of one of the store managers in Tesco.'

'Well, I'm not surprised. Who wants those disgusting flying rats and their crap everywhere?' Stefan wasn't surprised this man hadn't been too pleased.

'Great chalet mates obviously think a lot like each other.' It was now her turn to smile as Stephen and Mike hadn't ever seen eye to eye back in the day.

'Sorry? What are you on about now?' He finished his drink.

'The store manager was Mike Robinson. Don't you remember I told you the other night?' Stefan's face turned pale when Destiny reminded him of their conversation and his eyes glazed over. 'Anyway as I said then, I watched him chucking poor Roger out on the street. He looked in such a sorry state.' Destiny's curls danced once more prettily, as she shook her head. 'I went over to speak to him. I felt sorry for him, you know? And do you know what the funny thing was?'

'Destiny, there's nothing remotely amusing about any of this.' He picked up a drinks menu. 'I need another drink. Waitress, over here!' Once more he snapped his fingers but stood up this time, to make himself more easily both heard and seen.

'Despite what had just happened to him, Roger was concerned about me. He assumed I was homeless and he was worried that I was cold.' She finished the remainder of her Purple Pornstar, which had been very nice.

The waitress arrived. 'I'll have a *Watercooler,*' demanded Stefan. This was a watermelon and cranberry, vodka infused gloop of a drink. Stefan didn't need to look at the menu. He was au fait with the Peacock's splendid selection of drinks. 'What do you want Destiny?'

'Anything.' She couldn't be bothered reading the drinks menu and was more concerned with continuing her story.

'She'll have a *Summer in Seville.*' He knew this was a gin and orange based cocktail which he was sure she would like.

'So, to get back to Gateshead, you recognised him but he didn't know who you were. That's very odd isn't it?' Stefan watched out for the waitress returning.

'I was dressed as an old woman. Why would he? Anyway he told me that he used to work as a Bluecoat at Pontins.' If Stefan had thought she looked a fright as Martha. God knows what he would have thought of her Bird Woman get up.

'Oh yes.' He added sarcastically. 'That's a topic that falls naturally into any conversation.'

'He was explaining how he knew Mike. That's all. Anyway he seemed like a nice man and I felt sorry for him.' Destiny noticed the place was getting louder, as more people started to arrive. She wondered if they would be noticed and was pleased she was wearing her lovely dress.

'Poor Roger.' Stefan pulled a face. 'I don't think so. I mean, it's him that's set this whole ball in motion. Aren't you worried Destiny? I mean, one of us could get sent down for this you know?'

'Can I ask you something Stefan?' She bit the bullet. 'Was it you Stefan? Did you kill Tony Noble?'

Once more the waitress arrived. 'Here's your drinks,' she said placing the one with an odd pinkish green tinge in front of Stefan and Destiny was given a bright orange cocktail, decorated with a little yellow parasol.

'Just put it on my tab.' He swished her away with his hand and he too noticed with some alarm that the place was beginning to fill up. 'No, it wasn't me.' His voice fell to a whisper and Destiny heaved a sigh of relief.' I know I had good reasons to but it wasn't me. I swear on my little brother's life.' He paused for a moment, reflecting how inappropriate this comment was. 'I tell you what though. I wish it had been. So if we're laying our cards on the table. Was it you Debbie because you had your motives too?'

'No, it wasn't me. I hated him also, not just for what he did to me but for what he did to you as well but I didn't kill him.' She thought about that horrible time in his office when he had called her a freak among other things. Now it was Stephen's turn to show his relief by once more by draining his glass.

'So, at least that narrows the field down by two. Let me see.' He pictured the suspects in a box with little windows as if in a prison or a game of Blankety Blank. In the top right hand corner he saw Jill. 'Jill was always a strong contender in my book. Not only because of her grubby dalliance with the man but also due her involvement with the charity tins and her very swift exit abroad.'

Destiny thought of Roger being bundled out of Tescos. 'I think Mike's recent behaviour paints him a very bad light also and, although I don't know what it was, Tony definitely had something on him.'

'There was Roger as well.' Stefan imagined him in the bottom left hand corner of his imaginary game show. 'He was off his head on drugs at the time and could have done anything.'

'Lots of people who weren't Bluecoats were suspects too. Tony had rubbed so many backs up the wrong way.' Destiny imagined a tabby cat yelping and scratching him because Tony had been stroking its fur in the wrong direction.

'But everybody knew how much I hated him.' Stefan's brow wrinkled and he looked worried. 'The very fact that he even stole the identity of my little brother to give credence to his scam was completely outrageous. It totally beggared belief and still makes me feel sick to this day. And I said on many occasion that I could kill him and I wish I had. That Destiny is why I'm so scared of this case being reopened. I might not have actually done the deed but it doesn't look good. And in these current times the media will have a field day. Come on Destiny. Let's go up to my apartment. I've had enough of this place for one night.'

Chapter 48

17th August 1984 - Sunny Dunes Holiday Camp – Tony's Office

Jill's Final Night

Jill was listening to her final Friday night sob story from Tony. He was laying it on particularly thick that night, hoping for good returns in the charity tins. She watched as the punter's eyes filled up before they feeling deep into their pockets. Thank goodness after tonight she would have to play no more part in this despicable fraud. By this time tomorrow, she would be settling in at the Holiday Club Poseidon in Greece and she wasn't going to miss this dump, not one little bit. She had fully intended to slip off quietly at the end of the night without explanation.

But she should have known that it was impossible and that Tony would be bound to get wind of it somehow. It was just her luck that he should have been chatting that morning with Stan blabbermouth Braithwaite. The camp manager must have been talking about her with the powers that be. Tony was just as furious as she knew he would be. Jill thought back over their earlier difficult conversation, the one she had been hoping to avoid.

'Bloody Pontinental.' Tony had roared with a face like thunder. 'Jesus Jill, I'd have expected a little loyalty from you of all people. I thought we were supposed to be a team. And who's going to be my bloody deputy for the rest of the season? After all I've done for you.' He thumped his fists on the table.

'I'm sorry but the position just came up.' Jill hadn't met his eye.

'Just came up, my arse. You've chased after Fred Pontin for this one and you no doubt twisted him round your little finger. Like you did me you little bitch.' He spat out the words, as if they were venom. 'Well don't think it'll be a barrel of laughs. You've not even got what it takes to be an Entertainment's Manager in one of the UK's poxy Pontins, let alone one of Fred's flagship Pontinentals. And don't think next season you can come back here with your tail between your legs.'

'Well, we'll just have to see about that one.' She tossed her mane of hair and wanted to stick her fingers in her ears and go *la la la* in his face .

'Don't be expecting a leaving gift. You were just going to slope off and not tell anyone weren't you?' He lit a cigarette and put the packet quickly back in his drawer not offering one to Jill.

Jill had shrugged her shoulders. 'What difference would it have made?'

'And don't be expecting half of the charity box money either. It's all mine now.' A greedy smile had formed on his lips.

'I wouldn't be too sure about that.' Jill had fully intended to take her full cut but nonetheless she reminded him. 'You've to give half of the money to the blackmailer tonight or the game will be up. Won't it?'

Tony had forgotten all about that and as Jill watched the nasty little weasel in full flow on stage, she felt nothing but revulsion for the man. She wondered how she had been able to stomach his advances for all these weeks. But if hadn't been the first time Jill had used her charms to get what she wanted and it probably wouldn't be the last.

Jill had been planning on moving the money from the safe to her suitcase that night but he would be probably watching her like a hawk. A taxi wasn't taking her to the airport until the morning. She still had her keys and all things considered, early morning was a much better option for collecting what was left in the safe.

17th April 2014 – The Lazaridis'' House, Jesmond

Fancy Chocolates

From her bedroom window Jillian was watching her husband talking to Carl, and imagining the worst. Teddie would obviously be asking Carl what he knew about that murder at the holiday camp all those years ago. Judging by the length of the conversation and from the look on the gardener's face, he obviously knew a thing or two. Upon catching a glimpse of her tousled hair and panda eyes, Jillian was reaching for a tissue from her dressing table to repair some of the damage when she heard a heavy foot on the stair. Well it couldn't be Teddie because he was outside.

Then there was a knock on the door. 'Mrs Lazaridis'. I'd like a wee word.'

'Not now Elaine. I'm busy.' She wiped off the unattractive black patches under her eyes.

'Yes now.' Elaine opened the door and boldly walked into the room.'

'Well what is it?' Jill smoothed her hair with a brush.

'You know who I am, don't you?' Once more that threatening edge was in her voice.

'Yes. You are my cleaner Elaine.' Jill continued brushing her hair.

'Come, come Jill. I think you can do a little better than that.' She moved closer towards Jill, until their two faces were inches away from each other.

'What do you want Elaine?' She could see the menacing glint in the fat woman's breath. 'You see now's not a good time so if you could just …'

'Shut up. I know who ye are Jill McDonald.' She folded her arms. 'I know where you come from. I don't know why you think yer so high and mighty. With all of yer airs and graces. I mean yer no better than I am.'

'Excuse me? And what is your point?' How dare this vile specimen speak to her in this way.

'Well yer think you're something special but you're no. You're just one big fraud. And yer know what? You're from the exact same slums as I am. Don't you think yer pulling the wool over anybody's eyes. And as me mam used to say *You cannae make a silk purse out of an old sow's ear.*' Elaine spat out the words.

'I think you can leave now.' Jillian walked across the room, the words stinging in her ears. 'I will send your wages through the post. I don't ever want to see your face again. Just go.' She held the door open.

'I don't think so. You dinnae get rid of me that easily. Ye see I ken all about you and yer nasty ways. I just want what's rightfully mine.' Elaine plonked herself down on the bed and it creaked.

'What on earth are you on about?' Jillian hung around the door wishing she could leave the room herself.

'Well, I remember only too well everything that happened at Sunny Dunes Holiday Camp in 1984.' She challenged Jillian with a knowing look.

'I know it was awful what happened to Tony …' Jillian began.

'I'll come tae that presently but first … there's the matter of those charity boxes. They must have been a nice wee spending spree for you before you went off all Pontinental. Mustn't they?' She helped herself to one of Jillian's fancy tissues and loudly blew her nose.

'Elaine. I never got any of that.' Jillian remembered discovering the empty safe along with Tony's body. Then, she thought back to the day that Elaine had come into the office and caught her with the safe open.

'Don't make me laugh. You and Tony had been conning those poor punters all season. It made me sick.' Elaine kicked off her crocs and made herself comfortable on the Lazaridis'' marital bed.

'I never got a penny of that. It all disappeared when Tony was found dead.' Jillian watched in horror as Elaine spotted a box of Jillian's favourite chocolates on her bedside cabinet and ripped off the cellophane.

'And ye expect me to believe that.' Elaine opened the lid, sniffed the insides, studied the contents list and popped a truffle into her mouth.

'Well it's the truth.' Jillian pictured the tartan carpet bag lying next to the safe. She had supposed Tony had been going to take the money to the Regency Lounge when he was attacked. Suddenly a chord was struck. 'You wrote that letter didn't you?'

'What letter?' Elaine asked nonchalantly while helping herself to a strawberry crème.

'The one with all the letters glued on to the paper. It was you wasn't it?' The image of the grubby, nasty letter flashed into her mind.

'Yes it was,' Elaine admitted. 'And I never got a penny of what I was owed did I?' She scanned the chocolates, wondering which to eat next.

'You do realise there's a policeman outside.' Jillian moved towards the window. Carl was busy once more with a spade and there was no sight of her husband. That meant he must be in the house.

'I think our dear friend Carl has more important matters to deal with and I am sure yer dear hubby would love to hear about ... well where shall I begin? Oh yes, well there's yer wee slutty days in Glasgow, then yer sordid affair with the married man Tony. There's yer charity box fraud and finally I think ye are the most likely person to have murdered Tony. So you could have all the dosh for yerself. Am I right?' She deliberated eying the contents of the box and decided on a caramel.

'You bitch.' The tears welled up in Jillian's eyes

'So who do ye think Carl would be more interested in? Your accusation of me of writing a wee letter which has long gone and of which you have nae proof or your charity box swindle and more than likely murder of your ex-lover.' Elaine was delighted with both the power she felt from the progression of the conversation and her realisation that the chocolate box had a second layer.

'I never murdered Tony.' Jillian sobbed.

'So you say ... but if the cap fits." Elaine clacked her tongue. 'And what do ye think Teddie would think of his darling wife's tawdry past. I'm pretty sure a wee divorce would soon be on the cards.'

'What do you want from me?' Jillian was at her wits end.

'Just what is rightfully mine. Give or take a little interest.' Elaine smiled.

Chapter 49

16th August 1984 – Sunny Dunes Holiday Camp – The
Princess Ballroom

The Heavy Velvet Curtains

Roger could think of nothing else but the need to feed his drug
habit. He desperately craved his next fix but he had absolutely no
money left. Despite having just been paid that day, once he had
settled his debts with *The Knife*, his new cocaine supplier in
Cullercoats, there was nothing left but a few meagre pounds.
Certainly not enough to score anymore drugs and he wondered
where he could get his hands on some more dosh.

He had been given the name of *The Knife* by a begrudging Kevin,
but Roger had been sworn to secrecy about his source. He assumed
that The *Knife* wasn't the man's real name but that he used this title
as a warning to anyone who crossed him. The drug dealer was a
bald Chinese man of around 40 with stubble, tattoos of various
weapons all over his body and an angry scar across his left cheek.
Although Roger was terrified of the man, he was even more scared
at the prospect of him not supplying him his essential medication.
Once the meddling and profiteering by Tony had stopped the
lifeguard's little side-line, Roger had been left utterly in the lurch.
As a result, in only a few short weeks, his visits to *The Knife* had
gobbled up all of his savings.

Roger felt as weak as a wet paper tissue. He trembled and felt
queasy. As his legs turned to jelly, he relied on leaning against a
column to keep himself upright. Watching Tony leaving the stage
and the takeover by Larry Lawson, he saw just the blurring of a
black suit into dazzling sequins. When the pounding disco music
began his head started to throb. Unaware of the odd looks punters
were giving him, he slid to the floor and began crawling across the

carpet. Making his way towards a large window, he pulled the heavy velvet curtains over his aching body and sat in the darkness.

18th April 2014 - Tesco, Trinity Square, Gateshead

Mike's Discombobulation

Mike had taken a break and got himself a much needed coffee in the staff canteen. He didn't know what was happening but he did know that he didn't like it one little bit. Firstly, there was the business of him being haunted by Roger's ghost. Something was sadly wrong in that man's life. In fact, he had felt scared himself when he recalled the look of sheer terror on his face, when he had run across the square earlier. It was as if he was being pursued by the Devil. The fact in itself that Roger was regularly in such close proximity was worry enough but now there was more.

No wonder there had been something that seemed familiar about the smart lady he had helped find the book the other day. He knew that there was but he couldn't place it until he had put her and Elaine together in context. No wonder Elaine had been trying to threaten him over the conversation with Roger. She was just being true to form. It hadn't just been a stab in the dark on her part because she knew fine well what had happened. Elaine had been that horrible cleaner who had spent much more time listening at doors and spying on people than she had done doing her job. It seemed leopards didn't change their spots.

He recalled that early on in the season of '84 she had been making sheep's eyes at him and much as he would have liked a girlfriend at that time, he wasn't scraping the barrel that low. Once her advances had been rejected, he was just another possible opportunity for her to make mischief. She probably knew fine well that Tony had been exhorting money off him and the reason for this. In fact, if her recent behaviour was anything to go by, she probably would have tried playing the same game as the Entertainment's Manager but she knew he had no money left. This was added justification for Mike engineering her dismissal from Tesco and the sooner the better.

But that wasn't all. Now he realised from where he recognised the pretty lady who he had helped find the book. It was Jill, Tony's Deputy Manager and it seemed she had worn very well indeed. It was difficult to believe that she, Elaine, Roger and he were of a similar age. In fact if anything, Jill had been slightly older than the rest of them. He wondered if she had been under the knife or just had an easy life. Clearly, she hadn't recognised either Elaine or himself because she would have been just as freaked as himself any by the prospect of any mutual acquaintance renewing. The very that fact none of their names had ever been cleared from being suspects in a murder was enough for them all to avoid each other. The case over who had killed Tony, had been eventually suspended because even after months of wasted police time, they were no nearer to solving the crime than they had been the day he had died. However, with the more sophisticated procedures of today, who knew what the outcome would be? And more than often the true killer wasn't necessarily the person charged. Jill should be very worried indeed if she knew the true identity of him and Elaine. Also, the very fact that Roger was running amok close by, only made matters worse. All those years ago, Jill had been only too keen to escape from it all away to Greece and he wondered what on earth had made her ever return. Although, he had his own strong motive for killing the bastard, surely her position was even more damning. She had actually been equally responsible for the charity box scandal. Once Tony was out of the way, the money would have all been hers and its whereabouts had never come to light. Judging by her appearance, she certainly wasn't short of a bob or two and he wondered as to the whereabouts of its source.

Having finished his coffee, he went back down on to the shop floor. He went over to the magazine and book section to look out of the window. The Old Bird woman hadn't been spotted for a few days and he wondered what had become of her. As he scanned the store to see if there was any evidence of further wrong-doings by Elaine. His eyes fell once more onto the copy of *Follow Your Dreams* and then to his complete amazement, a woman who was the exact double of Destiny Chambers just walked into the store. His jaw dropped because she was just as lovely in the flesh, as she was on the cover of the book. As she continued walking towards him, in a fetching royal blue suit with flared trousers and bat-wing sleeves, he could see people nudging each other, pointing at her and staring.

'Well, hello there, Mike Robinson,' she gushed.

Her voice sounded smooth to him, just like honey. However did she know his name? 'Destiny Chambers my goodness. What can I do for you?' He fell to the floor in a curtsey.

'Oh, we are being civil today, are we?' She even chastised him sexily, as if he were a naughty school boy.

'Sorry. Have I offended you? If so I can only apologise.' Mike was confused because he couldn't ever recall having met this gorgeous novelist before. This would have been something he wouldn't have forgotten in a hurry.

'Don't you recognise me Mike?' She raised an eyebrow.

'Yes, I have seen you on the covers of your books. There are some over there.' He pointed and thought to himself that one thing was for sure, given half a chance there was no way he would kick Destiny Chambers out of bed.

'What about this?' From inside her large designer bag she pulled a battered old envelope and out of this she produced some bird seed. 'And this?' She waved the packet in his face.

Mike gasped. 'Do you know the Old Bird lady?' Mike wondered if something bad had happened to her and felt a little guilty. How could she possibly be a friend of Destiny Chambers?

'I am the Bird Woman.' She gave him a dazzling smile that was as far removed as anything that the ancient crone could have produced.

'Don't be silly. You are ... beautiful and she ... well she was an old bag.' Mike was still staring at her in wonder.

'But you probably remember me better as Debbie Carter. Now, when's your break because I think we both need to pay Roger a visit. Don't you?' Destiny told, rather than asked him.

Mike was completely discombobulated. He remembered his last encounter with Roger and how he had treated him so shabbily. Meeting his former colleague once more was not a prospect he relished but how could resist the opportunity of spending more time in the company of the delectable Destiny, Debbie or whoever she was?

Chapter 50

17th August 1984 – Sunny Dunes Holiday Camp – The Princess Ballroom

A Monster

Once more, another Friday night was drawing to an end. Everyone had just joined hands together and sung Auld Lang Syne. Very few of the punters had a dry eye between them. At the prospect of the ending of their yearly holiday and the return to their hum drum existence, they were at their most gullible. As the unscrupulous Tony Noble took to the stage, Debbie imagined herself in 1930s Nazi Germany, about to be addressed by Hitler. Next to him was his despicable accomplice, a hard faced Eva Braun. She looked across the room to see the complete look of anguish on Stephen's face. After what she had learnt earlier that day, the full abomination of Tony Noble's swindling was completely beyond belief.

'How that man has the audacity to even open his lying gob is beyond me.' Siobhan hissed into Debbie's ear.

'I know and look at all those people.' Debbie looked round the man's captive audience in utter despair. There was now a Mexican Wave of full blown sobbing, as the toxic lies spilled with ease from his conniving mouth. 'They've got no idea whatsoever that he's just lining his own filthy pockets.'

'To be sure we've got to do something Debbie. But what? If we say anything to anyone we'll just lose our jobs.' She linked her friend's arm.

'I think this is all more important than our jobs.' With her friend close by, Debbie felt her strength gathering. 'Tomorrow we should go and see Stan Braithwaite.'

'But he's Tony's big mate.' Siobhan couldn't see what good this would do. It would more than likely just seal their own fate.

'The evidence against them is all there in the safe and the probably large deposits in both of their bank accounts. Siobhan don't you see? He's Fred Pontin's bigger mate and if the papers get wind of this it could bring down the entire Pontin's Empire.'

17th April 2014 – The Ex-Policeman's House, Heaton

A Mystical Experience

Carl couldn't get out of his head the conversation with Teddie Lazaridis. The fact was that the case of the unsolved murder of Tony Noble had always bugged him and now that particular thorn in his side was now giving him some serious jip. It had been so out of the blue, when Teddie had brought it once more to the forefront of his mind. How uncannily that so many of the suspects were now living close by to the very scene of the crime. The whole investigation was just begging to be reopened. Thanks to his new friend and ally Teddie Lazaridis', the whereabouts of many of those Bluecoats would be easy to find and one of them would finally be brought to justice.

However, this was going to be no easy ride for Teddie. The man was clearly unaware of his wife's earlier dodgy dealings. Who would have thought that the elegant Jillian Lazaridis', patron of many local charities, had once been involved in a sordid little scam? Lots of vile information regarding Jillian would be bound to come to light. Still, Mr Lazaridis' had clearly opened up his own wife's can of worms and there could be no going back. Carl, with the long arm of justice on his side and the conviction that no crime should be left unpunished, had one last duty to do. And if Jillian Lazaridis' was the murderer, (he had always felt she was the one), then it was only right that she paid for her wrongdoings. Nevertheless, he did feel sorry for his eavesdropping friend who clearly had no idea of the hornet's nest he had stirred up.

Although Carl had been retired for a good few years, he still had plenty of friends down at the station. Nobody working there now would have first-hand experience of the case like him. They were all much too young but if he could help them to finally solve the mystery, he could think of no finer final swan song for himself.

Carl and his wife Christine were watching *Endeavour* on the television that evening. He always enjoyed watching crime dramas, as they reminded him of his days in service. She wasn't so keen on the programme and was playing *Candy Crush* on her phone at the same time.

'Christine, do you remember that murder down at the coast at the holiday camp back in 1984?' He asked his wife when the adverts came on.

'Well, hardly Carl.' She put down her game detecting a worrying excitement in her husband's voice that she hadn't heard for some time. 'That was years ago. I mean, I'd have only been a teenager then.'

'Yes, but it was big news at the time.' He rubbed his hands together. 'The Entertainment's Manager had been brutally stabbed and they never got the culprit. It was at that Pontin's camp just outside Whitley Bay.'

'That was pulled down years ago Carl.' She thought back to when she was a girl and remembered some talk of a murder in the playground at school. 'I might remember something vaguely, I think. Why are you interested in that old case all of a sudden?'

'Well, I was talking to Teddie Lazaridis' earlier on today.' He was now oblivious that his programme had resumed on the telly.

'Is that the Greek bloke that owns that fancy Greek restaurant in Jesmond?' Christine had known he had been doing some work for a rich couple over that way and she had felt distinctly jealous when he had shown her photos of their posh house on his phone.

'Yes, I've been doing some gardening for him and his wife. Do you remember I told you about them?' He shuffled forward and was now sitting on the very edge of his seat.

'Why don't you ask him if we can a have a free meal at their ...' Christine was quick to suggest.

'Well, it only happens that his wife Jillian was one of the suspects in the case.' His eyes brightened and were blinking unnervingly like an answer phone when it has a new message. 'And you'll never guess who else was?'

'Go on then.' Christine replied, although she would have much rather be playing with her phone than listening to her husband's ramblings. He was even missing his favourite programme.

'Well, that Stephen Sondheim who's never off the telly.' Carl was sure this couldn't fail to impress her.

'The music producer that's always so full of himself.' Christine could never take to the man. He was far too big-headed for her liking.

'Yes, that's the one. And, that book over there.' He leapt across the room, which was quite a feat for a man his size and picked up the paperback his wife was currently reading. 'This woman on here ... Destiny Chambers. She was a Bluecoat there too at the time.'

'Wow.' This she did find of interest. 'I'm really enjoying her book. It's great. In fact I don't want it to finish. And you say she was a Bluecoat at Pontins too.' Surely Destiny couldn't be old enough to have been working in 1984 thought Christine. 'How's all of this information just landed in your lap?'

'Mr Lazaridis' heard them talking about it all in his restaurant.' He said as matter of factly as he could and sat back down once more in his chair.

'They must have been speaking down megaphones or the man must have ears like a bat then.' Christine was sure there was something about all of this that didn't ring quite true. 'I mean, I've never caught all these details off the conversation of two people in a restaurant even if they are sitting at the next table.' The thought of Mr Lazaridis' creeping around listening to his customers while they ate was starting to sound a little pervy.

'Christine. Wouldn't it be marvellous if I could help to round them all up, get them down the station and help convict the murderer?' He stood and pulled himself to his full height with fervour as if he'd just had a mystical experience.

'Carl. You are no longer a policeman.' She compared him unfavourably with Endeavour on the screen, who was not yet a late middle-aged man. 'You've been retired now for at least five years.'

'But with all the new technology. We would be bound to catch the murderer.' He wondered why Christine always had to be so negative.

'Don't get involved Carl. I mean we've got that Mediterranean cruise coming up next month.' And, she returned once more to the game on her phone.

Chapter 51

16th August 1984 – Sunny Dunes Holiday Camp – Tony's Office

Roger and the Knife

When Roger came round he could hear the awful racket of everyone singing 'Auld Lang Syne', which would indicate that it must be round about midnight. That meant he must have been passed out for about four hours. Although still suffering horribly from intense cold turkey, he at least felt a little more normal than he had done earlier. He guessed people must have noticed him missing but there was really nothing else that he could have done given the state he was in. Considering there would still be punters about for the next few minutes at least, he thought he had better stay where he was for the meantime, before venturing back to his chalet. Once back there, he planned to search through all his drawers once more with a fine toothed comb, in the hope of finding some mislaid drugs.

Eventually, when the coast seemed clear, he emerged from the crimson chrysalis of his curtains and crept towards the doors. Thankfully, nobody was about and the building hadn't yet been locked. On the way back to his own place, he noticed a light was on in the Entertainment's Office. He had not expected that and he thought he would take a quick look at tomorrow's rota. As he opened the door, he noticed an untidy knife lying on the bench next to a pile of crumbs. Someone must have been cutting bread for some toast earlier and hadn't bothered to clear up. It reminded him of his dealer so he picked it up and once more he began shaking.

Then he saw it. Tony's office door was open and so too was the safe. Not only were the charity tins with tonight's takings there but

Tony's hoard was absolutely crammed with the largest amount of banknotes he had ever seen. There must have been thousands of pounds lying there. An endless supply of cocaine, all up for grabs. There was even an empty tartan bag by the side, just waiting to be filled with the money. But Roger could see that it was nowhere near large enough for all that cash. He couldn't believe his luck and he wasn't thinking straight. This was indeed a most welcome gift from the gods and suddenly Roger was firing on all cylinders. He went into the drawer in the Bluecoat's Office where some cleaning products were kept and pulled out a big black bin bag. Then he ran into Tony's office holding both the knife and bin bag in one hand. With the other he started scooping the five, ten and twenty pound notes into his swag bag.

'What the ... what the hell do you think you are doing?' yelled Tony. The Entertainment's Manager had been at the far end of the room getting another can of beer from his filing cabinet and when he turned round he couldn't believe his eyes. What the bloody hell was Roger doing?

'Leave me be. I'm not going to take all of it.' Roger's eyes, in his searching-for-drug-crazed-frenzy, were wild and his speech staccato like that of a darlek.

'Too bloody right. It's all my money and not yours for the taking.' He moved across the room to shove Roger away from the safe but his Head Bluecoat, amazingly back on form, jumped deftly out of the way.

'I need money.' Roger screeched. 'And I need it now. Stand back, I have a weapon.' He transferred the knife from his left to his right hand and started waving it in front of Tony's face.

'Give that to me. You arsehole druggy.' Tony tried to pull the knife from Roger's hand and the two of them became locked in a tussle. As their limbs flailed to and fro they looked like one giant spider wriggling its legs.

'No, you bastard,' yelled Roger and somehow both of them became entangled in the black plastic bag.

Tony lunged forward to try and steady himself with his desk but Roger fell on top of him. The breadknife plunged down stabbing straight into Tony's back.

Both men screamed. Tony as a result of the excruciating pain from the blade and Roger because of the scarlet fountain squirting out of the Entertainment Manager's back. He jumped up in horror, saw he too was covered in blood and watched the life ebb out of the vile man's body. Roger's feet were rooted to the ground. What should he do? Clearly, Tony was beyond any help. Self-preservation kicked in and he returned to the safe. He filled the bin bag with every last scrap of the money, including all the contents of the charity boxes. Then he crouched over the body, calmly wiped his prints from the knife's handle with a tea towel and got the hell out of there.

18th April 2014 – Destiny's Flat, Jesmond

Shocking News

Destiny couldn't pretend she hadn't revelled in the puppy dog adoration she had seen in Mike's eyes when she had introduced herself. She had always enjoyed male attention and female too, for that matter, but she had never really sung from the Sapphic song sheet. Still, it was good to be back in Destiny's skin once more especially after the experience in the coffee shop that had signed Martha's death warrant. Nevertheless, she hadn't forgiven Mike for his diabolical treatment of her alter ego or the brutal way the bully had thrown Roger out of the shop. She could have only supposed that his attitude towards Roger was based on fear of the investigation being re-opened, but he didn't seem particularly phased by her re-introducing herself as Debbie.

Anyway, she had little difficulty in persuading him to go and check on Roger. He too seemed to be genuinely concerned for the safety of the man. Destiny herself was growing more fearful by the moment especially, when Mike had told her of the sheer terror he had seen on Roger's face and the speed with which he had fled past the store. Obviously, he was in some serious danger and their old friend desperately needed their help.

But when they had gone inside the cinema complex, there had been no sign of Roger anywhere. They assumed they must have mistimed his shift but when they asked about him, a rude man informed them with some glee. 'Don't know where the bugger is. He just hasn't shown up today. No phone call or nothing. It's just typical of him. I always said that man's just a complete waste of space.'

So, she had told Mike that she would return the next day and try again. He told her he usually had his coffee break about eleven and that they should go once more together. Then, before they parted company for that day, he shared with her further unsettling news. Not only had he spotted Jill McDonald of all people, Tony's Assistant Manager in the store yesterday but he had just found out the old cleaner from Pontin's — Elaine, was actually an employee in his very store.

How could Jill McDonald be here in Gateshead thought Destiny? The last she had heard, Jill had gone over to Greece and come over all Pontinental. Still, she supposed Jill would now be a bit long in the tooth for that type of thing, especially as she had been a good few years older than most of them. Destiny wondered how Jill was coping with the aging process, as the woman must be nearing sixty. And Elaine the cleaner, she hadn't given that woman any thought in over thirty years. She did recall though that she hadn't really liked her and that nobody had. The woman had clearly been resentful of the Bluecoats because she was jealous and wanted to be one herself. Another spooky coincidence though. This was all too much for her to process at once.

The journey on the Metro back to Jesmond didn't take long and Destiny thought once more of her Bluecoat days. It seemed such a long time ago that she had been plain Debbie Carter and the only person from those times who she was still in contact with was Stefan. It had been such a relief when they had admitted to each other, that neither of them was the killer. For years she had feared it might have been Stefan but she believed him when he had told her that it wasn't him. He had always been a useless liar. Nevertheless, if the case was opened the odds wouldn't be stacked in his favour regarding the hard evidence. He wasn't the murderer but somebody was and there was still a price to be paid.

She wondered if Mike and Stefan met once again they would like each other any better than they had in the past. Somehow she didn't think they would, as they had both become more extreme and not necessarily nicer versions of their younger selves. What about her? Was Destiny worse than Debbie? She guessed they were both silly and vain. She decided she had better leave those thoughts there.

Once back in her flat, she was relieved to retreat into the fantasy world of her latest book. Her new storyline was about a gorgeous ingénue and her adventures in the heady New York of the 1980's. It was true to Destiny's usual format. This would please Sorchia no doubt and she had to admit she was feeling quite inspired herself. Finally, she had put all that pretentious serious novelist crap to one side. She was what she was and did what she did very well. Although, you couldn't make a silk purse out of a sow's ear you could still make a very functional and practical one. In the same vein, she might not be Virginia Woolf but she was able to write an excellent page turning and crowd pleasing best seller. It might not win any literary awards but it would please Sorchia, her readers, and most importantly, make plenty of money.

The phone went and she fully expected it to be her agent. At last she had some news to shut the woman up. She could see the pound signs lighting up in Sorcha's greedy eyes.

'Destiny. Oh my God. Have you seen today's news?' It was Stefan and he sounded shocked .

'No. Whatever's wrong Stefan? What's happened?' Had someone written a bad review about Stefan's latest protégé band?

'It's Roger,' he gasped. 'They've pulled a body out of the Tyne and it's believed to be that of the once multi-millionaire night-club owner Roger ….'

'Noooo. Surely that can't be right.' Destiny couldn't believe what she was hearing.

'Put the telly on Destiny. I'm coming straight over and pour me a very large gin.' Stefan was already on his way.

Chapter 52

17th August 1984 – Sunny Dunes Holiday Camp 17th– Roger's Chalet

The Solution

Roger felt such relief when he slammed shut his chalet door but he knew that he needed to keep focused and think straight. Behind the wardrobe he knew there was a gap in the floor boards where the wood had become rotten. So, he yanked out the heavy piece of furniture and pulled up the piece of wood from the skirting board. For the time being at least, this would have to be the home for the money. The timber crumbled easily and revealed the perfect space. Although he didn't have time to count all the notes, he knew that there were a lot. He would have to deposit it in dribs and drabs into his various banks over a long period of time to avoid suspicion. Into a drawer, he shoved a couple of hundred, to take care of some immediate expenses and smiled. He pushed the closet back into position.

Next he ran himself a hot bath, peeled off his bloody clothes and then it hit him. He was not only a thief but he was a murderer and after plunging down to these depths there was no further level to sink. His once pristine white uniform shirt now branded him, with its incriminating red of a killer. If this was to ever be discovered, it would point the finger of blame unequivocally in his direction and would provide the police with the perfect noose for his neck. There was no way this piece of evidence could ever be seen again and it needed to be destroyed. But how? He could hardly shove it in a bin for it later to be found or light a fire without drawing attention to himself.

Once more, Roger moved the heavy wardrobe. He bundled the contaminated shirt and trousers inside the plastic bag to bury them deeply underneath all the money. Then he sat in the bath and scrubbed his own skin until it was almost the colour of the death soiled clothes. Next, he pulled on some jeans and a sweatshirt and headed off to Cullercoats. *The Knife* kept late hours and he needed a little something to get through the night and next day.

18th April 2014 – Ramsey Court, Central Gateshead

Elaine's Plans Go Up in Smoke

Back in her flat, Elaine was sitting with her family and wishing she had another box of those lovely chocolates of Mrs Lazaridis' to eat. Although, they had been quite delicious and probably very expensive, the best part for her had been the experience of enjoying the sweetness of the fancies while watching her employer squirm with mortification. It had been perfect, like sprinkling salt on a slug and then standing back to observe the results.

'What are you smiling about Mam?' Kylie noticed that her Mam was smirking.

'Nothing Kylie. I was just thinking a few wee thoughts about that snotty bitch I'm forced to clean for. But it won't be for much longer.' Elaine's grin became broader.

'Why? Is she going to give you the sack?' Kylie had never been fired because she'd never had a job.

'I don't think so somehow. Not if she knows what's good for her.' Elaine thought back with relish over her second experience of boss torturing. She could develop a taste for this.

'I've told you before Mam. When you're cleaning for Lady Muck just let me in and I'll nick a few things. That'll serve her right.' Scott repeated a previous suggestion of his.

'You'd get caught. I'd get nicked. That'd just be stupid Scott. But let's just say I've got a wee something up my sleeve.' Elaine tapped the side of her nose, knowingly. 'A little plan of mine is coming nicely to fruition so to speak.' Then Elaine's eyes were drawn to the television where the local News was on. On the screen was a photograph of the Head Bluecoat Roger. It was a grainy picture but she recognised him instantly. The news reader informed everyone that apparently, not only had he been responsible for the theft of the charity boxes all those years ago at Sunny Dunes Holiday Camp, but he had also stabbed the Entertainment's Manager Tony Noble. Now his dead body had just been pulled out of the Tyne.

'Bloody Hell,' Elaine wailed. Once again, she could see all her plans going up in smoke.

Chapter 53

18th August 1984 – Sunny Dunes Holiday Camp – Tony's Office

Jill's Discovery

Jill woke up feeling excited because this time tomorrow she would be at the Poseidon Club in Greece, far away from horrible Tony and this Sunny Dunes dump. Her belongings were all packed in her expensive new crocodile skin cases, ready for her late morning flight. She took a quick bath, before sliding into her new designer jeans and the crisp white shirt she would be travelling in. It was still early and with any luck she wouldn't bump into anyone she knew. She picked up a large bag and put the bunch of keys in her pocket. She was planning on taking as much of the money from the safe as she could. On the way to the airport, her taxi would wait outside the bank for her, while she deposited the money into her account. The main branch in Newcastle would definitely be open on a Saturday morning because she had checked it. Life felt good, her plan was moving forward with clockwork precision and Jill practically skipped along to the Entertainment's Office.

She was surprised when the door wasn't locked because Tony was usually pretty fastidious about that sort of thing. Nevertheless, last night he was probably out of sorts, dwelling on what he saw as her betrayal coupled with having to begrudgingly deliver the money to the blackmailer. Jill still couldn't fathom who it could possibly be but she wouldn't need to trouble herself with the niggle as to the bastard's identity any longer after today.

As she walked into the Entertainment's Office, she saw the usual mess and she noticed that the door to Tony's room was slightly ajar. So she opened the door and then gave a spine chilling scream. Not only was the safe open but it was empty and there was a sea of red all over the floor. Most shocking of all although was Tony's body, lying in a pool of blood with a knife sticking out of his back. Jill recognised it immediately as the Bluecoat's bread knife. This couldn't be happening. She blinked several times hoping she could make the image disappear but it refused to budge. Then she ran to the main office looking to find Stan Braithwaite or anyone awake or alive. Where had all her money gone? Who had killed Tony? But the most important question of all now hanging in the air was, would she be catching today's flight to Athens?

18th April 2014 – The Police Station, North Shields

The Pandora's Box

Carl walked back into the familiar Police Station in North Shields whistling cheerfully, and with a fine tale to be told. Behind the reception desk, the two police officers he knew well, Martin Clayton and Tom Cooper were engrossed in a game of chess. Carl smiled, these two needed something to shake them up and he was going to be just the person to do it.

'Morning lads. How's tricks?' Carl looked round the room, pleased to see nothing much had changed since he had retired,

'Hi there Carl. How are you doing?' Martin, a dark haired man in his forties was pleased for a distraction from the game, as he was getting beaten.

'Not seen you for a while mate. What have you been up to then?' Tom was a little older. He and Carl had got on well together. They had often gone for a pint or two after a shift.

'A little bit of gardening and a few odd jobs. You know how it is.' Carl leaned on the counter. 'Me and the wife are off on a cruise next month. I can't grumble.'

'It's all right for some.' Tom said with some envy and folded his arms. 'I can't wait until I'm retired.'

'Must be great. I can't wait till it's my time to see the world.' Martin sighed. He still had a while to go until this plan of his could come to fruition.

'Well you two don't exactly look rushed off your feet do you? Anyway I was just passing so I thought I would drop in and say hello.' But Carl had a certain edginess about him that didn't imply this was a casual visit.

'Always good to see you.' Tom smiled to himself, sensing a checkmate wasn't far away.

'The thing is I was talking to Teddie Lazaridis' the other day. 'Carl sat himself down on an empty chair. 'You know the one that has all the Greek restaurants. I've been doing some gardening for him recently. Do you remember years ago when there was the murder at that holiday camp that used to be near Whitley Bay?'

'No, that was way before my time.' Martin went over to the vending machine to get himself a can of coke and a bar of chocolate.

'Well it only transpires that Teddie Lazaridis' wife used to work there at the very time of the killing.' Carl pulled a knowing face.

'Isn't that funny though? The boss was only talking about that case earlier.' Tom reached for a nearby newspaper.

'Yes.' Martin made the connection with the recent breaking news story. 'The bloke that was found guilty of the murder at the holiday camp in the 1980s has just been discovered dead.' He took a sizable bite out of his chocolate bar.

'It's all over the papers today. What was he called? Oh yes Roger Henderson.' Tom pointed at a blurry photograph in the paper of a youthful Roger in his Bluecoat uniform.

'But I thought they had never caught the killer.' Carl was shocked, his grandiose sleuthing plans were evaporating in front of his very eyes and he just couldn't understand why he knew nothing about any of this.

'There was something funny about the whole business I believe.' Tom reached for a newspaper to show Carl the headlines. At that very moment in walked the Chief Superintendent. Quick as a flash, Tom opened the paper up and slid it over the top of the unfinished chess game. 'Here's the boss. He'll probably know more details about what happened.'

'Morning again lads. Morning Carl.' The Superintendent, Brian Baxter, was a thick-set man with a steely grey thatch of hair and a no nonsense approach to policing. He was carrying a thick file.

'Brian what's the information on that bloke that was pulled out of the river? Wasn't he the one who did that murder at the holiday camp?' Tom hoped his boss hadn't noticed their chess game on the go.

'Ah yes it was all a bit shady.' Brian Baxter scratched his head. 'There were some funny goings on at the time and things the police wanted kept quiet. That's what's in this file. I've just been checking on the details myself. I've printed off some stuff from the computer so I can have a proper look.'

'But when was he convicted? I thought the case had never been solved.' This was not the way at all that Carl had imagined the morning panning out.

'It wasn't at the time Carl.' The Superintendent sat down at a table, opened the file and spread out the papers. Tom, Martin and Carl all pulled their chairs around. 'It was much later that the arrest was made. In fact Carl, I seem to remember that you had already retired by then. It was when at last they finally pulled the eyesore down. That holiday camp hadn't been used in many years. There were rats all over the place and it was becoming a health and safety hazard. So, anyway, when they were knocking down the chalets they made an interesting discovery. They found heavily blood-stained clothes in one particular chalet. When it was discovered that this was where Roger Henderson had been living the summer of 84, he was immediately taken in for questioning.'

'But why didn't I hear about this?' Carl watched the TV news daily without fail. No way would this have escaped his attention.

'Well, this is where it gets kind of sticky. You see boys, over the years Roger had kept some pretty unsavoury company. And when he was charged, his sentence was made … sort of … less severe than it would have been.' Brian looked uncomfortable relaying this.

'Why? This man had committed murder hadn't he?' Carl was definitely confused.

'Well, it was found out to be manslaughter rather than cold-blooded killing. Roger had been in the process of stealing the charity money in the safe when Tony had discovered him. There had been some scuffle and Roger had discovered him. There had been some scuffle and Roger had accidentally fallen on him and stabbed him.'

'Hang on,' said Carl. 'Then all this could only have been a few years ago. After a conviction of fraud and manslaughter, he couldn't possibly have been released yet from prison. The man should have been locked up and the key thrown away.' from prison. The man should have been locked up and the key thrown away.'

'This would make an excellent programme on the telly.' Martin had by mistake spoken his thoughts aloud. The three other men glared at him.

Brian continued. 'Have you heard of turning the Queen's evidence?' All the three men shook their heads. 'It's when evidence for the prosecution is given by a person also on trial. Well a deal was struck. He gave the police lots of valuable information about some heavy duty drug dealers and as a result many important arrests were made.'

'So that's why the sentence was reduced.' Tom was now as interested in all of this just as much as Carl.

'And that's why he's ended up in the Tyne. It was payback time.' Carl sucked in his cheeks. At last he understood.

'From the moment he stepped out of jail after his short sentence, Roger was a sitting duck. If the actions of the police were made public I don't think this would look good for anyone.' Brian shook his head.

'So this was all about revenge?' Martin asked, as he had now also been pulled into the drama of the terrible cautionary story.

'But of course,' Brian said. 'I doubt very much if Roger had been made aware at the time he struck his bargain with the police, that his actions would be bound to have consequences. Whether he had or not, Roger Henderson has indeed paid for his crime.'

Although, at first Carl was disappointed that his final blaze of glory wasn't to be. Upon reflection, maybe this was all for the best. He was generally fond of both Teddie and Jillian Lazaridis' and dragging all this up again would have been disasterous for both of them. The revealing of her past actions would have broken Teddie's heart. Even when Jillian had finally been found innocent of both the murder of Tony Noble and the embezzlement of the charity money, the damage would have already been done. The opening of that particular Pandora's Box would have had disastrous repercussions not just for them but for others too. Tonight, quite a few people would be sleeping more easily in their beds and perhaps sometimes it was best to just leave well alone. After all, Carl was soon to be off on his cruise.

Printed in Great Britain
by Amazon

37366028R00202